The Best AMERICAN SHORT STORIES 2024

GUEST EDITORS OF THE BEST AMERICAN SHORT STORIES

1978 TED SOLOTAROFF
1979 JOYCE CAROL OATES
1980 STANLEY ELKIN
1981 HORTENSE CALISHER
1982 JOHN GARDNER
1983 ANNE TYLER
1984 JOHN UPDIKE
1985 GAIL GODWIN
1986 RAYMOND CARVER
1987 ANN BEATTIE
1988 MARK HELPRIN
1989 MARGARET ATWOOD
1990 RICHARD FORD
1991 ALICE ADAMS
1992 ROBERT STONE
1993 LOUISE ERDRICH
1994 TOBIAS WOLFF
1995 JANE SMILEY
1996 JOHN EDGAR WIDEMAN
1997 E. ANNIE PROULX
1998 GARRISON KEILLOR
1999 AMY TAN
2000 E. L. DOCTOROW
2001 BARBARA KINGSOLVER
2002 SUE MILLER
2003 WALTER MOSLEY
2004 LORRIE MOORE
2005 MICHAEL CHABON
2006 ANN PATCHETT
2007 STEPHEN KING
2008 SALMAN RUSHDIE
2009 ALICE SEBOLD
2010 RICHARD RUSSO
2011 GERALDINE BROOKS
2012 TOM PERROTTA
2013 ELIZABETH STROUT
2014 JENNIFER EGAN
2015 T. C. BOYLE
2016 JUNOT DÍAZ
2017 MEG WOLITZER
2018 ROXANE GAY
2019 ANTHONY DOERR
2020 CURTIS SITTENFELD
2021 JESMYN WARD
2022 ANDREW SEAN GREER
2023 MIN JIN LEE
2024 LAUREN GROFF

The Best AMERICAN SHORT STORIES® 2024

Selected from U.S. and Canadian Magazines
by LAUREN GROFF
with HEIDI PITLOR

With an Introduction by
LAUREN GROFF

MARINER BOOKS
New York Boston

HarperCollins books may be purchased for educational, business, or sales promotional use. For information, please email the Special Markets Department at SPsales@harpercollins.com.

FIRST EDITION

ISSN 0067-6233
ISBN 978-0-06-327595-9
ISBN 978-0-06-327596-6 (LIBRARY EDITION)

24 25 26 27 28 LBC 5 4 3 2 1

"Seeing Through Maps" by Madeline ffitch. First published in *Harper's Magazine*, June 2023. Copyright © 2023 by Madeline ffitch. Reprinted by permission of the author.

"Democracy in America" by Allegra Hyde. First published in *The Massachusetts Review*, volume 64, number 1, Spring 2023. From *The Last Catastrophe: Stories* by Allegra Hyde, copyright © 2023 by Allegra Hyde. Used by permission of Vintage Books, an imprint of the Knopf Doubleday Publishing Group, a division of Penguin Random House LLC. All rights reserved.

"Engelond" by Taisia Kitaiskaia. First published in *Virginia Quarterly Review*, Fall 2023, Fiction. Copyright © 2023 by Taisia Kitaiskaia. Reprinted by permission of Brandt & Hochman Literary Agents, Inc.

"P's Parties" by Jhumpa Lahiri. First published in *The New Yorker*, July 3, 2023. From *Roman Stories* by Jhumpa Lahiri with Todd Portnowitz, translation copyright © 2023 by Penguin Random House LLC. Used by permission of Alfred A. Knopf, an imprint of the Knopf Doubleday Publishing Group, a division of Penguin Random House LLC. All rights reserved.

"A Case Study" by Daniel Mason. First published in *The Paris Review*, issue 243, Spring 2023. Copyright © 2023 by Daniel Mason. Reprinted by permission of the author.

"Just Another Family" by Lori Ostlund. First published in *New England Review*, volume 44, November 27, 2023. From the forthcoming collection *Are You Happy?*, Zando, April 2025. Copyright © 2023 by Lori Ostlund. Reprinted by permission of the author.

"Privilege" by Jim Shepard. First published in *Ploughshares*, volume 49, number 3, Fall 2023. Copyright © 2023 by Jim Shepard. Reprinted by permission of the author.

"Baboons" by Susan Shepherd. First published in *The Kenyon Review*, volume 45, number 2, Spring 2023. Copyright © 2023 by Susan Shepherd. Reprinted by permission of the author.

"Extinction" by Azareen Van der Vliet Oloomi. First published in *Electric Literature*, Oct 2, 2023. Copyright © 2023 by Azareen Van der Vliet Oloomi. Reprinted by permission of the author.

"Mall of America" by Suzanne Wang. First published in *One Story*, issue number 301, May 25, 2023. Copyright © 2023 by Suzanne Wang. Reprinted by permission of the author.

"Valley of the Moon" by Paul Yoon. First published in *The New Yorker*, July 3, 2023. From *The Hive and the Honey* by Paul Yoon. Copyright © 2023 by Paul Yoon. Reprinted with the permission of Marysue Rucci Books, and imprint of Simon & Schuster LLC. All rights reserved.

Contents

Foreword

SERIES EDITORS, AT least the editors of *The Best American* series, are different from other book editors. We do not suggest corrections or changes to text, or work with marketing and publicity departments to help guide publication. We do, however, read. A lot.

In my research for *100 Years of the Best American Short Stories*, published back in 2015, I learned about four people who weren't often explored publicly, the four previous series editors of this longtime book. The first was Edward J. O'Brien, who had fallen in love with reading as a child with a heart condition; Poe, Dickens, and Balzac became his companions during those times when his illness flared. At only twenty-three, he set out to create a yearbook of American short stories. In order to stay on top of the flood of magazines that submitted their fiction to him, O'Brien devised elaborate filing and tracking systems, indexes of periodicals and every story that he'd read, relevant articles, and even a necrology of writers. He spent weekends reading short stories, stopping only for meals. Martha Foley helmed the series from 1941 to 1977. She had been coediting *Story* magazine when she took over the series after O'Brien died, and she herself wrote fiction and had had stories appear in *The Best American Short Stories.* Her system of reading and tracking was less orderly than O'Brien's. She rated each story as "superlative," "quite good," "above average," and "the others I try to forget," and she tracked them all on colored index cards. Foley read in bursts and often fell weeks behind schedule, to the chagrin of her publisher. Next came Shannon Ravenel, who had been passing along stories to Foley as a young editor at Houghton Mifflin, something that Foley did not always welcome. After the latter died, Ravenel edited the series from 1978 to 1989. From South Carolina, Ravenel "was the only child of older parents . . . We had no money, but we had this good Southern name, Ravenel. I grew up reading. I had very, very bad eyes and was told that I shouldn't read too much, but I did anyway." Ravenel was the first to work with guest editors, but this did not lessen the number of stories that she read. Guest editors chose 20 stories from a pool of 120, a number winnowed from thousands by series editors. Ravenel later cofounded Algonquin Books, and in 1989, she resigned from *The Best American Short Stories* in order to focus on the new publisher. Her replacement was Katrina Kenison, another young editor at Houghton Mifflin. "I have to confess I had always been a novel reader. And I don't think I took short stories all that seriously when I began, which is a terrible thing for an editor of short stories to confess. But I had just become a mother . . . and there was something about the form that really attracted me in my new life, because I didn't have a lot of time ever to sit down and read at a stretch." Kenison was another keeper of file cards, but she managed to stay on top of the fast flow. "Failing to stay on top of the tide was to drown in unread literary journals." Kenison oversaw the series until 2006.

It was not easy to find information about my predecessors—one scholarly book about O'Brien that largely focused on his religiosity and the poetry that he'd written; a partially written memoir of Foley. I interviewed Ravenel and Kenison, but reading through my notes, I saw that there was much I hadn't thought to ask and I hated to trouble them for even more time. In the end, I wanted to know things that maybe even they would have been unable to answer or remember: Who *were* these people who'd taken on the same challenge I had? What kept them reading all those stories year after year? What kept them confident in their ability to choose "the best"? How would they describe the experience of suddenly coming across an excellent story by a first-time author? And where did they read—was it always at home? At a desk, or in a den, an office? Did they have one chair that they preferred? Did their minds ever wander? What tenses or points of view, if any, made them itch? Were these four people influenced by politics, literature, culture, something else? How about their own moods? Did an unexpected bill or a sick child or upsetting news make it difficult for them to follow the threads of so many stories? Editors are meant to be objective arbiters of taste, curators, but can anyone really be objective about what they love?

I admit all of the following with hesitation: I've never had training to be an editor of any type. I have no degree in literature, although I do have a master's in Creative Writing. Reading past volumes of the series was my only real training; there was no handoff or passing of the torch between Kenison and me. I was lucky that I'd been the in-house editor of the book for years and could jump in quickly. Here's something else: there were moments when reading even one more short story is as appealing as plucking out my own eyeball. And this: sometimes I cannot tell you with any sense of certainty whether a story is brilliant or terrible. Sometimes I deliberate with a guest editor, whose reaction or non-reaction is the same as mine, and together, we take a deep breath and jump, usually onto the side of "brilliant." And: my mind wanders all the time. Focus has gotten harder for me over time. I have envied the other series editors (less so Kenison) for not having to contend with the internet, the world's most effective distraction. I am very much influenced by politics, culture, my own mood, the moods of my children, the moods of the country. I read everywhere. At home sprawled on my couch, in waiting rooms, in libraries and coffee shops. Instead of index cards I use a plain old Microsoft Word document, where I list and grade all the stories that pass muster to me. It is one way to make something that is by nature amorphous and subjective and unruly seem more manageable.

In my eighteen years as series editor, I have thought of O'Brien, Foley, Ravenel, and Kenison often. I can think of no other people who have known the strangeness of reading American short stories (no translations or excerpts!) alone day in and day out. No coworkers or friends or family members have had the experience of taking in all of those voices and narratives over such a long period of time. If I could have a dinner party with anyone from history? No question: it would be those four people. Though we've lived through different times, vastly different moments of history, and though the writers we've championed as are different as Ernest Hemingway and Roxane Gay, Dorothy Parker and Ha Jin, I suspect that like me, my predecessors experienced profound awe at the sheer multitude of people—writers, characters—trying to speak and to be heard in this world, all those people trying only to be understood.

Reading is quieting the mind and making room for another voice. Reading is listening. It is a form of witness. Being a series editor is nothing less than a measure of love for the very human act of storytelling and making meaning. Reading is watching, and reading for this series is watching for words that have been set together in just the right strange and surprising and resonant way that causes a reader to feel and/or think something. Reading is recognizing something about oneself or a loved one or a nemesis, something about history or the future, something about humanity or nature or technology that one had not known or understood yet in the deeper tissue of one's body. Reading is even, I'll say, the cure for loneliness, meanness, narcissism. The joy that comes with the discovery of a piece of writing that stops my breath is the reason that I have done this job for so long. I have always been a picky reader, easily bored, easily critical (this job has only made me more so), but in the face of vibrant, authentic, fully inhabited writing, I'm a child again, a stranger on the earth, clay in the hands of this writer. We five series editors have been close witnesses, undoubtedly grateful witnesses to 109 years of human truths and storytelling. Between us, we've been some of the first to lay eyes upon the fiction of Sherwood Anderson, F. Scott Fitzgerald, Thomas Wolfe, William Saroyan, John Steinbeck, Richard Wright, Saul Bellow, Philip Roth, Flannery O'Connor, Vladimir Nabokov, Eudora Welty, Ray Bradbury, Shirley Jackson, Jack Kerouac, Charles Baxter, Amy Hempel, Mona Simpson, Robert Olen Butler, Andrea Barrett, Aleksandar Hemon, Jhumpa Lahiri, Nathan Englander, and many, many other authors.

One paradox of life is that we achieve peak confidence about all that we know as teenagers, and at least for me, getting older has been a process of realizing what relatively little knowledge I will forever have. The more open I can remain to what I don't know, the better I am as a reader, editor, and writer, but also as a friend, partner, and mother. In reading thousands of short stories each year, I've learned that I may never know the following:

- The standard definition of the length of a short story and how this differs from flash, short shorts, and novellas.

- My own taste. I'm more Catholic than I knew. Sometimes. Although this series began as a platform to highlight literary short fiction, genre-blending has always played a part, from the ghost stories written during the world wars to the more speculative stories that appear in this volume.
- What makes writing or a writer American. Do they have to live here? What if an author lived here for most of their life but holds citizenship from another country? I admit that I've erred on the side of inclusivity, and I am even including my first story in translation this year, written as it was by an author who grew up in the United States, Jhumpa Lahiri, who first wrote in English before she taught herself Italian.
- The best way to tell a story. I'm not a fan of the present tense, as I feel it hamstrings an author by holding them to a very small period of time, but stories like Shastri Akella's "The Magic Bangle" prove me wrong. Present tense can be used to create a greater sense of urgency. In Akella's story, a character wants only to feel safe in his skin. What is more necessary and urgent than that?

In my tenure, this series has published early stories by Karen Russell, Rebecca Makkai, Manuel Muñoz, Lauren Groff, Danielle Evans, Jamel Brinkley, Téa Obreht, Maggie Shipstead, Lisa Ko, and Sarah Thankam Mathews. It has also published later-in-life stories by Alice Munro, Steven Millhauser, Joyce Carol Oates, John Barth, Tobias Wolff, Mary Gordon, Louis Auchincloss, Alice McDermott, John Edgar Wideman, Denis Johnson, and Wendell Berry. I want to talk about the mid-lifers and oldsters for a moment, those whose new books may arrive with less marketing money, fanfare, or public interest. Without them, without Mary Gaitskill or Barbara Kingsolver or James McBride, where would we be? With age comes a different perspective, wisdom, hard-earned truths. We are a culture and a publishing industry focused on the young, and an asset of this series is in fact the element of discovery. My guest editor and I get to offer new writers a portal to a larger audience, a prize in a cutthroat business and a very loud world. But here's a warning to young writers: if you think that publication, an added item to an author bio, a prize, or a proud post on social media will bring you sustainable satisfaction, you will be disappointed. The highest highs and the truest and most lasting joy comes with reading and writing itself. To the writers in this volume: be sure to read the other stories here. To others who are reading these words: after you're done reading this book, pick up one of the past volumes.

Try one from a decade or longer ago. See if you can find a writer you've always wanted to try, someone you just never got around to reading. A story is a great place to start.

When I think of what I most love about short fiction (which happens to be what I love about any writing), it's an easy sense of balance. It's risk with depth. It's one eye to the future with another to the past. It's low- and highbrow side by side. It's the marriage of young and old, showing and telling. We cannot write without reading. We cannot write well without a deep and broad sense of the other writing that has come before us.

This year's volume brings an assortment of new and established voices, slow builds and explosions, rural and urban settings, earthly and surreal, young and old characters. Amidst the promising newcomers—Alexandra Chang, Katherine Damm, Susan Shepherd—comes a previously unpublished story by Laurie Colwin, who passed away in 1992. Established writers like Jhumpa Lahiri and Jim Shepard appear alongside new voices like Suzanne Wang, whose first published story appears here and is guaranteed to make you rethink the relentless inhumanity of artificial intelligence. The new and old appear together within stories, too. Steven Duong addresses the horribly age-old plague of racism with fresh vulnerability and intimacy. Selena Gambrell Anderson takes an unemployed jeweler for a ride on an old slave slip. Allegra Hyde is, as she says, "someone who often likes to write about the future by way of the past, which is how I got it into my head to reimagine Alexis de Tocqueville's travels around America in the nineteenth century." A Russian bureaucrat living in Texas sets off for a ranch and bonds with animals in Taisia Kitaiskaia's fairy tale–infused and electric "Engelond." Paul Yoon beautifully brings to life a man leaving a settlement and returning to a destroyed home after the Korean War. A woman who lives on the fringe of society tries to reconnect with her grown son in Madeline ffitch's astonishing story, about which the author writes, "sometimes words have so much power that you can't talk about what you're talking about. You have to talk about something else." Another woman returns home to help her mother after her father's death in Lori Ostlund's "Just Another Family," a story written with irresistible humor and pathos, patience and energy. Marie-Helene Bertino gorgeously explores the hazards of eternal life. Jamel Brinkley brings us a group of high schoolers who reconnect with an old friend over rescue rabbits. Molly Dektar offers up a father and daughter holding tight to their own versions of the past. A therapist gets in touch with a former patient years after their work together in Daniel Mason's emotionally acute story, "A Case Study." Azareen Van der Vliet Oloomi manages to balance humanity and mysticism, beauty and illness in her story about a woman's trip to a medieval city located near the Pyrenees.

This is my final volume of *The Best American Short Stories*. It's time to devote myself to a different form of allyship with writers and writing. A couple years ago I started Heidi Pitlor Editorial and heidipitlor.substack.com in order to do just this (flagrant self-promotion here). I've missed the other kind of editing, the longer, deeper engagement with authors and their work. That said, I will greatly miss reading for this series. I still remember the moment I came across Lauren Groff's story, "L. DeBard and Aliette," her first to appear in this series. It was also my first year as series editor. Groff's use of language and sense of story and character and motivation were stunning—I could not believe that this was a young writer. Stephen King, the guest editor that year, agreed. What a gift to have Lauren as my final guest editor! I sent her the first of three batches of stories, and she read these forty pieces in warp speed. She sent me a lovely, grateful email saying that she'd hoped for more stories that took "wild swings, risks, pushing against narrative expectations." I happened to be teaching at a conference in Kauai at the time, and after my initial chafing—*Let* her *read 3,500 stories every year, dammit*—I was soon overcome with the sense that she was right. I had phoned it in, had sent along quality but ultimately safe stories. After eighteen years of reading, I had finally shifted into cruise control. I promptly went back and reread certain stories. I read the subsequent stories with different eyes, and soon after, I came upon Steven Duong's "Dorchester," and we were off. Lauren agreed. Thank you, Lauren, for giving me the kick in the pants that I needed. We must be fully awake in order to read well. We must be fully awake when we write, too. If anyone writes with more alertness and focus and energy than Lauren herself, I've yet to come across their work.

I write this in April 2024, and the upcoming presidential election grows uncomfortably close. By the time you hold this book in your hands, someone, inevitably an older man, will have been elected president again. Most likely the partisan noise will have risen to a fever pitch and will continue this way for too long. Each of us longs to and deserves to be heard—but let us not forget to listen, to allow space for each other. To serve witness. In her story in the following pages, Laurie Colwin writes, "It occurs to me as I sit that everyone in the world is born with a personality and is fully entitled to express it. The planet is a-spin with notions, phobias, inclinations, tastes, ideas, creeds, beliefs, and behaviors of all kinds. Often this thought is uplifting and fills my heart with what feels like rich blood. If I stopped any of these people and questioned them closely, we would be sure to have a friend, an experience, a relative in common."

The stories chosen for this anthology were originally published between January 2023 and January 2024. The qualifications for selection are (1) original publication in nationally distributed American or Canadian periodicals; (2) publication in English by writers who have made the United States or Canada their home; (3) original publication as short stories (excerpts or novels are not considered). A list of magazines consulted for this volume appears at the back of the book. Editors who wish their short fiction to be considered for next year's edition should send their publications to The Best American Short Stories, Mariner Books, Attention: Jessica Vestuto, HarperCollins Publishers, 195 Broadway, 23rd Floor, New York, NY 10007, or links or files as attachments to thebestamericanshortstories@gmail.com.

Heidi Pitlor

Introduction

WHERE IN THE world does the short story come from? If we rifle backward through literary history, we snatch up one possibility for the primary ancestor, only to discard it when an earlier precursor reveals itself. One possibility, Giovanni Boccaccio's fourteenth-century *Decameron,* in which wealthy people quarantined against a raging plague tell stories to pass the time, gives way to the Islamic Golden Age's dazzling compilation *One Thousand and One Nights,* which gives way to ninth- and tenth-century Persian fables, and on and on back into misty prehistory. The bite-size tale seems simply always to have been here, to have risen in tandem with human language. Though the radical technology of the written word is still relatively new in the grand scheme of our species, the short story is atavistic. For thousands of generations, there was little else to do but share a story or two during the long cold nights, hyenas yipping somewhere just outside the cave opening, the only stays against the darkness a fire to warm the body and another human mind to warm the soul.

The short story as we know it today—let's call it a chunk of literary fiction short enough to read in one sitting—is a river flowing out of many sources, including biblical tales, fables that gesture toward morality, fabliaux and chansons and lais and other stories in verse, and fairy tales transcribed from the work of oral masters of the form. In Germany in 1795, Johann Wolfgang von Goethe contributed a few short tales or stories to Schiller's journal, *Die Horen,* but they didn't seem to take. An innovation with few copycats is no innovation, alas.

Perhaps because of the new development in cheap printing, which gave rise to periodicals in the early nineteenth century, a great eruption of the form happened at about the same time in multiple European languages. Now ideas could pass boundaries of space and language in a way that had previously been difficult. In 1819 in America, Washington Irving published "Rip Van Winkle." In 1829, in France, Prosper Mérimée's "Mateo Falcone" appeared in the *Revue de Paris,* and by 1936 was being hailed by the critic Albert Thibaudet as a new literary form that did not exist before Mérimée birthed it. In 1831, Alexander Pushkin published his collection, *The Tales of the Late Ivan Petrovich Belkin,* and 1832 the Ukranian Nikolai Gogol published the two volumes of stories called *Evenings on a Farm Near Dikanka.* Also in 1832, the American Edgar Allan Poe published his first short story, "Metzengerstein: A Tale in Imitation of the German." Poe was one of the few early American writers who would have a powerful influence across the Atlantic, primarily because his translator was none other than the poet Charles Baudelaire. Poe would go on to make powerful inventions in mystery, science fiction, Gothic fiction, and horror.

In the late nineteenth century, two paths opened up for short fiction, as demonstrated by three practitioners who lived contemporaneously: On the one hand were extremely popular plot-heavy tales often with surprise twists or endings, written swiftly and meant for daily or weekly journals or newspapers, like those by O. Henry in the United States or Guy de Maupassant in France. On the other hand, there was the model that arose from the stories of the Russian doctor and grandson of a liberated serf, Anton Chekhov—who had begun, like the two others, writing stories for journals and papers for money—but soon developed a cool, keen, nonjudgmental, character-centric form of the story, in which plot is secondary to emotional truth. The latter style quickly took precedence as the highest literary form of the short story. To this day, nobody has had a stronger influence on contemporary American short fiction than Chekhov. Great living story writers, from George Saunders to Danielle Evans to Alice Munro to Lorrie Moore to Yiyun Li, all owe an obvious debt to the subtle, generous doctor.

It's possible that the heyday of the short story came and went in the twentieth century, when slick magazines paid what, in 2024, appear be absurd prices for the short fiction of geniuses like F. Scott Fitzgerald and John Updike. Both writers could support their families with a yearly handful of stories sold to places like Scribner's and *The New Yorker.* In 1929, the *Saturday Evening Post* paid Fitzgerald $4,000 per story, today the equivalent of $72,500, or a downpayment on a nice house. Even the best-paying magazines for short stories these days only pay a fraction of that. It didn't hurt the form that, after the Iowa Writers' Workshop was founded in 1936 and copied thousands of times at universities across the country, the workshop model for fiction, in which a writer sits silently (freaking out) while the rest of the workshop goes to town on the work at hand, was only effective when it used the short story. It is almost impossible to meaningfully workshop a novel in progress; I believe, deeply, that it's cruel to expose novels to such harsh and deforming light when they're so tender and fragile and young.

When the internet came along, it reversed the technological advances that cheap printing had brought to the form in the early nineteenth century. The internet has had a chilling effect on the market for the short story, because, though there were now infinitely more places to publish one's work, the places that paid for short fiction mainly lost interest in publishing them. It is expensive to put out a literary journal in print, and, though there are more people than ever before in this country, we have exponentially more places to scatter our attention, and it is hard for most journals to get enough subscribers to pay the bills. Short fiction, already closer to poetry than the novel in its intensity and size, has begun, for the most part, to be published like poetry. That is to say, in small journals run with passion, the writer repaid with pride in their work and a few contributor copies.

Let me say, here, that I don't think this is necessarily a bad thing. I want all writers to be able to make a living from their work, of course! But if publishing short stories provides very little opportunity to make money, the people who would only be in it to make money won't bother with the form. This leaves the short story writers of the world to be the ones who love stories most deeply, who see in the form something taut and urgent and profound. Just as there is no shortage of poets in America, there is no shortage of short story writers, thank god. It makes me happy to know this, and to have seen such overwhelming evidence of it in my role this year as guest judge, because the short story is the literary form that I love the most. Though a writer has the time over the course of their lives to write many more short fictions than they can write novels, in my opinion, it is far harder to write an excellent short story than it is to write an excellent novel. A story is unforgiving in a way the more capacious novel—Henry James's "loose, baggy monster"—is not. In William Faulkner's 1956 *Paris Review* interview, the Nobel Prize winner most famous for his novels, said, "Maybe every novelist wants to write poetry first, finds he can't, and then tries the short story, which is the most demanding form after poetry. And, failing at that, only then does he take up novel writing." I'd quibble a little with this, because I think it's possible for a writer to love all three forms with equal intensity. That said, it's vanishingly rare for all three forms to love the writer back. I know this from personal experience, to my chagrin; I began writing as a poet when I was twelve years old and a friend gave me the collected works of Emily Dickinson. In the Amherst poet's words, I felt physically as though the top of my head were taken off. Emily Dickinson fomented thousands of poems in me, though all were sickly, feeble little things. It wasn't until college, when I took a short story class, that real, vigorous, richly oxygenated blood began to run in my work. I could finally stretch and breathe and feel the good strong muscles of the words working the way I wanted them to. I adore writing novels—they are the first souls I see in the early morning when I get up, and over the years that they take me to write, they become my intimate friends—but short stories are heady, wild, passionate little beasts that I write the first drafts of with a fevered joy and a great single burst of energy, with infinite rewrites and revisions afterward. The part of my brain that hums with short fiction is the same part that hummed with poetry when I was a shy, tormented twelve-year-old, and that hums when I read the poetry of great writers now. The difference is that, from the first, short fiction loved me back.

Here's my wholehearted plea: if you love short fiction, if you want it to thrive as a form, and have the means, please take the opportunity to look at the wonderful list of outlets for the short story in the back of this book, and choose a few to subscribe to. Better yet, ask your local libraries to subscribe to them, and read them when they come in. Nearly every prose writer I adore got their start in small, scrappy journals; only when readers support said journals can the next wave of brilliant prose writers work their way into the world. Amen. End sermon.

There has never been a time when the deep knowledge of craft of the short story has been so prevalent, so faithfully and constantly and prolifically practiced. This is because of the constant accumulation of ever more short stories that have been written through the years, the vast population of writers working today, and the number of MFA programs in which the short story is treated as something of a training exercise (unexciting to many, but necessary for building strength and endurance: literary squat-thrusts, narrative planks). It follows that there have never been as many exquisitely built stories in existence than there are now. Most of the stories I read for this year's edition of *The Best American* Short Stories were faultlessly crafted: balanced, symmetrical, thoughtfully designed, the windows and doors true in their frames, nary the smallest gap under the door for a palmetto bug to crawl through, no crack at the roofline for a hurricane wind to yank at with its invisible strong hands. There were so many well-made stories, in fact, that I grew a little bit tired of the well-made story. Such ingratitude, Lauren! I scolded myself: Wouldn't you rather have an airtight story than a mess of words slung willy-nilly onto the page? Absolutely. Yes. Of course. And yet, I often found myself, when reading, yearning for something perhaps less carefully made, something rawer, meaner, spikier, something that made me uncomfortable. I was hungry for stories that absolutely shouldn't work but that, somehow, did.

What I tried to draw together for you, here, are twenty stories that buzz with their own strange logic. There are some stories that made me question my own understanding of craft, honed for more than twenty-five years in my own relentless writing and reading of the form, and some stories that revealed their authors as more artist than artisan. Art has a kind of magic in it, something that sets the blood on fire, that speaks to planes of existence deeper than the individual one. Art speaks out of the previous art that others have made; art speaks back into time. I have come to wonder if true, resonant art in the form of the short story is possible without some kind of exquisitely controlled imperfection. This is not to say that there are no stories in this edition that are beautifully crafted, of course, because there obviously are; but that those stories also have that ineffable something else, a weird discordance thrumming up under the perfect harmony of the sentences, a tang of dread, a moment the story takes a flying volta into the unknown, a feeling that both the author and I were simultaneously discovering something together.

But *how* do you *know* that what you're making is *art*? I can imagine so many writers yelling right now in their garrets and garages and beds and desk chairs, wherever they may be reading this. *How* do you do this? *How* do you go through craft into art?

Welp, that's the perennial question, I'd say. I don't know.

But that maybe if you listen hard enough, the work you are trying to make *does* know.

And that, eventually, if you are patient enough and listen to the story attentively enough, you will figure out how to make a particular story into art.

And that you will have to figure out how to do it every single time you write another one, because you have to figure out how to create magic anew. Just because you did it once doesn't mean that you can do it again.

Good luck!

Ciphers and koans; riddles and magic. You can teach craft, you can teach legerdemain, disappearing tigers and daring escapes from locked immersion tanks, but you can't teach real magic. Here's an even more frustrating thing to say: the magic in a short story is not merely subjectively there, not merely objectively there, but, somehow, both at once. It is highly dependent on the receptivity of the reader: their familiarity with other short stories, their affection for the form, whether the particular voice dovetails with the reader's taste, as well as other uncontrollable factors like barometric pressure, hormone levels, mood, dips in blood sugar, vitamin deficiencies, whether the dog was grumpy in the morning, etc. That said, the presence of magic is just as objective as it is subjective. This is highly unfashionable to say, but I'll say it: there *is,* in fact, a difference between good art and bad art. *À chacun son goût* is a perfectly acceptable philosophy when it comes to the way a person takes their morning coffee, or how to match one's socks with one's hat, or even when talking about most television shows, but it is in no way sufficient when it comes to talking about art. It's only a keen understanding of the history of the art form at hand, plus careful attention, plus openness, plus frequent self-interrogation, plus time, that can teach people how to recognize objective artistic power.

That said, even after all that time and training, the imp of the subjective can come moseying along and ruin everything.

Of the many stories I read this year, I'm positive that I missed some utterly astonishing ones. Perhaps I had just read a story in which a mother is dying of cancer, and couldn't immediately handle another; perhaps my phone rang in the middle of a truly great story and broke the spell, and my feathers were too ruffled by the outrageous intrusion of another human's needs into my solitude to get the flow of the story back. Perhaps a story contained one of my pet peeves or irrational dislikes, like too many subordinate clauses starting the sentences, or the body of a dead girl, or cats. (I said it.) In addition to this year's *Best American Short Stories*, I had the privilege of reading for the O. Henry Prize last year, which means that during the past two years, I have read hundreds, if not thousands, of contemporary stories. Through these two experiences of judging short stories, I have come to feel an almost physical reaction when I pick up a story and I discover that it's in the first person. It's not quite an allergy, but maybe something along the lines of a spiritual intolerance; my readerly gut starts to churn, my skin itches, I have a flight response. Don't get me wrong: the first person is often a very good choice. In any case, it's one of the three we've got. I use it myself, sometimes! It's fine! I believe quite firmly that I would not feel such a strongly developed intolerance of the first person if 90 percent of the stories I've read these past few years hadn't been in the first person. The second person has felt, ever since Lorrie Moore and Jay McInerney dazzled the world with it in the 1980s, a bit of a copycat move; the third person has become vanishingly rare. The first person is, simply, wildly overused.

A cynic might say that the overwhelming tsunami of the first person has something to do with the solipsism of the contemporary age, the navel-gazing age, the age of selfies and social media influencers. I dislike modern-day cynicism, especially among literary types (though I deeply admire the OG, Diogenes, naked and defiant in his *pithos* in the marketplace), so I refuse to believe this is the cause. Instead, I think a slow earthquake is taking place. Bedrock authority is being shaken and broken up. America is secularizing, which is not in itself a bad thing, but with this loss of a greater authority looking sternly back at us, the god's-eye view of the world may feel false to the contemporary writer. The institutions that hold us accountable—the mainstream media, the Supreme Court, the presidency, academic institutions (just look at what that vindictive fingerling potato Ron DeSantis is doing to

Florida's state educational system)—are being loudly and visibly corrupted. This is shaking our collective faith in said institutions. This last sentence made me uncomfortable to write it, probably because, as a result of the earthquaking of authority, it feels a little wrong to speak in generalizations. Perhaps the only authority that many of us have come to feel secure in is the authority we have over our own lives. We speak out of our personal experience so we don't trample on the experience of others. Plus, *I* contains its own plausible deniability.

The problem with the first person is also its strength: it is tethered ineluctably to the individual. This means that it is inherently limited. The limitations can give a first-person story immediate accessibility and credibility: here is a single story, recorded by a single mind, that has its apotheosis when another single mind—the reader's—encounters it. There is no obfuscating authorial consciousness getting in the way, complicating things. At the same time, this tight anchoring to a singular consciousness can also make many stories feel way too safe, as if the writer is absolving themselves from engaging in systems or injustices larger than the self. The first-person voice contains its own excuse for the blinders hindering its sight; after all, there's only so much one person can do or see or experience or know. The first person also makes a lot of stories sound rather samey-samey. It turns out that when hundreds or thousands of people sing the same vowel sound together—*IIIIII*—even if each voice is radically different, they blend together into one very loud musical note.

That said, I did include a bunch of first-person stories in this anthology. In our paranoid, kinetic, hyperspeed year 2024, I just couldn't escape them. I do want to honor the first-person stories that made it into this edition because they're exceptionally strong; they felt new and strange, they subverted my expectations, they overcame my instinctive initial impulse on seeing the dreaded *I*, which was to fling them across the room. They are proof that it is not really the fact of the first person that I object to—in the right hands, it can be a thrilling choice, as it is in the stories here—but only the fact of its overwhelming contemporary preponderance.

I'd love to take a moment near the end of this essay to celebrate—roll in the champagne, the dancing dogs in tiny costumes, the mountains of roses!—our *BASS* queen, Heidi Pitlor, who, after her eighteenth year, is gently setting down her crown as series editor of *The Best American Short Stories.* It boggles the mind how many pieces of short fiction that Heidi must have read throughout her nearly two decades as series editor; in fact, I tried to calculate it for you, but gave up when I started to feel a panic attack coming on. I have been lucky to work with Heidi with some regularity during these eighteen years, having had seven stories selected for her *Best American Short Stories* series, one reprinted in her *100 Years of the Best American Short Stories* anthology. Her name brings a swoop of happiness every time I see it, even now, after the intensity of being a guest judge, when one might assume that I'd be a little bit tired of hearing from Heidi. Never! I came out of the stint admiring her even more deeply. It has felt like an extraordinary stroke of luck to get to read and discuss and think through this year's stories with her, that she still will answer my calls after the innumerable and confusing emails I have sent trying to specify what exactly it meant when I said I was looking for stories that sent blue lightning through my nerve endings, what I meant when I wanted stories that felt a little raw, a little dangerous, a little new. I can tell you that Heidi is so tough and smart and razor-focused that she would never have stayed so long in the role if she did not love short fiction with every particle of her being; she has a vast memory for short stories; she is, and will remain, one of the world's greatest advocates for the deeply strange and oft-overlooked form. Also, and this should be heartening to many writers out there, I was so moved to see how passionately she looks out for so many writers, how she works very hard, year after year, to bring them to the attention of her guest judges. Some of these writers have not yet had a story in *BASS,* so they may not know of the true admirer they have in Heidi. I do, now, and I'm in awe of her enormous heart, which can hold so many eloquent and complicated strangers in it.

Now, a word about the stories you are going to read, all of which Heidi first loved and passed along. I have come to dread the word *masterful,* particularly when it is applied to art: it suggests an outrageously oppositional relationship between artist and art, one in which the art is a subordinate to the artist, either resentful paid servant or, far worse, forced to bend its will and life to the artist, and, as a result is perhaps rightfully full of an acute and wounding rage. Who in their right mind would want to fight with art like this? The nomenclature of the master of fine arts—for people who trained up into an exquisite sensitivity in language!—falls with a clunk. What actual human, having spent two years reading and writing in a workshop, suddenly comes out the other end having wrestled their art into submission? Oh, darling, please! Using the language of hierarchy is a goober-headed way to talk about something that is one of the great gifts of being human; art is a lifelong companion that one creates oneself; art is a slowly accumulated rarified atmosphere in which one can breathe freely; art is a way to sing back into eternity. So, let's never insult the short stories in this collection by calling them masterful. Let's call them what they are: authoritative, intelligent, musical, often risky. They are gorgeous, generous, three-way collaborative acts between the writer, the work, and the reader. You.

You, the reader, are the final element in all art. A story or poem or song or painting—any piece of art—cannot fully exist until the audience meets and finishes it. So please come to these stories with your ears tuned to the music of the sentences, your eyes open, your soul receptive to the strangeness and beauty here. You may not like all of them (the imp of the subjective rides!). But I hope—I trust—that if you can meet these stories where they live, you will be as dazzled by them as I am.

LAUREN GROFF

SHASTRI AKELLA

The Magic Bangle

FROM *Fairy Tale Review*

KARTIK MAKES A decision the day his father strikes him: on workday evenings and weekends he'll pretend he's a tourist in his hometown. His real home—where he belongs—is a place, he imagines, where it's safe for him to love men.

That Thursday after work he visits the Golconda Fort. He enlists the services of a tour guide, who takes him from the watchtower on the rampart to the courtroom in the heart of the fort. The tour guide tells Kartik about the fort's many tricks. Alcoves for soldiers to hide in plain sight. Unseen vantage points from which to pour hot oil on intruders. Kartik likes the clap trick best. When the watchtower soldier clapped, the sound traveled all the way to the courtroom: two claps for an approaching friend, one clap for a foe.

A happy future is the sound of two claps, Kartik thinks.

On Friday he tells his parents he's going to the Delhi office on a work trip and leaves home with a suitcase. At work he tells his colleagues he's going to see the Taj Mahal for the long weekend. The office will be closed on Monday for Holi.

He takes an Uber to his hometown's old district and checks into a hotel. His fourth-floor room has a balcony that overlooks the Charminar. He changes into a red kurta, straps his camera across his shoulder, and goes down to join the street traffic: scooterists, pedestrians, buffaloes, and peddlers of steel vessels, velvet pursers, and plastic roses. The air smells of jasmine and stagnant water. He crosses the Jama Masjid, whose stone courtyard is packed with Friday devotees. Men in kurtas lean towards one another, haloed in dusk's violet glow, their murmurs a collective buzz. The women's praying quarters, he guesses, are tucked away, out of sight.

He takes a right and enters the Bangle Bazaar. He pauses frequently to click a photograph. In a shop empty of customers, a man sitting behind the counter holds his attention. Camera to one eye, Kartik zooms in on him: his face in profile, illuminated by phone light, his skin the color of chai. A manicured stubble dots his angular jaw. There's a slight shift in his posture, as if he knows he's being watched. Not immediately, but at length, he lifts his head and looks. Kartik hones in on the man's green eyes, framed by his thick lashes, punctuated by a mole on his temple. *Click.* Kartik lowers his camera and walks into the shop. He occupies the chair the green-eyed stranger points to.

What kind of bangles are you looking for? the man asks Kartik. Glass? Enamel? Metal?

He speaks a mixture of Urdu and Hindi, and his voice brings to mind the sound of a stone skimming the surface of water.

What do you recommend? Kartik asks, holding one hand up. He points to his wrist.

The man rubs his jaw. He knows it's his most attractive feature. He knows Kartik finds him attractive. Kartik can tell, from the tilt of his neck, from the slow movement of his gaze.

Bidar, he replies. Silver, with an antique look.

A man shuffles out from behind a curtain that leads to the back of the shop. He has a small white beard and wizened coffee skin. He nods at Kartik, then says, adjusting his skullcap, I'm off to pray, Shahrukh.

The man's departure seems to unknot Shahrukh. His shoulders relax under his brown kurta; his face opens like the door of a cage. My parents met at a Shahrukh Khan film, he volunteers. Ammi was selling tickets, and Abbu was buying.

He stands and opens the display rack. His hand darts with practiced ease. He extracts six bangles. They release six sonorous clinks as he places them on the glass counter.

Which one? Kartik asks him. You pick.

Shahrukh sits down and leans forward. Kartik smells the perfume on his neck. A scent full of smoke and wood. His left cheek is scarred somewhat; the tip of his tongue gleams against one side of his mouth. They hear the azaan. The singer's voice is husky. Shahrukh points to the bangle third from the right.

You didn't even look, Kartik protests.

I knew, Shahrukh tells him, when I pulled it off the shelf.

He places the bangle in an envelope like it's a letter.

Kartik pays, takes the envelope, and asks Shahrukh out to dinner. He suggests Shadab. It's nearby but not fancy, he acknowledges.

It's unique, Shahrukh says. Two men going to Shadab on their first date? Janab. We'll make history in the city's oldest biriyani joint.

He reaches under the counter. An object flashes between his fingers. He slips it into his trouser pocket.

Shahrukh points to the Lakshmi temple abutting one of the Charminar's minarets. He says, The first Nizam king propitiated the goddess. When she showed up, pleased with his devotion, he tricked her into staying.

How? Kartik asks. He knows the story, but he wants to hear it again.

Shahrukh replies, He tells the goddess he's got an urgent errand to finish. Before leaving, he extracts from her a promise that she won't leave until he returns. And he never returns. The goddess knows, of course. She finds the ruse clever and blesses the Nizams with wealth that sees them through the rise and fall of the Mughal and British empires.

They take a corner table at Shadab. On the opposite wall is a framed quote from the Quran, white Arabic letters sewn into a green cloth. The place is crowded with the men who were at Jama Masjid. They're immersed in food and conversation. The air is thick with the scents of hot spices and cardamom. A qawwali plays on the speaker, the poet Ghalib's words punctuated with rhythmic, forceful claps: *Allow me, Imam, to drink in the mosque or show me to a corner where God isn't there.*

After the waiter serves them their food and takes their money, Shahrukh picks up the envelope from the table and extracts the bangle. He takes Kartik's hand and slips the bangle down his wrist. Shahrukh's teeth gleam in Shadab's orange glow. It feels to Kartik like magic, affection expressed in the open.

Do you want to meet Samosa? Shahrukh asks.

I'd like to eat one, Kartik says.

Samosa is my dog, Shahrukh says and laughs.

They eat from the same steaming plate of biriyani with their hands. They imbibe sweet tea from the same hot steel cup they pass back and forth. It's a place of communal eating. No one blinks an eye at them.

They lie next to each other on the hotel bed, fully clothed.

What are you doing in Hyderabad? Shahrukh asks.

I'm *from* Hyderabad, Kartik replies.

He recounts the incident: he in the kitchen, refilling his glass with water; a notification sounds from his phone, left on the dinner table unlocked; he's out in a flash, the tap left running; his phone in his father's hand; on the screen, the dating app: a private message and a picture attachment; his mother sees it next and grips her head; she cries; his father stands, returns his phone, and strikes him across the face before sitting down; he says, I'm giving you a year to get this hobby out of your system. After that, you're getting married. Clear?

He called it a "hobby," Kartik says. In a year, prospective brides will sit in my drawing hall with their parents and ask me what I studied, where I work, how much I earn. I play tourist to forget that future.

Shahrukh turns and places his foot on Kartik's ankles. A wave of electricity shoots through Kartik's body.

Will you take your kurta off for me? he asks.

Shahrukh yanks his kurta off and tosses it to the floor without breaking contact.

I have an enchanted bangle, Shahrukh tells him. Its magic is real.

He taps his trouser pocket.

Kartik runs his fingers through the hair on Shahrukh's chest. He's heard what Shahrukh has said, but what's more magical than a beautiful man whom Kartik desires and who, like some miracle, desires him back?

This bangle, Shahrukh continues, is made of mirror. If you look into it and ask a question, it will give you the answer. If you ask a question about the future, you must do what the bangle shows. The djinn who controls the bangle's magic doesn't like being wrong.

Kartik laughs. He touches Shahrukh's jaw. Let's call it a night? he says.

Shahrukh mounts Kartik, and Kartik wraps his hands around Shahrukh's warm back.

*

Kartik befriends Samosa the next day by feeding her ice cream. One spoonful at a time. She has large brown eyes, a thick white tail, and caramel fur that glows in the sunlight. They bring her to Kartik's hotel. The manager, Su, doesn't object. She knows Samosa. And she *knows.* Her eyes shine as she watches Shahrukh and Kartik as they wait for the elevator, their shoulders touching.

Kartik points to the GRE workbook Shahrukh holds.

I want to do my Masters in New York, Shahrukh says. Right now the book is a ruse. Abbu thinks I'm studying with Zaid, who, incidentally, thinks I'm on a Tinder date.

Kartik aches for that future: a room in Brooklyn with Shahrukh. Kartik's parents moved in with him as soon as he started working. If he had objected, his family would have branded him an ungrateful wretch for not caring for his aging parents. The real problem, Kartik knows, is that he's internalized their way of thinking.

Samosa naps on the balcony. Shahrukh sits on a chair next to her and spreads his legs. Kartik sits between his thighs. Shahrukh takes out the magic bangle. It reflects the Charminar behind them. They stick to safe questions.

Whom am I falling in love with? Kartik asks.

The reflected reality doesn't fade. But soon Shahrukh's face appears over it: first as an outline, then fully pronounced. It is a snapshot from last evening, when Kartik saw him through the lens of his camera.

Creep, Shahrukh teases. He asks the bangle the same question, and Kartik's face from the restaurant appears.

The answers are broader than the question. Now they each know the point at which the other fell for him.

A fakir gave it to me at an Eid fair, Shahrukh says.

He had a crush on you, Kartik says with a grave nod.

Stop, Shahrukh says, laughing. I was *eighteen.* The fakir looked like he hadn't seen a shower in some time, but his shawl smelled of new cotton. I bought him a plate of biriyani—he said he was hungry. He took out this bangle, looked into it, and murmured in a language I didn't understand. He smiled after a moment. A bangle for the bangle seller's boy, he said, holding it out. He told me it was magic. You're the first person I've showed it to.

You met him again? Kartik asks.

Shahrukh's answer confirms what he already knows.

*

They walk to Shadab for biriyani and chai, Samosa in tow.

What if your parents show up here? Shahrukh asks.

They won't, says Kartik.

Shahrukh looks at the bangle. Do Kartik's parents like Muslims? he asks.

Kartik apologizes for the bangle's answer.

We can't apologize for our parents, Shahrukh says, his smile sad.

Kartik wakes in the night, cold. Shahrukh is asleep with his hand wrapped around Samosa. The dog softly snores. Shahrukh's black hair shivers in the breeze of the fan. The room is drenched in moonlight. Kartik gets up and puts on a T-shirt and pajamas. He notices the bangle on the bedside table. He picks it up and addresses the djinn.

I bet you are as powerful as Aladdin's djinn. Who are you anyway? he asks.

After a moment, he puts down the bangle and climbs into bed, covering Shahrukh, Samosa, and himself with a blanket.

Who is he, the djinn? Shahrukh asks, his eyes still closed.

Not he, Kartik says. *She.* She lives in a minaret in the middle of a desert. The Thar, I'm guessing, from her outfit. A choli-lehenga. She plays a sarod and has a pet camel.

Shahrukh says, Our mullah said that if you use djinn magic to get what you want, a hundred different things will have to realign to make the new reality happen. You'll lose a lot in the process. It's the price you pay for defying fate.

His eyes open. His irises, emerald by day, are moss by moonlight.

Am I worth that price? Shahrukh asks. You don't even know me.

I know I like you, Kartik replies. And you're a man. That's better than marrying a girl of my parents' choosing. There's a price to pay either way.

Under the blanket, Shahrukh places his foot on Kartik's ankles.

On Monday they stand on the balcony and watch people on the street smear one another's necks and faces with color and water. The sectarian difference, made particularly volatile under the current regime, vanishes. The only riot is that of colors staining the air pink, blue, and green. The only guns fired are water guns. The only shrieks are those that rise from throats drunk on bhang: milk steeped with cannabis, ginger, cardamom, and rose and served cold. Kartik and Shahrukh don't partake in the festivities. They want to spend their last day together exclusively in each other's company. Su has brought them a jug of bhang. They take turns drinking from it directly.

They sit with their backs to the balcony wall. Shahrukh holds the jug away from Samosa, who's eager for a lick. Kartik tells Shahrukh a story. Two boys fell in love a long time ago, but they knew their elders wouldn't let them get married, so they fled to the forest and hung themselves from the oldest tree. But the tree spirit, moved by their love, reincarnated them as plants. Tobacco and cannabis. Lovers bound forever in a wedlock of intoxication.

Shahrukh smiles and leans forward and claims the white liquor mustache on Kartik's upper lip.

The next morning the light from Jama Masjid radiates a glow where dawn has colored the sky blue. Kartik books an Uber, and Shahrukh packs his bag. Samosa stands up, shakes herself, and stares at Kartik.

She knows, Shahrukh says, zipping the bag. He leaves it by the door.

They lie next to each other on the bed, their fingers laced. Samosa lies next to Kartik, her paw on his chest. When Kartik's phone beeps, informing them the car is three minutes away, they sit up. Kartik kneels on the floor and slips Shahrukh's sandals onto his feet. Shahrukh slips Kartik's bangle down his wrist. It feels like a wedding.

They walk to the balcony. Shahrukh holds out the magic bangle.

Kartik poses the question that's on both their minds.

They wait, and from the corner of his eye, Kartik sees the car cruising down the street. It stops in front of the hotel. Samosa woofs. The light from the mosque gleams on the face of the bangle. The sound of the future fills Kartik's chest. A clap sounded twice.

SELENA GAMBRELL ANDERSON

Jewel of the Gulf of Mexico

FROM *McSweeney's*

SPRINGTIME AGAIN. AFTER ten o'clock. And I was deep in pine tree and cricket land, in the glass orangery Olivia's father had built for rare occasions of decadence and gluttony like this one: his fiftieth birthday. I sat where I'd been assigned, where the geraniums used to be. Waiters poured generously, so I drank. Hors d'oeuvres of every culture sailed past on polished silver, so I took bite-sized pieces of everything. But at twenty minutes past the hour, Uriah was still a no-show. Olivia and over three hundred of her people looked around, bug-eyed for scandal, and it was anyone's guess why her father, the original big-timer, would ditch his own party. Catching the bland face of another waiter, I motioned for a double—a double Malbec that is, because I'd recently come to appreciate the importance of seizing opportunity in those ask-and-receive type of atmospheres, whenever they weren't choking me, I mean. Choking wasn't my problem. I had gotten to where I could almost breathe without air. My problem was asking for the wrong things, or maybe being dumb about what to ask for, or maybe asking for anything in the first place. The waiter's face went canvas with recognition, and that's the look of a professional. Regardless, he topped me off again.

Eventually there comes a time when you say, *To hell with this.* That time came for me about a year ago. That was when my bid at the jewelry store had sort of run its course, due to some creative differences between the owner and myself. The situation progressed in such a way that in order to keep falling into the hole that had materialized under my feet, I wound up selling my car and breaking my lease. Excessive maybe. But sometimes you need to commemorate what's even happening. And Olivia, God bless her, Olivia who'd been demanding a happy future for years, she warned me against experimenting with her dreams too. And then she changed tactics, upping the ante, threatening progeny. "Maybe a boy," she'd said in her flip, fed-up way. "Someone to get your line in line." Whatever that meant. Now she was three weeks pregnant, celebrating with sparkling cider.

"We should've left," I told her. "You don't wait for anyone longer than fifteen minutes."

Hysterically gorgeous, she eyed the clock, then me. A half-orphaned pillar of black tourmaline, cotton candy hair backlit, eyebrows, dagger nose, and chin pointed at my heart. "Who told you that?"

"God."

She looked me up and down, with lashing winds. "I don't know what's keeping him," she said. "Out of everyone here, he wanted to see you. He wants to talk to you about your situation. He said he can relate. I think he wants to help."

My glasses started to fog the way they always do when I realize I'm about to get in trouble.

Olivia's father has never really liked me. Maybe because I couldn't rub two cents together, yet he's rich like he invented the color green, like he at least held the patent. That's how he made his pile of money. Patents.

Once he'd established a regionally famous rap label and trademarked the words "hootie who," Uriah went on to make his real fortune by purchasing the patents for all kinds of retailable junk—from foldable cameras to barbecue tags to light-up eyelashes to watches that transformed bad juju into positive ions. And like those who have the capital to fund the darkest regions of the imagination, over time Uriah had acquired some strange obsessions too. As of today, he owned the nation's largest collection of slave memorabilia. Nobody alive has more.

When Olivia and her brothers were in high school, he used to educate them on adversity by leaving them in hallways filled with muzzles and old farm equipment. The lessons stuck. Back in college, her party trick was to bum everyone out by naming all the slave ships that had ever sailed into Galveston Bay. I loved it, how cool she was with receiving high levels of attention, how she knowingly volleyed it back to other people who just couldn't do what she could. She'd caught me watching and said, "You're looking at me." A challenge.

I surveyed her mouth, breasts, and neck, shoulders, breasts, and legs, wrists, hips, and breasts again before finally getting to her eyes. Their power was almost feral. "You're looking back," I'd said. That's how it got started.

Early on, Olivia mentioned that her father had gotten into collecting as a way of ingratiating himself with a certain social circle. I recalled an interview in *What's the Word* magazine where Uriah discussed the trials of navigating the bougie set as an outsider, learning to react civilly to their class sympathies. "I had climbed a different ladder," he'd said, "and I guess they felt that nullified theirs." On the next page, he knelt in the prison break pose—leaning asymmetrically with praying hands—but the combination of a pin-striped suit, fur coat, and bowler hat made him look like a villain in a silent film who only wanted to be your friend. Who knows why he didn't make any?

"Want to know a secret," Olivia had said then. "He's in the market to buy one." *One* being a real slave ship that gave off the odors of sea salt and tragedy in the translucent green waves.

"You can't buy that sort of thing," I'd said, and even to myself I'd sounded naive, like I hadn't known since forever that everything is for sale.

So now her elder rapper, venture capitalist daddy wanted to have a chitchat?

"Cool," I said, which is garbage because when I'd met Uriah for the first time and he reached to shake my hand, I plucked my own glasses off my nose and broke them in two.

"Oh, you're a cool guy," said Olivia.

Under slightly different circumstances, if we were completely different people, I'd feel relieved, to be so acknowledged, embarrassed at my own happiness. But in reality, there's no such thing as mutual understanding. You're a chump to want it.

Somebody's mama took the stage singing one obituary ballad after another, looking at every face in the crowd but mine. The audience clapped at the right times, but as soon as possible, they looked for Uriah. This time I looked for the big man too.

"I want you to know it wasn't my idea," said Olivia, holding my eyes and then not. "I have nothing to do with it. But I agree with him. You lack direction."

"You only need directions if you're lost," I said.

Olivia let the comment slide, stabbing a tomato with her fork. "You know this. You're becoming a flop—by choice. You're a man who has become committed to making bad choices," she said, and I liked that logic. In her mind, the patient was restored to health simply from hearing the proper diagnosis.

Another negotiation was happening across the table. A man dug his nose almost sexually into a girl's ear. She let him linger before elbowing him away. Twenty-three maybe. A washed-up ballerina. The world is full of them.

"I mean, who are you trying to be?" Olivia said.

Dopily, I said, "I'm a jeweler."

Of course, I wanted to be important. My grandparents took the literacy test. I'm college educated. I'm an artist.

"You were never interested in that. And now you're not interested in anything." Above her salad, she became resigned, as if all my disappointments were hers to remember.

My ex-boss Gilbert was a tyrannical dweeb who took an hourly inventory of jewels and checked pockets and purses anytime employees attempted to leave the store. He'd promised to move me up from melting and casting to actually designing something, but there was always some delay. I got to the point where I couldn't handle the polite brush-off any longer—me on the other side of someone else's work, someone else's stupid yet realized dreams, my own face twisting in a fraud of geniality. One day, at the end of a particularly soul-crushing shift, I clenched my fists as Gilbert searched my wallet for a 0.0009-carat topaz that only existed in his mind, and I realized that the options available to me were to jump him or quit. So I quit.

"A flop," Olivia said. "It's floppy."

"It's complicated," I said. "I want to do my own thing, but timing isn't great, you know? With the economy and everything." I'd wanted to be a sculptor, making huge kaleidoscopes full of sapphires and setting them on mountaintops in Africa somewhere. "I'm working on stuff—lots of stuff. So much of this is beyond my control."

A waiter came around with a giant bottle of black wine, and the sound of pouring gave us something practical to listen to. Olivia smiled at the waiter and then looked at me like I'd just killed five people.

Onstage, the mother turned away from the applause and then her grin turned into a smear of disgust and all-knowingness. I don't know why, but I thought that if she looked at me, something would shift.

Olivia leaned in and grabbed my hand, nerves sparking. "You feel that?" She was referring to her engagement ring, a pear-shaped amethyst that had survived two fire sales. "You made a promise, you ugly possum. Snap out of it."

That's when the man leaned in to pay his ballerina a compliment. "Your perfume reminds me of gravy," he said. The girl pulled a double take—we all did.

"What did I do?" He held her hand, kissing the knuckles. "At least tell me what I did?"

"You don't tell a young lady that her perfume smells like gravy."

"I said it *reminds* me of gravy!"

The man recovered quickly, rising with a pair of empty glasses in one hand and buttoning his tux with the other. For some reason this gave me a reason to get up too.

I wrenched my hand free from Olivia's. "I need to think."

"Oh yeah." She angled back in disbelief. "By all means. Think! And use your *entire* brain too!"

Wiping my face, I took a seat at the bar, the orangery's windows making a glass and steel womb around me. Outside the night purpled and purred with scrappy looking pine trees looming in. I piled my plate high with the kind of food that made me feel privileged and guilty. Nobody even noticed me, which was what I'd half expected.

Quitting your job, I found, wasn't such a hard thing to do. If you made up your mind to just quit, you could quit anything. And once you got to the quitting place, you realized just how much could go. Quitting was a matter of protest. I had tried to remind Olivia of this if I'd ever need her to pay the tab, or if my phone were to get disconnected, or if I'd ever need a new kidney. That last one was supposed to be a joke meant to charm and annoy her, like I used to do without even trying. But as I spoke, I saw her face change. She was frightened for me.

At once the crowd erupted with a different applause. A spotlight hit the exit door and in came Olivia's old man. I had to get where I could see. Regardless of the screams, people didn't seem that happy for Uriah. His neighbors, his exes, his friends. The men looked alike, like stress fractures, scheming. They tried to seem friendly and familiar but stood back while they were doing it. You can only congratulate a person so many times. You can't be happy about the other person's good fortune forever. It's actually inhumane.

Uriah cut across the room like an old gangster, pausing to dap up the men and kiss the women, no matter who they were or who they were with. Founder of Swamp Bottom Records. Father of two hundred patents and the most spoiled black kids I'd ever met. Negro Clause to my unborn. I felt simple by comparison.

Later, Uriah snuck up like a quiet fart. "You going to see all there is to see tonight or what?" he said. I turned my head quick, catching the humidity of my own sweat and edge wax. He was right there in his clanking chains and steel-colored suit, floating in all those metallics. "I mean, what's really going on?" he said. The way he eyed my drink sort of hurt my feelings.

"You made it," I said.

"I been looking for you, man." Uriah looked at me and stepped closer. "It's good to see you. How are you? What you doing? What's happening?"

My guts started yelling: *I can explain! In bed, together, your daughter and I fornicated, to secure our love bond, as we've been doing for almost ten years, but this time, the worst possible time, we got pregnant—it was both of us.*

Uriah let the smile creep up, and when I tried to copy him, he only shook his head. "You remind me of this dude who used to come wearing a panda mask to my concerts," he said. "He came to every damn show like that."

Uriah snapped his fingers, and the bartender came whizzing by with two more drinks. He pounded, I sipped. He crossed his arms, so I pounded too. "You don't got to wear the mask around me, man. It's better for our friendship, you know? If you speak freely."

"I don't have many friends," I said, body threatening to go supernova.

I was afraid to look away. Somewhere in Uriah's weakness-seeking eyes, I saw reflections of the twelve-year-old me surrounded by chains and bear straps, singing the National Negro Anthem at his compulsory request.

"Somehow that doesn't surprise me," said Uriah. "You got that rare talent for thinking *and* talking way too much. We probably wouldn't have to go through all this if you didn't."

"Go through what?"

"So many questions," he said. "What you think this is, an interview? It's *my* birthday."

Like a dummy, I wished his horrible ass a happy birthday.

"I'm in the mood to make friends, and as a token of my friendship, I want to loan you a present." He gripped my shoulder in foreboding. Or in support. Or in a secret that included both.

"I'm sorry—go through what?"

Uriah winked at me as though I'd asked an obvious question. "Well, let's start with this hallway. Shall we?"

"Hallway?"

What was it they used to say in church? Until God opens another door, you praise Him in the hallway. Uriah began to ferry me in that direction.

The hallway he spoke of was paneled in oceanic slabs of blue agate sourced from the Abismo Anhumas caves of Brazil, purchased at auction on the computer. Less than two ton remaining in the world and Uriah had squirreled away a small percentage for himself. In the crystal I watched a better and brighter version of myself drift by, radiant as an aura. Still, I couldn't forget where I was. Any holy visions of my reflection just served to remind me that I had visiting privileges to someone else's dream. Eventually the dreamer would have to wake up, and I would have to see my way out.

Uriah was talking. "When I'm between decisions, like earlier tonight, I take a walk down this hallway, and I always find a solution. Your problem is that you haven't found a solution like I have."

He paused so I could consider all the problems with how I was moving through life. But the effort of imitating thought under his gaze caused my glasses to fog up again. In spazzy movements, I dropped them into my shirt pocket. Don't judge. This was the best I could do to keep from staring at Uriah's collection, because by the way, we were *in* it.

Half a millennia's worth of torture toys dangled from the ceiling in a dense assortment of chains and muzzles. There were handheld cotton gins, hooks, gelding knives, masks, garrotes built for six, each piece flaked with rust. Somehow their stillness and weight—

not to mention their position over my head—made it impossible to see with total clarity.

Closing my eyes did little to keep the burning sweat from rolling in. Behind the orange glow of my eyelids, Olivia sat cross-armed, turning stank when she realized I was the one staring. I opened my eyes, and the blur of Uriah's collection took on a new shape: a big trap inside the even bigger trap of the hallway.

Uriah was still talking. "Sometimes you feel like everything is running from you. Your insides become swampland. You catch yourself on a curbside staring at thrown out furniture and getting poetic about it. When it gets that deep, I shop. Add a piece to the collection. Collecting has become my substitute for golf or therapy or teaching myself how to make a bomb."

Glancing up at a neck brace, I considered what he meant. That shopping for this colossus of antebellum nightsticks had kept a project kid from making a bomb.

"But now I quit," he said. "Starting today, I am no longer a collector. I've gone as far as I can go in this enterprise. I've outdone myself," he said, stealing glances until he had the confidence to go on. "Want to see what that looks like? To outdo yourself?"

At the end of the hall, Uriah cracked open the back door grinning timidly. "What I'm about to show you," he said, "might seem strange."

We looked down the length of his arm, squinting into the feathered darkness. At the end of the dock, next to a couple of candy painted speedboats and a Jet Ski, the outside world dissolved behind a three-hundred-year-old slave ship.

Maybe you've seen them. Drawings of our ancestors packed like anchovies in one of those prototypes for the ocean liner. Head-to-foot under a cannon. Surrounded by dried goods in cotton sacks, barrels upon barrels of rum.

The *Berthea* was much smaller than I had expected, about the size of a two-car garage. Crafted entirely of mildewed oak and a big girl set of coffee-stained sails, she nodded in weary salutation. Taking that first step on the deck, I held my breath. The floorboards interrupted every move with a vibrating om that seemed to echo into space. Uriah had taken the time to decorate a little. In the wheelhouse, there was a gray sectional sofa butted against the far wall, and angled in front was a glass coffee table covered with books on Kemetic yoga, under which lay a cowhide rug dyed buttery gold. A grill was wedged into a corner next to a box of cleaning supplies, a stereo system, and a limited-edition pair of headphones.

Then the wind kicked up. The moon sifted into the gulf and the gulf folded into itself, into white scribbles of moonlight. It turns out, the sky above a slave ship is no different than the sky above a baseball field or an alley. I kept expecting to catch a ghost staring in disapproval, but there was nothing like nothing had ever been. Nothing could accommodate the fact of that nothingness. It poured into my stomach like sand.

Uriah lit a pipe and played a record that I only knew from its samples. He talked about how the ship had changed hands over the centuries and had reinvented itself as a vessel of philanthropic good, displayed in a world-class museum. And when that museum fell on hard times and had to liquidate its assets, the ship assumed another life as the crown jewel of Uriah's collection.

His three interns hurried over to introduce themselves in quick succession: Bob, Bobby, and Bert. Mentally, I christened them the Bobbies. They had small, waxy faces and wore identical green windbreakers and took on a hungry, happy demeanor when Uriah was speaking. I couldn't tell if they even noticed me. On one of the big man's silent cues, the Bobbies got back to work, pulling up the anchor. "Don't get too attached," he told me. "Those three aren't included." Like a great dad, he laughed at his own joke.

There was a way of sailing the ship that relied on trade winds and reading the stars, but Uriah and his interns weren't about to do all that. The Bobbies had researched the basic stuff on the computer, studying a few videos that gave them enough confidence to coast along the harbor while Uriah steered the way. The whole trip would take no more than thirty minutes. That was the plan.

Berthea drifted past the end of the dock and, catching sight of the harbor, took courage coasting onward. I turned to the gulf. Out front lay a panorama of Port Aransas: three elbowing islands lurching toward the shore. At this distance the orangery was already disappearing in a stubborn twinkle of light. In no time, it went out.

I tried to make conversation, but that's not something I can pull off. Uriah acted his part as an interested listener anyway. I started blabbing about Olivia and couldn't stop. I was repeating myself. Uriah tried to pause me with a look. I couldn't be helped. I was talking to keep from talking, telling whatever came next. Uriah waited. I kept saying the same things, for my own benefit. When I realized what it sounded like when I was trying to explain myself, I became quiet. Uriah let me stay that way for a long time. More stars came down in an eavesdropping sort of way.

"Congratulations," Uriah said. He really looked like he could throw me overboard. "Y'all obviously know where babies come from. That chat is over."

"No, man. She said you wanted to talk to me, like, tell me something."

Uriah gave excellent side eye. "I must be in the spirit tonight," he said. "Giving gifts. Priceless advice."

When I closed my eyes, Olivia materialized once again. She reached a hand back, fingers splayed, to scratch a precise spot at the back of her head, only it felt like my head was the one getting scratched. That's how close I'd wanted to get to her. She signaled for my attention and jab-pointed in her father's direction, mouthing, *Where are you going?*

Uriah drummed his hands on the wheel and marshaled his attention into the sea. He was talking about being a collector and how collecting was the most vibrant form of expression. "The collector is always reflecting his deepest self," he said. "He reveals his deepest interest through the things he collects."

Like a creepy ass slave ship? I rolled with it. I stood up from the sofa, walking softly until I was next to Uriah again. "So first you have to find out what you're even into," I said.

"That's easy," he said. "Jealousy. Pain. I wanted to control how I was seen."

Uriah nodded at the gulf, at the past, at himself when he was my age, after the critically acclaimed *Last Rites for Dry Snitches* had left him with a kind of thanks-a-lot-but-that's-enough-from-you status. I remembered the era well. Uriah would show up to radio interviews dressed as the cross between a dandy and a lawn jockey, awkwardly trying to break in his new end-of-career persona.

INTERVIEWER: Tell the streets what's next for the King of the Swamp.

URIAH: Oh, well you know. Front office type stuff. Major music management. Lyrical therapeutics. I'm transitioning to that next mountain, as they say.

INTERVIEWER: So you're like Moses?
URIAH: How's that?
INTERVIEWER: Like Dr. King too, I suppose.
URIAH: Come again?
INTERVIEWER: I mean, you *do* admit you never made it to that mountaintop. You wouldn't make your own top five, would you?
URIAH: Well, I always believed humility was a virtue . . . Anyway, I'm doing the front office . . . Plus, I got this patent hustle I'm working on too.
INTERVIEWER: Uh-huh. Is it true D Records killed your concept album? You was doing some wild and wack shit on that record like playing some maracas and a drum that you made.
URIAH: I stay in that experimenting mode. I mean, that was after my pilgrimage, man. My content had matured. I found all these new sounds. A lot of dudes don't get the chance to connect with the earth on that level.
INTERVIEWER: You right about that.
URIAH: Say, man. What are you trying to do? Why does this feel like a gotcha interview?
INTERVIEWER: [*Playing instrumentals of the classic hit*] I guess that depends. Is you saying I gotcha?

This was the last picture Uriah's remaining fans got of him. Soon after he was fraternizing with the talented tenth, the same smug bastards who raised my core temperature at every wedding and graduation. They spoke in refined tones about traveling to Nairobi, or about how the poor could avoid the perils of instant gratification by opening a savings account. Uriah held on to every syllable. But when he spoke, using a double negative with the dictionary word of the day in the same breath, they curled their faces. Their eyes went dead.

Uriah had access to money, sure—but not to books. He was too colorful, too needy, always one remark shy of cracking their rock-solid sense of complacency. Each man had his own collection—this was the sole feature that distinguished one from the next—of hideous little objects that had come to represent all the ways they felt shut out from society. They convinced Uriah that collecting was the worthiest endeavor. They almost got him to admit he really didn't know what the hell he was doing, but when Uriah started hanging artifacts in the hallway, these men nodded in stunned approval. But approval isn't acceptance. There's really no substitute.

Uriah fantasized about cornering the weakest one to find out what the rest of them said about him, but ultimately, he accepted the fact that you can't fight the people you'd always wanted to become. His only option was to show them up. He showed everyone up until there was nothing left to see.

"You're still mad about it," I said.

"I'm jealous." Uriah dispatched the kind of frank sadness you see in the eyes of abandoned kittens on television. "My jealousy built my fortune. It's how I built my collection. Jealousy became my guiding light," he said.

I turned away, then back. I had recently gotten to the point where the only way I could see myself was through the eyes of others.

Behind Uriah, the Bobbies worked to untie the mast. The pole tilted upright as the wind pushed over the islands, drawing us farther from the coast. Nobody said a word about this. One by one, the Bobbies glanced into the wheelhouse, locking eyes with me. We must have been a mile out, maybe more.

Realizing that it was my turn to talk, I stammered gracefully. "I . . . guess that can be a great talent."

"More like an obsession." Uriah moved his shoulders, but he wasn't really laughing. "It doesn't go away. Even when you leave, you still want control. Can't you see?"

"I don't know, man."

"No, I mean, can you see? Put your coke bottles back on if you can't."

I slid my glasses up my nose. "Coke ain't come in bottles in a long time."

"So why you bringing them back?" Uriah laughed like laughing was going out of business, like laughter was bad for the environment. But his rigid movements contradicted the cool killer persona he'd been cultivating since before I was born. His habit of checking my face for possible collusion—because he both needed and abhorred it—his impressively rude way of laughing at me or, worse, flat-out ignoring me because he could, lent him a disjointed vulnerability that was equally intimidating and endearing. I liked the guy. And he liked me too. It was weird.

"The jewelry store was just something for after college. It was never my passion," I said, suddenly unsure that I still had one. "I knew the job was a waste of time, but at least I was making something of value to someone."

"I felt the same way about *Swamp King Part IV.* Believe it or not, at the time that album was worth something." Uriah eyed me before going further. "I was jealous of the people who bought that trash. Jealous that they could like it."

I pictured my ex-boss Gilbert at the workbench holding a filigreed ring up to the light and smiling to himself. "I know what you mean, man."

"You would," said Uriah. Then he explained to me my own personal problem, that I was into jewelry because jewels and gems were the closest thing modern man had to the preternatural experience. That without knowing it, I was deeply envious of the visionary's worldview. But due to my circumstances, the closest I could get was the jewelry store. He understood this predicament, since a similar feeling had possessed him years back, when with his first advance, he'd bought himself a rose gold Jesus medallion, weeping big ruby tears. He got into it again after his career ended. He wanted to mix with respectable people.

"You're probably giving me too much credit," I said.

"Well, who else gone give it to you?"

The Bobbies stood around conspiratorially, their voices bouncing through the wind. One was telling an involved joke, which became clear only when they all started laughing, their hair doing cartoon orangutan things.

Uriah said that as my collection grew, so would my level of tolerance and understanding. "Your perspective too," he added. "Possess or be possessed."

Berthea hummed her centuries-old misery into the darkness. Moonlight pressed down with its lunar intensity, amplifying the ship's ugliness and decay, the moldy embellishments, the deck speckled in starbursts of bird shit. A few seagulls soared by on some instinctive miracle, guided into flight.

For the first time in months, I felt my heart do its little tap dance. I kept nodding. It was better to agree and be liked. I had negative thirty-four dollars in my bank account, but what I needed to do was collect jewelry. I ran my hand down the armrest of the sofa, going against the grain until I'd rolled a few strands of lint into nap. Then I covered my face with my hands, thinking, So I should just collect jewelry?

When did this start? Was it that night I'd first seen Olivia sulking into her plastic cup? Or on Thanksgiving ten years before, when my drunk uncles set hands on my shoulders and told me what all I couldn't do? When did that busted feeling really kick in? How did it become just another thing I'd gotten used to?

Then I remembered way back to when I was thirty minutes younger and Olivia's father had offered me a ride on his slave ship and I'd said, *Huh?* but went along with it thinking that somewhere en route, he'd reveal to me some secret to my own success, when really all he could tell me to do was what he and his fake friends had done to put their shortcomings in perspective. Stay mad. Collect weird shit.

I laced my fingers behind my head and lay back, smelling cedar. "Instead of a slave ship," I said, "you should have bought a spaceship."

"A spaceship?" Uriah turned the idea over carefully. "A spaceship?"

"Look, man." I stood up from the sofa and walked to the doorway. "It's nothing I can solve—not really. I don't think I can do anything with it. I don't have to feed it or talk to it every day. But I probably have to live with it, if I'm going to go on living, I mean." Uriah never asked what *it* was, because he already knew. The real ones always know. "What I'm saying is, I don't think I can be like you. Not this go-round."

Uriah slashed me up with looks. "I offered to *loan* you my ship. Don't think I was just giving it away." He spoke with a humored bitterness. The humor lasted for a second, but the bitterness played for keeps.

Berthea wailed again, trying to get some sensible person's attention. When I turned to see what was wrong, my ears started to burn.

We had drifted far from the narrowest part of the harbor to a place where the islands reached toward one another into the gulf. The waves out front swelled and heaved. We had gone too far, and the ship couldn't take it. She pushed on anyway.

"Where are we going?" I asked, though the answer was painfully clear. There was nothing left to confront but sky and ocean. "Should we turn around?"

"We should," said Uriah.

He muscled the wheel and our course took a wild diagonal. The sea looked ugly. Waves leapt up across the side of the ship, splashing across the deck. I looked over the edge and the water appeared capable of anything. It was like the entire Gulf of Mexico was trying to jump into the ship.

Berthea belched woodenly. Beneath our feet the planks jostled and snapped. The force of another wave knocked me over. More waves piled up into mountains of dazzling foam.

Up ship the Bobbies sprang to useless action, mounting the masthead and fumbling with bundles of rope. The waves crashed, winds and currents rocked, and we were listing badly. Still, *Berthea* pressed on.

Something like an arrangement of chords tingled across my chest. "You're fixing to get us killed," I said.

He shrugged. He looked up at the stars. Dudes like that never admitted to failure. It made me feel bad to know why. "Honestly," he said, "I didn't think you'd mind."

Then he leaned back as his recent acquisition, his jewel of the Gulf of Mexico, started to fall the fuck apart. At each dip, another crucial piece of construction crunched and splintered to bits. The floorboards buckled and split too, and with another crack, water sprayed upward. The Bobbies splashed around trying to plug the leaks.

Another thing was happening, a noise unlike the ones we'd been hearing. It was singing, a whole mass choir of squeaky laughter. Dolphins. A dozen glistening, conspiring, brown dolphins popped up beside the ship, turning flips and showing their bellies, laughing. Foolishly, I thought they'd come to save us. All of them were looking me in the eye, all at once. And they were all laughing.

I didn't know what I was about to do until I was doing it. I grabbed the spokes and cut to the right. Water as green as mouthwash flooded the deck. I held on. I hooked right again, tipping *Berthea* up on her working hip. The Bobbies scrambled through deep water, cheering me on in moral support.

Uriah rushed out of the wheelhouse to check our progress. The northernmost island was behind us, and we were speeding back toward the harbor. I'd angled too far and the ship was heading straight for marshland. The deck shot upward, tossing all of us into the sky, before dropping us back to the ground. The ship cracked on impact, and then it started to break in half.

"You broke my ship!" Uriah cried. "You broke my ship!"

Batting through the water, I watched the last of the Bobbies jump over the bulwark and down to the marsh. I grabbed for one of Uriah's ankles, but he pushed me away, steadied himself, and stalked down the deck. The mast and sails fell as he climbed up to the edge.

"Thanks," said Uriah. It took me a second to realize he was talking to me. "Thanks for being a friend," he said, and we were friends now. I gave him the thumbs-up. He froze in stunned disgust.

Then the big man took a flying leap into the gulf.

Post-shipwreck, a few diehards from the party gathered on the dock as Uriah explained what had happened. The Bobbies fetched him a folding chair and draped a blanket over his shoulders, and as he paused, allowing himself to be cloaked, I couldn't help but think what a great cover of a failing magazine this picture would make—the CEO in exile, telling his own adventures, by himself too.

Olivia stood beside her father with her hands clasped, looking on church-faced, a subtle cue for anyone listening to do the same. Security yawned. Middle-aged ladies shook their heads. Uriah laughed and his mouth looked like he'd bought it at a garage sale. Catching my stare, he pointed a finger as though the two of us shared some deep, everlasting secret.

Olivia came my way, glowing in real time. This woman had let me get her pregnant. And her crazy daddy had almost gotten me killed. Feeling floaty, I told her, "You smell like gravy."

Olivia paused, which made me laugh, which made her sock me in the arm. Then she eased herself under my blanket like she'd been traumatized too. "Anyway," she said. "I'm glad you're alive."

"Me too. Me three, me four, me five."

She didn't laugh. She studied me closely, as if balancing an equation. "How do you feel?"

I shrugged. "Like a kitten left in a mailbox." I could have told her I was okay with that. We were family after all.

Olivia smiled and I could tell she was about to say something. She stepped all in my vicinity, grabbing me by the earlobes. She searched the different parts of my face, settling finally on my eyes, and a sparkling confetti happened behind hers. That's how it is when you find what you're looking for.

"Crazy fool," she said.

MARIE-HELENE BERTINO

Viola in Midwinter

FROM *Bennington Review*

THE MARGARETVILLE SHOP & SAVE stays open twenty-four hours as a service to hunters, hospital employees, sex workers, and other creatures who work at night. Viola in pre-dawn debates poppers and Pharaoh snakes in the fireworks aisle. In the checkout line, hunters discuss a bobcat one saw on his drive into town. A mama, probably, looking for food before the real snow arrives and locks the county in place. Seeing her, their talk zips closed. Viola knows they call her Dark Lady, which she sometimes enjoys. The cashier rings up her purchases (poppers, a small axe, mint tea for sleep), still talking to the men collected under the announcement board though they've gone silent. They watch her pay and leave, her puffed black coat trailing like a cold remark. Viola feels a numbness in her forehead framed in pain, a cricketing in the temple. She is always on the verge of a headache: the Shop & Save is always open: she is always forty-nine.

Outside, pale light crowns the higher mountain peaks though the parking lot is dark. Other hunters low under a streetlight. Viola positions her bags in the trunk, overhearing ideas in their mumblings, *I was going to, she would,* until one of the men, emboldened by her lack of attention, calls out. "Need help?"

She keeps her gaze on him and swings the trunk closed.

"Trying to say hi," he says.

"Being polite," his friend adds.

She pulls a cigarette from a pocket and pauses as if waiting for a light, an extinct ritual from a former life. The men blink. She finds a lighter in another pocket.

The original hunter seems to decide the smoke is meant to anger him and blooms. "Where you from?" he says. "Not here."

She exhales smoke toward where they move from foot to foot like deer that cannot smell the origin of disturbance. The Shop & Save doors whistle. A man wearing hospital scrubs emerges carrying groceries. He walks toward a different part of the lot, then, seeing them, changes course for the encounter that had for the men changed from something they understood.

"Everything okay?" the EMT asks her. Blank eyes. Poised posture.

Viola spits loose tobacco onto the ground.

He turns to the men. "Everything okay?"

They push one of their own forward, a lantern thrown in front. "Just being friendly," he says.

Viola uses this interruption as cover to get in and start the car. The men move aside. The EMT stands under the streetlamp, holding his bags. In the rearview mirror, she watches him. Do-gooder, maybe. She takes the road that leads into the foothills and parks at the base of the woods she heard the men discussing.

Viola follows the tracks down the county road, in and out of the tree line until it jags into an embankment by the creek. Another awareness grows alongside hers as she walks, royal blue and not solitary. The bobcat is pregnant, Viola thinks, watching it move along the frozen stream, slow and exposed. It must be injured, but there is no blood on the trail. She follows it, avoiding the mudcrust, whose sound would give her away. The movement of a cat's shoulders out of sequence with its forward motion pleases her. The cat slips on its way up the other bank. Her grasp is firm. She pushes a blade into its neck.

A pink dawn, flurries beginning. The animal draped like a bride over her legs. Viola sits in the snow and drinks.

Viola was forty-nine in 1917 when she met the woman who would immortalize her. Viola's husband, a temperless Swede, was fighting in France. Their seven-year-old daughter Bea had been good-natured before her father left, but now it was like living with a gathering storm. Always some petulant, bruising remark, a brush hurtling through the air. Every morning Viola left for the factory, buoyant with relief. She loved the simple purpose of a job.

The neighbors viewed Viola with suspicion for waiting until thirty to wed. She preferred the factory women who discussed how they'd shore up the line better than that sack of shit Haig, and at the end of sweat-ridden shifts, how they missed their husbands rarely if at all. Under the factory's wasting lights Viola met more kinds of women than she knew existed. One or two were married to hitters and joked that these years were the clearest their faces had been. Viola didn't know women could speak so candidly, but she'd never been among so many, protected by war's isolation.

Samarra was the pinnacle of that candor. Her administrative role at the factory allowed her to walk the line and chat. Her wide, expressive mouth made everything she said sound scandalous even when she let the younger girls go to catch some school. She befriended Viola and her storm-cloud daughter, bringing them food and clothes they could never afford. During the summer of 1917 they'd drink Samarra's whiskey in Viola's cold-water walkup, the smell of the Greenwich Street fish shops souring through the windows. Fanning themselves only deepened the stink, but it made them laugh. Their friendship loosened whatever fist always seemed to grip Viola's breastplate. She confessed to Samarra that a longing rose inside her whenever she walked a street with a view of the river. Sometimes she feared it would split her in two.

Samarra said she knew a way to lessen that woe. She called it The Occupation. Typically, the conversion procedure was harder for women. The men could bite each other on the neck, but women had to receive permission. The subject had to be certain.

A week after the hunters, the EMT approaches Viola in the Shop & Save.

"I'd love to know your name," he says. "So, the next time those guys bother you, I can at least say, 'Hey, don't bother . . .'"

In the moment that passes his smile reconsiders then strengthens. "This is where you say your name," he says.

"Men aren't new to me," she says. She says, "Viola."

He takes a few glancing steps back, pretending to be moved by beauty. It is meant to seem corny. She smiles, in spite of herself. His basket is filled with honey, bread, and yogurt. Soft, sweetening things. If he had known he'd run into her, they'd seem designed to woo.

Outside they load her car. "How many fireworks does a woman need?" he says, gesturing to her bags.

"You never know when I'll need to shove one up a hunter's ass."

He laughs, apologizes for the hunters as if he is their mayor. He has already drawn the line between her and the town she's lived in for half a century. She says, "I've been through it before."

"Ten times today, I bet."

"A hundred."

She likes that he laughs when she curses. She wonders if under his scrubs his biceps are defined. His hands look strong and soft, and while he speaks, one rests on his lower stomach. She knows it is where he wants to touch her.

Later, Viola watches him park in front of her property. He is not a stand-up straight man but hovers lower in his body; the glancing steps at the Shop & Save and these chastened ones, crossing her lawn as if clearing a series of boughs. He's young, mid-forties maybe, but like many white men in middle-age he looks floured, older. Viola meets him on her porch and asks what he thinks of her house.

He makes a show of considering. "The yellow and white reminds me of my grandparents' cottage. We spent summers swimming in a stream like yours."

"You see the stream?" She is pleased.

"It's running a bit low because of the cold. But healthy," he hastens to add. "Beavers are working it, that's a good sign. I didn't know it came out this far. And so loud."

"You can hear it too?" Noting his confused look, she explains, "Sometimes I think only I can see how pretty it is here."

"How long have you lived up this way?"

"Forever."

She tells him that every night more icicles grow from the gutters, and he says it's because the house isn't properly winterized. "You're not protected."

She doesn't offer him dinner. They sit on the couch with tumblers of whiskey. She asks what it's like to be an EMT and he says it's a lot of waiting until it's not. He says he has healer hands and she says, "You have healer hands," so he hears how ridiculous it sounds. He asks to touch her. She places the glass on the table, removes her sweater, and lies on the carpet. This seems to cue a tuxedo cat who comes around to sniff. She motions for it to leave.

The EMT drains his drink and crouches near her. She is pleased that he seems cowed by the sudden exposure of her skin. He places his palms against her back. When was the last time anyone touched her? He digs in with his fingertips, beginning at her spine's base. She has what he calls an ancient coil in her lower right back. It's where she keeps people she loves. An old wound activates. She dislikes so-called healers but dislikes more that he's right.

"I'll make you a steak for your trouble," she tells him after. "Do you eat meat?"

"You cook?" He gestures to her kitchen, the sink and counters covered in plants.

Viola sets one place at her table and prepares the meat on an outside pit. She serves him the steak, pours herself more whiskey, and sits across from him.

"You're not going to eat?"

"Not hungry," she says.

He cuts a forkful and swears that the area's hunting helps its animals.

"A progressive and a hunter?" she says.

"There's no way around the body craving meat."

"The body craves protein, not a sirloin filet. I bet the animal prefers to live. I'm too old to pretend."

"You're so old." He grins.

"Middle-aged."

"I'm middle-aged too." He seems happy to be connected by this. "You're not a vegan, are you?"

"No," she says. "I'm a hunter, too."

He takes off his shirt and jeans. She sits astride him on the couch. He drags a flat tongue over her breasts. He whispers, pushing into her, that he wants to build her a house. She doesn't want him to build her a house but doesn't mind the sentiment. It's been decades since someone has pressed their cheek against her heart and shuddered against her.

On the night Viola ceased to age, she'd received a letter from her husband in France, outlining his plan for return. They'd move in with his family. She would quit the factory. It angered Bea that he mentioned the thickness of the fighting, the ranks obliterated by rot and illness, but not her, not once. She spit food and threw her plate. Finally, she lay in the back bedroom performing occasional, pitiful whimpers. Viola and Samarra shared a bottle of rye on the fire escape.

Viola was grateful for Samarra's unblinking company. She'd never seen a woman move through a room like a cleaver.

"It's hard to be forgotten by a man," Samarra said about Bea. "She doesn't know that the letter sounds like it does because he's scared and not admitting it."

The rye worked her mood loose until the fish stink seemed participatory. She asked about The Occupation. Samarra said that inability to handle sunlight was a myth. It was more of a strong aversion that had been exaggerated by men who couldn't handle it. "Like most things, the truth has contradictions that don't fit neat theories," she said. "We don't turn to ash. We've just usually had long nights and are nursing plasma hangovers."

Human blood was not the only way to receive sustenance. They could hunt animals, though Samarra considered this beneath her. She was raised by maids in the Philippines in an affluent political family. She made deals with meat factory bosses and had first pick after the slaughter. "You'd be surprised how easy it is for an older woman to go unnoticed. They either assume I have a family somewhere or I'm there to clean."

The war was ending. Survivors were coming home. After her husband returned, she'd be with his mother and sisters all day, mending, darning, keeping polite. Samarra reached over and untied the top of Viola's dress. Viola felt the chill of her skin meeting air. Samarra leaned over and pressed her lips against the skin she'd exposed. She pushed her fingers inside her. From the top of her hill, the river looked indistinguishable from the clouds. The feeling made Viola want to choose something for the rest of her life.

"Are you sure?" Samarra said, and Viola said, "Please, yes."

In the morning, the EMT does not leave but chooses a contemporary collection of short stories from her library and reads to her. The next day, he works his hospital shift and returns with a bag of groceries. Flowers, mint, salt. She places her lips against the hollow of his collarbone. He works another night shift. She goes with him: newness makes joining someone at work seem fun. He opens a wall-sized cabinet revealing racks of blood, shining in bags. A genital pulse overwhelms her, her vision pinwheels. He holds her up against a wall during sex. He pulls a hammock from the attic and hangs it outside. She watches him from the shadows on the porch. The sun makes his eyes go clear. He leans against a pine, pulls his arms overhead to stretch. The crescent of pellucid skin above his belt adds itself to the night shifts and blurs time. She doesn't know how many nights have passed since the first when she made him a steak. She likes pressing moisturizer she doesn't need into her cheeks while he reads in the other room. Viola writhes, cries out, fixed in place by the softest pin. The joy of having a tongue inside her that knows what it's doing.

"It's not fair," she says, meaning: thank god life can still hold this joy.

Samarra would call this "love jail." Viola thinks she knows how it feels to wear nothing and lie beneath the sun.

In the waning days of war, Viola's new appetite became a second body. In the pale, drenched moments before satiation she could watch it as if she were a bystander. How it swerved and knuckled down on an unsuspecting figure. She engaged in nocturnal benders that ended at Samarra's apartment where she stopped herself in ice baths.

Plague shuttered the city. A telegram from France arrived. Her husband was missing. Bea retreated into the room of herself and Viola became a foe.

Viola was the oldest she'd ever be and no longer needed food. She registered the loss of her husband in an unlit part of her brain. She was a novice immortal and though Samarra was a veteran she was unwilling to teach. She didn't want to explain, for example, why the longing to leave had not lessened but hardened. She hadn't anticipated that The Occupation alongside Viola's age would combine to quadruple desire. Samarra was in her sixties, safely beyond middle age. They didn't argue but backed away from one another.

Viola and the EMT hunt.

His gear and blinds amuse her. He lines up a shot to find she's been streaming in from another direction. Both methods prove effective. Bodies pile up. Their love is bad for the animals.

Showing off is new to her, as is someone anticipating her tricks. Even in deepest cover, he finds her.

He says, "If you think you're being watched, you are."

One night, a whiff of impermanence makes her crave concrete answers. Does he want to stay with her? No town? No job? Just his body and hers.

"Always," he says.

She says there is a way, but he must be certain. "It will be for a long time."

The future tense makes him grow still—a squirrel sensing movement freezing at the base of an oak—until she doesn't know what is him and what is tree. She thought she'd been following the path of their desire. He makes an excuse and leaves.

Though Viola's aging halted, other parts advanced. Her hair and nails grew so fast she could shave her head and have floor-length hair within weeks. Menstrual blood disappeared for months then, as if to compensate, returned with painful hemorrhaging. No longer able to care for Bea, Viola took her to live with her Swedish relatives. At sixteen, Bea began work as a boarding house waitress.

One evening in the middle of the century, mother and daughter passed each other on the street. It took Viola a moment to understand that this hard woman was her daughter. Bea had exceeded her in age and looked to be in failing health. Viola realized that the girl with her was Bea's daughter, who'd inherited her grandmother's lavender eyes. Bea belonged to another time that moved like a barge away from where Viola was pinned to the dock. She'd already forgotten Bea's birthday and her own. Split with regret, she left the city.

In the 1960s, Viola worked as a flight attendant. She hunted in the Scottish Highlands, prowled the bars in Golden Gai, visited the battlefield where her husband had fallen. For a while travel allayed her restlessness. Samarra was right about one thing—it was easy for a middle-aged woman to go unnoticed. The other flight attendants were on their own thresholds—after college, before marriage, before babies, after changing careers.

But Viola was pursued by a sensation of vanishing. She worried that instead of being freed, she'd been forgotten. She longed for her chin to sag, any indication she was still alive. Perhaps this was why people invested in religion or children or causes. To pass time pleasantly while watching something grow. Instead, Viola noticed how human tendencies genuflected through time. Hemlines and mothering trends advanced and receded. The tendency of women to wound their own. The nucleus of the house became the child who even had their own room for toys. It sickened Viola to watch mothers be controlled by toddlers.

Age's boundaries were occasionally recalibrated. At the turn of the century, the idea of youth reached the age of forty. Viola's body seemed newly valued. Men's gazes, once trained solely on college-aged asses, lingered on hers. Factories, planes, space travel, the Internet. Though the structures varied, they were built from hubris. Stitched with greed.

New mandates after 9/11 required flight attendants to submit to regular reviews and Viola could no longer fly with anonymity. She returned to America and moved to the Western Catskills, where she spent the rest of the century in and out of hot flashes, chased by an unleavened smell, fertile and not, fertile then not, joints swelling, trapped in a developmental doorway. She kept routines she did not need like market shopping to tend the last ember of being human and lived timelessly in the woods that were silenced by snow for half of every year. She'd been middle-aged for a century, intuitions deepening, minor and major knives growing along the walls of her understanding. She had become a cave purpled with stalactites. She could smell feelings in a room.

The EMT shows up after two weeks carrying chanterelles he's foraged. Viola had missed him so she participates with a few bites. Worm-thick, spiced by earth. Since it serves no purpose, food is something she understands but doesn't enjoy, like perfume and holidays.

"What do you do for fun?" he says. He seems distracted. The question belongs to an earlier stage of courtship. It sounds like he is returning to an improperly filled-out form to correct mistakes.

She shows him her arsenal of fireworks, he lines up an impressive display. Colorful sparks soar above the woods. A tornado of snapping around their ankles.

"I'm surprised you don't get noise complaints," he says, gazing over the trees toward town. She notices a stab of effort in his voice, as if he is trying to recall what brought him here.

"No one would come all the way out."

She's been with local men before, though none from the EMT's generation. A dirt farmer with soft hands. His wife. Two brother lawyers. Their wives. Her favorite was a married door-to-door vacuum salesman she saw for a year before his shame grew too large. Occasionally she sees him slow on her road—elderly but still possessing the same dazed, blinking calm—trying to determine her house amid whatever glamour appears. But she never loved him, or the others, or even Samarra. She never lost breath when leaving them, or when they stayed away too long.

In the 1960s Viola was traveling through the Midi-Pyrenees when she met a woman who taught her the spell to glamour homes.

If what appeared to the visitor was a pleasant memory, they'd get along. If it was troubling, the connection wouldn't last. One lawyer she'd been excited about was startled back into his car by whatever he saw. She never had a chance to ask. His bumper took a chunk out of her hedgerow when he roared away. Most guests couldn't see the stream, the feature that was dearest to her. Powered by some relentless turbine, every so often it would produce a cherubic black beaver, moving its weight front-to-back, front-to-back over a lichen-thick rock. Before she met the EMT, these rare sightings had been the highest delight of her endless life.

A week, a month, no visits. Viola finds him in the home of a local bartender, a generous pourer. Their bodies are pearlized in television light as he pumps into her, whispering. Maybe this is the woman who wants him to build her a house, Viola thinks, hovering outside the window.

She drags her firework arsenal to the lawn and lights each one. The sky fills with fury. Sparks ignite in the dusky growth. The arriving firemen cannot find a house but hear laughter spiraling in the hollow. Amid the damage a centuries-old hemlock falls, bisecting the county road. For a week the locals must travel longer on the highway to avoid it.

Heartbreak slows the hours as months creak by. Viola's hair grows past the floor. She dyes it Lights Out black from a Shop & Save kit. Doubles up on face creams she doesn't need. The memory of her birthday returns. She spends November 15 shivering in a scalding bath. She cloaks her house so he'll find only ankle-breaking ruts if he tries to visit. Adds a few cats to her home and one tall dog named Oberon who stands like a masthead in the yard, every so often conjuring a single, day-splitting bark.

When she had just moved to the mountains, Viola came across Death on a train platform in Arkville. Death wore an impeccable hoodie under an acid-washed blazer. She stood beside an elegant suitcase, checking a timepiece. Sensing Viola's stare, she looked over. Her gaze was a climate. She raised a delicate hand and saluted.

Viola returned the gesture. She imagined they could be friends since neither needed anything from the other. They were workers who shared a commute. It must get lonely being that essential. Viola thought she knew how that felt. The train arrived. Viola watched Death move through the car of sleeping travelers. She selected a window seat, removed her watch, and gently laid it on the tray table in front of her. No passenger stirred. No one notices remarkable women.

Viola watched the train leave then bought a newspaper and a bottle of pills that promised to alleviate the ankle swelling that accompanied her like an assistant.

A little boy gapes in the firearms aisle of the Margaretville Shop & Save where Viola wears remnants from her past lives. A corset shows under a one-shouldered dress from the eighties belted in the style of the nineties. Bobby socks. Boots from her first life's job.

She misses the factory. She misses the women who snuck flasks, spit seeds, bit, demurred to the bosses then exposed their asses for laughs. She hadn't known there were women like that. Since then, she has been them all.

The little boy's mother snatches him away but he steals glances from under her arms. He wants to keep looking at the Dark Lady.

Viola points one glowing shoulder at him, shows her teeth. Then zips it all—her mirth and misery—under the purple coat, makes her expression into a storm cloud, and leaves through the whistling doors.

That evening, Viola wakes, struggling for breath. Her sheets are soaked in sweat. The wind swirling in the hollow sounds like a passing big rig. Gun powder fills her nostrils. She checks outside but there's no one in the meadow blanketed with snow, or on the hill milked in the waxing Wolf Moon. No deer lolls in the copse of hemlock that stubbles the crest. More icicles have grown from the gutters. One side of the house shines in the dark.

Viola repots plants in her kitchen, uneasiness growing. Finally, she feels a presence behind her.

"Devour me," it says.

Samarra stands in the center of the room, arms raised for a hug. She is in town to check out the "whole upstate thing."

"Girl," she says. "You look rough."

"I could use a party," Viola admits.

"You could use a haircut. No matter. Party's here, babe."

They are naked for days. They throw a log into the fire. They finish the whiskey.

Samarra, addressing Viola from between her legs, tells her the word for the EMT is narcissist. "My seventh—no, eighth!—husband was one. Diminishing returns. They leave you starving." She laughs. "Which is the worst thing you and I can be."

"What did you do to him?" Viola says.

"Poor man. He did not go easy."

Samarra suggests they kill the EMT too, but Viola refuses. Killing him would bring no relief, she says. Who she wants to kill is deathless.

"Well, I'm going to have to eat something," Samarra says. "I'm not here to ski."

"I know where we can go," Viola says.

They drive to the Shop & Save and chuck tote bags and firewood into a jangling cart. Samarra humps the bear statue and tries on fluorescent hunting gear. It is good to be with this unruly woman in a cheap grocery store at night. They've been friends for a hundred years.

When they'd arrived the parking lot was empty but when they load their bags into the car hunters watch from under every streetlamp.

"Hello, boys," Samarra calls, driving away.

Viola directs her to the unmarked door at the back of the hospital. She leads them through a series of hallways, avoiding night nurses who glimmer in deeper rooms. Viola reveals the cabinet of blood.

Samarra leans on the counter for support. "Why do I have the urge to bless myself?"

They fill the tote bags with the plastic sleeves, retreat through the hallways, and load the car.

"Hurry," Viola says when she hears the door open behind them. Samarra climbs into the car.

"Wait." The EMT approaches, face mapped with pain. "Talk to me. Viola. Why have you disappeared?"

"Babe?" Samarra lowers the window and observes him with flat, gray eyes. Her pallor has been flawless for centuries.

"Who's that?" he says. "Who is that?"

She gets into the car and Samarra drives away. "That's the guy?" She says, "You need to leave the woods more."

Samarra predicts the EMT will show up again, and on a moonless night in midwinter, he does.

Viola reveals her house (she's been drinking). He stands on the porch and speaks quietly into the closed door, while on the other side she listens in the dark, Oberon beside her keeping a low growl. She watches him walk to his truck. His headlights scan her as he pulls away. Viola drains every fisher cat on the mountain.

The EMT takes up with another local girl, homely with pretty eyes. Another progressive who insists that hunting is fair to the animal and who defers to him, unlike the bartender he keeps fucking even after he and the pretty girl marry.

They have two boys, indistinguishable from the other county kids. One moves to Canada, the other marries a local girl like his mother, hunts with his father on weekends, pulls the sightless deer onto the car, sings down the mountain. The girl gets homelier though her pretty eyes stay. Every year the EMT decorates their house with blow-up snowmen. His property backs onto an overgrown section of woods that connect the hamlet.

One night toward the middle of the century, the EMT administers to a pile of steaming meat in his backyard. He is in his seventies, lymph nodes stuffed with cancer. She smells it coursing above the meat stink; metallic, salted. It seems unfair that he gets to die.

A windless rustle, a certain un-sound. He doesn't have to see her standing inside the tree line, owl quiet. If you think you're being watched, you are.

She meets him again, in this town or that, a man or not, employed or jobless, sick or well, a doctor, a stoneworker, and he runs his systems on her. Sometimes, she doesn't have the energy. She tells him she's been through it before. Sometimes she accepts his dances, his tongue, attempts to summon love's old frictions until, inevitably, the drumming subsides.

A girl on the verge of adulthood arrives in November when the forest's reddish growth makes the mountains appear rusted. She has compiled a map from four semi-accurate ones procured in visits to town hall. She has sweet-talked a hunter who liked her lavender eyes. This determination paired with a hard countenance has separated her from everyone she's ever known. The girl walks onto the empty meadow and the word ancestor occurs to her as if from clear air. Each foot presses it into the moss. *Ancestor,* as icicles gleam on rocks that pin the stream. *Ancestor,* she feels the Devonian gaze of hemlocks. She speaks to her hammering heart (the house will arrive or it won't, and if it doesn't, she'll return home). Nothing in her life has prompted such breathlessness. Something in the meadow seems to unlock and turns toward her. The stream begins a louder chatter that sounds like, hello. I won't leave. I'll wait forever.

JAMEL BRINKLEY

Blessed Deliverance

FROM *Zoetrope: All-Story*

WHO KNEW THAT old-ass Headass was capable of even greater feats of headassery? Our little crew had become accustomed long ago to his foolishness, the imbecilic way he walked around Bed-Stuy with his lips swelled up, duh-duh, all the various look-at-me antics. We were bored with him, he was dull, the five of us paid him no mind. He might as well have been a fire hydrant. It had ceased to affect us when he interrupted our hangs in the park by barking out one of his nonsensical jokes, every punch line a non sequitur, or by unzipping his dusty jeans and pulling forth from the opening, inch by inch, the ashiness of his dick. By the time we started high school, his pratfalls on the basketball court while a couple of us tried to hoop were no longer amusing—we just dribbled around him and told him to go bother people his own age—and when he would dig in the trash for scraps of pizza or the half-eaten remains of fried-hard chicken wings, it wasn't worth clowning anymore, it was no longer worth the breath for one of us to say to another, *Hey bitch, hey motherfucker, hey, peep it, there he goes again, you see him right, look, there he is, there goes your father.*

Truth be told, we didn't even know Headass was still around. Word was he'd been framed for armed robbery or some such and was doing a bid. Others said he'd been tracked down by a very distant relative and was living in Louisiana among his people, if it's possible for near-strangers to be your people. The most dubious and therefore most prevalent rumor contained some version of him plummeting tragically into the East River from the hive of coffin-size, bike-chain-bound plywood shanties that sheltered the homeless just below the upper deck of the Manhattan Bridge. What had actually happened, we eventually found out, was a police raid of an abandoned building on Lefferts, a former hotel where Headass, among others, had been squatting. Nothing had changed about the status of the building—it hadn't been sold to some developer, at least not yet—but for whatever reason (we knew the reason), certain cruelties of the law were now being strictly enforced.

By senior year, however, it didn't really matter. The five of us weren't thinking about Headass at all. Other things were on our minds. College, for instance, was becoming a thrilling prospect, though we were each interested in different schools, and though the guidance counselor had cast a puckered frown at our lists, striking out the Harvards and Yales, and the Howards and Spelmans, meanwhile telling us through his teeth that despite our grades and vocabularies and test scores, we shouldn't get our hopes very high. Our parents all seemed to be going through it, too, some losing their jobs, some suffering the very first symptoms of what would be fateful illnesses, some separating divorcing reuniting testing new loves, and while we avoided talking to one another about these things in any explicit way, there was an awareness among us of a common feeling, disgust but also bafflement that we had so little sense of who our mothers and fathers really were, and that despite our trepidation about growing dull with age, life apparently would never stop with the excitement, leaping from the gray shadows of alleyways to jump you, knocking you to the ground and seriously kicking your ass. Still, we weren't old yet. Far from it. Which meant that our bodies, unbeleaguered, and intact as far as we knew, weren't dull at all, they were fascinating. Which meant that we could do whatever, or whoever, we wanted with them, and who and what we wanted to do could change from week to week or day to day or moment to precious moment, suddenly and consumingly, such that each new desire was, in essence, the first-ever desire, with every one prior to it cast instantly into a pitch-darkness as formless and empty as the original canvas of the earth. Much of what we (a few of us, at least) wanted to do was sex. For the most part we (a few of us) hooked up, or approached doing so, with those outside our crew, but since the summer we (again, a few of us) had also developed new and irresistible interests in one another. The fact that we were friends, that we had grown up together since we were kids, didn't make these particular desires strange, it made them strong. While some awkwardness ensued, some friction, there had always been trust among us, you see, and with trust comes the gift of an ample room, or better yet, of an open field, like those in the Botanic Garden or in Prospect Park, where on warm days, when things had seemed simpler, we would lavish time, each field providing a volume of space in which to flex and stretch ourselves freely, to play, to recognize that our bodies absolutely belonged there, among all the other fragrant and colorful organisms surrounding us.

One afternoon, during a balmy October weekend, the five of us assembled for the first time since school had started up again and took a walk, something we used to do frequently. Call it an act of nostalgia. We stopped outside the new store just across from the street of brownstones that always placed decently well in the annual contest for the Greenest Block in Brooklyn, and stood as one, peering in through the windows. A sign indicated the store was open, but it looked nowhere near ready to welcome customers yet. Inside, among towers of large, haphazardly stacked boxes, were intricate arrangements of junk, each surrounded by four low, unattached grids of metal wire leaning precariously against one another. A strong sneeze could have sent them all clattering down. Every arrangement contained variations of the same stuff: plastic bins, downy cushions, blankets, bowls, pellets of dirt. A trio of white people—two women and a man, all wearing tan aprons—moved slowly within the delicate maze, carrying large bags of what appeared to be desiccated grass. As they began to toss the twirling grasses here and there, everything around their feet twitched into motion, the entire floor leaped to life. The cushions weren't cushions at all, we saw, but living things, animals—rabbits—grouped inside rickety, makeshift cages.

We stared as we realized how many there were. About twenty cages, each housing two or three rabbits, so maybe fifty in total. Most were hopping around or furiously nibbling, but some settled quickly back into absolute stillness. There was something striking about these in particular, the assurance of their repose, the serene confidence that everything they wanted would eventually and inevitably arrive.

In response to all this, we slipped easily into our trademark goofiness and banter. Riffing on our old script felt like a form of solace. When Walidah, incredulous, expressed her opinion that the animals were too large to be rabbits, that the somber droop of their ears meant they were something else entirely, Roni told her to shut up and then teased, "We all know your ideas about the world still come from cartoons."

"They *are* plump, whatever they are," Antonio said, putting an arm around Cherise. He eyed her with the overwrought expression of hunger he'd developed during the summer. "You should find out what they eat," he added. "We can put you on their diet."

Cherise, who had always been self-conscious about her narrow frame, watched with a slight frown as the animals ate. She seemed uncertain whether Antonio's words amounted to criticism or encouragement. "Guess they do look happy," she said finally, and then slipped the pleasing fat of her lower lip into her mouth to suppress a smile.

"They are indeed rabbits," a man's voice announced, "but actually there are guinea pigs and chinchillas, too." The voice sounded peculiar, like something massive pressed densely small, simultaneously loud and restrained. The white man with the apron was peeking out of the open door. "Come on in, kids," he said. "Let's introduce you to them."

Shrugs. As we followed him inside, the two women were cheesing maniacally at us, and for reasons we couldn't discern, they kept nodding their heads. When we separated and looked around, the man explained that the place was actually a rescue, and then began rattling off the names of the animals—"That's Oreo, that's Marshmallow, Sasha's over there, and that's Balthazar . . ."—but he spoke too quickly for us to keep up. He had a pronounced underbite and a highly suspect chin beard that might as well have been a glued-on strap of mangled pelt. His face and skull were captivating, to be honest, but it was in our best interest—in the best interest of *us*—to focus on what made his features hilarious, to imagine his onrush of words as, say, a waterfall flowing over the jagged precipice of his bottom teeth. After naming all the animals for us, he mentioned, almost as an afterthought, that he was Cyan. He neglected to introduce the women.

"They eat grass? Dogs shit on grass."

"Technically, it's hay," Cyan said, pointing a finger upward. "But they can't subsist on hay alone. It doesn't provide all the nutrients." He offered us an opportunity to feed the animals some lettuce.

"So you can really get thick like that on lettuce and hay?" Antonio asked.

Cyan gave a heh-heh laugh, false and uncomprehending but good-natured, and called toward the back of the store for someone named Reginald. A moment later, this Reginald walked in, except Reginald wasn't Reginald. Reginald was Headass. He stood there, also wearing an apron, and looking even taller and lankier than usual, though a bit more youthful, with a semblance of a healthful glow. Against his chest, he held a clear-plastic bin filled with wet, brilliantly green leaves. His pants and kicks were clean—well, clean for Headass, anyway, meaning they weren't filthy—and his matted hair was parted oddly on one side. The part itself, which revealed his pale skin in a broad strip, glistened with some kind of grease. We gaped at the sight of him, he yawned at the sight of us. Then, in a snap, a crooked grin stretched the left half of his face, like the banner of some new country tautened by a sudden wind.

"Y'all hired Headass?"

Cyan pursed his lips and then gave his heh-heh laugh again. "It was always our intention to engage people from the community," he said in his funny voice, with enough brightness to blind us. "Reginald here was the perfect person to help us out."

The sound of that name had the effect of a magical incantation, activating Headass again. He stepped forward, but instead of distributing the food among the animals in any way that would have made sense, he set the bin on the floor, grabbed a handful of the greens, and vaulted over the tremulous perimeter of a cage in two easy strides, then lowered himself until he was sitting cross-legged with three rabbits, which, after a moment of wariness and agitation, reacted surprisingly well to him. Headass carefully lifted one of them—portly and auburn-colored, with flecks of black—and set it on his lap. With evident pleasure, he began feeding it.

"It appears that Reginald and dear Chicory have made a love connection," one of the women said.

Headass was imitating the rabbit now, with rapid, pulsing movements of his nostrils and mouth, as though he were eating, too. His fingers slowly stroked the air just above the fur, never touching it. The gesture made you feel the animal's heat. When one of us started laughing, a moment passed before we could all figure out why, but as we did, the laughter became reassuringly infectious. The pellets scattered in the cage with Headass—scattered in all the cages—weren't made of dirt. He was sitting gleefully in a pile of rabbit shit.

We left the rescue and walked shoulder to shoulder to shoulder and so on, incandescent with jokes and cackles, five lit bulbs on a string. It's ridiculous, but seeing Headass, genuinely taking notice of him, really witnessing him rooted there in that playpen of dung, seemed to bind us in a way we hadn't been bound in months, at least since the end of junior year. We walked and without speaking agreed on which direction to turn at which corner, and on where (the pizza parlor) and what (a pepperoni pie) to eat for lunch, and as we ate we expressed one enthusiastic opinion about the new album everyone was talking about, which had been released without warning the midnight before, and we quickly agreed on which song was the best, which possessed the most fire, and after lunch, as we played it aloud on one of our phones, we stopped walking and claimed a little pocket of Marcus Garvey Boulevard, making it gorgeous as hell with our singing and our shouts and the perfectly synchronized dance steps we devised right on the spot. Even the two of us boys who had grown increasingly shy about that kind of display, especially in the last few months, were completely into it for a minute, gleefully popping our butts along with the girls until we all leaned into one another and roared in a spirit of gratified exhaustion, without a trace of cynicism, irony, or embarrassment.

As we resumed our walk, one word seemed to come to all our minds at the same time: *Reginald*. Why were those white people referring to Headass as *Reginald*? we screamed, which sent us into more fits of laughter. And then—again, all at the same time, it seemed—we invoked Toby (for Kunta Kinte), SoHa (for lower Harlem), DoBro (for downtown Brooklyn), all the examples we could think of that illustrated the ways they claimed the right to name and rename whoever and whatever they pleased. We agreed without debate, without an utterance of doubt, that Reginald could not under any circumstances be his government name, but we did not acknowledge the fact that we, too, had named him—we'd done it, or our uncles and older cousins, who'd grown up with him and gone to school with him and who were also, sometimes, a part of us, had done it—and so it was easy to avoid that particular complication since he'd always, as far as we knew, answered to Headass, and after all, it was a different thing entirely to speak of what we, whoever we comprised at a given moment, decided to name ourselves. We avoided the complication of that, too, the idea that Headass was also, sometimes, in a peculiar way, a part of us, because in that moment, all that really mattered was the beautiful, hazy dream of we-the-five restored to harmony. But then, when it was suggested that we go over to Antonio's apartment, which is exactly what we would have done before, back when things had been normal, Antonio hesitated. In the span of a silence like that, you could hear the breeze plucking a yellowing leaf away from its stem. He looked down at his hands as they gripped the sides of his jeans. He said we shouldn't. His place was messy. Things were still weird there. Lately his mother had been feeling even worse. He started to say something more, anxious to offer additional excuses, as if he needed them, but instead let his voice trail away. "Yeah," he added uselessly, rubbing the splendid bulb of his nose. Cherise cleared her throat and said she, too, had to go. Then the two of them said hasty goodbyes and walked off as if holding hands, in a direction where neither of them lived.

"So," Roni said to Walidah, "what was it you were gonna show me? One of your cartoons?"

Walidah nodded, her eyes shrouded beneath their lids. "Yeah, that's right . . ."

Then the girls, who'd developed a new and hard-won intimacy, left, as well, a careful distance maintained between them, together but apart, and just like that, with inexplicable ease, our reunion, our alliance, was again, however lovely the bond, broken.

Two weeks later, though, our dormant group-text lit up with a message from Cherise, telling us all to come by the animal rescue to see what was happening. She was already there, a second message said. So was Antonio.

Walidah and Roni arrived last but in time to witness some of the spectacle: Headass in a bulky costume, stalking the sidewalk back and forth. The intention was probably to attract people who were, or could be, lovers of the Leporidae, but he was playing it all wrong. From where we stood along the curb, the fur was convincing enough, smooth as though someone had diligently combed down all the fibers, and aside from a smudge here and there, it gleamed a solid silvery-white. At the extremities, however, the color graded to the hideous, fleshy pink of skinned game. As Headass moved his feet and hands mechanically up and down, he seemed to carve the air with his pointed, yellow nails, his fingers rigid and spread, his posture that of a demon giving chase. For some reason, he was also wearing a stiff, plaid vest, which jumped on his body like an ill-fitting shell. But the strangest thing, the thing we couldn't stop whispering to one another about, was the way his face peeked out of the creature's open mouth, as though he were being swallowed, or bizarrely birthed, through a frightening crown of sharp buckteeth the same awful yellow as his nails. Up top, the eyes were garish rings shaded pale blue and pink. If not for the ears, which were as languid as those of the real rabbits inside, it would have been reasonable to think Headass was pretending to be a rat with albinism.

Behind him, Cyan stood at the doorway of the rescue, leaning within the threshold and chewing loose fistfuls of peanuts. He must have been listening as we discussed Headass and the strange sound emanating from him. "Little-known fact," Cyan called, "but rabbits have the ability to purr, just like our feline friends. It's much cooler, though. You know why? Rabbits do it with their teeth."

Headass wasn't doing anything with his teeth, and the sound wasn't one bit like purring. It was more a drawn-out, melancholic moan, which hardly ceased long enough for him to breathe.

Cyan wiped his hands on his pants and came over to us, specks of papery, brown peanut skin stuck in his beard. "This was Reginald's idea," he said. "So we let him choose whichever costume he wanted. It's perhaps not what we would have gone with, but there's something to it."

Maybe Cyan wasn't all bad, for an invader.

"It was cool of y'all to hire a homeless dude."

Cyan seemed taken aback by the comment. "Well," he said, "technically speaking, he's a volunteer."

"Wait, you don't pay him?"

He listened to Headass moan and nodded regretfully. "If only we could."

"Do you feed him?"

He balked. "*Feed* him? Actually, there's usually lots of leftover romaine, not to mention—let's see—bok choy, watercress, kohlrabi . . ."

Maybe not.

We watched Headass stop, spin on his heels, and start again in the opposite direction.

"There haven't been as many adoptions as we might have liked," Cyan said, changing the subject. The two white women who worked there were the only people inside. "Not a single one so far, in fact. But folks seem curious, that's for sure. They slow down when they pass. They glance in. Building interest is always step numero uno."

"You can't really expect a lot of rabbit adoptions in the hood," Roni said, with a razor in her voice.

"Why not?" he replied. "History tells us that rabbits appeal to people from all walks of life. Certain rodents, too, studies have shown. Besides, this isn't really *the hood* anymore, is it?"

Cyan was right about that last part, though he spoke as if he had absolutely nothing to do with it. We stared first at him and then around at the drivers parading by in their eco-friendly cars, the cyclists in their actual helmets and biking shorts, pumping their nickel-bright knees, assaulting us with their show of law-abiding goodness and safety. But all that was oppressively dull—we knew it too well—so we didn't comment on it. What was interesting to us were the people and places that were gone. After Cyan went back inside, and as Headass persisted in his marching and his moaning, we found ourselves scrutinizing the rescue itself. What exactly *had* been there before? Any of us could have gone in and asked Cyan or the two ladies, but none of us would. Information from them, from some records they had dug up as part of a business plan, would have been merely that: information, data. No better than an internet search. The thing was to remember, to use our minds and their keen, branching tails, and our sparking, scintillating connections, to recollect. But despite our efforts, all we could conjure was a sign in a clouded window that read *commercial space for rent.*

Suddenly Headass pivoted and stomped toward us, as if all his back-and-forth had just been a way of winding himself up. He stood directly in front of us and peered down into our faces, fully inhabiting his bestial role. The teeth of his costume pressed pinholes into his worried brow.

"What's up, Headass."

When his eyes narrowed in disapproval, we glanced at one another.

"What's up . . . *Reginald*?"

He shook his head emphatically. Then he sucked a deep breath through his mouth, pressed his lips together, and moaned with even greater force and resonance. We all laughed, but it was thin laughter, tentative, nervous. We didn't hide our bewilderment. Headass could talk, we knew, but he was refusing to use his words. He did it again: deep breath, tensed mouth, long, plangent moan. He pointed one of his frightful nails at us and nodded briskly, the ears of the monstrous rabbit flopping, the sickly eyes atop his head seeming to look down at us, too, his multiplied vision holding us in place. One by one, we came to understand. What started with the incredulous stares of the other four became, gradually, through a process of reluctant submission, our unanimous choral response to his call. He moaned, and we moaned—Antonio so loudly you could feel the vibrations of his chest—and for a while, it went on like that, antiphonal, until finally all six of our voices coalesced.

In the quiet that followed, satisfied perhaps, Headass turned and retreated into the rescue. We took another look through the window. The towers of boxes were gone, but the rest of the interior appeared as it had before, just as perfunctory and helter-skelter, still unsure of its purpose. Headass stood at the same cage he'd sat in two weeks earlier, the claws of his costume curled into the gaps between the metal, staring raptly at a fellow creature within.

We left but didn't get very far together. Just reaching the corner required a colossal effort. What we (some of us) had felt coerced into doing with Headass had cast us into a net from which we (some of us) were eager to escape. The excuses came so quickly. Antonio's mother was still sick, he said, Cherise had chores to do, she said, Walidah and Roni had to study. And then they all left, and the street that would one day win the honor of Greenest Block in Brooklyn was, at least for the immediate interval, also without question the loneliest.

We returned to the rescue a week later, on a cold day that could have been special but was depressingly ordinary. After the interminable hours at school, we found ourselves going in the same direction at the same time, so we just gave in to the accident of being together. The conversation, if you could call it that, was halting and slight, much feebler than small talk because we were the ones having it, because it was us. Our hands stayed balled in our pockets, our chins tucked into our scarves.

"It's brick outside today."

"It was brick *inside* today. How you gonna make kids come to a school with no heat."

"Write this long-ass essay, but you gotta do it with mittens on."

"It's fucked-up."

"Yeah, it's fucked-up."

"It's brick as hell out today."

"For real."

Outside the rescue, Cyan was sweeping abscised leaves into a pile. He greeted us warily, without a word, barely raising a hand to wave. His mouth dropped open, and the heft of his jaw turned this expression into a shock of surrender. For a while, we watched him work, listened to the swish of the broom and the rasp of the leaves.

Finally it was asked: "Where's Headass?"

Cyan froze. "Why didn't anyone tell us he was troubled?"

"Troubled?"

He lowered his voice. "Mentally disturbed."

"Wasn't it obvious?"

"We thought he was a little eccentric, quirky maybe, but generally fine, totally within the range of our expectations. You guys could have said something."

"Why would we?"

"Is there a good reason why you wouldn't?" Cyan asked. Since none of us could muster a response, he continued: "Anyway, it doesn't matter. Please don't mention him to us anymore. From now on, consider Reginald persona non grata here."

"But what happened?"

His face became strained and then relaxed into a grimace. "There are things called zoning ordinances, OK? There are *rules* that have to be followed. And your friend, he put us in violation. If we hadn't found him by chance the other night, there could have been serious consequences. He was staying here, sleeping here behind our backs, agitating the animals when we weren't around. He totally and completely abused our kindness."

"Where is he now?"

Cyan looked genuinely aggrieved by the question. "Who knows! And more importantly, who cares," he said. "As long as it's far away from us." Then he began to sweep again, fitfully, the bristles uncomfortably close to our feet.

None of us moved, though. We just stared holes into his head. But even this communal act of aggression couldn't hold us together for long.

"Man, fuck this place," Antonio said. "We out." But *we* didn't mean all of us.

"Wait, this stupid bullshit can't mess up our day. Let's get into something, go somewhere. Don't you guys want to do anything?"

His eyes got dull. He exhaled loudly. "The day was already messed up. It was a dumpster fire the second the fucking alarm went off," he said. "There's not a thing we can do about it, and not a damn place to go but home."

And there they were again, suddenly, the realigned configurations. Cyan watched as we separated, two by two by one, and went every which way. After a minute, he yelled something to us that had the striking ring of optimism, but we weren't close enough to hear it.

Later on, at home, Dad was waiting. "Happy birthday," he said. He held a brown paper bag, crisply folded and sealed with a square of tape. It was obvious that a book was inside. "Couldn't get what you really wanted—you know how it is—but next year, next year . . . Anyway, it may not look like much, but the lady at the store guaranteed you'd like it."

"Thanks, Dad."

"'Preciate you, Son," he said. "Lord knows what things would be like without you. Without the rock. Sturdy and steady, no matter what."

"Dad, you know that place that opened up a little while ago, the animal rescue?"

"Animal rescue?"

"Yeah, with all the rabbits and stuff."

"Oh, that place. Talk about a sore thumb. What of it?"

"Do you remember what it used to be?"

He made himself look thoughtful, one of his playful displays of effort. Anyone who really knew him knew that his chief affliction was an inability to ever forget. After hamming it up like this for a while, he snapped his fingers. "It used to be a church. One of those storefronts, you know."

"That's right . . ."

"The Cathedral of Blessed Deliverance. That's what it was called."

"For real?"

"Lying is dying," he said. "You'd walk by on service days, and the singing that came out of there would bring you to your knees. That one's gone, but there are still plenty of others around. More than ever, it seems. Cathedral City, that's where we live." He handed over the bag. "Now come on and open your present. And guess what your dad's whipping up for dinner tonight? Your favorite."

Not long after we ate, Dad started crying in his room again. His weeping had always been legible, and easily classified. There had been a taxonomy to his tears. Angry heaving meant his attempts to get a second job had resulted in some new humiliation. Pathetic quavering meant he wished Mom would change her mind and come back to us. And so on. But the sound he was making that night, which shot directly through the poster of Sun Ra on the wall, was some kind of hybrid. Usually you can't decide what to be sad about. Usually you don't get to decide. Sometimes it all hits you at once. Sometimes you don't even know what all is hitting you.

Better to let people be when they get that way, though. Earlier that summer, Antonio had made a similarly horrible sound when he'd learned exactly how ill his mother was, and how little time he had left with her. Who knows what else he was figuring out, what else was baffling him. When you hear someone you love make a sound like that, the problem isn't that you don't know how to respond, it's that you lose all your reserve, the discipline and self-restraint that were actually keeping everything intact. So you take liberties. You close the door to your friend's room and begin gathering the dented soda cans and empty water bottles, arranging them in rows on his desk. You pick up every loose bit of soiled, funky clothing from the floor and the chair and drop them into the hamper in his closet. You stack the crusted cereal bowls on top of the smeared plates and neatly arrange all the used spoons and forks. With nothing but the palm of your hand, you wipe the dust from the screen of his TV. You understand completely the power in the illusion of order, so you clarify the shapes and lines around him. When he makes the sound again, you sit on the bed where he's crumpled into a heap. You clear the dust from your palm and lay your body down beside his. You put your arm around him and pull him close and hold fast, your chest knocking against his back. When he turns toward your body and its offering, you kiss along a meridian of his face, first on his eye, then down beneath his cheekbone, then lightly on the leftmost edge of his mouth. You say you're sorry, but he doesn't understand what you mean. Or maybe he doesn't want to.

So, no matter how wretched the sound, it's best to stay very quiet and avoid calling any attention to yourself. It's best to do absolutely nothing.

But if you must do something, scroll through the old photos saved on your phone. Read the first few pages of your new book. Lie there gazing at the poster of Sun Ra on your wall and think about the perfect silence of outer space. Attempt to go away, to get lost. Try, as a means of control, to obliterate yourself without violence. Try to endure the long waking hours and then slip unnoticed into sleep.

Nearly three more weeks passed. The calendar on the refrigerator at home said so. Otherwise how could you tell? The air outside felt the same as it had the previous month, with the single exception of that one notably raw day, and people had yet to bring out their thickest gloves and heaviest coats. We did see one another at school or on the street, two or three of us at a time, in passing, but never all five. And the way we interacted during those random encounters, with shrugging superficiality, seemed to acknowledge that this was it, this was what life did, plain and simple, nothing profound so maybe don't worry too much. It pulled bodies apart.

But then one morning brought us back together. It was the Friday before Thanksgiving. The sun hadn't yet risen very far in the sky, and Bed-Stuy was still waking up: people on their way to school or work, walking listlessly, sinking down to the subway, or languishing on corners, waiting for the bus.

Near Halsey Street, a chubby stray cat leaped from behind a tree and made an odd purring sound. At second glance, however, it wasn't a cat but a rabbit, of course—one from the rescue, the one they called Balthazar. It jumped again, moving in reaction to a different sound that came within earshot, a distant clanging. Along just the next couple of blocks, more than a dozen of them became visible, hopping or dozing, as if our little slice of Bed-Stuy were like some town out in the Midwest, teeming with wildlife.

It didn't take long to find the source. Out on MacDonough, beside the open door to the unlit rescue, Headass stood with a large metal spoon in one hand and an empty pot in the other. Among the people gathered there: Antonio and Cherise, Roni and Walidah, standing together-apart in their pairs. As Headass continued to bang the spoon against the pot, more loudly and rapidly, some began to warn him. Others, to cheer him on. More rabbits came into view, as though summoned.

Over the next few minutes, the crowd grew, and the cheers intensified, punctuated with random shouts of *Yeah!* and *That's right!* but also *Be careful!* and *Don't get got!* It wasn't clear what the crowd, as a collective, was hoping to articulate. Everyone seemed to be smoldering in their own private fire. The cautions were easier to understand than the encouragements, but it all made sense somehow. It made sense that it didn't make sense, and when the five of us exchanged glances and nods, perhaps granting one another permission to join the shouting on either side, it felt good. We-the-five weren't a thing anymore, and we wouldn't be ever again, but for a little while, as long as Headass kept up the intensity of his racket, we could be part of another thing, a large and incoherent body that had plenty to say and no need or desire to justify itself.

Still, such things tend not to last, and sooner than we might have expected, it was done. Without warning, Headass stopped the banging. Truth be told, he may have just gotten bored. He looked at the pot and spoon in his hands as if they no longer held any interest at all. He dropped them to the ground, and the crowd started to disperse. People had to return to their lives. Roni and Walidah, Cherise and Antonio, too. They walked in the direction of school, as if the routine had never been in question. They walked until they were gone.

"Headass, you should go, too. It's not safe for you to be here."

But he paid the concern no mind. Instead he crept over to a car parked directly in front of the rescue and ducked behind it, disappearing completely for a moment, before rising again with a rabbit nestled in his arms. Grinning, he approached with it. The rabbit struggled a bit, flailing its little limbs, then relaxed as he got close. Headass didn't smell so good. With great care, he extended his arms, offering the animal for affection. He seemed so proud as he held it out. Its nose fluttered.

Its fur was stunningly soft, its warmth an astonishment. It was the same rabbit from that first day, the one he'd held and obsessed over. "This is Chicory, right?" The words came automatically, blurted at the exact moment of remembrance. But he shook his head and responded, "No, no," his voice richer and more sonorous than before. He smiled broadly and said a word, pronouncing it slowly, savoring each of the syllables, sharing the true name he'd given the rabbit out of love.

Then he told me his name. Then I told him mine.

ALEXANDRA CHANG

Phenotype

FROM *Electric Literature*

PEOPLE SAY THAT we don't really know each other and that's why we're still together, but what everyone doesn't see is that we understand each other perfectly fine. It's true he's Korean and I'm not. It's also true that I'm an undergrad in the same lab where he's a grad student. Yes, he TA'd my cell bio class, but that was before, so I deserved my A. The age difference isn't as much as it looks. My parents are orthodontists. I have a lot of jaw issues, so I've worn braces since freshman year of high school. He's never had braces. He doesn't believe in cosmetic alterations. He says he's traditional in that way, not like most Koreans these days. His teeth are small, tinged yellow, and crooked.

"I bet her parents keep her in braces to keep the boys away," a grad student says.

"Oh, God, like a chastity belt in her mouth," says a post-doc.

"Didn't work on KJ. Guess he's into it. Or girls who look like they're still in high school."

"Or any mediocre white girl."

The two of them burst into heinous laughter.

Another thing people don't know is that I hear a lot in lab. They think because I'm quiet that means I'm also deaf. Here I am, taking photos of mutated yeast, having to listen to them talk about me.

"Oh. Hi, Judith," says the grad student when she walks into the microscope room.

"How's it going?" says the post-doc.

I look up at them and smile to show off all my braces, rubber-banded in gold.

It didn't take me long to figure out that not everyone who gets a PhD is a genius. KJ is not a genius. He's in his sixth year, and the mean time for completing a doctorate in this department is 5.4 years, which makes KJ about average among his peers. This isn't even the best graduate biology program in the country. Last I checked, it was ranked eleventh. I'm as smart as, or smarter than, any of the grad students and post-docs in the lab, including KJ and maybe even my PI. I haven't reached my full potential yet.

My plan is to become a real doctor. Not like my parents and not like KJ will be eventually, when he graduates. I will be an MD, a doctor of medicine. My other plan is to get far away from this town, maybe even to another country, like Korea. I was born and grew up here, and because the university is one of the best in the country for undergrads, *not* the worst Ivy League, I stayed. I lived at home. I took the bus to classes. I took the bus back home. I ate dinners with my parents every night.

Until KJ.

I joined the lab last year, my junior year. It is in the newest building on campus, a sterile white and metal structure that looks like it's made of giant kitchen tile. At first I didn't notice KJ. He sat in a distant bay. All the grad students seemed the same back then. Overworked and undernourished adults plodding around in sneakers and blue gloves. I work for one named Drew. After months of having me grow yeast cells and wash dishes, Drew let me do real experiments, and the PI invited me to attend lab meetings. I sat there at the first one with my mouth closed and back straight, trying very hard to look deserving as the grad student of the day stumbled over their PowerPoint slides. I don't remember anything anybody said because I was so worried about my mouth opening and making me look dumb. It has a tendency to hang open when I'm not paying attention.

KJ approached me after that meeting and asked if I liked to eat Korean food. Those were his first words: "Do you like to eat Korean food?" I'd never had any, but I said yes. When he walked away, I noticed he waddled because of his thick, stocky legs. He is not a small person; he is shaped like a brick.

The next day he brought me a Tupperware of pork and rice, and we ate it together in the fourth-floor lunchroom. I didn't know what to say as I sat across from him, so I didn't say anything. KJ was quiet, too. We sat there eating in silence for a long time, and I remembered an article I once read that said silence between people indicates that the people are comfortable with each other. Most people like to talk a lot when they're in front of you. I preferred the quiet. It was how I ate with my parents at home.

KJ had a deliberate way of putting each bite of food in his mouth and chewing, like he was thinking really hard about it. I was studying his forearms, hairless and bronze, when he said, "I'm a very good cook."

He did not say it like a question. I took another bite to show that I agreed.

"You are very smart," KJ said. "Top five percent in cell bio."

I knew this, but it felt different, special, to hear it from somebody else.

"Did you grade my tests?" I asked.

"Yes," he said. "I enjoy your handwriting. It is crisp and excellent."

We sat in silence for a moment, chewing the food he'd made.

Then he pointed at my mouth.

"Your hair," he said. "You're eating it."

"Oh." I yanked the strands out of my mouth, unsure how they'd gotten there.

"Has anyone ever told you that you have pretty hair?" said KJ.

Nobody had ever told me that. My hair is limp and dry and the color of wet sand. In fact, in elementary school, the kids used to call me Scarecrow. I always think of my hair as one of my worst features. That and my fingernails, which are short and stubby from when I bit them down in high school.

I blushed.

Hearing his compliments felt like stepping into the lab's cold room on a humid summer day. It felt great.

That's when we started dating. We didn't tell anybody, and we limited our interactions in front of others. KJ said it should be kept a secret, at least for a while, and I agreed. We did not want people to think we were a stereotypical grad-undergrad couple. We also did not want the PI to know until we were sure he wouldn't flip out and kick one of us out, most likely me. KJ said he cared about my future. Our PI is fairly unpredictable, which KJ attributes to his being from Argentina. I'd never met anybody from Argentina before joining this lab, and now I know seven Argentinians: the PI, his wife, his two daughters, the one graduate student who is an idiot, and the two post-docs, who are too depressed most of the time to notice anything around them. Before KJ, I did not know anybody from Korea, either.

It is difficult to have a secret relationship, especially when one person lives at home with their parents and the other lives with grad school classmates. The only times I could see KJ were during intramural soccer and in lab. Since both of those spaces were occupied by our labmates, we had to be careful, always watching ourselves, sneaking time for quick lunch walks (always leaving the lab staggered), and hanging around after soccer until everyone else had gone. He would send me texts that said, *You are good at science* and *You are pretty today.* I didn't read into the syntax (am I pretty today but not yesterday or tomorrow?) because he's ESL. I have met a lot more foreigners working in the lab and have gotten very good at understanding ESL people.

What I loved was going to soccer and watching KJ get into fights. I still love it. He's quiet and calm in lab, but on the field, he is frightening. He rams into people. They yell at him. He yells back and pushes. Other people on the team have to pull him away. Sometimes he runs off and pushes somebody again. It is fascinating. It is like watching a nature show about my boyfriend. I think it has to do with him having been ranked very high up in the South Korean military before he came to graduate school. He says everybody smoked cigarettes there, which is why his teeth are yellow. He went from two packs a day to quitting completely when he came to the United States.

"I have incredible willpower," he said when he told me this thrilling detail of his life.

In those early months, when he wasn't overwhelmed with work, we'd meet at the far end of the parking lot outside our building, and he'd drive us to a restaurant for dinner. He chose places far from campus, places we didn't think anybody else would go, like the Arby's on the outskirts of town. I had to tell my parents that I was busy running experiments in lab. Yes, I lied to them, too, at first. It was the biggest secret I'd ever kept.

Our first kiss—my first kiss ever—happened in the Arby's parking lot, before one of our meals. KJ is very conscientious about his breath and hygiene in general, and that first time, he handed me a piece of gum when I got in the car. We both chewed and chewed. The minty scent filled the cold car. When we arrived in the parking lot, he leaned over and held out a napkin for my gum. I spat it out. Then he put his mouth on my mouth. His lips were softer than I'd expected. The whole time, I thought about my braces and my tongue. Was one of them poking him in a bad way? KJ pulled back.

"You'll get better with practice," he said.

He ordered two Arby's roast beef sandwiches, and we ate them at a sticky linoleum table inside. The only other customer was a middle-aged man wearing a tank top with a graphic of a smiling cartoon hot dog wrapped in an American flag. I thought he looked like my uncle Robbie, who lives in Horseheads. The man stared at us the entire time he ate, sauce dripping down the corners of his mouth. I wiped my mouth furiously.

KJ stared back at the man. They went on like this for a few minutes. I waited for a fight, like KJ was on the soccer field. Instead, KJ eventually said, "Let's go."

"You have something in your teeth," he said once we were back in the car.

I flipped open the passenger's-side mirror and saw clumps of wet bread stuck behind my braces. Mortified, I dug the stuff out with my finger and tongue. "Don't worry," KJ said. His tone was matter-of-fact. He was not disgusted or ashamed. He rested his hand on my knee to let me know it was okay. That's when I knew he accepted me as I was.

The parking-lot intimacy progressed. KJ was right. I did get better at kissing. I didn't think about my braces the whole time. I thought about other stuff, like sex. He started to ask, "How much today?" meaning, how far did I want to go. He was very considerate. "Second base, okay? That's what Americans say." I said, "Yes."

I wasn't an expert. I didn't know anything about baseball, and he was a huge fan. KJ said Koreans love baseball, which surprised me. I was always learning new things about his culture. I let him reach under my shirt and into my bra. I kept my hands in my lap. He seemed satisfied. When the occasional car drove in or out of the lot, we shot apart and stared out the front window, then laughed into our hands. Outside, small birds hopped around, pecking at crumbs and garbage. It was not a romantic setting from the movies, but it felt special to me.

After three months of this, KJ decided it was time to tell the people in our lives. He said he was very serious about me. Also, someone had figured out about us. Another Korean PhD student named Jun-ho always wanted to know about KJ's love life. Question after question at our soccer games. KJ avoided answering until, finally, he conceded that he was dating me. KJ said that the Koreans in America find each other wherever they go, and they are obligated to spend time together. That's why he and Jun-ho were friends, even though KJ said he hated Jun-ho's nosiness.

These days KJ says he doesn't want to associate with the Koreans on campus anymore. He wants to be more than just another Korean graduate student. He says he has me now.

Still, he invited Jun-ho to the announcement party. KJ said it was very important that we tell everyone at the same time and place. The message would be consistent and clear. He invited people over to his apartment complex for a barbecue, but somebody else suggested the park, and KJ complied. He confirmed everyone's attendance. He told people 6:30 p.m. sharp. I didn't care much about anybody, but I liked to see KJ in this meticulous mode. I overheard him talking to a grad student on the floor below ours.

"Oh, Cassandra's barbecue thing? Yeah, I'll be there," the guy said.

"No. My barbecue," said KJ. "Be on time, please." "Uh, okay. Sure," the guy replied.

We arrived at the park a half hour early and laid out everything we'd bought on one of the picnic tables by the lake. A tablecloth, chicken breasts, water, soda, napkins, plastic utensils, paper plates, coal, ice, and a cooler. KJ did not know how to start the grill, so we waited for somebody who did to arrive.

KJ took my hands in his. "We will surprise them with the announcement," he whispered. I hated surprises, but I liked KJ, and this was for us. I wasn't going to be the one surprised.

Many of our labmates had been invited but had texted KJ minutes before, saying they couldn't make it. They had too much work. They were tired. They weren't feeling well. KJ tried very hard not to look disappointed. Finally, Jun-ho arrived five minutes late. My supervisor, Drew, showed up with his girlfriend, Cassandra, who plays soccer with us. She's also a grad student, except in a social science department. There were some others, but I knew them only in passing. These people meant nothing to me, and I wasn't sure they meant much to KJ, either. But as I said, we do understand each other. And that evening, I understood that to KJ this was more symbolic than anything else. The *we* and the *us* would be more real after an announcement.

The picnic table became crowded with other people's snacks, even though KJ had bought enough for everybody. People busied themselves with activities. I stayed put, sitting there picking a brownie bite into smaller pieces—pieces that wouldn't get stuck in my braces.

"Judith, want to come hit a Wiffle ball?" Drew yelled, and waved his arms to indicate I should go over to a grassy area where people had gathered.

I had been watching them, happily remembering a fight KJ had on the soccer field the previous week, when he'd ripped an opponent's shirt at the collar and gotten kicked out of the game. Wiffle ball, however, was a children's game. I looked around for KJ, trying to see if I could get out of this. He wasn't paying attention. He was still standing beside Jun-ho at the grill.

"Judith? Did you hear me?" Drew yelled.

I nodded.

"Well? Do you want to come hit the Wiffle ball? It's not much harder than soccer!"

I shook my head.

Cassandra laughed loudly, and the sound hurt my ears. "She doesn't want to," she said. "Leave her alone!"

I hated Cassandra. She came into lab with Drew in the evenings and on weekends, even though she wasn't part of the lab. She just sat there on her computer, "working," she said, but it looked to me like she only watched videos and chatted with friends. I couldn't even remember what department she was in, what she was researching, not that it mattered. Social scientists aren't real scientists. The worst part was that she talked a lot and she sat at my bench, even when I was doing experiments in lab. I tried to leave my stuff on the desk to hint that she shouldn't sit there, but every day she moved my things aside and sat there again. Now she was walking up to me at the table.

"I'm so hungry! We should tell them to grill faster," she said.

"Heh heh, yeah," I said.

"KJ! Jun-ho! Hurry up! We're starving over here!"

KJ walked over and stood opposite me. "There is so much food here," he said.

"We need protein!" said Cassandra. "So when is this girlfriend getting here? Is that why we're still waiting to eat? Because she's late?"

KJ made a small smile and looked at me. "She will be here," he said. "The food is ready soon."

"How rude to come late to your party, where all your friends are waiting to meet her," Cassandra said.

KJ let out a little laugh, like a little bell, and walked back to the grill. I tried to give him a look to tell him not to leave me alone with Cassandra, but he had already turned around. Cassandra looked at me. My heartbeat picked up a little bit.

"What a weirdo," she said. "I told him I could help with food, but he kept saying, No, it's my event, it's *my* event. It's a barbecue!"

"I—"

She cut me off and called out to everyone that the food was almost ready. Soon everybody was sitting at the table with a paper plate in front of them. KJ walked over with the chicken breasts.

"Interesting. Did you season or marinade this in anything?" asked the guy who worked downstairs.

"There is ketchup," said KJ.

"So, where's your girlfriend?" Cassandra asked again, in front of everybody.

"What girlfriend?" the guy downstairs asked.

"That's why we're here! Because KJ has a girlfriend and wants to show her off to everybody."

Drew slapped KJ on the back. "Finally got one to go out with you, huh, buddy?"

As KJ was doling out the chicken to everyone, he said, "She's here."

"What? Where?"

"What did he say? Talk louder, KJ."

"He said she's here."

I was staring at the chicken on my plate, determining how many pieces I'd have to cut it into so that it wouldn't get stuck in my braces, when KJ said, "It's Judith."

"Ha. Ha. Good one," said Drew. "Judith, can you pass me those brownies?"

"What did he say?"

"Speak up! Why do you talk so quietly? I can't hear anything!"

"Judith is my girlfriend," KJ said again, louder.

I looked up and was about to smile to everyone, the smile of a girlfriend. I was relieved and satisfied that this was finally over. But then Cassandra started ferociously slapping KJ's arm while yelling, "No, she isn't! Stop saying that! She's an undergrad! It's not funny!" On the third slap, the chicken on KJ's plate flew onto the table and knocked a beer over into Jun-ho's lap. People jumped from their seats. They all started handing napkins to Jun-ho.

"I'm fine, I'm fine," he said, dabbing at his shirt and pants.

"Look what you made me do," said Cassandra.

KJ looked over at me. I felt my mouth opening a little and a heat rising up my neck into my face. I put a small piece of cut-up chicken in my mouth. I didn't want to say anything anymore. I wanted everybody to understand what was happening, but nobody understood us. I wanted everyone to go away. They all stared at me with confused faces. KJ repeated what he'd already said.

"Are you serious? Judith. Are you really KJ's girlfriend?" Cassandra said.

I nodded.

"I'm sure this is just a prank or something," said Drew.

At this point, Jun-ho got up and said something about grilling more chicken. KJ gave me a thumbs-up before heading to monitor the grill as well. Everybody was silent for a while. We all ate our chicken peacefully. I thought that was the end of it, that everybody finally understood, but then one of them said, "So, I don't really know KJ that well. What was that about?"

I've noticed that once one person starts talking, it's as though their voice opens the doors for everyone else to start pushing words out, too, even if they're useless.

"He just said he's dating Judith," said another person.

And another: "Okay, so, what does that mean?"

Drew: "Judith, this is a joke, right?"

I shook my head. I was starting to feel a heavy weight behind my eyes, like I was going to fall asleep from being so tired.

Someone else: "Stop bothering her."

And another: "Of course it's real, why would they joke about this?"

I was searching for words that might communicate everything

more clearly but realized there weren't any for me to use that would work. I worried KJ and I might have to kiss in front of them for them to believe. It was a terrifying thought. The publicness of our relationship now felt so wrong.

"So how long have you been dating?" Drew asked. "Like, a couple weeks?"

"A few months," I managed to answer.

"Wow. Okay, wow. Congrats." He started tapping his fingers incessantly on the table. "I need to use the bathroom. Cassandra, will you help me find it?"

The two of them got up and left. The others followed suit, getting up to go back to their pre-eating activities, leaving me alone. Finally.

I looked around for KJ, but he was nowhere in sight. I started to panic that he, too, had left, embarrassed by our relationship. Then I felt hands on my shoulders. It was KJ. I looked up to see him holding a single pink flower.

"I got you this," he said. "To match your teeth."

"Thank you," I said. I had pink rubber bands on my brackets that week.

"Now everybody knows. We are official. I am so happy."

Nobody really spoke to us after that. They hit the Wiffle ball around and talked to each other. As we packed up to leave, KJ told people how much they owed him for the food. They said, *Congrats. Great barbecue. See you later.* Cassandra looked me in the face and apologized for her earlier "explosion."

"I'm happy for you," she said.

"Yeah. Anyway, see you two in lab tomorrow," said Drew.

Back in the car, KJ said, "That went very well. A great success."

I agreed with KJ. Nothing else mattered.

For days, I overheard people whispering in the halls and in lab about the barbecue. They told people who had canceled last-minute what had happened. They told people who weren't even invited. They went over the details with each other. They complained and rejoiced and wondered.

"God, it was painfully awkward. Most awkward thing I've ever had to go to."

"I can't believe he made us pay him ten dollars for that shitty-ass chicken."

"Why did they do that? Why did they want to make an announcement that they were dating, like it's an engagement party or something?"

"Definitely a top-five grad school experience right there. Remembering that forever."

"Is this even allowed? What is she, eighteen? Isn't this against school policy?"

"Have you ever seen them talk? I've never seen them interact."

"They just stand real close and whisper at each other in lab, like they don't want anybody to hear what they're saying."

"KJ should know better than to date an undergrad. I mean, she's so naive. I feel bad for her."

Nobody needed to feel bad for me. I felt bad for them. I appreciated what KJ had done. They didn't understand that I'd fallen in love with KJ that day. I didn't care about anybody else.

Having KJ changed my worldview. It was as if a tiny but incredibly important piece of my genetics had been changed, and the phenotypic result was a shiny new me. I told my parents I wanted to move to the dorms. I wanted to have independence. I had a boyfriend after all. I wasn't a kid anymore. They invited KJ over for dinner, and afterward, my dad said he was happy I'd found somebody polite and mature. And surprisingly handsome, my mom added. I'm not sure what was surprising about how KJ looked, if it was that a Korean man could be handsome or if it was that somebody as handsome as KJ would date somebody like me. It didn't matter either way, because KJ *is* handsome, and he is with *me.*

My parents gave me a card the next evening. There was a freckled little girl who looked like me on the front cover. She was smiling with all her teeth. I opened the card and saw one of the familiar office stamps. It read, *Hooray! Time to take off your braces!* in the shape of a circumzenithal arc. My parents said my jaw was finally fixed.

"You're a woman now," my mom said, her voice shaky.

"I've been a woman for a while now," I said, feeling confident.

"Yes. Now you'll look the part, too."

"How about we keep the bottom braces on, just in case you need another round of headgear?" my dad said when I sat in the patient's chair the next day. My dad never got emotional, so I was surprised to see his eyes watering. He cleared his throat. "It's up to you now, of course."

I told him to take them off. I was a new person, and I could make decisions of my own. After nine years, all the braces would go. When they came off, my teeth felt slick and slimy, like wet rocks along the lake.

I moved into the dorms soon after. I got a single room a third of the size of my room at home, furnished with a skinny bed, a short dresser, a small desk with a weird rocking desk chair upholstered in scratchy green fabric, all made of the same pine. Short gray carpet speckled with white covered the floor. It was perfect. On the first day, I lay down on the floor and imagined all the geniuses who had come through, people who had become doctors, like I would. I wanted whatever leftover particles of these people to seep up into me and make me brilliant.

Now I am totally free. KJ lives alone, too, and even though my parents said living with a man is only for marriage, I started to spend every night at his apartment. We stopped going to the Arby's parking lot after the barbecue event. We go to nicer restaurants in the center of town and close to the university, places where we can sit at tables with cloth napkins and a flower or candle between us, places where people can see us, though we have yet to run into anyone we know. When we sit in booths, KJ sits beside me because he says he saw it in a movie, where the man put his arm around his girlfriend as they ate. Sometimes people look at us strangely, but neither of us cares. We care only about each other.

Back at his apartment, we kiss and touch, and every night he asks if we can go to home base. To be honest, I would have had sex with him a long time ago. It's mostly what I think about when around him. What his thick, stocky legs will feel like rubbing up against mine. The problem is, I don't know what will happen. I don't know how much I will bleed, and the unpredictability makes me tense. What if I bleed all over his mattress and he needs to replace it? But he doesn't have the money for another nice mattress on his grad student stipend and has to sleep on a futon? What if blood gets all over him and he throws me out? What would I do afterward? Run away, leaving a bloody trail behind me? I don't know how to tell him, so I shake my head each time he asks. I wait for him to understand. He stares at me with his small eyes, looking like a hungry cat. Then he pats me on the cheek, turns away, and falls asleep. I stare at his ceiling, trying to figure out a way to have sex that will not be embarrassing.

I finally come up with an idea and feel light-headed about not having thought of it earlier. My dorm room. It is not romantic, but it is functional. I don't care about the university's mattress. If it gets stained, we can flip it and nobody will know for a year or more, hopefully after another person moves in and can be blamed. The amount my parents are paying for the room should cover these kinds of damages.

Hours on Google looking up articles on how much girls bleed their first time turns up many answers. It seems too huge a range, from no blood (hymen broken at an early age on a bike or in some sport) to streams of blood. One girl commented on an article, *Im bleeding alot! Im freaking out and don't know that to do! Im worried im dying!* What was she thinking, seeking medical help in the comments section? She might have gone crazy from blood loss, then died. I did not want to be that girl.

Soon KJ calls and asks to be let in.

"This room is sad," he says when he walks in. "It has no life."

He hands me a bouquet of flowers. There is nowhere to put them, so I empty out the pencil holder on my desk and stick them in there.

We sit at the edge of the bed and start kissing. Then we lie down and he gets on top of me. For a moment I think his face looks like a giant saucer looking down at me from an alien world. I push the thought away and we undress. He sits up briefly to take his socks off, roll them into each other, and places the sock ball gently at the foot of the bed.

"My favorite socks," he explains.

I consider grabbing a towel to put beneath us, which I read about online. Then I realize a towel would do nothing good. Blood would only ruin the towel. KJ returns to crouch above me. From the long distance between my eyes and my vagina, I look at his hanging penis, nearly touching me, the sprout of black hair surrounding it, and this time I see it as a branch wanting to reach into and grow inside me, but my body is on a different track than my mind, because KJ looks up at me and smiles. He's stuck a finger inside me and pulled it back out, slick. I try not to think about my teeth.

"Good," he says. "You're ready?" I nod and brace myself.

It hurts only a little, then it feels good for a little. I think it lasts around a minute. I don't feel any differently afterward. KJ apologizes. "It has been a long time," he says, then gets up, takes the condom off, brings it to eye level to examine its contents, ties the top off, then places it gently into the small trash bin beneath my desk, in the same loving motion as he had with his socks. I hope he is thinking, *My favorite condom.* I take the time to glance at my bed and am relieved to see no blood at all. KJ catches me looking around, then looks around as well.

"Hmm," he says, frowning.

I realize I now have a different problem, remembering another comment from an article online. A girl hadn't bled, then her boyfriend had accused her of lying, then he'd started crying. KJ stops looking on the bed and stares straight at me. Are those tears forming in his eyes?

"It must have been a bike or something," I say after thinking for a moment.

"A bike?"

I wonder how to put it. KJ's face is vibrating. He looks like he did in the photo he once showed me, him in his green military uniform, no glasses, black serious eyes pointed straight at me.

"I must have ridden my bike very roughly one day, and that's why there's no blood now," I say. This is what a commentor had told the girl to say. It is a valid and believable reason. Most bike seats are not engineered for women and are very painful to ride.

KJ looks at the ground. He is processing. His face vibrates some more, and I can almost see the gears turning behind his eyebrows.

"Okay," he says. He does not cry. He lies down on the bed, then motions for me to lie next to him. He wraps his arm around my naked body. We are both slightly sticky, but he doesn't let go. I don't want him to let go, either. "I was worried I would hurt you," he says. "I wouldn't want to hurt you. I love you."

I am so relieved, I start giggling. He asks what's so funny. I think about telling him all of my fears, my dreams, my ambitions for my—no, our—future, seeing what will happen if I let all of the words pour out of me, and how much they will make us understand more or less about each other. But then I don't. There is nothing to say, except one thing: "I love you, too."

We don't talk, and soon his breath deepens into the sound of sleep. When I'm certain he is not going to wake up, I slowly lift myself up to a sitting position. He doesn't stir. I look over at his crotch, where his penis lies soft and shriveled in its nest, unassuming and harmless, a tiny baby animal. I bend over so that my face is an inch away from the thing, then I sniff. It smells of sweat and dust and like the yeast we use in lab. This is what we smell like mixed together, two foreign elements in one, and it is not an unpleasant smell at all.

LAURIE COLWIN

Evensong

FROM *The New Yorker*

THIS IS NOT an account of a love affair, and it is not the story of a religious conversion, although elements of both pertain. Of course, in life, which is full of surprises, it is hard to know what anything is.

My husband, John Felix, and I live, with our ten-year-old daughter, Alice, on the bottom two floors of a brownstone, in the neighborhood of an Anglican seminary, a collection of Gothic buildings and a lawn. In the spring, it is possible to watch priests and their families playing croquet on the grass. In summer, vaporous smoke from their tiny barbecues wafts through our front windows. If you were a complete psycho and could not tell one thing from another, the orderly workings of this place—its piper on St. Andrew's Day, its Christmas procession and Easter picnic—would remind you that the season had changed, and you would know, because the hours are marked by bell ringing, what time it was at least five times a day. Even those who pay absolutely no attention to the institution are affected by it, if for no other reason than because on clear nights you can hear the organist practicing in the chapel.

Our lives—the lives of the Felix family—are also informed by Louis and Emily Billiards, whom we have known for years. Louis is a dealer in fine antique English and French furniture. His shop is in our neighborhood, and it was he who found the wonderful place in which we now live. Before we lived here, we lived right next door to the Billiards family, and we are very connected. Emily, who is the head of production at a publishing company, helped me get my first job as a book designer. When I became pregnant with Alice, Emily sent me to her doctor, and when Alice was a baby, Emily and Louis's daughter, Janet, babysat for us. Meanwhile, their son, Peter, graduated from college and needed advice about banking, which my husband, John, who works on Wall Street, was happy to give. When I quit my job, Emily helped me find freelance work. Louis also sold us our walnut dining-room table and fruitwood sideboard at a good price. How much we owe to Emily and Louis! Sometimes when I cannot sleep at night I am tortured, as if by bedbugs or red ants, at the size of this debt.

This account of what we owe the Billiards family is one of many lists. I am by nature a person whose constant battle against encroaching chaos is fought by list-making and organizational thinking. I make grocery lists that cover our immediate needs, our staple needs, our long-term needs, and our long-term needs of a special nature, such as a dinner party a month away. I *know* what I will serve at a dinner party a month away. Of course, in order to make these lists, plans must be made. My family tells me that I can sometimes be seen baring my teeth or muttering to myself as I make these lists.

For a while, my list-making was complicated by the fact that I had stumbled into a love affair with Louis Billiards (some way to pay Emily back for all her kindness!). Louis likes ginger ale, for example. No one in the Felix family will touch it. The same goes for gherkins, which Louis adores, and liverwurst. The trick was to coordinate the bringing of these items into our fridge with Louis coming for lunch.

I spent many hours of each day thinking as follows: If Louis turns up for lunch and eats the boiled potatoes, we will have to have rice with parsley and butter with dinner, but if he does not eat the potatoes we can have potato salad, which goes so much better with roast chicken. If Louis does not drink the ginger ale, or eat the Niçoise olives, or if he finishes the broccoli soup—and so on.

On the other hand, John and I are sort of hopeless around the house and are constantly paying workmen to come and do simple things like change the screens in the spring or fix the filter on the air-conditioner in the summer. It was Louis who eventually did these things. He made the list. He put Mortite around the back windows in the fall, and he put the screens up in the spring, and one day, when John was away on business and Alice was on one of her overnight class trips, Louis took down the pantry door and planed it. When he re-hung it, it opened and closed perfectly.

Emily, who is extremely competent, often beats Louis to the punch when it comes to household work—doubtless the reason he was having an affair with me.

In a love affair, it is usually the lover who is handsome and the husband who is not, whereas it was just the reverse in my case. John is exceptionally good-looking—tall, wavy-haired, lean, and fine-featured. Louis is a little shorter than I am, and bald, with a fringe of white hair. He has been weather-beaten to the color of teak and smells of cigars and furniture polish. Unlike my husband, who looks ravishing in his banker's suits, Louis plods around in worn chino trousers, blue work shirts, an old corduroy jacket, and suède desert boots. During the many hours I spent pondering my activities with Louis, it occurred to me that elements of the father-daughter relationship must obtain in an affair in which the man is old enough (or almost old enough) to be the woman's father. Of course, it also occurred to me that Louis was nothing whatsoever like my father, who was not bald, did not smoke cigars, was pale, and preferred to be rather formally dressed. But of course it does not matter if the person is like one's father. It matters that the person be *fatherly*. As I watched Louis weather-strip our back windows, I could not help but feel that he was something of a father to both me and John, although I knew that couldn't be right.

It is said that there are always four people in a love affair of this sort, the lovers and their spouses. It is also said that when two people go to bed together their parents are right there with them. Moreover, there is a saying that it often takes three to make a marriage. What a mob! And all because Louis and I were having a love affair.

Louis is a descendant of someone named Francis-Hugo Billiards, one of the founders of the neighborhood seminary. It was either coincidence, or fate, or divine guidance that led Louis to have a shop almost directly across the street from this institution. This forebear is the author of the hymn "In His Pasture May I Graze (That His Love May E'er Secure Me)," No. 214 in the hymnal supplement. One is encouraged to sing it "with flowing rhythm."

All these connections prove that everything, somehow or other, is in order. Life is infinitely rich, and infinitely interconnected. In the twilight of an early-fall or spring evening, I like to sit on the front steps with my daughter and watch our neighbors. Our street pulsates with individuality: rare breeds of dogs, strange modes of dress. No one even walks like anyone else. It occurs to me as I sit that everyone in the world is born with a personality and is fully entitled to express it. The planet is a-spin with notions, phobias, inclinations, tastes, ideas, creeds, beliefs, and behaviors of all kinds. Often this thought is uplifting and fills my heart with what feels like rich blood. If I stopped any of these people and questioned them closely, we would be sure to have a friend, an experience, a relative in common.

There is just no getting away from the complexity of human life. We are a tide pool, teeming with varieties of species. No matter which way you turn—on the bus, in the supermarket, sitting in a coffee shop—you are surrounded by people making idiosyncratic choices about this and that. Sometimes this all gives me a headache, and I reflect on what a pain in the neck people are.

My love affair with Louis began when he started to renovate his shop. He acquired a second shop next door and broke through a wall to connect them. Since I live in the neighborhood, and since I felt I owed the Billiardses so profound a debt, I volunteered to open the shop early in the morning for the workmen. It was the least that I could do. Had they not found us our dwelling? Our doctors? Did we not use products recommended by them? Their daughter as a babysitter? Had they not helped us get a good price on our beautiful Persian rug?

The renovations began early in September. One day in late October, I stopped by to see what progress had been made and to have a cup of tea with Louis. It was Alice's afternoon to have her ballet class, after which she always had dinner at her little friend Annie Shepherd's. After their afternoon of field sports, Annie Shepherd often came to us for dinner. How beautifully ordered are the lives of children!

The workmen had gone home. The street was empty. A thought flew into my head and I expressed it. I said, "I think I come to visit you too much." After all, I honestly had no interest in Louis's renovations, and yet I felt drawn to his shop.

Then Louis said, in a tone I had never heard from him before, "I don't think you visit often enough."

I was covered with shame to find that my heart had begun to pound in my chest. Louis got out of his chair and locked the door.

He hung up a sign that said "CLOSED." I followed him into the musty basement where he stored new shipments and furniture that needed repair or reupholstering. There, under a clean packing quilt, on a wide chaise that was to be reupholstered in pale-blue linen, we committed adultery. Nowadays, it gives me a pang to walk into a neighbor's house and see some piece of furniture that Louis and I once misbehaved on.

As to the cause of this love affair, well, cause was not my thing, really. Feeling was more up my street, as they say. This alliance had a preordained, familial feeling to it that I found irresistible—the combination of innocence and intimate knowledge you get at a family reunion.

One winter afternoon, when Louis and I had emerged from a tattered empire sofa in the basement, the seminary bells began to ring, reminding us that it was five o'clock.

"You know," I said conversationally, "we've lived here for almost ten years and I still don't know what those bells signify."

With this, Louis dragged me to my feet, wrapped me in my coat, switched off the lights, locked up his store, and led me out into the street. He walked me right through the seminary gates and toward the chapel.

"From couch to church!" he said jauntily.

I stopped on the path and would not move. Louis seemed right at home on the seminary grounds—being, after all, the descendant of a founder—but I was not. Furthermore, it was clear he was going to take me into the chapel, and I did not think it right to enter a religious structure after having been to bed with a man who was not my husband.

"Furthermore, I am not a Christian," I said.

"Pish-tush," Louis said. "You're a poor excuse for a Jew, and so is that husband of yours."

This was certainly true. John and I were the most watered-down of Jews, raised by diluted Jews who did not know how to be Jewish at all. As a result, John was sent to a Quaker school, I was sent to a school that embraced all faiths, and the two of us had put in some time at the Sunday schools of reformed congregations where, for the most part, we passed notes, chewed gum, and saw our little friends from dance class. Out of a sincere but confused longing to establish in our child some sense of cultural identification, we sent her to a Sunday school from which she appeared spouting the names of holidays we had not known existed, and patiently instructing us in various religious matters as best she could. Each year, we had a secular Christmas, and more advanced Jewish friends invited us to Passover dinners.

"I won't know where to put my feet," I said, balking at the chapel door.

"We'll sit in the back and no one will know what an infidel you are."

"Infidel does not cover what I am," I said.

"Now, now," Louis said. "No melodrama. God loves us in our sins. Be a good girl. Take a deep breath and move." He gave me a little shove and I flew up the stairs and into the chapel.

The last light came through the stained-glass windows, but the rest of the chapel was dim. The altar was lit with candles. I was immediately overcome with that undeniable, elevating melancholy so many people feel in a religious setting.

I found myself sitting in a pew, staring in panic at the row of books in front of me: the hymnal, the supplement to the hymnal, a book of canticles, the Book of Common Prayer, and a paperbound book with the seminary's name stamped on it, which when opened revealed itself to be full of hand-transcribed music.

"What am I supposed to do?" I said.

"Just look at the nice pictures in the windows and then stand when I stand and kneel when I kneel."

"Kneel?" I said. "Do I have to kneel? I feel it would be a betrayal of my Jewishness to kneel."

Louis gave me an indulgent look. "What future for the Jews?" he said. "You can stand. It's the alternative method."

I sat in my place and watched the community file in. Many of these people were familiar to me—recent or long-time neighbors whom I saw at least once a day. And yet they had been going about this particular piece of business right under my nose. How secret are even the open lives of others!

I saw the nice red-haired man I always said hello to at the newsstand, although I had never seen him in a clerical collar before. He was standing with his wife, whom I always saw in the supermarket. At the last minute, a tall Black man in flowing African garb walked in. This man lived on our street with his wife and two daughters. His wife, too, wore African clothes, with a winter coat on top when it was cold. In this costume she looked terribly homesick, and seeing them on the street as a family made me homesick, too. You would not find this woman having an unexplained love affair with an old friend.

The organist began to play. Louis elbowed me in the side to get me to stand. As I stood, I could see a procession emerge from the back of the chapel—a line of people, mostly men, in academic robes.

"Who are they?" I whispered, as they took their places.

"The deans and teachers," Louis said into my ear. "Now hush. It's beginning."

A disembodied male voice floated from the back of the chapel and began to chant:

> O God, make speed to save us.

The congregation, Louis included, chanted back:

> O Lord, make haste to help us.

Tears came into my eyes. I wanted to throw my coat over my head and sob. The chant continued, but I was too concerned with not disgracing Louis by crying.

The organ then played a note, and a pure, high woman's voice began to sing:

> O gracious Light,
> pure brightness of the everliving Father in heaven.

Louis had opened all the right books to all the right places, but the print swam in front of me. During the singing of the Psalms, a line hovered up before me: "Do not hand over the life of your dove to wild beasts." And during the singing of the Magnificat I was brought up short by the line "He hath scattered the proud in the imagination of their hearts."

I stood there mute and awash in emotions of many sorts, among them shock that Louis knew this service like the back of his hand and seemed on very chummy terms with his Creator.

We heard readings from the Old and New Testaments. We chanted prayers both standing and kneeling. Then the organ sounded and a hymn was sung. To my surprise, the tune was familiar, the chorale from a Bach cantata.

Finally, we received a benediction and filed out into the autumn night. The air was crisp and filled with woodsmoke.

"John is in Chicago, isn't he?" Louis asked.

"Until tomorrow." I felt I was having trouble speaking.

"And Alice?"

"She's at Annie Shepherd's for supper."

"Well, then," Louis said. "Feed me. Emily's at an A.G.A. meeting." The A.G.A., of which Emily was chairwoman, was the Association of Graphic Artists, to which I in fact belonged—at Emily's suggestion—although I never went to meetings. I did not want to have a meal alone. In the darkness, the seminarians looked like furtive animals scurrying for home. The windows on the other side of the street were full of warm, yellow light. All this made me feel the kind of awful loneliness you feel in childhood at twilight.

In the fridge I had leftover stew, eggplant-and-pepper conserve, and rice salad. I wished Louis had not been my lover, so that I could have the luxury of sharing leftovers in a guilt-free atmosphere with an old friend.

We had our meal, during which Alice called to ask if I would pick her up or if I wanted the Shepherds to walk her home. I said I would pick her up.

"If only she knew what her mother was," I said to Louis.

"What is her mother?" Louis said blandly. "Oh, I see. A woman taken in adultery. Now, now. You're a nice girl, and you're not much different from anyone else."

"Do you think those seminarians go around having sexual encounters in the afternoon with old friends?"

"I wouldn't be at all surprised," Louis said. "That place is a hotbed of all sorts of emotional misbehavior."

Louis's perspective on life was very consoling to me. He was old enough to take the long view. Life unrolled before him like a Persian runner. He observed and enjoyed, without filling his head with a million unnecessary questions.

"How does anyone keep all those books straight?" I said.

"Practice," Louis said.

"How come you know that service so well?"

"I went there," Louis said.

"You what?"

"When I was a little boy," he said. "I mean a little boy in my twenties. I thought I might become a clergyman, but I decided not to."

I was stunned by this piece of news.

"Why did you decide not to?" I asked.

"Oh, Papa was getting on, and he thought it would be nice to leave such a flourishing trade to me. I love furniture, and I liked having an excuse to go to England and France three times a year. It's a nice, civilized business. The life of most clergymen is a nasty one. They are either constantly saying what they don't mean or searching to find out what they do mean, and they don't make any money and they lose their faith. Besides, I'm too much of a sybarite."

"Nobody knows anything about anybody," I said sadly.

"Nonsense," Louis said. "People know plenty. Do you really want to know every little thing? Don't you ever want anyone to surprise you?"

Actually, I did not. I wanted to know everything all at once. In fact, I was often brought to tears by the thought that my darling Alice, my own flesh and blood, had dreams, and a school life, and thoughts to which I had no access whatsoever.

"For instance," Louis said. "I didn't know you knew any hymns."

"I didn't, either," I said.

"Well, hymns are like that," Louis said. "Catchy."

It was time to pick up Alice. Louis walked me into the night, up the street, and to the Shepherds' corner. I thanked him for taking me to Evensong.

"All that standing and kneeling," he said. "Just like exercise."

From that time on, my life assumed a slightly different pattern. I had tea, or what we euphemistically called tea, with Louis a few times a week, and on the days that Alice stayed late at school for French conversation, or sports, or went to ballet or to her piano lesson, I found myself in chapel for Evensong. Perhaps I was merely killing time. After all, I did my work in the morning; my child did not come home some days till after five; my husband did not come home until seven; and Louis was not always available. Besides, I was fond of music and liked to sing. Evensong gave me plenty of both.

One afternoon in Louis's basement, I said, "Isn't it funny, Louis? Here we are together, and your Janet used to babysit for our Alice."

"An arrangement that could easily be revived if we ran off together," he said, leaning over me to get a cigarillo out of his jacket pocket. A chill passed over my heart. The tip of the iceberg is a most terrifying sight. I looked at Louis, who was smoking contentedly, and said, "Do you really think we should run off together?"

"Certainly not, you silly girl," he said. "I was attempting to make an entertaining remark."

Who knows why this entertaining remark set off such a depth charge in me. Perhaps I harbored a longing to run off with Louis. After all, if the other is unknowable, then the self is unknowable as well. It is almost better to go through life with eyes half closed than to have unpredictable parts spring up out of oneself like mushrooms after a rain.

Walking home from the shop, I came across the African family strolling down the street. The father, splendid in his batiks, with a brown overcoat; the mother, wearing a short coat with a fur collar over her tribal dress; and the two little girls, in braids and school uniforms. You won't find any love dalliances going on in that mob, I thought.

At the start of spring, Louis went abroad on one of his buying trips, and when he came back it was clear that he had made a decision about me: our love dalliance was over. He did not lead me down to his basement to entwine illicitly in packing quilts. Instead, we sat upstairs and had tea, which Louis brewed on his hot plate. I did not question the wisdom of this decision, doubtless because I was relieved not to have had to make it myself, and because emotional scenes were spared. Also, I deferred to Louis's fatherly guidance.

But when I was alone I was often assailed by fear. Perhaps I had done or said something Louis found disgusting. Perhaps he found *me* disgusting. Perhaps he was ill, or Emily had discovered our affair, or he had told her everything. In a more paranoid moment, I imagined that Louis had had an affair with me solely to get me into chapel and thereby convert me.

One afternoon, I blurted, "Why did you drop me, Louis?"

"I didn't drop you," Louis said. "We're having tea, aren't we?"

"I mean, why don't we ever sleep together anymore?" I said.

"It was never the right thing to do," Louis said. His eyes were mild and kind, and it was quite impossible to see behind them. He was not going to say another word on the subject, and I was going to be left to contemplate this welter of possibilities forever.

And so I saw Louis for tea once a week. I picked Alice up at school. I attended Evensong. The service became an addiction. Was it the fact that only the music changed, that certain prayers followed certain canticles which followed certain readings? Or was it the music and the setting, which were so curiously soothing and emotional? I puttered around the house singing "O Blest Creator of the Light." At times, I said to myself aloud, "Lighten our darkness, we beseech thee, O Lord," which, according to the Book of Common Prayer, is part of a collect for aid against perils.

As the light changed, the stained-glass windows revealed themselves. As the buds came out, little leaves made a speckled pattern on Adam, Eve, and the serpent. It occurred to me that it would be hard to explain what a Jewish girl, even a very watered-down one, was doing at five o'clock in the afternoon in a chapel singing "O Trinity of Blessed Light." It did not seem to be the religious angle that I was after. I had quite enough trouble with the concept of one God. Three-in-one was much too confusing to contemplate.

Then one day I had an actual revelation. It came to me that I might never know very much about anything. It might never be imparted to me *what* I was doing at Evensong. "The thing about the unknowable," I said to myself, "is that you have to accept that it just isn't knowable, and that's that." I found this very relaxing.

On a beautiful evening late in April, I came out of Evensong and bumped right into my husband, my very own John. I was amazed to see him, and he looked back at me with pain and puzzlement on his face.

"Oh, hello!" I said brightly, as to a new neighbor. "How did you know where I was?"

"Last night, when I came home early, I saw you come out," he said. "I got home early tonight, and I thought I'd come and pick you up and find out what's going on."

"Nothing's going on," I said.

"You're not converting, are you?" he asked. He looked terribly worried.

"Of course not, silly," I said. "It's nice in there. I like to sing. It reminds me of my Jewish heritage. I've been thinking that we ought to take more part in Alice's religious upbringing and go to

Friday-night services every once in a while. I also think we should have a proper Passover next year."

"That's a wonderful idea," John said. He was very relieved. God knows what he had thought. I was not going to know; I was not even going to know what *I* thought.

I took John's arm, and we walked slowly down the street toward Alice's school. It was a sports afternoon. The school was a nice, brisk walk away. It was a treat for her to be picked up by her father. It was a treat to have him home early on such a lovely spring night. We walked with our arms around each other. When we got to the school, we would find Alice in her sports clothes, with her school uniform in a canvas carryall. Her answer those days to the question "What did you do today?" was "Nothing very interesting."

Then we would walk home, the three of us, through the front door and into our privacy, as close and as distant as any connected people are.

KATHERINE DAMM

The Happiest Day of Your Life

FROM *The Iowa Review*

WYATT AND NINA were at Nina's ex-boyfriend's wedding reception in the Grand Ballroom of the Drake Hotel. The groom worked at a law firm that competed with Nina's, a friction that hadn't been the source of their split, she'd told Wyatt, but hadn't helped, either. The bride was quite high up at the Federal Reserve Bank of Chicago. At a Fourth of July barbecue, Lillian had explained to Wyatt that her group did some of its own lending, but mainly functioned as a contingency office, meaning they were perpetually preparing to take the reins in the event of a "No New York Scenario." How morbid was that! He loved it.

This was the second ex-boyfriend's wedding of the summer. Wyatt had only ever had clean breaks with his girlfriends, but Nina's exes were often around, picking her up from the airport or accompanying her to the college film society to watch long foreign movies—the kind that bored Wyatt to sleep, often literally. Nina's favorite was Greg, the groom, whom she'd dated the longest and who'd helped her quit smoking with long-distance running. Wyatt's favorite was Rico, the sculptor, because Wyatt had never met anybody like him.

"I've met a million Ricos by now," Nina had said, when he'd mentioned it. "You can have that one."

In addition to a full bar, the wedding guests were encouraged to order a Greg, which was wine floated on a Manhattan, since Greg was from New York; or a Lillian, which was vodka, triple sec, and egg white served up with a key lime garnish, since Lillian was from Florida. The ingredients were joyfully lettered on a pair of medallion-shaped chalkboards alongside outlines of champagne bottles bubbling over with hearts. In Wyatt's opinion, this was a great wedding, and he had been to many great weddings in the past couple of years, most notably his and Nina's own. The celebrations ran the gamut. There was the one in Kentucky where they all sat on haybales. There was the giant Indian wedding at the Yale Club of New York—another of Nina's exes. There was the one on New Year's Eve where the two grooms kissed right at midnight. There was the one during a Minneapolis blizzard where everybody silently hoped the electricity would go out, for the sake of a good story. That ceremony had looked a little strange to Wyatt because the people on the bride's side were mostly Black and the people on the groom's side were mostly white, and it was uncomfortable to see a church split down the middle like that, but of course everyone came together for dancing, and the more Wyatt drank, the more the reception struck him as a really nice metaphor.

Greg and Lillian's was classic from start to finish. The ceremony was at St. Michael's, which the card next to the hymn book listed as just one of six buildings to survive the Great Chicago Fire; a propitious history for a wedding venue, Wyatt and Nina agreed, in light of the divorce rate. Lillian's father walked her down the aisle to Pachelbel's Canon in D, and Greg's brother read from Corinthians 13, including the part about the noisy gong, which not everybody included. The newlywed's first song was "Can't Help Falling in Love," and the entrée for all but the vegetarian guests was salmon. Wyatt appreciated this appreciation for tradition. All of these choices were timeless for good reason.

That said, Wyatt also loved when people got creative: when couples wrote their own vows, or when the bride wore yellow, or the groom wore Chuck Taylors. The fact was, he just loved weddings.

He wound his way through the numbered tables, careful not to spill the Greg he'd brought for Nina or the Lillian he'd gotten for himself. He liked fruity drinks, and Nina preferred hers alcohol-forward. As often as not, they needed to switch when the server who brought their orders turned away.

He'd barely had a chance to talk to Nina since the cocktail hour—had barely even seen her, since the sprays of Queen Anne's lace in the extensive floral centerpiece had screened her from his view. Their table was composed of four couples, all seated apart, though their pairs were shifting and reuniting now that the main course was over. In Nina's place was a round-faced British girl whose frequent laugh distorted her face like a sob or an orgasm. Even from across the table, she seemed like a lot of fun. Her boyfriend was finishing a story—"I'm serious, he thought it was a real word!"—and she leaned on his shoulder and laughed like her heart was breaking.

He set the drinks down. Nina's purse was still at her place, its silver chain reflecting the light of the many tea candles. He pulled it over to save the seat next to him, then stood with a hand on the back of his chair. They'd rented the same ones for their reception: gold-painted wood shaped to give the impression of bamboo. He gazed over the table's post-meal disorder, pleasantly tipsy, until his eyes drew together on his place card, which was set in a notched pewter pawn. His name looked briefly unfamiliar, such that for a moment, he wasn't even sure it was spelled correctly. In the elaborate calligraphy, it was like a knocked-over tree, the large W a system of flared, denuded roots, the y and t's like splayed branches. He tilted his head until the tree was right side up.

"Hoot, hoot!" The man two seats down was hooting at him. "You look like an owl with your head like that."

"I'm Wyatt," said Wyatt. "I think I had the pleasure of sitting next to your wife."

"Connie! Where is Connie?" The man turned in his chair until he located her a few tables over, chatting with another couple. "Look at her. Isn't she just the most beautiful woman you've ever seen?" The man was red in the face, and Wyatt couldn't tell if he was naturally ruddy or had been overserved. He finished his Lillian while he considered the question.

When the man introduced himself, Wyatt instantly forgot his name and tried subtly to get an angle on his card, which was set in a rook.

Over dinner, Constance had described herself and her husband as a doctor-philanthropist couple, and Wyatt wasn't sure if the red-faced man was a doctor, a philanthropist, or if both were both. They were older than the others at the table, and he knew that Nina would say this meant she and Wyatt had been at the bottom of the guest list, like lone socks at the bottom of a drawer. She'd said something to that effect at another wedding, when they'd been seated with two family friends and a grab bag of miscellaneous colleagues. This would bother her more, though, as she and

Greg were close friends, an intimacy she described as informed by, but separate from, the one before.

Nina had a lot of ex-boyfriends; at least two were at the wedding. They weren't short relationships, either, but rather had been packed efficiently into her life, with little space in between. Most surprising to Wyatt, besides the high number and the fact that she'd maintained good relations with almost all of them, was that the men were all wildly, undeniably unalike. While Wyatt's girlfriends all felt very different to him, he acknowledged that from an outside perspective, they might come across as very similar. "I guess I have to hope I'm the apotheosis of your type, and not the latest in a series," said Nina, the first time she scrolled through his old photos. She then explained that she found comfort in giving things a teleological shape.

"So, are you the doctor or the philanthropist?"

"A little of column A, a little of column B."

"What type?"

The man thumped his chest with a loose fist. "I'm a heart guy."

"I have a cousin who's in fellowship for pediatric cardiology."

"See, that's good. Even if you take the most cardiological of pediatricians, you end up with a pretty nice guy, or woman. Unlike your average cardiologist. People tell me all the time, 'John, you're the only cardiologist I know that's not an asshole.'"

John! Wyatt held on to the name like bus money. "So, John, how are you enjoying the party?"

"It's spectacular. Of course Paul and Jackie are going to throw little Lillian a good one. This is a good place, too. A lot of history, I'm sure."

Wyatt had read about the venue beforehand, and he remembered things. "The mob was based here for a while. The chef is one of three who claim to have invented Thousand Island Dressing. There's one famous ghost, The Woman in Red, from the twenties. She found her husband cheating on her after a New Year's party and killed herself."

"Just one?" asked John.

Wyatt took a sip of Nina's Greg and revised his assessment: he remembered things he learned *when he was sober.* After only a few drinks, information like people's names was free to come and go.

John went on. "I'm surprised a place like this isn't more haunted. Have you ever seen a ghost?"

"No," said Wyatt, "but I'd like to."

"They're beautiful and diaphanous."

"So you have?"

"All the time. We had this old house up in Winnetka with this one teenager in particular who was pretty active. She scared the babysitter one night. Connie had to chase the kid down to pay her because she ran right out the door when we came home. And I go upstairs and there's this ghost floating between the girls' beds—we have two girls—and she's just looking at them, because she's curious, right? And I told her, 'You can hang around, but you can't go scaring the babysitter.' And she listened, she settled down after that."

Wyatt couldn't tell if John was earnest, drunk, or messing with him, but he really liked the guy. "What did she look like?"

"Kind of shimmering. Wearing flapper stuff: beads and feathers and all that."

"I'm jealous."

"It'll happen for you. If you want it to happen, it will happen."

Wyatt thanked him. "Can I ask you something personal? Have you ever seen the ghost of one of your patients? One that, you know, didn't make it?"

John looked off in thought as if the answer wasn't immediately available. "You know, I haven't. Most people don't even want to come to the hospital when they're alive. That's part of the problem."

"One other question. Is it bad if my heart sometimes feels like it actually skips a beat?"

"You wouldn't believe how many patients come in asking about palpitations. Most of the time it's totally normal. Every once in a while it's a problem. Every once in a blue moon. So where does this Lady in Red haunt?"

"The tenth floor, I believe."

"Then that's where I'm headed," said John, and his eyes flicked to the pawn. "Wyatt, it was nice to meet you. I've got to go see about a girl." He paused to kiss Constance on his way upstairs.

Wyatt enjoyed the Greg more as the ice melted. He scanned the crowd for Nina. A research psychologist he'd gotten to talking with at a retirement party had explained that within split seconds of birth, babies react more quickly to human faces than any other stimuli, and it had changed the way Wyatt looked at people. It felt like a superpower how quickly you could spot a face.

Recorded music played during dinner, but Frank Wonder and the Good Time Players were back now, fiddling with the microphone stands and pulling the straps of their instruments over their heads. Each member wore a splash of purple, and Wyatt pictured a rainbow stack of fedoras in Frank Wonder's closet to accord with any palette.

The father-daughter dance was a winsome jitterbug to "Isn't She Lovely." Lillian and Paul had clearly practiced; they were chatting and laughing as their feet moved in sync. The bride's expression, made visible at a distance by her dark makeup, was at turns sunny, sentimental, and girlish, and it occurred to Wyatt that this was the first time he'd seen her with her hair down. The photographer came right up close and snapped pictures.

Greg and his mother joined them for "God Only Knows." These were tricky songs to choose: Wyatt remembered from his own wedding. Often a single romantic lyric would nix an otherwise winner from the list. He'd seen one mother-son pair dance to "You Are the Sunshine of My Life," a pretty innocuous choice, but at a stray "baby," the whole audience had rippled with Oedipal discomfort. Or maybe it was just Wyatt.

If you should ever leave me, though life would still go on, believe me . . .

The mortality stuff in this song had kept him from selecting it, though it was on several mother-son dance lists.

Greg's mom was little. Nina had mentioned that in passing before, but she was, she was really little, and she had a great face, crinkly, with every line expressing joy. Her son could scoop her up and put her down if he wanted to. He could tuck her into bed like a daughter.

Wyatt wanted to be the kind of son who took care of his parents. As an only child, he would have to be. Still, when he was being honest with himself, or with Nina, he admitted that he didn't want to. She felt the same way, and the plan was that they'd switch: Nina would take care of his parents when they got older, and he would take care of hers. The plan was a joke, but he hoped they did it anyway.

Now the in-laws joined hands, and the bride and groom fetched their other parents. Wyatt took another Lillian from a passing tray and sat down to enjoy it, watching the crowd go up by factors of two as dancers split and recruited new partners from the crowd. The low yellow light of the first two dances gave way to pink and purple gels, and a machine in the middle of the ceiling threw bright patterns across the room.

A woman near Wyatt sighed loudly through her nostrils. She'd angled her chair towards the dance floor, and her foot was bobbing erratically, completely independent of the music's tempo. Her unstrapped satin heel bounced in half-sync below it. She watched one couple in particular, pushing her hair back and sweeping her dangling earring behind her ear along with it. A caterer circled the table, bearing wine. He spoke up over the music to offer her merlot from his left hand or chardonnay from his right, to which she responded, "Please."

"Please which?"

"It doesn't matter," she replied.

"I have merlot or chardonnay."

"It doesn't matter."

"Would you prefer red or white?"

"It makes absolutely no difference to me."

"There are two options . . ." he pleaded.

At last, she thrust her glass at him and said, "Here, red, I don't care." The band played on.

Wyatt tactfully averted his eyes from the exchange and observed the woman's leg, which stopped moving as she spoke. The dark roots of her hair were visible through the pale skin of her calf, and a small patch behind her ankle had escaped the razor altogether. Wyatt loved stubble on women's legs for a couple of reasons. The first was that he'd never felt the texture on his own body—facial stubble being a whole other species—and all his formative experiences with it had been in a sexual context. His high school girlfriend was Greek and never quite smooth, and when he first ran his hand over her leg the whole thing felt so real he thought he was going to lose his mind. And the appearance, too, was intimate, especially an imperfect job like the one on his table neighbor. It made him imagine the woman—any woman—in a state of preparation, expectation even, a record of a private moment displayed like it was nothing at all.

"Merlot or chardonnay?"

Wyatt shifted his mouth as he considered. He liked red better, but he'd had white with his salmon and his glass still had the dregs. He'd drunk Nina's Greg and thought he'd get her some consolation wine. She'd been gone for some time now. A little turned on from his leg reverie, he thought vaguely of being inside her, a desire that was only partly localized, or even sexual at all, since there was an opposite and equal urge to enclose her. He decided that what he was really in the mood for, though physically impossible in three dimensions, was occupying the exact same space as her, molecule for molecule.

"Sir?"

"Sorry. Red for me, and white for the glass—" he squinted like the mark he was pointing at was far in the distance, "—three seats down. And then pass it over here, please."

He drank half of his, then covered each glass with a cocktail napkin and went to find his wife. His chair tipped over when he stood.

First stop was the men's room, where he relieved himself for what he knew to be the first of many times that night. He washed his hands, then his face, then drank water by the palmful. Clean and hydrated, he surveyed himself in the elaborately beveled mirror. He'd reached the age where people started to look . . . not like older versions of themselves, which would have been alright with Wyatt, but rather like worse versions of themselves. He'd stayed vigilant. He'd developed a small belly when his metabolism first slowed down, but he'd been quick to reel it back in. His hair had thinned, but judging from his uncles and cousins, it had reached low tide and would recede no farther. He stuck his tongue out. It was blue-black from wine. He looked better in a suit than he used to. He loosened his tie and popped his top button.

He held the door open for a man who was entering the bathroom and saw that it was Austin, the other ex, Nina's sophomore boyfriend from ten-plus years back. Austin knew Lillian from a postgraduate year at Cambridge, completely independent of Nina. He hadn't even made the connection until he saw Nina and Wyatt at the welcome party the night before, living, as he did, off the grid as far as social media went. It was a small world, they all agreed.

One by one, some passing comment had rendered each of Nina's exes irreparably three-dimensional. In Austin's case, it wasn't that he'd had a sick mother, or that he wrote plays, or that Nina had spent a summer with his family in Eagle River. It was that he'd made Nina feel "feminine," a remark that Wyatt wished he could unhear as soon as she said it. That Austin wasn't obviously hunky only made it worse, because that meant he possessed some other *je ne sais quoi* animal magnetism. Usually when Nina spoke favorably of a former flame, Wyatt listened for the implied request of him. But what could he do with that?

He said hello and asked if Austin had seen her.

"Wyatt!" Austin clasped Wyatt's hand, which was still wet. It was a good handshake. How many things like that added up to make someone feel feminine? "I did actually, out in the lobby. I think she was on her way back in to find you."

Austin had a geometric tattoo that extended onto the back of his hand, which, to Wyatt, implied that Austin knew what he would be doing for the rest of his life. There was no hedging in case of future employment.

"I'd love to catch up with Nina while I'm in town. It's been a minute. Maybe the three of us could get coffee."

"That would be nice," Wyatt said, and he meant it. As uncomfortable as Austin and his ambiguous masculinity made him, Austin had worked on an oil rig for a year, and Wyatt had a lot of questions about that.

"I won't keep you in the bathroom," said Austin.

"And I won't keep you from your business."

They shook hands once more.

Back in the ballroom, Nina was nowhere in sight. He checked their table, finished his wine, and was considering making his way to the second-floor balcony for an aerial view when Frank Wonder called, "Now we want everyone on the floor!" The Good Time Players looped the same few measures as he spoke. "Every single person in this room. Grandma, Grandpa, you too. If you don't know the dance that's just fine because we will tell you the moves."

The female singer spoke over the ambling bass. "If everybody fits on the dance floor, it means we've got too many wallflowers. I want spillover. I want to see people on the rug." There was a touch of elementary school teacher in her cadence—the kind who's not afraid to cancel recess—and the remaining holdouts filed obediently onto the floor and loosely arranged themselves into rows.

Wyatt followed the bare feet of the teenage girl in front of him. After two quarter-turn hops, he was in front, and presumably it was his feet that were watched now. The couple times he messed up, he made up for it by owning his mistakes: smiling and shrugging and doubling down on his own enjoyment. He glanced around for Nina.

The song ended, and with the singers' implied permission, half the dancers returned to their seats and conversations. Not Wyatt, though.

First, he liked dancing. He'd been at the center of the dance floor at his fraternity parties and at bars after college. A normal floor would often become a dance floor just by virtue of Wyatt's presence. Then there were the fallow years, when everyone he knew—himself included—turned into a homebody. But now people were getting married, and he could get down once a month, twice during summer. Nina said he danced like Jerry Lewis, and when he asked if that was a compliment, she said, "Oh yeah."

Second, Wyatt liked Greg, and had a great rapport with Lillian. It was all good. He knew that. Nina knew that. Greg and Lillian knew that. But the other guests didn't necessarily know that, and he wouldn't pretend it hadn't crossed his mind that people might be glancing to see how he was doing.

Third, eventually Nina would appear, and she'd either find him loitering around the table or having a great time on his own. Which kind of husband would anyone choose, given the choice?

There was nothing like a live band. True to form for Greg and Lillian, most of the selections were fun-for-the-whole-family classics. Now Frank Wonder was singing "More Than a Woman" in admirable falsetto, and in speculating whether he himself could hit those notes, a bright yawp escaped from Wyatt's throat. The timbre was nothing to write home about, but he'd hit the pitch. High notes were easier to reach as the day went on; he'd learned this from an opera singer he'd met at a gallery opening. Well, case in point.

He made it his mission to dance with the very young and the very old. He rescued a sulking niece from her own tantrum during "Build Me Up, Buttercup." He supported a matriarch through "Let's Stay Together." He instigated a conga line for "Love Train" and accepted no one's excuses for sitting it out.

He was so happy. He was so happy! This was what he wanted his funeral to be like: a celebration. Who could he tell? Who put this thing together? How could he include instructions in his will for the party planner of this event without spooking her? Or "him," of course. Men could plan parties, too.

But probably "her."

He loved thoughts like that: little let's-be-honest asides between him and himself.

He would ask the man and woman of the hour, who had just swirled into view. Funny how little time a person got to spend with their new spouse at the reception. It was probably funny to this bride and groom, just as it had been funny to him and Nina.

"Greg and Lillian. Gregory and Lil." Wyatt made two finger guns, one for each. "Is that ring titanium, Greg? Mine too."

"It's tungsten carbide."

"You're a dancing machine," said Lillian.

"Fire on the dance floor," said Greg. "Hot! Literally and figuratively, my man. Maybe you should cool down a little before you get back out there. My brother will help get you some cold water and the best seat in the house, won't you, Stephen?"

Wyatt felt himself propelled into the best man's arms. "The Great Chicago Fire on the dance floor. That's me."

"That's you." Stephen looked like a tall version of Greg.

"I am hot," Wyatt admitted.

"You're burning up, big guy," said Tall Greg.

"You're the big guy. Look at that wingspan. You ball?"

"I swam."

"That's a good sport. Easy on the knees. You can do it your whole life."

They were at the bar now, where the bartender filled a plastic cup with soda water from a nozzle.

"I love fizzy water. It's like breathing and drinking at the same time," Wyatt told them, then decided it was time to escape from Stephen.

The curtains behind the band had been opened during dinner, and he remembered being curious about the view. When Stephen turned away, Wyatt set a course for the south wall. He ducked and dodged and picked and rolled through chairs and tables and people. He passed through the loud cone of sound in front of the speakers into the relative quiet behind, found a part in the gold drapery, and insinuated himself into the folds.

It was snowing outside, and night. The street was a glassy obsidian, lit white and red as cars passed casting wet, beige piles aside. He rolled his forehead from side to side on the cool pane. The script on the awning across the street read *The Grand Ballroom.* "If you're there, then where am I," he wondered, then remembered that he was at the Drake Hotel, looking over Walton Street at the Knickerbocker.

Wrapped in the curtain's white plastic backing, he was reminded of hiding in round racks of clothing as a child while his mother shopped.

The parallel ballroom was hosting its own wedding. On the curb, a man smoked while a woman stood apart from him, shivering in a thin wrap. They looked off toward separate places until she spoke as animatedly as possible in the cold, gesturing with her elbows still locked against her body. He smiled, took one last drag, and stamped out his half-finished cigarette. They went inside. Another woman, this one in a coat and voluminous scarf, looked from her phone at the passing cars. During a break in traffic, her eyes moved across the Drake, up to the second floor, meeting Wyatt's. She laughed; she waved. It took a moment for him to figure out how she was able to see him, but of course, he was on her side of the curtains. She confirmed her ride with a driver and disappeared. He'd been too slow to wave back.

He still went to the department store with his mother. That's how she did Christmas: she'd fill a stocking with knickknacks and then take him to Bloomingdale's.

How many more Christmases would he spend with his parents? His mother was a spry sixty-six, and the Moores had long lifespans. His father was sixty-two. It could be as many as thirty, even thirty-five Christmases. That seemed like too many. Numbers like five or ten, however, were unequivocally too few. He tried to locate the sweet spot—sixteen? twenty-two? seventeen? twenty-one?—until he realized what he was doing, and he shifted his attention back to the Knickerbocker. A woman in a tight dress and miraculously tall heels passed the main entrance in chilly, mincing steps. The doorman watched appreciatively, then snapped for the valet's attention to share the experience.

From the world he'd left behind, Wyatt heard the long diphthong of an "O" buttressed by arpeggiated chords. He loved this song! His eyebrows lifted as high as they could go. The corners of his mouth and tops of his ears perked up, too. He unwound himself from the drapery and made his way back to the room.

I've hungered for your touch, a long, lonely time.

Frank Wonder crooned, fedora pulled low over his eyes. The female singer oohed in the background, tambourine slack at her side. Wyatt looked through the dark crowd. People were holding each other close and moving in their own personal circles. Some kissed. A few women looked asleep standing up. It must be what they looked like in bed together, when they were at ease and alone.

He was sure that the dancers would part and Nina would be there. He envisioned the two of them, spotlit, approaching each other from opposite sides of the floor. He swayed side-to-side like they were already together.

I need your love. I need your love.

He was almost crying. Needing love was the purest feeling in the world. Everybody needed love. He was having a profound aesthetic experience, and his knowledge of that did nothing to diminish it.

The song ended and Nina hadn't appeared. Instead, there was Lillian.

"How are you feeling, Wyatt?"

The Good Time Players transitioned into an uptempo song, and Wyatt's mood transitioned with it. The lights in the room brightened. Everybody was bright pink.

"Lillian! Let's find the photographer and take a picture, you and me. The beneficiaries of the Greg-Nina split." He tried to take her by the hands.

"I don't know that we need to document exactly that."

"You're the best, Lillian. Without you there's no me."

"That's very sweet."

"I mean it! I owe you so much for the right of first refusal thing. How that whole thing worked out. I lay my life at your feet."

"Oh, Wyatt, stand up. What are you talking about?"

"The right of first refusal."

"I don't understand what you're saying." She looked down at him like he was speaking nonsense.

"You know, you know, when Nina called up Greg and said, 'Greg, I'm at a point in my life when I'm ready to get married, and I'm giving you the right of first refusal.'" Wyatt held his thumb and pinky between his ear and mouth, then remembered an actor he'd met at a fundraiser had explained that a more professional telephone pantomime was to grip the air as if holding an invisible receiver. He switched.

"Stop that for a moment. What?"

He got to his feet. "Oh, you know, he thought about it and got back to her and said, 'No thank you, not right now,'—because you two were dating—and next thing you know she meets me and the rest is history."

"When?"

"After you but before me. So, three years ago? Three point five?"

"He never told me about that."

"He never told you? In a way you're the hero." He added the last part because Lillian looked perturbed. It was a happy sequence of events, and he worried that he'd mistold the story. "Heroine. If it had been the other way around, and Greg had right-of-first-refusalled Nina when we just started dating, I don't know what would have happened. You guys were rock solid from the beginning, is what I'm getting at. You're a special lady, is what the story means. Your love story made my love story possible, is the point."

"Who told you?"

"Nina did." It was a funny question. He liked Greg, but it's not as though the two of them had heart-to-hearts.

Lillian shook her head for so long that Wyatt almost giggled. "Lies of omission are that man's specialty." Then she nodded for just as long and said, "But you're right, it doesn't matter. It really doesn't matter. It's not a big deal. It's not a big deal."

"Exactly."

"Excuse me," said Lillian.

"You're excused," said Wyatt gamely, and they parted.

Where was Nina? At least three songs had just played that they always made it a point to dance to: "September," "Shout (Parts 1 and 2)," and he couldn't remember the third.

Now the music stopped and Greg and Lillian were cutting the cake while everybody, including Wyatt, cheered. Now Wyatt was at his seat, resting, eating a piece of that very same cake—or a piece from a larger, cheaper sheet cake in the kitchen, if they did it like he and Nina did. Now he was back on the case.

"She was out to the lobby, but that was a while ago."

This was fun, like he was on a quest.

It was confusing that the lobby was at once brighter and quieter than the ballroom. It seemed like it should be one way or the other. How could a place with a chandelier that sparkly and a plant that big be so still? Even his footsteps on the blue carpet were muffled. Nina wasn't there, but Wyatt saw a friend of Greg's that Nina had briefly dated, pre-Greg, holding one of her green strappy shoes and speaking with the receptionist.

"So she's close!"

"I'm seeing if they have something for this," said Chase, showing him where the heel had detached from the sole.

"You're the guy to fix it. The guy!" Wyatt turned to include the receptionist in the conversation: "This guy knows all about glue. But where is the woman that belongs to that shoe? That rhymed."

"She went that way maybe fifteen minutes ago."

"Glue, shoe. Thanks for the clue."

"Are you alright, Wyatt?"

"Toodle-oo!"

He turned down the hallway. Like anyone, he often considered the ways his life could have gone differently. Sometimes he imagined what it would have been like if he and Nina had met earlier: what it would have been like to know her in college, or high school, or even childhood; what if it had been her at all those points instead of Emily, or Sasha, or Hannah, or nobody. Rarely did he think about what it would have been like to have not met Nina at all. They'd been seated together on an airplane; it would have been easy.

Vertigo spun up from his stomach. It was like he was looking at the bridge that connected his life before they met with his life after they met, and seeing for the first time how narrow it was and how steep the drop was below. He almost fell over in real life, but he steadied himself by remembering that they *did* meet and by pressing his hand to the wall.

There she was at last, outside the glass door of the Business Center.

"Taking care of business?" he asked, approaching.

He could see now that she was crying, but it didn't matter because they shared everything—legally and spiritually—and soon she would share his happiness. She had a million ex-boyfriends but only one husband, and that husband was him: Wyatt. Wyatt the knocked-down tree. Wyatt the dancing machine.

He tried to restrain his expression into one of concern, but a smile spread heedlessly across his face. He was a dog, that, in wagging its tail, wags its whole body. He waved at her and she kept crying.

It was simple. He loved her more, and the realization thrilled him. Nina loved Wyatt more than she'd ever loved anyone, and yet still he loved her more, because he was good at love. He was expansive: he could fit the entire Drake Hotel into his capacity for love. He could take in the whole city of Chicago, large and looming, like the Stay Puft Marshmallow Man of love. He vomited benevolently onto the floor. The lemon buttercream and the raspberry jam, barely digested, were still sweet. A little dill-imbued acid followed. He rested against the millwork and watched the liquid settle on the carpet, which was brownish-yellow and composed of abstract, tessellated shapes anyway. They could buff that out, no problem.

"Wyatt!"

"You missed the cake. I haven't seen you in—" He scrutinized the hands on his watch. It was either eleven thirty or twelve thirty. "Hours."

She drew her ring fingers along the bottoms of her eyes, more or less smearing her mascara back into place. She'd been crying daily for months: in the mornings, in the evenings, after sex, on the phone from the bathroom at work. Wyatt had almost forgotten it was unusual. "Hours?" She took his wrist to confirm. "Not *hours*. I'm sorry, though. Something about the music made me flip out. I kept starting to come back in, and then I'd hear it and flip out again. We should do something about this," she said, of the pale, fragrant patch on the carpet.

"Tomato, to-mah-to. What's up?"

"It's not even worth talking about."

"I vomited. Now I want *you* to vomit." He reached for her face but undershot and swept the air.

"I don't know. I just feel so lost lately, and then tonight especially."

He knew about the lately, so he asked about the especially: "Are you sad about Greg?"

"It feels like that a little, but I know that's not really it."

Wyatt waited for her to gather her thoughts.

"I feel like a drag," she said.

"You're not a drag."

"I experience myself as a drag. I just feel so bad lately. It's something different every day."

He nodded. He knew this.

"Tonight, I'm jealous. Not jealous of Lillian being with Greg: more jealous of Lillian being Lillian. She's so fucking successful, and I peaked in law school. And I wouldn't compare myself to her except for Greg, and so I get angry at him, and myself, and even you. But tomorrow it will be something else. Do you love me, even when I'm like this?" Her red cheeks and nose greened her hazel eyes. Mucus in various states of evaporation rested on her upper lip.

"Of course."

"Would you love me even if I were always like this?"

He knew this wasn't the first time she'd asked someone this question. It wasn't even the first time she'd asked him. She wouldn't always be like this. He knew she'd had periods like this during every one of her relationships, and he could see each boyfriend saying yes, one after the other, just as he was doing now.

She brushed something off her dress. He blinked, and at the end of the blink it was morning and he was in bed.

Nina was still wearing mascara, and a small slash of black marked her pillow. He watched a small hair go in and out of her nostril for a while until she breached consciousness with a long, lugubrious groan. They regarded each other. Nina spoke first.

"If I have a hangover, you must be dying."

But he felt fine, which meant he was probably still a little drunk, and consequences were still to come. He said as much.

Lying on her side, her top breast hung like a paisley swirl. He reached under and pushed it up a little.

"Perv."

He responded with a Nixon growl: "I am not a perv."

They hadn't pulled the shade down, and the flat winter light made their bedroom unfamiliar, like the comforter and the bookshelf and the fiddle-leaf fig belonged to other people. He rolled toward his night table to check his phone. At the first bit of pressure, sparklers of pain burst all down his right side.

"Why do I hurt?" he asked.

"You ate it hard when we walked out to the car."

What percentage of broken hips occurred from dark ice on dark sidewalks outside winter parties? Orthopedic surgeons probably made their quota for the year during the holidays, he thought, just like retailers. "What else did I miss?"

"I had an existential freakout and you said we should have a baby, like that would solve it, and I got mad at you for being sexist. You threw up a few times. You also apparently told Lillian about that time I tried to get back together with Greg. He just texted me."

"Oh, Jesus." Wyatt rubbed his eyes. "I remember that one, mostly. Totally inappropriate, but I did think she already knew."

"That's Greg for you."

They gazed at the light from their phones until Wyatt spoke. "Can I ask you something?"

"What's up?"

He was embarrassed to look at her and kept his eyes on his screen. "If it had been the other way around, if Greg had come to you when we first got together and said, 'Leave him for me,' would you have done it?"

"You asked me that last night."

"What did you say?"

"Among other things, I said I would only answer that question once." He looked at her. She was pleased with herself.

"Please, Nina, I can't remember."

"You've got to drink less at these things, Wyatt. You don't want to end up like your granddaddy."

The hangover was settling between his eyebrows like snow. Jealousy, too. He found himself growing petty, earthbound. He wanted equality. He wanted to go back to the night before, when it didn't matter.

"I think you would have done it at the very beginning, and that's okay. My revised question is: what is the last date you would have done it? After what point would you have definitely said no?"

She shrugged as though mystified.

"After that Yellowstone trip we were probably in the clear. Anytime before that? Like that June? We had a great June." He watched for any reaction, but Nina's poker face was airtight. "Nina Nina Nina Nina. Nina Nina Nina Nina."

"That's not going to work."

Nina had it, whatever "it" was: some trade-secret proportion of need and gratitude and intelligence and who knows what else that made him do terrible things, like feign illness to get out of friends' birthday parties, or log onto an ex-girlfriend's email in front of Nina to show her that, no, Lauren didn't disparage her in her biweekly notes to her mother.

"What about Austin?"

"Austin who I dated for nine months when I was twenty? That Austin?"

She talked about her exes all the time but darkened at any mention of his, saying, "No, go on, I'm interested," but with an unmistakable clip.

She went to the bathroom and called to Wyatt over the sound of the faucet. "I look like I escaped from a mental institution. Please tell me I'm pretty."

"You're pretty."

He loved her more; she needed him more. Was that, then, equality? The patience, the commitment, the stability. Without Wyatt there would be no it. He held the means of production, so to speak. Or was it the other way around? Was he the labor? It had been thirteen years since Sociology.

The toilet flushed.

"You look unsettled. You look like you need coffee," she said from the doorway. She was pretty.

"And water."

"Coming right up. But first I'm going to belly-flop on you," and she did, naked and graceless and warm.

MOLLY DEKTAR

The Bed & Breakfast

FROM *Harvard Review*

OUR NEW HOME was an old stone farmhouse, cold inside, filled with dust and boards and trash, bottles, burlap, and nests. Despite having just ushered us through a trip involving three planes, a train, a bus, and a cab, my father was leaping with excitement as he led us from room to room. In the indirect light from the windows in the thick walls, my brothers looked as pink as plums. There was no electricity, no furniture, no kitchen, just a dark fireplace and a black stove in a room on one end and a line of empty, dirty rooms and then a room with hay at the other end.

The house was built on a hill. It had one story on the uphill side and two stories on the downhill side. On the slope above was the old garden with a broken chicken coop. The slope below was pasture for animals. My father said that he would fix the house up by the time the weather got cold. And then, over the winter, we would paint it, tidy it, and go antiquing, and by the spring we would open it as a bed and breakfast. I asked what that was. "A little hotel," my mother said. I felt bad for my parents, because I didn't see why anyone would stay here.

We moved from the Blue Ridge Mountains to Italy because my father wanted to. Around the time I turned ten, my father began to change the way he dressed. First, he exchanged his tie-dye and music festival tees for long-sleeved white button-up shirts. "Keeps the sun off my arms," he told our mother. Then he switched his athletic shorts to long navy blue pants. "Better for fieldwork," he told our mother. Then he bought suspenders. "They don't cut into my waist as much," he said. He grew a big beard, and one day shaved just the mustache. This, he could not so easily explain.

It was the fall and winter when I was eleven that my father began to work to convince my mother. He went much more frequently to the library and returned with books on cottage restoration and Italy and the hospitality business, which I thought meant hospitals. My mother liked North Carolina, her vegetable patch, her church friends. She often told us that God was watching us, and she had us sing grace before dinner: "For giving me the things I need, the sun and the rain and the apple seed."

In North Carolina, my parents slept in the front room, my brothers and I in one big bed in the attic. I was the middle child. My older brother Lewis fed and brushed the horses, I fed the goats, and my little brother, Lindsay, fed the rabbits. The three of us were essentially one person. I was the holy ghost.

All that fall and winter, we could hear them talking and arguing. And then for a few nights they were quiet, and then the nights were full of my mother laughing and the song "I've Got You Under My Skin," and one morning we woke to a big bouquet of store-bought roses on the table. That morning they gathered us and told us that we were moving very far away. It was springtime; the school year wasn't even over yet.

"Your father wants to build a business," my mother said, "but he promised me that he will also make it a home for us." At the time, none of us were concerned. We didn't understand. We thought if you lived in a place, it was a home. How could it not be?

We gave our firewood to the neighbor with the internet. We gave our dog, Sally, to one of my school friends. We sold the horses, goats, and rabbits. Even our table, chairs, pots, and pans men bought and stacked in their trucks and pulled away.

As soon as we came to Italy my father switched back from his white button-ups to tie-dye shirts. That first week, he cut my brothers' bowl cuts. He cut them short on the sides and left them long on the tops, and slicked them up with water from his water bottle from the airport. Lindsay looked at Lewis and laughed.

"Louise, do you want a haircut?" he said.

I said I would keep my braids.

"I think you would look lovely with short hair," he said.

I shook my head.

"Come on, Lou, short is better for the summer time," my mother added.

"I can just keep it in braids," I said.

"Come here," my father said in a new voice. So I sat down on the stone wall on the hill and he didn't even undo my hair from the braids, he just cut through them. It took a long time and made oddly a lot of noise, my hair crackling like a fire underneath his scissors. Then my two braids were in the grass and that was when our neighbor Claudio, *cloudy-o,* came to visit us.

"*Ciao, ciao, ciao a tutti!*" he said. "*Benvenuti!*" His face was so tan it looked metallic. He was a tall, rangy man, and he wore a brown felt hat. He switched to English, which I found hard to understand, and Lewis whispered to Lindsay and me what he was saying: he was so glad that someone had bought the old stone farmhouse, and he was so pleased to have new neighbors. He said that we should visit his farm; we could walk on the gravel road all the way or take a shortcut over the grassy hill. He told us about our property: when he was a boy, the peasant family had lived on the top level, and their animals had lived in the stables below. "What a beautiful family you are," he said. "What a beautiful family." He ate us up with his hungry eyes. Claudio had a clever face, with a dark beard and short gray hair. He was not much like my father, or like our internet neighbor, who'd always worn a mesh-backed baseball cap. He reminded me of a wizard, dressed all in gray with his lumpy, soft hat.

My father invited him to look at the state of the house. Lindsay asked Lewis and me, "Is Dad going to start dressing like him?" Lewis said shhh, so we could hear Claudio. In the house, Claudio was saying, "You will get wet under this roof, better pray the drought lasts."

"The whole roof is screwed?" my father said.

"In the kitchen, it's okay," Claudio said.

After a long while Claudio came out with my father and mother, who were laughing. He looked at my face and then at my braids in the grass. "Are you all right?" he said to me. I began to cry just from being taken seriously. I was a somewhat manipulative child—I thought he must not know many children, how we were always manipulating, working partly from true emotion, and partly from conceit. I wasn't really so upset about my short hair. But also no one ever gave me much attention or sympathy.

*

A day soon following, my brothers and I followed Claudio up the hill and onto the dusty path. I remember the golden boil of bees and butterflies over the abundance of flowers I had never seen before: purple hairy flowers and tender red poppies on threadlike stalks amidst the yellow and white waving fields. Dust rose around my brothers, who made dark paths in the meadow. Below us, the distant hills were pale shades of blue. The valleys were poured with mist.

Claudio had huge fields and a small house that used to be a shepherd's cabin. He was a woodsman from one of our forest survival books. Shiny knives and shears hung against the wall and, most prominent, his great-grandfather's hunting bow. He talked about how around here, he saw hedgehogs and wild boar, and once as a boy, he'd seen a unicorn, luminous and white. He talked about his great-grandfather, who shot with that very bow a boar almost the size of an elephant and fed the whole town on it, a feast for two hundred.

His four-poster bed was hung with red draperies, and he pulled back the drapes to show us his bed with its tidy quilt. And he also had electricity and a refrigerator. My brothers and I exchanged looks. We all wanted to live with Claudio, not our parents. He called us a *beautiful family* again.

From the freezer he took out a small coffin-shaped Styrofoam container of gelato. It had only a little bit of chocolate left and larger amounts of *frutti di bosco*—berries of the forest—and cream. My brothers and I all wanted the chocolate. He said I could choose first, but my brothers would not allow it. So he had us pick playing cards from a deck and the person with the highest playing card could choose their scoops first.

His cards were strange. Lewis drew the two of swords. The two swords were blue, with gold handles and a red ribbon wrapped around them. Lindsay drew the *Fante* of coins. Claudio didn't know how to translate *Fante*. It was a young man with long curly hair and a Robin Hood hat with a feather in it, standing by himself, holding an ornate gold disk.

I drew the Horseman of Cups, a man with a big ruff on a pink horse, and won, or so Claudio said. I took all the chocolate.

"The house has a good foundation," my father said many times. "Doesn't matter that it's out of level. It's a good foundation."

"If you don't have at least the roof, the walls, the stove, the electrical, and the plumbing by September," said my mother, "your children will freeze and starve in the winter and fail all their classes."

"We'll get it done," my father said.

Claudio came from his house with a few tomato plants for us, and he sat with my parents on the low stone wall of the garden. When Claudio came, we all stopped playing and came to listen. It was supposed to rain that day, but it didn't—my brothers and I had been praying against rain, as Claudio had suggested. Down in the valley, the lightning moved like a glowworm, and on our hill the wind blew, our shirts contorted on the clothesline, and the gray cat and the black cat stalked each other.

Claudio leveled with my father. "You can get the roof, the walls, and the stove," he said. "Electrical and plumbing, no." The wind flapped his hat's felt brim, and he pulled it down low against his forehead.

"I can't get through this winter without a sink," my mother said.

"Fine," my father said. "I'm dropping electrical. But not plumbing."

"Can you hire some people?" Claudio said.

My father glanced at my mother. "Obviously, the thought has occurred to me," he said. "I appreciate it, Claudio."

When my father turned his head I saw a huge green spider was climbing right next to his ear. I yelled and pointed and in an instant Claudio had risen and swatted my father on the side of the head, hitting off the spider.

There was a moment of confusion for my father and mother and brothers. Then Lewis went to find the spider. It was still alive, as large as a tarantula but with slim black legs and a green body. Gray-green like the storm clouds in the valley, which we had prayed against.

"You didn't need to do that," my father said. I looked at Lewis to see if he had noticed: my father was angry.

"Your girl was scared though," Claudio said.

He didn't know how it worked, how I could be scared and not scared at once. And how the fear was for my father to resolve. My father's arms were stiff at his sides. He opened his hands from their fists.

Claudio was quiet for a moment. He gave my mother a small smile.

"Claudio, do you have any thoughts on laundry?" she said.

"There's a place in town," he said. He pushed his hat back on his head, in a gesture of resignation, and the shadows left his face. "All I want is for you to let me know how I can help."

When he was leaving, my father made a sort of apology. "Just getting our arms around everything here," he said.

"I've never left the place I grew up," Claudio said simply.

My father shook his hand.

I remember my mother with her face in her hands, and my father saying, "Sara, don't worry, I will have the plumbing in by fall."

In the beginning, we slept on old hay in the hayloft part of the house, with its slotted walls that let the breeze in. To use the bathroom, we dug little holes in the woods.

My father said that we children should be responsible for filling a few plastic jugs each morning with water from the pump. My brothers competed over who could do it fastest, while I kept time. Then we brought the jugs inside in the wheelbarrow.

My father went to town and returned with hundreds of paper plates and napkins and plastic forks and knives, and foam pads for sleeping with knobbly bumps all over them, and one pillow each. He also brought our mother a blue broom and a pack of yellow sponges. We started sleeping in the kitchen instead of the hayloft, in case of rain.

In that first period, we didn't eat any hot food. My parents stirred instant coffee crystals into the well water in their paper cups. We ate bread, and cheese all warm and sweaty from the sun, and raw carrots and tomatoes in olive oil, and off-brand M&Ms that squirted out of their coating when we bit them. My father was happier now. He pumped water faster than Lewis and came up behind Lindsay and me as we stood on the garden wall and roared to frighten us. His hair had grown over his ears. My mother had a different kind of happiness. She found old glass soda bottles in one of the old stables, scrubbed them out with the well water, and arranged little bouquets in them—daisies were the only flowers I recognized, the rest were yellow dragon-heads and little pink rose-like things that were not roses and so many bright indigo trumpets. We bathed in a big plastic bin next to the pump. My brothers and I all used the same water, taking turns for who would go first. Too much trouble to pump it each time. If I went third, the bottom of the bin had a layer of lavender dirt on it that spun up dreamily when I agitated it. It was impossible to wash the soap off all the way.

Soon, Claudio and his friends had dug us an outhouse, and cleaned out the stove in the one room that was our kitchen and bedroom. My mother lit a fire in the stove and our first hot meal was Brunswick stew with half its ingredients different from at home. Claudio ate it with us sitting out on the stone wall. My father had come around to him by then. "We're making a house sandwich!" my father exclaimed. "Foundation and roof first. They are the bread of the sandwich. And the rest—the walls, windows, plumbing, another stove, furniture—is the delicious ingredients. And the foundation is all good!"

Claudio laughed and they conversed vigorously about foundations and roofs. My mother cleaned the kitchen with the water from the pump, and then went into the garden to weed the patch she'd begun to tend. She kept her shirt on under her overalls.

"How old is Claudio?" Lewis asked her later.

"The same as your father," she said.

We all found this shocking. He seemed so much older.

I'd found that we could walk along the garden wall until it ended, then there was a field with no fences, and across the field, the hill turned down suddenly. I didn't like walking alone, so I made my brothers come with me. I liked to feel like we were all one person. I had decided that I didn't like winning the chocolate gelato, or Claudio's good favor; I didn't want attention that pulled me away from them. And, equally, I didn't want the house to become a bed and breakfast, and all this dirt and strangeness to wash away.

We walked across the field and came to the steep edge. The hillside below was too steep to walk and covered with dry, tough brambles. There was a view of the whole valley, patched with sun. We looked down at it together for a while. Lewis looked for boys he could make friends with, and Lindsay looked for tractors, and I looked for unicorns and boars.

Claudio showed us a place where we could swim in the river. A gravelly incline, lined by very tan Italians, led down into deep green, unshaded water. "If the drought keeps up this pool will be gone by August," Claudio said.

"But we're supposed to pray for the drought," Lindsay said, "so we don't get wet in the house."

"Do what you like," he said, and shrugged. "The farms need rain."

I whispered my question to my brother. I was still afraid to talk to Claudio directly.

"Will our father fix the roof in time?" Lewis asked.

"Of course he will," Claudio said. "Your mother deserves it."

Within a few weeks, my mother had obtained an old round wooden table, with white paint flaking off. Candlesticks and a few long taper candles. A two-burner hot plate and a *bombola* of gas. She turned the second room into the children's bedroom. She made raised bedsteads from flat pieces of wood raised up on clay blocks. "Just make sure to fix the roof over their room," she told my father.

"I'll do it before anything else," he said.

He often tracked mud into the kitchen, and at night they had long fights about him being distractible and messing up all her careful cleaning, and about her focusing on small easy things and not helping with the items in the House Sandwich. He said she was wasting time roaming around the churches, and she said that she was getting back in touch with religion. They fought more here than in the Blue Ridge.

I went with my father to the tile store. We drove past tomato fields, then factories, with their acres of large empty cans, ancient farmhouses and barns with their perforated walls, huge rounded arches. Everything was so dry.

We entered a lot filled with huge ridged-clay tiles. A white cat with a big pink nose and small squinty eyes came over and rubbed against me. My father spent a long time negotiating the tiles with the man.

On the car ride back, he said, "What do you think of Italy, Louise?" I imagined telling him about Claudio's cabin with his knives and his bow. Or about how Lewis was starting to leave Lindsay and me alone, going on long walks, looking for something else. I wanted to apologize for being scared by the spider that had crawled over my father's big sunburned head. We were all barely holding on to each other.

"Do you like it?" he said. I told him yes. He smiled and pulled at the ends of my hair, which was starting to grow out. The truth was I didn't like being singled out and asked like this.

*

Right away my father started installing the tile over our bedroom. I overheard Claudio arguing with him, "No, no, that's not right at all."

Once he was done with our bedroom, he hired some workmen to help him with the other parts of the roof.

"Are you sure it won't leak?" said my mother.

"I'm not a fucking idiot."

"I know," she said.

"I built our old farm."

"You did."

The drought continued, but one night when a light misty rain fell no water came into our room, and my mother was so happy the next day she sat on his lap and kissed him right at the breakfast table. My brothers and I made retching sounds and went to eat outside on the garden wall.

Lewis got tall that summer and pink dots appeared around his nose. He was thirteen; Lindsay was nine. In the green pool in the river I saw Lewis's armpits had grown dark hair. My heart beat to see it.

We made friends with another group of siblings. The older sister was named Simonetta. She was fifteen and wore a beaded choker necklace, and she helped translate at first. Enzo and Tommaso were thirteen-year-old twins, but much shorter than Lewis. From them, we began to learn Italian.

We walked downhill to their apartment building. It was near the tomato-canning factory, on the flat plains. It was an orange building in a neighborhood of orange buildings. They had a soccer field nearby and a park with a slide, and a bakery with focaccia and a gelateria, but it wasn't quite a town. More of a stop on the way to the town where we would go to school. On their balcony, under the green-and-white sunshade, we ate pasta using Mickey Mouse forks. The whole time we talked about how we wished we could stay there. Simonetta's mother had us take showers, and even while I soaped myself, gray grime and sand came flowing into the tub. I hadn't been clean in months. She gave us each two euro coins with gold centers and silver rings, to go to the gelateria. I saved mine.

The new friends didn't play our forest-survival games. The twins liked war games. They liked to put on armor—goggles and helmets—and to carry toy guns and swords. We bruised each other's arms and necks. Their scent of fresh soap and shampoo was the scent of war. Lewis played with us only once. He wanted to walk with Simonetta.

I asked Lewis what he and Simonetta were doing when they crossed over the dry fields and disappeared behind the hills. He tried to scare me. He said, "Looking for spiders and feeding them flies."

Sometimes the new friends came over to our house. At the house we each had a box for our clothes. Lewis was outgrowing his but still too small for my father's. My mother told us to go ahead and look through his box and see whether we could find anything shrunken. While my brothers and the twins looked through his box, I looked through my mother's, and found a pink lace-edged satin slip. Lindsay and the twins laughed hysterically at it, but Lewis flushed and told me to put it back at the very bottom of the box.

My mother went to Ikea in our big truck—we had a car and a truck by now—and returned with masses of pink, red, and white candles, tin lanterns, colored gauze curtains—"What *are* these?" my father said and she said, "They were no more expensive than standard curtains!"—plus three small mattresses.

"Are these for the bed and breakfast?" I asked.

My mother laughed.

My father said, "No, the bed and breakfast will have all beautiful, antique things. No Ikea. We're going to get chairs from the Renaissance, you can still find them at flea markets. We're going to get four-poster beds with gilt on the wood. We'll get Murano lamps."

"It's too much," my mother said.

"The walls will be pristine white," my father said.

"Please don't talk about it anymore," my mother said.

"You think I'm jinxing it?" he said.

"We need to focus on what we have," she said.

She took our foam pads to the kitchen. We children got the good mattresses. She hung ropes along the ceiling of our bedroom and pinned onto them those gauzy curtains that had purple at the bottom and faded to pink and then yellow at the top.

At night when I pulled the gauze curtains around my bed I could see the vague shapes of my brothers, and through the window the night sky washed with soft cream, and when we woke our room bloomed with color. Even Simonetta, when she visited, was amazed.

My parents slept on our old foam pads. Three for her side of the bed, two for his.

Next my mother was finding us school desks and chairs, because we were heading into August. She bought us each one new pair of jeans and three new shirts.

At the height of summer, when the drought had reduced the river pool to a fiercely green puddle, Claudio helped Lewis, Lindsay, and me fix up the old chicken coop. We held the chicken wire against the beams while he stapled it. Then we tossed the hay into the nesting boxes. He brought us five hens, carried down in a cardboard box in the back of his truck. My mother came rushing out when she heard his voice. "How can we ever thank you?" she asked.

"I have too many chickens," he said. My father appeared behind my mother. He was less pleased than she was.

Lindsay ran to open the little door of the coop, and Lewis and I carried the meek red hens over in their box, then brought each one out and dropped it inside the coop. The hens fluttered away and regarded us with their twitchy eyes. My mother offered Claudio a coffee. Now that we had the two-burner stove and the *bombola* of gas it was easy to make.

Claudio sat next to my father on the wall. He was tall and thin with his striking beard and mushroom-colored hat. My father had long rockstar hair and muscular arms, a sleeveless shirt with a lightning skull on it, and a bright red, freckly face.

"I'm impressed with you for fixing up this place," Claudio said. "Americans always move here to try to take our tourist dollars, they start hotels and tour companies. But you, you're strengthening our local agriculture and our traditions."

"It's a pleasure," my mother said.

My father looked down at our clothesline. "Lewis," he said suddenly, "go re-pin your mother's shirt, it's coming loose."

Lewis kicked the dusty ground. He wanted to stay and hear what Claudio had to say. But he obeyed, and my father watched him go with an expression of satisfaction.

"Italy is a place of wonderful tradition," Claudio continued. My parents nodded. "The problem is, all of our farm workers these days are from dirty countries." He sighed and looked down over the hill. The sun illuminated the dust around Lewis. His legs were so long now, his shoulders still so narrow. "They're taking over Italy."

"Claudio," my father said, "I think those immigrants are the only thing keeping your country going."

"Sure, the economy," said Claudio, and shrugged. "But they're not Italians . . ."

"Neither are we," my father said. I didn't understand why my father was being so rude to him. Don't push him away, don't lock him out, I wanted to beg.

"Never mind about the coffee," Claudio said, rising. I had the sense that Claudio had been testing my father—and that my father had come up short.

"Oh, the coffee!" my mother said. She ran into the house. Claudio watched her go. Then he saluted me and Lindsay and shouted "*Ciao*, Lewis," and turned to climb up the hill without a look at my father, for which I was grateful because my father looked so unhappy.

My mother returned with the coffee pot. "What will he think when we tell him we're doing a B&B?"

"Asshole," my father said.

Lindsay giggled.

"Please don't tell him, Peter," my mother said. "It'll be at least two years until we open—well, at the rate you're going, maybe faster," she said. She kissed his cheek and the top of his head the way she kissed us. "Let's not see him for a while. But no need to tell him, okay, Louise? Lindsay?"

We nodded.

My father turned to us. "I'm not going to talk to him again," my father said. "And neither should any of you. Sara?"

She glanced at my father. There was a strangely triumphant look in her eyes, but her voice was quiet. "Yes, I agree," she said. "I think it's time we let him be."

The truth was, now that we had chickens, we had as many eggs as we could eat, and they were, to my brothers and me, the most delicious food on earth. Eggs with their edges lacy and golden, dripping with olive oil. Eggs and pancetta cooked in the same pan. Eggs on big rough chunks of bread.

I found a patch of clay by the stream that led to the swimming hole, and I made a few little model chickens and dried them on the windowsill. I put the best one in my pocket and walked to the gelateria with the two euros from Simonetta's mother, and I asked for a *barattolo,* I knew the word now, of gelato. Three flavors, the server told me. Aware that I was doing something illegal, I told him chocolate, *frutti di bosco,* and hazelnut, which he said was better than cream. When it was time to pay he asked for eight euros and I handed him my two. In Italian, he said, "I need six more," and now I pretended I had no idea what he was saying. "I've ruined all this gelato," he said. "You're not allowed to come back here." I started crying. "I would just give it to you," he said, "but my manager will be mad. You've made me spend my own money on you!" He put the Styrofoam container in a bag and told me to get out.

I carried it up to Claudio's. My tears quickly dried. It was a long walk up the dry golden hills, past the little hut filled with saints, and up his gravel path. I didn't like to be alone this way. The wind was much stronger now, almost shouting loud in the fields. It lashed the branches of the trees. The sky was blank and relentless. "The eyes of the Lord are in every place, watching the evil and the good," my mother sometimes said. I imagined the sky was the blue of His eye. I preferred to be under the cover of the trees. The old farm in North Carolina had been all cream, green, and smooth ovals—smooth pebbles in the creek, our round bellies. Italy instead was red, silver, and gold, and its shapes were stars and webs. The wind blew too strong here, and the dust filled my nose and mouth.

I knocked on the wall of his tiny house. The red curtains around his bed were drawn. I imagined the trouble I'd have if my parents were hiding behind them, watching me.

"Louise!" he said. "What a pleasure."

I placed the bag with the gelato container on his table, feeling suddenly shy. "Did you walk all the way here?" he said. "You must be thirsty." I nodded. He filled me a large glass of water, and I was envious of his tap, which was so much better than our pump.

We sat down at his table. I looked around at the herbs hanging from his ceiling. It was like the house of a woodland fairy, so beautiful and clean.

"Now, let's see what we have," he said, and opened it. The ice cream had entirely melted and become a red-brown soup with pale chunks of hazelnut floating at the top.

My eyes filled with tears again.

"Mmm, I see," he said. "What are the flavors?"

My throat constricted, and I didn't say anything.

"It's delicious this way," he said. We drank it out of cups. A clashing confused drink, creamy and icy, nutty and fruity. He patted his stomach.

I took the clay chicken I had made out of my pocket, and put it on the table.

"What's this, dear Louise?" he said. He picked it up and looked at it. His face changed. He looked nearly as upset as I felt.

"I have too much pride," he said quietly. "That's why you all have stopped seeing me, isn't it? I made an error of pride." He leaned his chin on his hand and looked away from me. "I've been thinking a lot about it."

"I don't know," I said. "I agree that not everyone can be Italian."

He sighed and tucked his chin down to look at me from his deep bloodshot eyes. Bloodshot from too much sun and sky. "Don't let yourself grow into an old man already, Louise."

"Okay," I said, disliking his serious tone. I did not like being corrected. I had been trying to comfort him.

"How did you afford this?" he said.

"I got in trouble."

He went to his cupboard and pushed aside many boxes of pasta and took out a *pastiglie* tin that looked heavy in his hand. He placed it on the table and when he opened it I could see it was filled with euros. He handed me two small pale five-euro notes. "Go pay him back," he said. "That boy is Giuseppe, he's a good boy."

I nodded. "Are you going to come visit us again?"

"No, no," he said. He saw my face. "Are you disappointed? Come here, Louise." He knelt on the floor and opened his arms wide. I walked toward him and he embraced me tightly, something my father never did. His beard was against my cheek. "Oh, Louise, I like you so much," he said. "I wish you were my little daughter." My tears wet the shoulder of his green shirt.

September arrived. We'd begun school at the *Liceo Scientifico,* the scientific high school. It was fortunate that we knew Simonetta and the twins, but I was still sad without any of them in my classroom. I tried not to say a single word.

My mother had told my father to have the roof, the walls, the stove, the electrical, and the plumbing by September. Claudio had struck the electrical. Out of the four that remained, my father had only managed the roof and the stove. They argued constantly about the plumbing, and about the walls—walls meant windows and doors too, and several of our windows had empty panes, and the doors let cold air under them. My brothers and I would eavesdrop on them and they were always talking about what they could afford.

"At least we have the foundation and the roof," my father would say. "That will get us through winter."

My mother told him to set up a second stove in our room or we would freeze. But he delayed. He was trying to do the walls first. Didn't want to waste all the wood, a stove in an uninsulated room. "They can always stay in here with us," he said. But she did not like that idea. "Lewis is a big boy now," she said. "You'll drive him out of the house if you make them miserable like this."

"They're not miserable yet," he said. "Just see, it'll all be good for the winter."

The first frost came, and the two garden cats came in through our broken window. We shivered and I was barely asleep when Lewis woke me for a midnight meeting. In the end we were too afraid to go into our parents' room. So we slept, the three of us, in Lewis's bed, the way we used to before he became what my mother called a big boy. Toward morning Lewis woke us and made us go back to our own beds. The stone floor froze my feet even through my socks. That was the last time the three of us ever slept in one bed. I recognized it as it passed. One body in front of me, one behind, their legs, bony and warm, tangled with mine, much more worth praying for than drought, much more an answer to my prayers.

Breakfast was unpleasant. "You need to go find and install that stove today," my mother said.

The next night was the decisive one. The storm finally reached us, the spider green clouds that meant the end of the drought. It was the night of icy rain. This was the first big test of our father's roof, and he failed. The water poured into our room and soaked my mattress and the mattresses of both of my brothers.

We had no choice. In the drenched dawn, we went into our parents' room. My father looked betrayed when he saw us. It was almost as though he'd wanted us to soak and freeze in our own room.

And we understood why, because our mother left the next day.

"I have put too much into this, Peter," she said. "I am not coming back until you do what you have to do."

"Their roof? Their stove?" my father said.

She shook her head.

We did not know where she went. It rained three nights in a row. My dreams those nights were deserts, hellmouths, because we slept so close to the stove. My father found other holes in the roof, but our former room was the worst. Our nice mattresses were waterlogged, even though we lined them up against the wall in the stove room to try to dry them. The sunset-colored curtains had come unpinned and lay against the stone floor with the gray water creeping up them.

She was gone for days. We ate only bread with cold things on it. It was impossible to do homework. My father was awake all night every night.

I was aware that what we needed was money. That was what was delaying everything—new roof tiles, workmen, new stove. I thought about discussing this with Lewis, but the family didn't seem to hold much interest to him anymore, and even when I determined I would talk to him, it was impossible to find him by himself. Either we were all lying near each other in my father's room, or he was disappearing over the hills. I would have to do it by myself.

When I realized this, I left school at break and went walking. It was a cold, beautiful fall day. I loved my new jeans and my sweatshirt that Simonetta had given me. I felt so grown up walking the four miles. The fields were shorn, their dancing insects and dust gone, the twinkling myths, unicorns and boars, harder to believe now in this tremendous raw coldness that was getting greener and colder by the day. I passed the saints and silk flowers behind the bars of their little white hut.

I looked in all of Claudio's windows first. The curtains were drawn around the bed but that was the way they usually were. But Claudio would never sleep in: he was a farmer. The little clay chicken I'd made sat on his table.

I entered his house. I listened for a moment. It was entirely quiet. I remembered my mother who always said, "God is watching." But if I completed my task, she would come back home. I wasn't, of course, going to take all of his money.

How would I deliver it to my father? I would just leave it folded up in paper in the kitchen somewhere. No, I didn't want him thinking Claudio had dropped it by. I would tell him I won a school contest.

I went to the cupboard and moved aside the jars and the blue cardboard boxes of pasta. There was the *pastiglie* tin. I pulled it out and brought it over to the table. He did not really have so many bills inside. A few fifties, a few twenties. Mostly fives and coins. I took one hundred euros total in a mixture of different denominations and coins. I replaced the lid and wiped it off with his dish towel, for fingerprints, and pushed it back into the cupboard.

I don't know why I stopped on my way out. Maybe I heard a quiet stirring behind the bed's drapes, or maybe I was just very nervous and wanted to be sure. I thought, if I find him there, I'll just apologize and explain. He might even give me the money. So I reached out a hand and tried to draw back the drapes.

They wouldn't pull apart. They seemed to be pinned—then I realized, there was a *hand* clasping them from behind. There was someone hiding back there. I tried a minute more to open them—a silent struggle between me and the hand—and then I darted around the side of the bed and opened the other drapery. And there in the dim little tent was my mother, in her pink satin slip.

When I looked at her, Claudio's quilt rumpled around her, I just wanted her to come back to us.

"Hello, Louise," she said, in a high, breathy voice. I thought she was going to scold me for stealing, but she said, "Are you going to tell your father?"

"Hello," I said. I didn't have a thought of pressuring her. This didn't feel like power on my side. I was thinking: *Oh, he likes her more than he likes me.*

Her face was flushed and crumpled.

"Are you coming home?" I said. "We're going to get another stove," I added.

"Your father won't take me back if you tell him about this," she said.

"Okay, I'm not telling him," I said. "What have you been doing here?"

She laughed and said, very sadly, "Oh, Louise."

I didn't understand why she was laughing at me. "Anyways," I said, "I'm taking the money."

This was a kind of test, but she did not, as I expected, tell me that I could not. "Claudio will notice, and then what will I tell him?" she said.

I thought about it. "Why not tell him you stole it for us?" I said.

"I'll tell him I suspect you or your brothers."

I shrugged.

"How much are you taking?" she said.

"A hundred," I said.

"Okay," she said, again with a sort of silent laugh shining in her face. Then she got serious again. "You're not telling your brothers or your father."

"I told you, I won't."

"I'll know if you do."

"I know."

"Then I'll come back once he has the stove and the roof fixed," she said.

I still don't know whether she had planned to come back or not—maybe my childish desire for her to come back changed her mind, or maybe she'd already decided not to abandon us.

I told her I missed her and asked for a hug. It was so different from hugging Claudio. Claudio's hug was a secret, I knew; there was something zinging in it, jittering around, something that needed to be contained. But my mother's hug was soft, sad, and desperate. Her chest was soft against me, and I felt the familiar embarrassment. She seemed to have forgotten that she was my mother and therefore I would obey her.

I never told anyone—not my brothers, not my father. It's possible that she told him at some point. We found her at home after school one day. Of her list, roof, walls, stove, the electrical, and plumbing, we only had partial roof, partial walls, and two stoves. I was worried that she would size it all up and leave again.

She kissed each of us on the head. None of us said anything about her absence until my father started, picking up a conversation we had interrupted.

"I thought you cared most about the children," he said. I hadn't understood this. That she didn't care most about us.

"I wasn't going to use them as bargaining chips," she said. "I can only make myself a bargaining chip."

"Instead of bargaining, you could simply communicate with me," he said.

"Peter, I have tried many times," she said.

We could tell they were going to have a whole long fight, and so my brothers and I went out into the fields. We agreed that if, in the night, the cold rain fell on our heads again, we would not tell anyone.

The bright afternoon nipped our necks and hands. The cats followed us along the garden wall. There were many perfectly geometric round webs growing on the shrubs and trees. We walked past the edge of the garden and across the field, shorn now, to the edge of the hill, where we could look down at the plains and all the broken old farmhouses that didn't have us to rescue them.

STEVEN DUONG

Dorchester

FROM *The Drift*

IN THE YEAR of the ox, my poem went moderately viral in some small but enthusiastic circles, the way a poem sometimes does. I wrote it after reading the news report about the old Vietnamese woman stabbed to death outside her home in Dorchester, which is where I was at the time, visiting Leah. These visits almost always involved her putting on a harness and me skipping dinner, so I was spent. When she went to clean up and get back to her paper on sexual dimorphism in Trinidadian guppies, I began drafting the poem.

The speaker was me, but barely—he could have been a cousin or something, a foreigner who shared my hair texture and general nose shape but lived a more exciting version of my life in a more expensive city. At the beginning of the poem, he is in a cab, coming home from the airport after visiting his mother in California. On his phone he reads a news report about an old Vietnamese woman stabbed to death outside her home in Dorchester, one in a string of recent attacks marking an uptick in anti-Asian hate crimes, and, stunned, outraged, he begins to imagine the life this woman might have lived: an untroubled childhood in Saigon; a marriage to a high school sweetheart; three tall, well-adjusted children; and, soon enough, a street of bombed-out buildings, a long and arduous voyage in a small fishing boat, a stint in a Malaysian refugee camp, and an eventual relocation to Boston, where she finds work as a house cleaner, where her children grow up and leave, where her husband passes quietly in the night, where she spends her days watching dubbed Korean dramas and strolling around her neighborhood, imagining another neighborhood in another country.

The speaker of my poem sees in this old woman his mother. The knife, the blood, the news. He imagines his mother at the grocery store, confronted by a man with wild eyes. He makes a decision then. He tells the cab driver to take him somewhere else. He goes to the old woman's house in Dorchester. To where she was killed. He sees a flock of pigeons on the sidewalk outside and tosses them crackers, watches them eat. When they fly off, he imagines them flying all the way across the ocean to Vietnam. The sun is sinking now. It swallows the birds. The speaker, with his luggage in tow, walks the full five miles back to his apartment.

This was the poem I wrote at Leah's place. Even then, before the poem was published, before it was widely shared by online literary types and blown up by the Chinese American congresswoman who retweeted it in May along with the appropriate hashtags, I knew that the best response to a horrific act of violence was not this poem. I told myself that I had to put my feelings into words, that this was how I dealt, how I coped and mourned. And it was. But there was also a thrill in writing about something so recent and terrible, a thrill, too, in connecting it to the various swirling traumas of my own life, however tenuous the connections. Even before I had a full draft on the page, I imagined people encountering my poem on a pristine website, sharing screenshots of it, chittering away in various comments sections, making careful conjectures about the relationship between the speaker and the poet. I wanted the noise. It was ugly of me to want it so badly, but I did.

At work, people demanded my thoughts on things. They were angry and sad about the old woman murdered in Dorchester, and so my poem became a professional whetstone, grinding me into myself but sharper. I was asked many times if I was okay. I was given opportunities to demonstrate my resilience. The day the poem was published, my job was to create social media graphics that would make people sign up for a six-week lyric essay workshop for eight hundred dollars. I was good at my job. It was a job anyone could become good at given enough time and Adderall. I answered to three different directors, toothy Gen Xers with pristine opinions on politics and literature.

Erica, our development director, told me my poem was brave

and gut-wrenching and necessary. She asked me if my parents were alright, and I told her they were. Matt, our programs director, asked me if I was going to the protest at the Garden that weekend, because he knew the organizers and could get me up there to read my poem if I was interested. I told him I would think about it, and he said, please do, take all the time and space you need right now. Kelly, our executive director, who had published a book of his own poems nearly a decade ago through a small but well-respected press, told me he would put me in touch with his editor there.

"It's easy to forget that everyone here is an artist, too," Kelly said. "That we all have our own individual practices. You get caught up and you forget."

"I know what you mean," I said, though I didn't. Everyone at work, from the directors to the assistants to the interns, was constantly sharing their writing online. It was unavoidable.

"Whenever something like this happens," Kelly said, "and I read something so incisive and painful by a writer in the community, especially one as young as you, it just reminds me. It reminds me why I do this work." He said the words *young* and *community* like they were serious illnesses.

"I mean it, Vincent. Thank you for your voice." When Kelly placed his hand on my shoulder, my shoulder became slightly damp. He had chosen to intercept me just outside the men's room, which had no working paper-towel dispensers.

"Wow," I said. "Thank you, Kelly. Just thank you."

I didn't know what else to say, so I pulled him into a hug, which seemed to surprise him. Kelly was a thin, bird-like man, but the muscles on his back were very firm. I wondered who he went home to. He never spoke much about home. At times, he seemed to me like a video game NPC, hard-coded with a dialogue tree, limited to a few encouraging comments and several dozen phrases about broadening the city's literary landscape.

"You know," Kelly added, "Matt was worried about putting out our solidarity statement this week, but when I read your poem, I knew we were in good hands." He gave me a look that said, I value you for reasons I cannot say out loud, and I returned him one that said, let's keep this arrangement going. In the bathroom, I crushed and inhaled a 10 mg Adderall. My phone seized up with notifications, most of them about my poem, and also a text from Leah, nestled between other messages on my lock screen.

Show me you're thinking of me

She always texted in short commands like this. It was a great power of hers. Her economy of language drove me into brick walls again and again. I calculated the risk of taking semi-nude photos in the bathroom mirror. It didn't take long.

Good boy

Afterwards, I finished my draft of our organization's statement of support for the Asian American community in the wake of the killing in Dorchester and forwarded it to Kelly and Matt. They liked what I'd done, but told me to mention South Asians, West Asians, and Pacific Islanders, who were almost always marginalized in statements by literary organizations. We could be better than that.

From Friday night to Sunday morning, Leah made me wear a collar and sleep at the foot of her bed. I wasn't allowed to want anything. All the wanting at her place was to be done by her. When I arrived after work, having taken a 30 mg Adderall and a half-tab of acid, I found her on the couch working on her paper. A Japanese animated movie ran in the background, something about a man with a sword and a pet crow. She wore a purple robe and didn't look up or greet me. Leah gave me nothing.

For a moment, I wanted her to get up off the couch and hit me, hard. I thought about telling her this, but then I gave up that want. I did what a therapist once told me to do with intrusive thoughts—take the thought, place it on a leaf, and allow it to drift down the river of my mind—which seemed like a poorly translated version of some Zen Buddhist practice. As corny as it was, I did it all the time, even though I wasn't sure how compatible Zen Buddhism was with the arrangement Leah and I had. I spent my weekends cooking her meals and doing her laundry while she attended to her research. Leah wrote about the sex lives of captive-bred guppies and killifish. She called me in every hour or so to dig through the notes she kept in the filing cabinet beneath her desk, sometimes ordering me to get down there myself and kneel under her. Once in a while, when I was organizing her notes, she would knock everything out of my hands and make me clean it up. She didn't do this as often as I would have liked, but that too was part of the game.

At first, I was concerned about how good it felt to be a thing Leah kept. We tried for a while to do it without the collar, without the cooking and the kneeling beneath the desk, to see if there might be another way. We tried it during the week too. Once, I even fastened the collar around her neck, the restraints around her little wrists. None of it worked. The alternatives made us stupid and violent and awful, both to one another and to ourselves, and so we resigned ourselves to the weekend, the only life it made sense for us to share.

That Friday night, I took my place at Leah's feet the way I always did. She looped the collar around me, fixing it tight with a small silver ring. She told me I was hers. When she came, the muscles in her legs clenching around my throat, hard and rhythmless, I felt my spine buzzing, a warmth seeping in, possibly the Adderall or the acid, but also, possibly, love. I felt my hair very acutely then, wound tight in her fingers. I was beneath her, always beneath her. She drew me in and came again. When the movie ended, we sat there, together and not together, the orchestral score fading into the low tumble of the dishwasher.

"I read your poem today," Leah said, finally. "I liked it, but it was hard to read."

I was still nestled in her lap, so I couldn't tell what her face was saying. Her voice was a plain, cold metal that never softened for me.

"The description of the murder?" I asked.

"The stuff about your mom."

Parents were the currency of our early days, before Leah and I had our arrangement in the city, before we even really knew each other. We met at a small college in Iowa, a place where students were constantly picketing the dining hall to protest the administration's unethical factory farming contracts. The first thing I learned about Leah was that her parents were from the same city in Vietnam as mine. We had shown up to the Asian American Association's first meeting of the year, and the leaders, a Korean senior and a half-Korean junior, encouraged us to tell stories about our families, in order to give us a handy set of shared, vaguely Asian experiences about which to commiserate.

After this meeting, Leah and I went to a coffee shop in town, where we learned several other things about our respective parents. Leah's lived in Albuquerque, worked at a Johnson & Johnson factory, went to church every Sunday, and sent her money in the mail, which she always sent back. My mother lived in San Diego, worked at a telecommunications company, practiced various forms of energy healing, and sent me emails I never replied to about my brother and his recent teaching accomplishments at a middle school named after a civil rights leader. For the next few months, Leah and I fulfilled the greatest wishes of our college's Asian American Association. I told her my mother used to hit me with a wooden spoon, and she said, mine too, and when she told me that kids at school used to make fun of her for the lunches her dad packed her, which always seemed to include a healthy dose of fish sauce, I said, same here. We're the same, I said.

It went like this for weeks, and then, one night, in the aftermath of a dorm party, when Leah and I were the only ones left in the fourth floor kitchen, sitting in desk chairs and smoking someone else's American Spirits, I told her the only thing she didn't yet know about my mother.

When I was finished, I found that she was staring at me, at my mouth, as if the answer she was looking for was behind my teeth. She flicked the remains of her cigarette out the window, the red dot sailing into the gravel like a live shell.

"Vincent," Leah said. "This might not matter, but I don't think I could ever lie to you."

"Okay," I said.

She told me to open my mouth. I did. She told me to look at her. I did. When she pressed two fingers against my tongue, pushing them down my throat, I tasted salt and ash and something I couldn't place. With her other hand, she took my head and brought me down.

This was when it began, not quite the way it was now, in Dorchester, on the carpet beneath the couch after a week at work, but something like it.

"It just felt strange to me," Leah said. "In the poem, you talk about your mom like she's someone you have this whole relationship with. Like, you visit her in the poem. You fly to California to go see her. I didn't get that."

"I guess the speaker is me in the future, maybe. Someone I could be one day."

"Do you really see that for yourself?"

"I think I might."

"Even after what she did."

"Yes."

"And when you heard about the murder, you thought of her?"

I didn't know what to say. I did think of her, because I wrote the poem, but I never called her or emailed her, never asked about whether or not she had heard the news. We hadn't spoken in months. It was too hard to love her and know her at the same time. I could only love her without knowing her, or know her without loving—never both at once.

"I don't want you to think I didn't like the poem," Leah said. "I like it. It was just hard to read, knowing what I know."

"I get that," I said. "You know me too well."

"Maybe," she said. "I just don't always feel like your poems come from a good place. Wherever they come from feels a little uncertain to me, a little painful and scary."

"It's not you," I said. "It's not in your control."

"I don't know," she said, and pulled me down again, this time by the ring of my collar. There was so much warmth at the center of her, I wanted to cry.

Leah was right. She always was. My poems came from a scary and uncertain place, and this was because they came easy to me. This was the most shameful part. It was easy for me to write in an angry way, using a large and prophetic voice I did not entirely believe in to describe the hurts I had accrued, to write the word *body* and mean a thousand imagined bodies, bruised and bleeding, to write the word *war* and mean some argument I had with my mother once over dinner. I wrote like this all the time. I wrote this poem about the woman in Dorchester in one sitting.

After she finished, I told her what Matt had said to me that morning at work, that I had a chance to read my poem at the protest on Saturday. She drew my chin up then, allowing me to meet her eyes, which were brown and murky and vaguely demanding. I almost cried again, looking at her. On my cocktail of prescriptions and supplements, I had many moments like this, when I stared at Leah in the warm aftermath of her pleasure and thought about what it would take for me to cry, physiologically speaking. Maybe if I was stabbed. Or if she was. I couldn't be sure.

"Maybe I'll join you," Leah said. "I'll see if I can finish my edits early."

The organizers set up their banners and speakers in the center of the pavilion, which overlooked the watery part of the Garden, the geese and turtles. The turnout was good—a few hundred people bundled up in hats and masks and scarves, most of them college students from the city's several dozen schools. They had painted their signs with slogans like *Stop Asian Hate* and *Protect Our Elders,* things we all believed in, because what else could we believe? We all wanted to keep Asians from being spat on and old people from being stabbed. The energy was palpable, electric. People were hurt. They were angry. There were names on some of the signs, Chinese names and Vietnamese names and Korean names, the names of everyone who had been attacked or killed in the past few months.

"You're on deck," Matt said. "How are you feeling?"

"I'm alright," I said. "It's cold out."

"It is," Matt agreed, "but people came out anyway. That says a lot. I mean, this is big, Vincent. You sharing your words with these people. It's big what you're doing."

We were all gathered on the marble steps together—me, Matt, the other organizers in their orange vests, and a few women in glittering dresses, Vietnamese women who must have been very cold. I was glad Leah wasn't there. She got nervous in large crowds.

Once, when we were at a theater in Des Moines, an alarm went off and Leah pulled me to the floor, convinced that there was a shooter in the building. She began texting a long and frantic message, I assumed to her parents, the glow of the phone illuminating fear on her face. I had never seen her like that. An usher came in seconds later, announcing that it was a faulty fire alarm, but the whole episode left her shaken. When we got back to our dorm, Leah put the collar on me and had me hold her in bed, the shades drawn, the white noise machine whirring like a swarm of gentle insects. I felt, for the first time, like a comfort, a small thing you touch when you don't know what else to do with your hands, when you have nothing to hold but must hold something. It was better, today, for her to be home.

The current speaker was a Vietnamese girl, a high schooler wearing a green ao dai. "We stand with all marginalized communities," she said. "We have to protect each other," she said. The people shouted and chanted with her. There were so many mouths opening and closing. It felt like a concert. I was impressed with her, this girl with her anger and her resolve, how young she sounded. Her voice was shaky but bright. What she said, she meant. It couldn't be faked.

"What happened in Dorchester," the girl said, "could have happened to any of us in this country. It might still. Any of us who look like this might one day be the targets of ugly, horrific, racist violence. We all know it. This pain is so big." Her voice shook again. This girl, this girl. People cheered her on when she faltered.

"At the end of the day," she continued, "as deeply as I feel this pain, it is not mine. This pain we feel today, it belongs to the victim and her family. It is their pain, and so it is their words we need to listen to. I am honored to invite to the stage Jasmine Nguyen, eldest daughter of Mai Nguyen."

The crowd simmered down to a hiss, then erupted. The middle-aged woman next to me stepped forward. I recognized her then. Everyone's face was a reflection of their mother's. I should have known. She had been crying this whole time, and still I hadn't connected this hurting woman to the woman in the video we all saw. I felt my stomach tighten like a coil. I thought of my own mother for the first time since I had spoken to Leah. I thought of the photo of her and my father and brother in front of the plane, dressed like they were going to church, when really they were uprooting their small lives and planting them elsewhere.

All my life, my mother had called us refugees, had told me and my brother tales of our escape: the boats, the guns, the dogs. The stories changed a little with each telling, but I learned to love the modulation, the shakiness of her voice, the guns becoming rockets, the dogs becoming sharks or Thai pirates. These stories were meant to teach me and my brother things like, *hard work pays off,* or, *do not trust the communists and their allies,* but all I heard was, *you, too, might be a series of stories.* In my college essays, I cited my mother as the reason I hoped to become a writer—to honor the stories of her life and thread them into my own.

The summer before I left for Iowa, I found a photo. My parents, together, young and fresh in their French pastels, standing on the tarmac with my brother, a fat baby in a stroller. They were surrounded by luggage, a dozen valises and trunks and leather suitcases. I was nowhere in the photo. The date scrawled on the back—March 19, 1984, nine years after the fall of Saigon, nine years after they had supposedly boarded the fishing boat at dawn, landing weeks later in the Philippines. There was no boat here. These were immigrants.

My stomach grew heavy then, my head warm and sweaty. I felt the lie in my body, the way I felt things like drugs and food and alcohol. I went to the bathroom and threw up. I thought about burning the house down, or grievously injuring myself and allowing my mother to find me bleeding in some corner.

I never confronted her about the photo. In Iowa, I answered her calls and emails less and less. I couldn't stomach her voice, the kindness and worry. I didn't want her lies to imprint on me, though I also figured that it might be genetic, that I had already inherited the liar's gene, the sequence of DNA that would one day compel me to tell my children that I was an alchemist or a high-powered lawyer or a refugee.

This was what I told Leah on the fire escape all those years ago. I gave it to her in a tumbling stream of consciousness that must have seemed erratic and mostly drug-fueled, and by the time I was done, I saw the lines in her face had been smoothed away. It must have pleased her on some level. For me to have handed her, so quickly, this great lie of my mother's, this heavy thing I carried with me all the time. It was then that I knew she wanted me. I had greased some secret machinery in her, whatever it was that allowed her to be who she was. When I told her my mother was a liar, I could feel it kicking to life.

Now, standing in the cold with the city's hurt pooled beneath me, I felt the great lie once more. I felt it in my gut, my head, my feet. I looked at Matt, who looked at me. I looked back to the woman on stage, adjusting the mic, crying still.

I couldn't read my poem for these people, for this woman whose mother had been murdered in Dorchester. It would cut me down, and even then, I would not be as low as she was, or any of the people here were, people who felt things with their hearts, who met violence with anger and sadness and one another, shivering on the lawn. I walked away, leaving Matt, leaving Jasmine, leaving the hum of the mic and the simmer of the crowd. I swallowed two Adderall and boarded the red line to Dorchester.

While I was assembling a banh mi for Leah, I heard squeaking from under the sink. Her kitchen had green tile and a mouse problem. I got down to find a mouse caught in one of the glue traps I had set out a week earlier. I drew the white sheet up, holding it to the light. The mouse's legs were bent at strange and ugly angles. I hated these glue traps, but this, too, was part of our arrangement. I had to make the place homelike, which meant keeping undesired houseguests out. I was so many things, all of them Leah's. It was a full life I lived.

"We could use regular traps," I'd suggested. "The kind that snap down. We could try cheese and everything."

"I'll leave it to you," Leah said. "Glue traps are easiest, but I don't care, as long as I don't have to see them. That's all I want."

I had decided to go with the glue traps. I'd read online that you could loosen mice from the traps by dousing them in cooking oil. But as I knelt there on the tile, I knew this one's legs were too far gone. It would be cruel to release it like this, only for the ants to swarm and colonize its body in the dirt, hollowing it out over the course of a day or two. The thing squeaked at me as I walked it outside, struggling pointlessly in the glue. I laid the sheet on the ground, mouse-side down. It looked like a page torn from a small notebook, shivering, quickened by an animal wind.

I considered writing a poem about the mouse with the broken legs, how I would have to crush it underfoot to put it out of its misery. The poem would concern this and more. It would implicate me in acts of terrible violence. It would gesture towards Leah and Matt and my mother and Jasmine too, the old woman's daughter in her white ao dai. I would write about what I knew, but I would write it all wrong. I would estrange the speaker from myself, giving him a mother who never left Vietnam, a partner who didn't leash him to the bed, a sister rather than a brother. I would draw upon great hurts. There were so many ways to write the true thing, but I wouldn't. I wanted the lie. I wanted what I wanted, and no amount of leaves and water could carry it away from me.

MADELINE FFITCH

Seeing Through Maps

FROM *Harper's Magazine*

I WAS SPLITTING wood at sunset when the cat jumped up on the chopping block in front of me, arched her back, and took a long piss. My axe hung in the sky. The cat stared at me, tail up. I put my axe down and squatted before her. I hitched my gown to my waist. I sent my own stream into the brown leaves. The cat narrowed and widened her yellow eyes at me, which is what cats do because they can't blink. Our eyes locked as we added our nitrogen to the landmass. She broke first, streaking back into the woods. I've never seen a cat piss or shit, not once they are out of their resentful kittenhood. Cats are private about such things. I have kept cats all my life. I say kept because my neighbor in these woods reminds me that no one can own a cat, not really. He says I should be more careful about language. He says that words have power. My hope every day is that he will leave me in peace.

I swung my axe, trying to beat the dusk. I am particular about firewood. Sometimes firewood can feel like my whole life.

Tulip poplar wants to burn but it doesn't give off much heat. I use it for kindling. It splits like a wooden xylophone. Listen for that muffled bell toll.

White elm is scarce now and red elm leaves behind clinkers. It will do. Across the grain, it's a rich color without being ornate, which some people appreciate.

Hickory rots at the center so you can split it in a circle, like unmaking a barrel.

If it's summertime and you're cutting live trees, you're screwed. You'll be burning green wood all winter. All those long dark days your wood will spit at you, refuse to catch, need constant tending, smoke you out of your place without keeping you warm, and that's not the worst of it. The worst of it is that green wood will build up creosote in your chimney, and your chimney will catch fire, and the fire will spread to your house, and your house will burn down and what will you do then.

My neighbor in these woods has already split, seasoned, and stacked all the wood he will burn this year. He did this last spring at the first thaw, as he has done every spring for the past twenty years. I don't cut live trees anymore. When I need to warm myself, I look for standing dead. All winter, I stay one fire ahead of the cold. I've never been good at planning. I don't know what's going to happen and I don't know why. I am, however, curious.

Oak will burn all night.

Persimmon is good hard wood but let it be. Wait for the first freeze and you'll get fruit like deflated jewels.

Ash was on the chopping block in front of me, soaked in the urine of the cat. The emerald ash borer, radiant and misplaced, has killed all the ash, so what to do but fell it and watch its bark fall off like meat from the bone. Green ash burns better than any other green wood, though it's useless to learn this. You should not burn green wood and you will not find an ash tree left alive.

Mid-swing, I saw it. Glistening in the piss. I bent to look. A drawing. A drawing in blue ink embedded in the tree rings. Nuanced borders, detailed topography, small as a badge. I had opened a tree and inside it found a map.

My neighbor used to have a book called *Seeing Through Maps,* written in a teacherly way that set my teeth on edge. "There are no rules for making maps," the book said, clearly a trick to get you to let down your guard. Of course there are rules. You'll be likely to break them. A map, by definition, is limiting. As with a journal, or any cavalier use of text, a map may help you remember things, but also invent a way of remembering them that makes you forget everything important. Instead of a journal, I made lists so banal that they unleashed my imagination in revolt against the tiresome record of my life. Instead of maps, I stayed home. I am certain my neighbor still has that book. He never gets rid of a damn thing that makes him feel good about himself.

There were two passages I could tolerate: "A map's quality is the function of its purpose." Also: "If you are making a map for your own purposes and do not care who else can read it—or do not *want* anyone else to be *able* to read it—the map need not even be intelligible to others."

I put my face close enough to smell the ammonia. The blue lines could be a stamp, a tattoo, an island, a spit, an isthmus, a lake, a mountain of two lopsided circles. As a map it was unintelligible to me. Which, according to *Seeing Through Maps,* meant that I was not meant to understand it.

Is what I was thinking, leaning on my axe, when my neighbor appeared at the property line. I had marked those trees with orange blazes yet still I was not left alone. I could see him there, out of the corner of my eye, his patched coat that he'd made from three other coats, his tattered hood, his dirty scarf. "Permission to cross," he said.

"Do it, then," I said, and then I saw that he held his left hand awkwardly with his right as if it were an object separate from his body, and I saw that his left thumb was hanging from his left hand and that all the darkness he was flinging around, darker than dusk, was blood.

"I'm not sure I can drive myself to the emergency room," he said, approaching. He had the pallor of someone in shock but still I could hear the recrimination in his voice. I waited to hear how his severed thumb was my fault. I was curious. My neighbor used to be my husband and neither of us has forgotten it.

"I was splitting kindling and the hatchet slipped," my neighbor said. "You know, the hatchet that you gave me because you gave my first hatchet away." He slumped against a sycamore, a tree that can give you a cough.

It's true that I gave him a hatchet when we were first married, a beautiful curved instrument with a handle of striped walnut and a razor edge. It's true that some years ago I reclaimed the hatchet so I could give it to our other neighbor, the younger one. When you give a gift, it's important to give the best of what you have, not the least of what you have. My neighbor's hatchet was the best thing I had. Of course I replaced it, but he remained angry. It's easy to give the best of what you have when the best of what you have belongs to someone else, he said.

Maybe so. But if you had seen our young neighbor, a radiant person, you too would have given him a beautiful hatchet. You would have given him everything you had. Before he was our neighbor, he was our son. But it had been so long since I'd seen him, so long since I'd heard his voice, I was no longer sure whether I should call him our neighbor or call him something else, or no longer refer to him at all.

"That ash looks wet," my neighbor said, squinting past me at the round as if it was his damn eyeballs that had been severed.

"Don't talk," I said. "Conserve your strength." I tore a strip of cloth from my undergarment. My neighbor grunted as I tied his thumb back on the best I could. The blood soaked through the undergarment. I tore another strip. I tried not to breathe him in.

"Is it green?" he asked.

"I don't burn green wood," I said.

"Anymore," he said. "You don't burn green wood anymore. Let's at least be accurate."

"It's cat piss," I said. I let him lean on me as I guided him to the truck. I buckled his seat belt because he could not do it himself. I told him about the cat leaping onto the log, the eye contact, the stream of urine. I did not mention the map. I could see that through his pain he'd found something to focus on.

"The problem with you is that you have no respect for anything," he said as I coaxed the engine. "When animals act like that, you should stop what you are doing. You should call it a day. You should go inside and shut the door tightly and stoke your fire."

"But I didn't have any firewood," I said. The shocks were shot. The struts were rusted. At the bottom of the hill, the forest ended, and we waited at the railroad tracks as the coal train crept past, hopper car after hopper car, though I always looked for a boxcar, curious to see if someone might be inside.

"Chopping wood out of season," he said, shaking his head. "Then the cat pees on the chopping block at dusk. Then you snub your nose at omens because you are desperate for warmth. Now you see what that leads to." He held up his thumb, trailing my undergarment.

Finally, the striped gate lifted. The light switched from red to green. I steered around the potholes, the ruts and deep ditches, to the highway. If my neighbor had bled out while waiting for the train to pass he would have found some way to reprimand me for that too. He wasn't one to let a little thing like death stand in his way. It must be comforting to my neighbor to know with such certainty how one thing leads to another. Causality is one of the major world religions, one of the last great articles of faith. To me, it is one of the great mysteries. And what is causality but blame?

The emergency room was full of all the people we tried to avoid, I mean any people at all, in various states of visible and invisible distress.

"You should go now," my neighbor said. "You've got no wood and it's going to be a cold one."

"And how will you get home," I said, "in the freezing middle of the night with blood loss? You can't hitchhike with a thumb like that."

The on-duty nurse, in her rolling chair, asked all the questions that my neighbor answered no to. No regular doctor. No phone number. No emergency contact. No insurance. No income, not this month at least. The nurse rolled her chair, rolled her mouth around.

"The doctor will still see you of course," the nurse said. "But you will be expected to make a payment at the end of your visit."

I lowered my neighbor into a chair like a blue plastic bucket so he could leave a grease stain, which, like I said, no longer had anything to do with me.

"We should go," he said, closing his eyes and forgetting to hold his hand up.

"There's no shame in resting for a minute," I said. I took him by the elbow and guided his injured hand so that his uninjured hand could hold it. I certainly wasn't going to. My undergarment grew crispy at the edges. I knew he wanted me to take him home and nurse him. I knew he wanted my entire damn undergarment, strip by strip.

In the adjacent bucket seat, a woman bluely changed her baby's diaper, and the baby was not grateful at all, in fact the opposite.

"When my son was a baby," I told her, "I told him I was going to change him. I meant his diaper. But my husband at the time said, Don't tell him you're going to change him because then he'll believe we don't accept him as he is. He'll wonder if the universe fashioned him wrong." The mother was about to respond, I swear she was, but her baby then kicked orange poop at her so I will never know what she was going to say.

"We hope you change," I said to her baby, watching its mother wipe away the creamy shit while the baby screamed. "Because right now you are less than two feet long and you can't focus your eyes.

You are entirely unreasonable and you are too loud for mixed company."

Words have power, my husband had said to me and to our similarly kicking soiled son. After that I stopped taking him seriously or I started taking him too seriously. Either one is the death of a marriage.

"There's no way I can pay for this," my neighbor said, grimacing.

"We could call him," I said.

"Who," he said, but I knew he knew.

Before he left the woods, our young neighbor had told us both to get health insurance, an easy thing to tell people to do. He told us many things, most of which I can't remember because I thought he'd be there to remind me. He wanted us to stop replying to Do Not Reply text messages from collection agencies with sentences in all caps such as, YOU WILL NEVER GET A RED CENT FROM ME. It had been our health care strategy while raising him but apparently it was no longer good enough. He had called me exactly one time after I found his lean-to empty. Just to tell you I'm safe, he said. And to tell you I want you and Dad to take care of yourselves. He told me he had a job. A paying one. Something more real than being a consultant but less real than being a carpenter. Something in the middle. I can't remember. But I remember that he made more in a year than I had made in my whole life. I remember when he told me, how gentle it was. I could hear the whole forest around me, wondering what the hell money was, what the word salary meant, was it close to the word salad or maybe salal. I want to be happy, he said. I want you and Dad to be happy, too.

Stupid forest, I said. Doesn't understand what's really important.

That's my idea of a joke. That's irony, which is like ironwood but easier for an axe to go through. My son has not called again. My text messages do not begin with Do Not Reply, but he does not reply.

A nurse called my neighbor's name. He tried to get to his feet but sat back down hard. I hauled him up and went with him into the back and the nurse put us behind a curtain, through which we could hear all the clamor and beeping, the frequencies and trouble and off-color jokes, the tapping and sighing and coughing that filled up that building, which is why we tried to avoid buildings, and each other. But here we were.

The nurse took my neighbor's vitals and asked him why he had filleted his hand. My neighbor looked at me as if I should be the one to answer.

"You're making me hungry with talk like that," I told her, because unlike my neighbor I understand humor. I understand that people who work in emergency rooms might want to use cooking or food metaphors to approach the horror that is human flesh. Unlike my neighbor I know that sometimes words have so much power that you can't talk about what you're talking about. You have to talk about something else.

The nurse left us alone, and my neighbor told me to reach into his pocket.

"Certainly not," I said.

"It's on my bad side," he said. "Help me out." In his foul pocket were six tiny persimmons. He used his good hand to take three of them.

"The persimmon tree is on my side of the line," I said.

"The fruit fell on my side of the line," he said.

We ate the persimmons. They revived my neighbor and they inspired in me a dastardly euphoria, unreplicable. They were exquisite.

When the young doctor came in, he tried to shake my neighbor's hand, then remembered, so he shook hands with me instead. "I'm Dr. Rahim," he said. "You must be the one making cannibal jokes. We love that kind of thing around here." Dr. Rahim and I shared a hearty laugh. He read my neighbor's name off a screen he held in his hand.

"Any relation to Duncan?" he asked, sitting down on his own rolling stool and unwrapping my blood-crusted undergarment. Neither my neighbor nor I said anything. "Had to ask," he said. "Same last name. Small town." My neighbor closed his eyes, as if it wasn't his damn last name spilled over onto Duncan and me.

"We are Duncan's parents," I said.

"How about that? I love Duncan," Dr. Rahim said, inspecting my neighbor's wound. "Jesus, I've seen bratwurst more alive than this." He winked at me. "Let's see what we can do."

"I also love Duncan," I said.

"We were buddies in high school," Dr. Rahim said. "Duncan's much better at staying in touch than I am. Some people are so good at keeping up old relationships. Those high school days, though. When I think about how much trouble we used to get in." He laughed. My neighbor opened his eyes.

"What kind of trouble," he asked.

Dr. Rahim stopped laughing. "It was a long time ago," he said.

"Still," my neighbor said. "We are his parents. If he gets into trouble we need to know about it."

"Just teenager stuff," Dr. Rahim said. He looked at me, as if for assistance. But what did he think I should do? That man was only my neighbor. Only a distant pain. My relationship with my axe meant more to me than my relationship with him. Petting the cat was more interesting to me than my neighbor was. I had worked to edit our relationship back and back so that I barely knew him. Strictly speaking, he was none of my business.

Once, when my neighbor was still my husband, he caught me Velcroing Duncan's tiny shoes, which Duncan could do himself by then but which I preferred to do for him when I could get away with it. My husband explained to me that Velcroing Duncan's tiny shoes would lead to Duncan becoming prone to vices unimaginable and irreversible. Velcroing Duncan's tiny shoes was in fact one of the primary ills facing our dying culture. My husband asked several questions, including what was wrong with me.

Where to begin. Mean mom, distant father, doesn't know which colors flatter me, bad at dancing, bad baker, can only sing on key when no one is listening, only apologizes in order to get an apology in return, sad when it rains, can't shake the childish sentiment that rain is God's tears, doesn't believe in God, inattentive pet escort. But by that time he had taken his hatchet and slammed out of the house. He was intuitive, imaginative, generous in his ability to link causes to events in the most expansive and unlikely ways. Yes, sometimes that could be difficult. You can do hard things, he told Duncan, refusing to Velcro his tiny shoes. No one could ever accuse my husband of shrinking before difficulties.

Dr. Rahim touched each one of my neighbor's fingertips, in a way I had never done even when he was my husband. "You'll need stitches, of course," Dr. Rahim said. "Likely surgery too if you don't want the nerve damage to be permanent."

"I can't afford that," my neighbor said.

"Which," Dr. Rahim said.

"Either," my neighbor said.

"There's a charity thing the hospital does for indigent or uninsured patients. You can grab the paperwork on the way out."

"I don't need charity," my neighbor said.

Dr. Rahim frowned. "I understand the two of you may need to talk this over. Why don't I give you a few minutes." He once again gave me that significant look, which I had rejected my claim to years ago and did not in any way want back.

Dr. Rahim left, and my neighbor and I ate more persimmons. They were like if you never had to eat again. They were anti-patriotic, anti-abundance. They were surrounded by blame but blameless. They were mostly pit, but all around the pit they were perfect.

"We should call him," I said.

"I did," he said.

"You did?" I asked. "When?"

"Before I came to find you," he said. "He was the first person I called."

"What did he say?"

"I left a message," he said.

"Do you think we were too hard on him?" I asked.

"No," he said. "At least, I wasn't."

"I actually meant you," I said. "I didn't mean me. What about when he climbed the persimmon tree and shook them all down before they were ready and as punishment you made him eat all the unripe fruit until he vomited? What about snapping him into his snowsuit and forcing him to play outside alone in a blizzard?"

"You call that a blizzard," my neighbor said.

"What about the nap tent? Knotting the zipper closed and letting him scream and cry sometimes for hours? Do you remember when he was too scared to hike with us in white fur coats along the ridge on a full moon and you made him do it anyway and he wet his pants? What about when you whipped him for insisting that everything was either a dog or a cat?"

Maple: cat. Elm: dog. Persimmon: dog. Dogwood: cat. Axe: dog. Hatchet: cat. Truck: dog. Creek: cat. Train: dog. Cat: cat. Squirrel: dog. Raccoon: dog. Spider: cat. It was a small thing, but it enraged my neighbor. Malingering, he called it. It was not honest, nor was it accurate. The one thing that stumped Duncan was a fox. To his father, he'd say that a fox was a dog. But to me he'd say a fox was a cat, because he knew I loved cats and he knew I loved foxes, although it's been so long since I've seen one that I think they might not live in our woods anymore, and Duncan doesn't live in our woods anymore either.

"The research shows it's not actually people's parents that make them who they are," my neighbor said. "It's other aspects of their environment."

"But what were the other aspects of Duncan's environment?" I asked. "You mean ash? Hickory? Oak?"

"His friends at school, for example," my neighbor said. "Dr. Rahim. You heard him, they used to get in trouble together, and we're only finding out about it now."

Dr. Rahim came back. He was looking at his phone. "I have some good news," he said.

"How much does it cost to amputate?" my neighbor asked.

"Duncan called," Dr. Rahim said.

"No, he didn't," I said.

"He texted me," Dr. Rahim said. "He said, *I hope you're taking good care of my folks. Let them know I'll pay for it. Don't let them try to stitch it themselves. Hahaha. But seriously.* I told him to contact billing, of course. I don't take care of all that. But I thought you'd want to know."

"He texted you?" I said.

"Yes," Dr. Rahim said.

"That's gratitude," my neighbor said. "Imagine that. The people who gave him life."

"He's paying your medical bill," I said.

"Money means nothing to me," my neighbor said.

"If you don't mind, I'm going to sew that up for you," Dr. Rahim said, taking his stool.

The nurse brought in a stainless steel tray. "From the cafeteria," she said, looking at me, but I was no longer in the mood.

Dr. Rahim readied the suture. The needle went in and out of my neighbor like he was a burlap sack filled with potatoes or sand. I could not believe such a bloodless man had blood beneath his cracked skin. He watched the suture, chewing on his filthy beard.

My neighbor and I never exchanged rings. Instead, I gave him the hatchet and he gave me the axe I swing to this day. It has some magic in it. I consider it the only other woman around because it's the only instrument that will do the work the way I want the work done. It's my only companion, now that Duncan is gone. When I gave Duncan the hatchet, he almost didn't take it.

It's Dad's prized possession, he said. How did you even get it from him?

I took it back, I said.

Does he know you have it? Duncan asked.

It belongs to you now, I said. But the hatchet did not make Duncan stay. He took it with him when he left.

My neighbor believes that blame, properly assigned, will bring our young neighbor home. What I wouldn't give to hold such a belief, or any belief at all. If I could rekindle my faith in causality, then what I would like is a map showing me how I got here. I would like a map directing me to Duncan. But no such map exists, or if it does, it's not a map I am meant to read. I stack wood for our young neighbor that is just the size for the woodstove in his lean-to. I keep his lean-to swept. I feed the cat, even though the cat is really Duncan's, even though no one can really own a cat. I wait. I'm punky on the inside, fungus-filled. I'm eaten away, barely standing. I'm dead, and I'm burning, burning all the time.

"You're going to have to stay off this hand for a bit," the doctor said. "Hope you weren't depending on it for anything." He chuckled.

"Just kindling," my neighbor said. "My wood's all in."

"That's right," Dr. Rahim said. "I remember Duncan used to talk about how his family heated with wood. I was always a little envious. To me it seemed quite adventurous. But didn't he say your house burned down? Or someone's house? Before he was born?"

"He was born," I said.

"I built that house," my neighbor said.

"Duncan was three when it happened," I said.

"Passive voice," my neighbor said.

"A hell of a thing to go through," Dr. Rahim said. To my neighbor he said, "Until the stitches come out, your wife's going to have to take care of your kindling."

"I'll split his kindling for him," I said. "But I'm not his wife."

My neighbor laughed.

"Forgive me," Dr. Rahim said.

"There's nothing to forgive," I said.

"Then I hope you won't mind me saying it's inspiring to see you two still have such a strong relationship, even after your divorce," Dr. Rahim said.

My neighbor and I stared at him. Divorce. What a powerful word.

Listen, we were like any other family. After the house burned, we took words apart and when we put them back together our relationship had changed. Our relationship to the word house. To the word together, to the word live, the word son, neighbor, family, to the word because, the word before, and the word after. Eventually we lived on opposite sides of the forest. We drew Duncan a map so he could travel between us. As soon as he could, he constructed a lean-to. Please, he said, consider me as you would any other neighbor.

"Maybe this is too much information," Dr. Rahim said. "But my wife and I are considering that right now. Conscious uncoupling." It was too much information. We were simple people. The words we had already didn't work and there was no indication that new ones with more syllables would work any better. "Please give Duncan my best," Dr. Rahim said, depositing his latex gloves and his suturing materials into the bio-hazard container.

I drove my neighbor and his rotten hand home. He wolfed a pill prescribed by Dr. Rahim. For once he didn't speak. What was there to say? It's hard to do what other people want you to do. It's hard to give someone your best. It's hard to give someone the best of what you have. It's hard to live with someone and also love them. I can do hard things. I can say things like, How was your day, which is effusive enough for some people. I can even say, When do you think this cold snap will end, or, Hey are we doing Christmas this year, or no just skip it, either way is fine with me. But words have power and mine were never powerful enough. Or they were too powerful. Either one is the death of a marriage.

Before the trees began, I steered the truck over the rise and dip of the railroad tracks, which made my neighbor curse. The striped gate was raised. The coal train was long gone. The animals hid in the dark of the forest, or they didn't.

When I gave him the hatchet, Duncan told me, You ignored what Dad did to me. You went along with it. Never once, he said. Never once did you stand up for me.

But just because you don't remember something doesn't mean that it never happened.

I do remember. Duncan was three. He was in the nap tent. He was meant to be napping. My husband had split and stacked two cords of wood. He'd told me which cord was seasoned and which cord was green. Burn the seasoned wood, he said. Let the green wood season, and I agreed. But in those days I had no relationship with the words cord, ash, hickory, oak, cherry, maple, let alone the word green or the word seasoned. To me those words were decoration, pleasant and folksy, with no real power. I must have been burning green wood all that winter, and into the spring.

That day, after my husband went out, I packed the stove. While the creosote built and bubbled in the chimney, I made a list:

Cat food
Lysol
Dish soap
Laundry
Propane
Diapers

I tried to remember what it took for me to get here and I wondered if I would ever leave.

I burned with curiosity.

After a while it became difficult to concentrate. I tried to stay curious, but my curiosity was interrupted by a noise.

It was a noise that had been there all along.

It was Duncan.

Duncan screaming in the nap tent.

Duncan growing claws.

Duncan clawing to get out.

Duncan speaking and speaking, speaking powerfully but without words.

That time, I heard.

I looked once more at my list. I opened the stove. I tossed my banal list inside and watched it burst.

Then I undid the nap tent knot and I gathered my red and sweating boy, my panicked boy, my soiled boy. He doesn't remember. He doesn't remember that I stripped him of his diaper, and I cleaned him, and I changed him, and I wrapped him up and snugged him to my back. He doesn't remember that we left. That we walked down the hill, out of the woods, that we came to the tracks and a train was passing. Dog, Duncan said. Dog. I watched a hopper car, a hopper car, a hopper car, then a boxcar. The train slowed so that we could walk alongside it. I climbed with Duncan into the boxcar and the boxcar picked up speed.

We were leaving, we were leaving, and with that wonder inside me, I watched our forest stay behind.

Cat, Duncan said, waving his hand, and there was a fox. The fox was trotting from the forest as if she had somewhere to go, but she stopped at the tracks. She waited for the train to pass, but the train lurched. Stopped. Started. Stopped again. The fox, waiting, spread her hind legs, put her ass down, and prepared to shit. Poo, Duncan cried, and the fox looked up and saw us. The fox saw us see her shitting. I saw her see us see her. She flattened her ears. The way she looked at us, angry, embarrassed, shocked, we knew it was wrong that we watched her deposit her black logs packed with feathers and bones, insects and fruit and seeds. High above her a column of black smoke plumed over the trees.

I may have no respect for anything, even the universe, but for twenty years I have wondered and wondered how one thing leads to another. I have wondered where my story begins. The fox is where I return. Everyone knows that if by some misfortune you see a dog shitting, you should hook your index fingers together or else there will be a consequence. Some say a wart will sprout. Some say it will be worse. But a fox is not a dog. A fox is not a cat. Should we have hooked our fingers? Duncan's fingers were too small, and mine were wrapped around my baby boy.

The fox shit and then she dashed up the bank into the woods. The trees stood still. The boxcar stood still. Away down the tracks, I could still see the striped gate, beyond it our path home. We hadn't made it very far. The train didn't move. The temperature dropped. The sun went down. The wind picked up. Duncan said to me, Hungry. The boxcar said to me, Are you actually leaving? Do you know where you're going? Do you know what you'll do once you get there? Do you even have a map? I smelled the smoke. I burned with curiosity. But curiosity is something quite apart from the desire to know.

All I want is for you to be happy, I whispered to Duncan as I carried him back up the hill, toward the smoke and the man who would be my neighbor. My boy slept against me heavy as a river rock. I told him to be happy, but what did that mean? Only that amid the terror of such attachment, words don't work. Now Duncan is out there somewhere, another happiness-pursuer, another person who may believe he deserves something, anything besides blame. For that and for nothing else I will apologize.

I parked the truck at the edge of the forest. I put the emergency brake on. I chocked the wheel. I helped my helpless neighbor out onto the forest floor. He used his good hand to switch on his headlamp and we wound through the trees we had marked with orange blazes to define a home.

My woman axe waited faithfully against the ash I had felled and bucked into mounds and wheelbarrowed to the chopping block so that the cat could piss on it, so that the urine could turn to crystals, which after long-term exposure can be mysteriously bad for your health. This is the type of causality you can watch. You can see it crystallizing. You may forget about it, but years later Dr. Rahim, or some other doctor who was a baby when your baby was a baby but who is now the one you trust your only body to, will look at you and break the bad news.

The cat slunk from the hut I built of particleboard and Tyvek near the burned-out foundation. Needily, she butted against my neighbor, who kicked her toward me. She put her rough tongue to my torn undergarment, curious.

My neighbor's beam caught the map in the ash.

"Spalting," he said.

"Spalting?"

"Those blue lines in the ash," he said. "Spalting. It's a process by which hard wood is eaten by fungi, requiring nitrogen, micronutrients, water, warmth, and air. It compromises the grain of the wood, but it's much sought-after by woodworkers, not for structure but for beauty."

"And for firewood," I said.

"You wouldn't catch me burning wood eaten up by fungus," he said.

"To me, it looks like a map," I said.

My neighbor bent closer, his thumb hovering upward. "You're right," he said. "It does look like a map."

What was I to do? And don't say be softened by the first words of affirmation he'd said to me in twenty years. Don't say invite him in.

What looked like a map was not a map. What looked like a map was spalting, which is a word like sparrow, like salt, like salary. Just a word that could be grown over and enveloped, repurposed and subsumed like all the others.

"Do you need help with your fire?" I asked.

"I'll manage," he said.

"Are you happy?" I asked. "I mean, living the way we do?"

"I'm not the happiness type," he said.

On that single affinity we had built a life.

ALLEGRA HYDE

Democracy in America

FROM *The Massachusetts Review*

> Where in the memory of man can one find anything comparable to what is taking place before our eyes in North America?
> —Alexis de Tocqueville

SHE WAS BEAUTIFUL, which made things difficult. The planes of her face cut to carry the light, liquid umber hair, pensive mouth, nimble body—she looked good even when shoplifting, sweatshirt-clad, her movements hunched. When I first saw her, stealing cashews from a convenience store in Massachusetts, my breath caught in my throat. I nearly missed my chance to follow her outside.

Honey was her name—or the name she gave me.

Her looks drew me to her, but they pained me as well. Soon she wouldn't be her. Anyone with eyes could have predicted this. Honey was beautiful and also broke. She was an ideal candidate for consignment.

Not that the future had ever stopped me from pursuing what I wanted in the present.

I had been in America less than a month—in Honey's weathered township mere days—but courtship isn't complicated. After a second casual crossing of paths, a clever remark, a half smile, I had her looking my way. And I knew how to hold a look. For my trip to America, I had packed light, but my two suits were impeccably tailored to my narrow chest, hips. A swagger lilted my walk. No one would call me beautiful, but they might use the word striking. Close-cropped hair, razor gaze; I possessed an androgynous cool that flipped hearts. And Americans went mad for accents.

Honey was no exception. After a round of drinks at the local tavern, then a twilit stroll, her hand found mine: fingers small and cold. I wanted to suck them warm, though I did not tell her that until later. And by then there were more complicated matters to discuss.

Honey's announcement arrived on a November afternoon. We had been seeing each other for several weeks by then; I had rented a room in town, and we had been meeting there mostly. We were resting in my narrow bed when she said: "So I talked to one of those recruiters who hang around the basketball courts—"

I pressed my eyes closed, braced for what I had known was coming.

"—and we actually had a great conversation," Honey went on, "about my future and my current financial situation. And, you know what? I think I'm going to consign."

From her tone, it was as if she had decided to dye her hair pink or get a tattoo.

"It just seems like the best choice for me. Especially right now, with how young I am and everything. It's a big opportunity. Plus, all my sisters have done it."

I kept my face impassive as she rationalized further: her oldest sister, Danika, had used her consignment payout to cover daycare for her toddler, which let her work full-time at the packing plant; Roxanne had used hers to buy a car, which allowed them both to get to the plant. And while she, Honey, didn't have a baby—and couldn't get hired due to her criminal record—maybe she would use the funds in other ways. She could start her own business. Or she could at least pay down her family's debt—her mother's MS wasn't getting any better, and the medical bills kept coming. Also their house needed a new roof.

I had once visited the family's house. A tired brick structure in a row of former mill homes, it leaned precariously over an eroded riverbed. Garish children's toys and dead lawn mowers lay scattered around an unkempt yard. The interior stank of chemically fake American cheese. The dereliction of the place had appalled me.

"What do you think, Alexis?"

I turned onto my back, my hands behind my head, pretending to ponder Honey's question. The rented room was above a local grocer and below us the register clanged with the afternoon rush, shrill with its clattering belly of coins, the swish of paper money, credit card beeps, as locals purchased pumpkin pie filling, mint ice cream, meat, for one of their culture's holidays. This was the kind of American town I had come to see, but it had not yet shown me what I wanted to know.

"My other idea," said Honey, "was that you and I could travel together. After consignment, I'll be able to pay my own way. More than anything, I've always wanted to see the world. I could even help you with your research."

She propped herself up on one elbow to gauge my reaction. The bedsheets fell away, exposing the smooth length of her torso. With a different woman, I might have guessed she had done this on purpose—to cow me—but from everything I had observed of Honey, she was guileless. Also: stubborn, striving, utterly provincial—a true citizen of her country—which did not change the fact that her body had a majesty of its own. Dark hair dripped around her shoulders. Her skin glowed. I ran a thumb along the ridgeline of her torso: down into the valley of her waist, then up the crest of her hip.

"Or do you only like me for my looks?" said Honey—emitting a loud, false laugh.

There was nothing to do except pretend her question offended me.

"Really, Honey?" I said. "You think I'm that shallow?"

She apologized immediately—relieved to be cast as the one in the wrong. I let her coax me back into her arms, our limbs entangling, the mood restored. Yet the ease of deception unsettled me. For all her rural coarseness, her petty criminality, Honey expected the world to be fundamentally fair and good; she expected me to be. And this expectation of hers moved me. It cut some ballast of detachment that had, until then, held me at a researcher's steady remove from the American experiment. I might have been worried—I should have been—but then, Honey's lips found my neck. Her fingers teased my thighs. And all worries faded against the landscape of her body, its infinite potential.

America had loomed in my imagination my whole life. Across the sea, yet ever present. An opposite and an endpoint. A fever dream and a nightmare—the force of its customs, values, ambitions, emanating outward. Consignment was a lever on America's slot machine of possibility. What if, it proposed, you could sell your youthful beauty? What if you could buy it back? Because in America, everything had a price. That liquidity pushed the nation down the river of equality—kept the country buoyant on its democratic raft—or so the story went.

I myself had grown up in one of Europe's obdurate second cities. You know the kind: with a decent cathedral, ruins a few tourists visit—though not with the vigor they might bring to a country's crowning metropolis. A city saved from tackiness by virtue of its elderly architecture and a stubborn commitment to constancy. A city with boulevards and outdoor café tables, small brutal espresso drinks; clothes shops selling cheap shirts, their prices in the windows. Dance music at night. Drunks. An old man on a bench, who has always been there. Schoolchildren in uniforms. Pigeons, papers fluttering. Cigarettes and crusty bread. Brisk winters. You know—I know, you know.

My family was well-off by many standards. They had afforded me the finest schools, access to the right circles, though most of our wealth was tied up in several crumbling properties too expensive to repair—a metaphor for most of Europe, really. My homeland longed to sit unchanged: comfortable in the ease of decay, drunk on its own history. Yet here was America, tugging on the reins of the new century, dragging the whole world with it. I wanted to know where she was taking us.

Officially, I had traveled to America on a government-sponsored fellowship, tasked with studying the nation's system of detention centers for undocumented immigrants. Europe was beset by its own refugee crisis; state officials were happy to have me research American methods—specifically, how America turned a profit on an outwardly intractable problem. I had been sent with a research partner, Beaumont—a longtime friend—but quarrels divided us early on. We had gone our separate ways in Boston. I cared little at the time. Detention centers were not my main interest. I wanted to understand America in its entirety; I had the idea that I would write a book.

Then I met Honey.

On the scheduled morning of Honey's consignment, she and I stood together in a strip mall parking lot, in a small city a half hour's driving distance from her hometown. Honey's father and a jumble of her sisters were there, too—a bleary smear of faces. We had arrived early. The sun was coming up, the parking lot nearly empty: endless asphalt except for a few enormous American cars. Spilled motor oil fumed around us and I inhaled willingly. There was a primal quality to what was happening, as if we were all standing before a volcano, a Delphic vent, a pit of lions, knowing something awesome—in the terrible, incredible sense—was about to happen.

Was it wrong that a part of me felt excited? Consignment was outlawed throughout most of Europe. One wasn't even supposed to talk about it: religious types got uncomfortable. Then, too, it was simply déclassé. Technically, consignment may have faced restrictions in a few U.S. states as well, though with the sitting president's deregulatory push, red tape had loosened across every sector.

Which is not to say that consignment was without stigma in America. For discretion, facilities were often embedded within other businesses. The site where Honey would receive the procedure was housed inside a travel agency—images of palm trees foresting the windows—the front innocuously positioned between a nail salon and a sporting goods store.

At ten minutes past the hour, the agent who would coordinate the financial aspect of the consignment had yet to arrive. Honey's father—a wan, poorly shaved man—scanned the parking lot. In his hands, he wrung a sweaty handkerchief. His face twisted, presumably as he calculated the family's potential loss of income.

I felt a dual pulse of disappointment and relief.

Honey seemed in a similar state: holding my hand tightly, her whole body vibrating. She had been impulsive, bawdy, the week prior. Appearing at my rented room at all hours, she demanded feverish sex, late-night visits to the local tavern; she binged on peppercorn cookies; she leaned out my second-floor window, catcalling men and laughing.

Her outbursts fascinated me—though they disturbed me as well. They were cries for help, no doubt: efforts to prompt me to admit that her beauty was what kept me close, that she ought not to go through with consignment. But while I was a flirt, a foreigner, I was no fool. To have made such a statement would have ended our liaison anyway, and I wanted to observe what would happen in the wake of the procedure. For all the discomfort that would come from seeing Honey transformed, the consignment process was uniquely American. My observations of Honey's experience could be included in my future book.

That our relationship would eventually end felt like a given—but that ending was far enough in the future so as to feel unburdensome. And when our ending did occur, I told myself, it would likely appear to be for reasons unlinked to her physical form. Honey and I might even part ways on good terms.

As we waited in the parking lot for the agent, however, my plan began to waver. Honey's manic stoicism had melted and her body pressed limply against mine. She thrust her hands into the pockets of my suit, as if looking for something. Reassurance? Commitment? My heart rattled, unmoored by apprehension. Meanwhile, her father and sisters stood to the side, muttering, shuffling—staring at us, then away. The family had never shown much affinity for me; we had barely said a dozen words to one another in the time I had known Honey. I do not know if this was because they were xenophobic, homophobic, or just rude.

Regardless, I tried not to look at them—especially the sisters, who were only a few years older than Honey, but who appeared many decades beyond that: their hair thin and white, skin mottled and creped, sagging.

I cannot claim expertise on the exact science behind consignment. From what I understand, the process was discovered by scientists working on a skin-grafting technology meant to serve chemically disfigured soldiers. Using AI surgeons, bioelectricity, a 3-D cartilage printer, and something called CRISPX, scientists transplanted the "multi-dermis" of cadavers onto soldiers of the same build. The precision of the resulting transfer was deemed "groundbreaking," "resurrectionary," and "blasphemous in the eyes of God."

The process was rapidly exploited by the private sector. Enterprising companies recognized that they could expand into one of the last frontiers of unmet consumer demand: youth at any age. All the Botox, plasma masks, and plastic surgery in the world could not truly replace what was lost to the passing of time—that is, until consignment. For the ultrawealthy who wanted it, a young, beautiful exterior could be purchased from a living youth, since "live consignment" turned out to be preferable to a procedure involving a cadaver. And for young people in financial straits—as many, like Honey, were—selling their external selves could grant them the start-up capital to transform their lives.

"She's here."

Honey's father pointed across the parking lot to where a blazer-clad woman was exiting a sedan, briefcase in hand. The agent had arrived.

To Honey, he said: "S'time."

Honey pulled her hands from my pockets but kept them in balled fists at her sides. The sun crested the strip mall roofline, illuminating the smooth planes of her face. My breath caught—as it had the first day we met—and I almost said to Honey: *No, no, don't throw it away, don't sell your beauty for anything, please, hold it tight, even as the months and years steal it anyway, and your youth slips from your grasp like water through fingers.*

And maybe I would have: the words right there, on the tip of my tongue, forged by a burgeoning tenderness. Because in the wash of that moment, it was Honey—beautiful, bighearted, sticky-fingered, naïve Honey—who felt most important. More important than any book I might write.

Yet how could I have explained myself? To advocate for her beauty was to admit the superficial dimension of my attraction. But to see her go through with the procedure—well, I discovered I might not be able to stand it. Though I had always planned on leaving Honey—our relationship a casualty of international travel—in that moment I realized just what, and who, I'd be giving up.

The anguish on my face prompted Honey to gather her own strength. She stroked my cheek, then said, with the confidence of any American: "It'll be fine, babe. The procedure is perfectly safe."

I wanted to laugh and to cry. Unable to do either, I felt compelled to give her something. With no preprepared gifts on my person, I slid off my watch—a weighty gold number from my grandfather—and held it out to her. Honey snatched the watch at once and put it on her wrist. Then she beamed at me, at her family, at the agent beckoning from across the lot. Everything was going as planned. We would see one another on the other side.

The day became more dreamlike from there. Standing in the parking lot with her family, I wondered: Should I have run after Honey? Was there time still to tell her to stop? Around us, the sound of traffic grew louder. The father muttered that I could wait with them in the nearby sporting goods store, which had TVs—it would be many hours before Honey's procedure was complete—but I could tell his invitation was not genuine.

The sisters huddled together, whispering. A breeze plucked at their white hair, the hemlines of their thin strappy dresses. Soon, Honey would resemble them. She would retain her same voice, eyes, organs, bones, and most muscle tissue, but she would otherwise appear as her sisters did—all of whom had sold their youthful looks to wealthy senior citizens. It gave me vertigo to picture this, a sensation worsened by the parking lot's motor oil fumes. My eyes began to water.

"Coffee," I said, nodding vaguely into the distance. "Will return later—"

The family said nothing as I hurried off, though I could feel their eyes on my back. The sun was higher now, spiking my vision, the city roads choked with morning commuters. America unfurled in every direction: honking and hectic. Fast-food restaurants exhaled grease. Billboards shouted their wares. Even the homeless pushed shopping carts here. I turned down one sidewalk and then another, concentrating on putting distance between myself and the strip mall parking lot. It seemed the only way I might steady my thoughts—decide what to do next. The farther I went, however, the more parking lots revealed themselves, often serving businesses identical to the ones I had left. To think I had believed America prided itself on originality and individualism; the nation was breathtakingly homogenous.

Near evening, I caught a rideshare back to my rented room above the grocer. My bed remained unmade, sheets frozen in the tumult of that morning. I felt awash in longing for Honey's embrace. It occurred to me that I might leave the bed untouched—in a kind of memorial—though as soon as this thought registered, the sentimentality appalled me. I needed to snap out of whatever trance I had fallen into. I needed to remember what I had come to America to do.

There was a text from Honey on my phone. I deleted the message without reading it. Then, before my mind changed, I blocked her number as well. A clean break was best for all involved, I decided; it might even be the more honorable tack. There was no reason to give Honey the hope that I would stay forever—after all, that had never been my plan. Also, despite the research benefits of observing Honey's procedure, consignment was but one aspect of American culture. There was so much about the country of which I still needed to learn.

*

My research partner, Beaumont, I found in Memphis, Tennessee. A bus, a plane, and a cab had returned me to him, the travel costs exhausting my remaining fellowship funds. Luckily, Beaumont had not been as careless with his. He also seemed to have forgotten about our prior quarrel in Boston, which had nearly ended in fisticuffs. When we reunited outside a sooty barbecue restaurant, he wrapped me in a thick-armed hug, slapped me on the back.

"You smell like a wet hound," he said, and pretended to fan the air. "Per usual."

Despite the troubling events of the recent past, I grinned. Beaumont and I had known one another since primary school and had grown up as an odd yet formidable pair: him bringing a rotund affability to most situations, while I contributed shrewdness and impeccable taste. This remained true even through our university years. And though tension occasionally rose between us—such as when I became briefly involved with his sister—we always sorted everything out.

We were a good team, Beaumont and I; he was, I suppose, my oldest friend.

The pair of us got right to work. We had three months remaining to research and write our fellowship report. And so, we rented a car. We made calls. We arranged tours of several of the largest immigrant detention centers, as well as the adjoining agricultural sites where detainees labored in exchange for special judicial consideration. We observed, among other things, the hand-pollination sweeps that had become essential since the extinction of bees in North America: detainees moving through orchards en masse, tickling blossoms into productivity. When Beaumont and I sat down to work on our report for the fellowship committee, we tried to communicate the surprising fact that desperation could be monetized. Detention centers were not mere stopgaps, but rather—as Americans deemed everything—opportunities.

The topic was a passion for neither of us, but it had gotten us overseas and closer to our personal ambitions. Like me, Beaumont had a career-making book in mind—his a "comedic novel of manners." He, too, was interested in interviewing Americans on topics beyond the scope of our fellowship. And so, in cafés and bodegas, mechanic shops and hair salons, we worked together to glean perspective and opinions from a variety of citizenry. More than once, our inquiries made us minor celebrities in some small town: we would eat dinners at the mayor's house, deliver short speeches in school auditoriums, even appear on the local news.

Hard work was a palate cleanser. I hardly ever thought of Honey.

This might have continued—Beaumont and I might have finished the project together, returned amicably to our homeland—had my former landlady not called, one afternoon, while Beaumont and I paused at a petrol station in South Dakota. Apparently, no one had rented the room above the grocery in the weeks since I had departed; my landlady, Ms. Pancelli, had just gotten around to cleaning the premises.

"You left a stack of guidebooks," she said. "Should I mail them somewhere?"

I told her no—irritated by the question. I had left a note saying the guidebooks could be donated to a local school. Also, I was in a rush: en route to Pierre for an interview with a U.S. senator who was among the president's inner coterie—"The New Frontiersmen," as they were known. The interview had the potential to accelerate my understanding of America's broader ethos and inevitabilities, but Beaumont and I still had an hour left of driving. Every minute ticked closer to the scheduled meeting time.

Phone to my ear, I paced around a graffiti-riddled picnic table. Beaumont leaned against our rental car, parked in the shade of an awning. He made a wrap-it-up motion.

I prided myself on my politeness, however. And Ms. Pancelli, I had always thought, possessed a touch of the old country. "Thank you for checking," I said. "Very kind of you. Yet, I must—"

"Wait a sec . . ."

A chill crawled up my spine; Ms. Pancelli inhaled the way a person does before addressing a sensitive subject.

To Beaumont, I held up a finger.

"I almost wasn't going to mention it," said Ms. Pancelli, "but I thought you should know that after you left, a woman came by. Knocking and knocking on your door. And when no one answered, well, she went back outside and climbed up the drainpipe to what was your window on the second floor."

An eighteen-wheeler roared past the petrol station, making the whole earth shudder. A buzzing line of motorcycles followed, impossibly loud. Beaumont mouthed: *Come on.*

"The woman looked—she looked elderly," said Ms. Pancelli, who was elderly herself, though not in the way we were discussing: elderly yet able to shimmy up a drainpipe to a second-floor window.

I needed to end the call—to shake the conversation off—but I could not help asking what I already knew.

"Was she wearing a watch?" I said. "A gold one, too large for her wrist?"

During the interview with the South Dakota senator, my concentration flagged. Beaumont did all the talking, which was no trouble for him. He loved to talk. Hamming it up in the company of American egotists was as much of a joy to him as mocking them in private. By the end of the meeting, Beaumont had the senator extending an invitation to his ranch. The pair shook hands, both red-faced from bourbon. I twiddled my pen in the corner.

As we exited the statehouse, Beaumont confronted me. "What is going on with you?" he said. "Did you even—"

He grabbed my notepad, surveyed the blank tablet.

His fleshy face clouded. The timing of the interview had cost us the chance to attend a professional basketball game, to which a prior contact had given us free tickets. This had disappointed Beaumont greatly. He agreed to do the interview only because I insisted it would help us write our prospective books. The senator, I'd told Beaumont, was a mouthpiece for a presidential ideology that would bring America into focus—and with it, the fate of Europe, the whole world. Wasn't it *interesting* that the president deemed himself an infrastructuralist and an "architect of opportunity" while also disenfranchising millions? That he had jump-started the U.S. economy with far-reaching deregulatory mandates, alongside massive investments in space exploration and deep-sea extraction?

With Beaumont, I glossed over the more nuanced aspects of the president's reigning rhetoric, though they fascinated me. For instance, when flash points arose around commercial development in America's national parks—Yellowstone, Denali, Joshua Tree—the president calmly offered critics one of his catchphrases: *All's fair in love, war, and business.* His supporters then celebrated his creation of thousands of jobs. Yet the president was most emphatically hailed as a visionary with respect to his promotion of "the frontier of the self." He advocated for self-empowerment in the literal sense. *See yourself as an untapped resource,* he told Americans.

Find your bootstraps and pull them. The idea was that any person, even those born into abject poverty, had a bounty of bodily resources at their disposal. Thus had the floodgates opened to legalized organ harvesting, a DNA market, penny stocks in small-time intellectual property, mind's-eye micro-cams, and, of course, consignment.

To the president's credit, America's GDP had soared—and at a juncture when the empire seemed doomed to fade the way most empires do, beleaguered by their own bigness. The American dream continued; no reason, yet, to wake up.

"You've got to get your head on straight," said Beaumont as we stood on the statehouse steps. "I don't know what's going on with you, but you can't fade away on me like that." I nodded, but my thoughts were with Honey—Honey as an old woman, climbing a drainpipe, looking for the lover who had promised consignment would change nothing.

A breeze rippled our suits, along with the row of regional and national flags positioned in front of the statehouse. A knot formed in my stomach—guilt twisting, tightening—and I reminded myself that Honey was an adult, capable of making her own choices. Was that not what America was all about: freedom of choice? This choice had been all hers.

Beaumont must have noticed the tension in my body because his face softened. I had told him a vague outline of my time with Honey when he and I reunited; perhaps he recognized that romantic troubles were the source of my agitation. He could certainly relate to distresses of the heart. In our youth, I had listened to him cry out his feelings over many a botched liaison. More clown than Don Juan, he was always falling for women out of his league. While this had never been my particular problem, and was not my problem at that moment, I suppose I should have appreciated Beaumont's perceptiveness—though of course, at that time, it only felt like an intrusion.

"You know what?" he said, slapping me on the back. "I think we've been going too hard for too long. All work and no play, right?"

Beaumont dragged me to a windowless discotheque on the outskirts of Pierre. In the forever twilight of the building's interior, laser lights speared the air. Everywhere: bare legs, false eyelashes, wigs, television screens. Cocktail waitresses distributed vials of noxious neon alcohol. Music ricocheted between the dance floor and bar. Already I was sweating. I tried to turn around and leave, but Beaumont pushed me forward.

"You need this," he said. "We need this."

I told Beaumont I would stay for an hour. At his behest, I downed a few of the neon beverages, as well as a handful of pale pink tablets that a waitress promised would take the edge off. ("And then the green ones add edges, if that's what you want.") From the bar, Beaumont purchased more drinks for a parade of spandex-clad dancers, some of whom fussed over our "adorable suits." One asked if we were Mormon. Another if our accents were Australian.

I glanced at my wrist to check the time—then remembered I no longer had a watch.

The knot in my stomach tightened. The drinks and the drugs had done little to aid my mood. The music crowed louder. Rainbow lights pulsed my eyes.

Beaumont leaned over from his bar stool. "Misty is going to request a song for us," he said—beaming at a twiggy woman in a bodysuit. When she left to find the DJ, he made a sad face at me. "Doing okay, old sport?"

The lights shifted to a stuttering silver blink. On the dance floor, everyone's face turned ghoulish, their eyes going hollow, bones pressing against skin, hair bleached white. I squinted, trying to see better—to see clearly—whether these dancers with their heels and bare midriffs, all grinding and leaping and drinking, were in fact young people in the bodies of the elderly. Had they been that way the whole time?

Then the light changed once more: softening to a mellow gold. Everyone again appeared young—or youngish. It had been a trick of the light, what I had seen. Beaumont sat beside me at the bar, tapping his foot, peering around for Misty.

And yet, it occurred to me that any of these people could be anyone else—at least externally—through consignment.

To Beaumont, I yelled over the music: "Do you ever wonder whether someone is truly who they seem to be? Or if they . . ."

"What?"

"Because of consignment," I said. "And—"

Misty was back. She took Beaumont's hand and led him into a fray of dancers. The pair bobbed and laughed; Beaumont's suit jacket rose like a cape when he twirled.

I got up from the bar intending to find the exit, then to get a ride to our hotel—but I could not find my way out. Dancers crowded every corner. The music blared too loud. The drinks and the drugs had muddled my navigational abilities, though I also would not have been surprised if the discotheque was intentionally designed to keep people inside.

Eventually, I found an unoccupied corridor. I wandered down it, relieved to put distance between myself and the music, the sweaty heat. No exit materialized, but an open doorway revealed the back room where workers took breaks. A bartender sipped water and sullenly watched a TV. On-screen, a news crew enthusiastically surveyed the latest presidential infrastructure initiative: One Big Lake.

The plan, evidently, was for all of America's Great Lakes to be bulldozed into one giant body of water.

"This new lake will be a symbol of unity," said a spokesperson as she posed beside a row of supporters and construction equipment on the shores of Lake Erie. "It will also create jobs. Most importantly, it will show that America is the greatest nation in the world—not just home to Great Lakes, but the Greatest Lake."

"Like we need to," muttered the bartender, in a tone I could not read.

On-screen, supporters chanted: *One big lake! One big lake! One big lake!*

The sheer nonsense of this country. I swallowed more of the pale pink pills I had acquired earlier, as well as a green one. Returning to the dance floor, I let the mass of bodies consume me: a democratic tide sweeping me in. Soon, Beaumont had his arm over my shoulders, his suit jacket long since peeled away. Misty twirled me. It felt as though someone had pressed a mute button on my brain; beneath the blinking lights, the writhing bodies were no one and everyone—everymans and everywomans and everypersons—sweaty and drunk and dumb and so damn powerful.

The dream goes like this: in America, anything is possible.

A sun-bright golf course spreads in undulating plains of viridescent lawn. A pair of twentysomethings in golf sweaters tip their caps. A third bends at the waist, club in hand, as he slowly, painstakingly, lines up his drive.

Farther on, beyond a row of swaying willows and a swan pond, sits a sprawling manor. *Cheshire Valley Luxury Retirement Village,* reads a sign. And in smaller letters: "*Because you earned it.*"

In the dream: if you work hard enough, paradise can be yours.

And, truly, inside the retirement village there are dozens of otter-sleek youths. Rosy-cheeked, dewy-lipped. Hair flipped and flopped. Hands smooth, necks smooth, legs smooth. They lounge by the pool; they gaze at themselves, at each other.

These youths: playing bridge. Shuffleboard. Napping. Knitting. Staying active.

A retirement home full of beauties, all dazzling right up until the end, dying like flames burning out. Because the end remains inevitable. Consignment is a purely cosmetic procedure; there are no known health benefits—except, perhaps, healthy self-regard: youth no longer wasted on the young.

I woke up gasping.

A bedside clock blinked red digits: 11:40 a.m. I was in a hotel room, though not my own. A body breathed next to me—long hair mobbing the pillow—but I did not bother to see who it was. I burst from the bed, scrambled to find my clothes. My mouth was cottony. My head zizzed. Half dressed, I lurched into the hotel hallway, holding my shoes.

Beaumont—recently showered and well coiffed—stood by the elevator door.

"Look who finally showed up," he said cheerily. "You smell like a—"

"I'm not in the mood, Beau," I said, stepping up beside him. "I just want to go back to the room."

The elevator door opened, but Beaumont blocked my path. He smiled as if this were a funny coincidence. "Excuse me," he said, "for showing you a good time."

I grunted, tried to circumvent him, but he stayed put.

"And for paying for all of your drinks—and pills—of which you enjoyed many."

"I never asked for you to—"

"Also for covering your tips. You seemed to have forgotten that particular American custom, despite all your 'research' on this nation's traditions."

That really touched a nerve. I glared at Beaumont, before replying in a cold voice: "I did not even want to go out."

Again, I attempted to push past him—and again he refused to move. His false smile fell away.

"That's the thing about you, Alexis. You take everything for granted. And you take whatever you want."

Beaumont's lower lip trembled. He always became like this—emotionally volatile, unfairly angry—when his own inadequacies reared into view. That was what had happened in Boston, when we first parted ways. A particularly charming MIT post-doc had scorned his try-hard jokes in favor of my casual bons mots. And while it would have been easy enough, there in front of the elevator, to stroke Beaumont's bruised ego—and get us back on track—I did not have the energy to do so.

"Can we discuss this another time?" I said.

Too late—Beaumont was staring over my shoulder, back at the hotel room I had exited. The door had opened and the person with whom I had spent the night poked out her head.

"Misty?" Beaumont said, his eyes widening.

Whether what came next was intentional or an uncontrolled spasm, I cannot say; what is certain is that Beaumont's open palm struck my face.

Beaumont and I parted ways again, this time for good. I suppose it was fortunate we had written enough of our fellowship report to turn in a sloppy draft, technically fulfilling the task we had set out to accomplish. The fellowship committee, however, did not send back its best regards or offer to fund an extended stay in America. Beaumont returned to Europe, but I could not bring myself to leave. I still had the idea that I might write a book—and that such a book had the capacity to launch my career as a preeminent cultural analyst by offering the world an unprecedented study of America, one that would serve global leaders and civilians alike.

But my understanding of the country had only grown murkier since I'd arrived. America made less sense by the day.

To further complicate matters, my nose was broken, and I had a complexion on which black eyes lingered. Interview subjects found this off-putting. Also, I had underestimated the research benefits of Beaumont's showy bonhomie. Always fake to me, he had clearly charmed Americans—compulsive smilers themselves.

Suffice it to say, I made little headway in my research efforts after Beaumont left.

Worse, my funds were gone. I suppose I could have called family members, begged, but that would have required pledging allegiance to one or another side in familial disputes that went back generations: messy business of which I wanted no part.

I had to find paid work. It was thus I joined America's sea of itinerant laborers, earning pay under the table as a dishwasher, ticket seller, sign holder, and marijuana harvester, among other roles. It occurred to me, in a cloud of dark humor, that with my state-sponsored visa expired, I could wind up in one of the detention centers I had come to America to study. For all of the nation's deregulatory initiatives—its promise of individual empowerment—the state could be punishingly restrictive.

I was no closer to making sense of what this meant. The ad hoc labor, meanwhile, made book-writing near impossible. Also, my new habit of taking the pale pink pills I had first imbibed at the club with Beaumont did little to aid my mental clarity.

The most significant impediment, however, was that I kept seeing Honey. Or more specifically: I kept seeing strangers and wondering if Honey's heart and brain and bone—Honey herself—was inside them. She could have been anyone by that point. Most likely she remained in the elderly body she had traded for start-up funds. But she might have made a little money, purchased herself a middle-aged body. Maybe she had somehow struck it rich: bought a young exterior—not her own, but someone who looked like her.

There was no way to know, though, unless she revealed herself.

All I could do was stare at strangers—on the bus, on street corners, in the dishrooms where I scraped plates clean—and imagine I was seeing Honey, that I might find a sense of peace if only I could explain to her the true contours of the situation.

Consignment was your choice to make—not mine.

You knew from the beginning that I was planning to move on for my research.

If anyone has suffered, it is me. Do you see the state I am in? How far I have been reduced? I was making excellent headway on my book; you threw me completely off course.

But these statements rang hollow even in my own imagination. I knew that if I ever encountered Honey again, I'd likely feel too overcome by shame to say much of anything at all. It was lucky I probably never would.

Except then—several months after Beaumont left—I did.

By that time, I had secured a job on an American cruise ship. The whole story is too long to tell in full, so let me say only that after a close call with U.S. immigration authorities, I signed on with the cruise line, taking advantage of a regulatory loophole for foreign workers at sea.

Pushing off from American shores, I hoped, would also grant me the perspective I needed to finally write my book.

My tasks on the ship were mundane and manifold but mostly involved cleaning. The captain held an ardent conviction in the purifying capacity of bleach. The work might have been called humiliating, chemically dangerous, but I was glad to be kept busy—even to be barked at by my supervisor—if only to distract my tormented mind.

The cruise ship's clientele was largely composed of the American nouveaux riches. Guests were wealthy enough to afford extended vacations, designer clothing, but not yet beyond the notion that enormous cruise ships offered a respectable form of leisure. They piled into their well-bleached cabins as families with matching luggage, or as couples pawing at one another, or as packs of friends—women mostly, bedecked in ruffled dresses, strappy sandals, sunglasses—who had gathered to impress and provoke one another.

The cruise line's selling point was that it took people to what was already gone. The marketing went like this: *What if a cruise could transport you to the most exclusive location imaginable: a place that cannot be reached by air, or car, or even other ships? A place that cannot be reached because it no longer exists?* To explain the conceit plainly: by using the latest holographic technology—and a suite of high-powered projectors—the cruise line re-created vanished locales. Thus, the ship seemed to sail past low-lying Caribbean islands—bird-covered, dolphin-splashed—that had been swallowed by rising seas. When the ship cut through the Panama Canal, the impression of a rain forest was projected on all sides. The truth of the canal—widened, industrialized, polluted—was obscured. *What's gone doesn't have to be! Live the Dream, the Myth, the Miracle!*

The cruise line was always making "Best of" lists.

It was near the end of a voyage that culminated with an illusional Alaskan ice floe that I saw Honey. I rarely worked front-of-house, but after a server dropped a tray of champagne glasses and toppled a flaming birthday cake, extra hands were needed for the cleanup efforts.

This particular incident had taken place in a guest lounge, lush with chandeliers that tinkled softly as the cruise ship made its slow heaves through the North Pacific. A group of young ladies lay sprawled on velvet divans, exhausted from doing nothing. They looked like Roman noblewomen, draped in silks and jewelry. A particularly wealthy set, this clutch of friends. All of them smooth-faced, shiny-haired, firm-bodied. A few watched the cleanup efforts with casual concern, though most ignored us workers, instead chatting together, laughing and bragging, throwing back more champagne. It was late and everyone was nearing intoxication; guests tended to drink more as the voyages wore on, and this was the final night.

I broomed a bit of birthday cake into a pan. When I looked up—to tell another worker we would need solvents for the frosting—I saw Honey.

She lounged amid the others, dressed like them in white silk and gold jewelry. She brought a vaporizer to her mouth, exhaled a plume of lavender smoke. Her hair had been teased high on her head, her eyes kohl-rimmed. Her face was sharper around the cheekbones, lips reddened, but I knew it was Honey. Not a hallucination—a speculation—but her in the flesh.

No, I reminded myself: this was Honey's flesh, but not Honey. The woman inside was not her.

And yet, not-Honey regarded me levelly.

I continued cleaning, but the broom shook in my hands. The other workers bustled around me. I glanced back at not-Honey: watching me as she lay stretched upon the divan. She took another long drag on her vaporizer.

The ship's bell sounded, alerting the guests to the nearness of our upcoming viewpoint—the last viewpoint, since the cruise would end tomorrow. There was a flurry of excitement. The other workers rushed to prepare the upper deck for passengers. Passengers rushed to their cabins to don warmer garments for the chilled air outside.

Only not-Honey remained unmoved.

She's probably tired, aching inside, I thought. Old bones.

She patted the ottoman beside her divan, maintaining eye contact all the while.

I went to her; in the rush of activity, no one seemed to notice. The ship swayed, chandeliers jingling like faraway laughter. I felt clumsy—oversized and gangly—as I sat down. I could not keep my eyes from her: this woman I had abandoned, looking radiant as she exhaled another lavender plume.

"Staring isn't polite," she said—in an unfamiliar voice, a voice that was not Honey's but deeper, gravelly with smoke and cynicism.

"Hard not to," I replied, because this was the truth.

A smirk crept over not-Honey's face. She must have intuited what I was thinking—that this exterior was the product of consignment—and she moved a hand to one of her breasts and squeezed it, as if to mock me.

"Worth every penny," she said.

I wanted to slap myself. I would get fired, cavorting with guests. And then what would I do? Return to my homeland empty-handed—a disgraced researcher? I would have nothing to show for my time in America except a half-formed book proposal and a ravaged conscience.

In my peripheral vision, bodies filtered in and out of the lounge, their voices a low murmur. Not-Honey exhaled more vapor and I sucked in a lungful—hoping it might numb my mind blank. Instead, a vast longing rose within me. The months since Beaumont had left had been lonely ones. I craved companionship—Honey's companionship, specifically. I missed her body, yes, but more than that I missed her grace and her gumption, even her small-time criminality. I missed the woman I'd chosen to leave.

Unable to resist, I reached out and took her hand.

"You certainly are forward," said not-Honey, though she did not withdraw. Rather, her eyes glittered; she was hideously beautiful.

My heart quailed. I glanced away—my gaze landing on the hand I had taken in my own: fingers ring-covered, elegant. I had heard that hands were the most difficult part of the consignment process to transfer. There was less fatty tissue to manipulate; scars could show up there afterward. But in the dim light of the lounge, I could see no scars. This woman must have had an advanced AI surgeon, been extra rich.

Or—a wild swell of hope hit me—this was Honey herself. The scenario was a long shot, and yet: might she be playing a game with me? Performing a lover's test? Why else would she be on this cruise ship, of all cruise ships, speaking with me now?

I studied her face again, my conviction mounting. A theory unspooled: perhaps Honey had been deemed unfit for consignment at the last minute. The operation's front—the travel agency—might have connected her with a wealthy widow who wanted travel companions: hence her presence on the cruise. And the elderly woman my landlady had seen climbing the drainpipe? That could have been one of Honey's sisters. Was it so impossible that Honey—loyal, generous Honey—could have given the watch to one of them?

I opened my mouth to reveal my understanding, but another bell sounded. The cruise ship had reached its final viewing point. From across the lounge, a voice called: "Are you coming? It's about to start."

My lost love withdrew her hand, pressed herself upright on the divan.

"Wait," I said. "Honey?"

She rose all the way to her feet, her silks draped around her, her gaze penetrating the dim distance of the lounge. More to herself than to me, she smiled softly—perhaps even a little sadly—and so I said her name once more, made the word a plea: *Honey*.

This time she answered, "Yes, darling?" and gestured for us to make our way to the ship's deck, as if this were where we had always been going, where we had always planned to be.

The cruise ship's deck was crowded with passengers. Everyone oohed at the projected visuals: the ice floe superimposed over iceless water, sculptural forms sparkling with the flickering colors of an artificial aurora borealis.

Honey leaned against me. She had asked that I carry her up the stairs to the ship's deck, saying she was tired—and I had been glad to do so, feeling heroic with her arms wrapped around my neck, her head on my shoulder, her body surprisingly light.

On the deck, my heart thrummed. I pulled Honey closer, even as—out of the corner of my eye—I saw my supervisor stalking the viewing platform.

I must have known, on some level, that I would soon be apprehended: an employee gone rogue. I had crossed a line I could not cross back. I would be fired and deported to my home country—if not immediately, then after a series of holding cells, paperwork, phone calls. Pleas. Fines. But this expulsion would turn out to be exactly what I needed, at least in one sense. Because by being made to leave America, I would finally grasp the truth of the country: America was a paradise no one could truly enter, a land of smoke and mirrors, a dream induced by the heady drugs of our greatest expectations. To wake from that dream is to see the brutal bed one has slept in—is to understand that the country has always been a figment of one's own mind.

This realization would allow me to write my book—the book I'd been striving to write during the whole of my journey—though the fact of the book's existence today brings me no joy. Even the book's ongoing success does little for me. In the years since departing America, I have found myself seated beside presidents, monarchs, celebrities, and CEOs—but I would give it all up to have Honey in my arms again. I would do anything for a few more minutes on that ship.

Honey pressed herself against me, while the ice floe glistened around us. Northern lights dazzled the skies. Belugas surged through crystal waters. A national song began to play, as was customary for the end of a voyage, but it seemed as if the song played for only us. Then fireworks broke open over the ocean like beguiling bombs. I leaned in and kissed Honey, warming her hands in my own. For that instant, paradise was ours: America the beautiful, from sea to shining sea.

TAISIA KITAISKAIA

Engelond

FROM *Virginia Quarterly Review*

THE ANTS ARRIVED on Marfa's first night at the ranch. They crawled into her bed in ceaseless organized columns. The creatures were harmless and died easily between her thumb and forefinger, but kept coming, and Marfa could not sleep. Around four in the morning, half awake, she realized why. They were all heading for the upper-left quadrant of her back, and she knew, with the certainty of dream logic, that this area was Engelond.

Not England—Engelond, of Chaucer's time. She heard her father's voice, reading the original Middle English out loud in his heavy Russian accent:

> And specially, from every shires ende
> Of Engelond, to Caunterbury they wende,
> The hooly blisful martir for to seke,
> That hem hath holpen whan that they were seeke.

Marfa's father had taught her to love Engelond. First through Agatha Christie, then through Chaucer. A wiry, philosophical engineer, her father loved the wickedness of Christie and the loopy rhythms of Middle English, a distortion of the language he'd learned late in life and thought very funny.

Pure, putrid Engelond, cows and dogs and foul undergarments. Milk slopping onto tables, infants crying. Wigs, sweaty lovers rutting in straw. Engelond!

The ants had smelled Engelond and marched, little crusaders in glinting armor.

Was this imagination? Lunacy? Marfa knew nothing of either.

Marfa was an ordinary person in her late thirties, indistinguishable from the other women at her government job. Marfa, too, ate organic frozen meals for lunch that were neither healthy nor tasty, and she, too, ambled silently home at the end of each day. Her looks were vague. Even her Russianness had faded; now that her parents were gone, she barely spoke the language. Texas had blurred the Russian right out of her.

"Marfa?" people repeated. "Like the town?"

And with these words, she became just another curly-haired person with a big face. Welcome home, the bodies of the Texans beamed, pushing their carts alongside her at the grocery store. But inwardly, minutely, she rebelled.

"My little bureaucrat," her father had often said, with his characteristic tenderness and total lack of delusions, when she went to visit her parents in Fairbanks, Alaska, a city so cold and far away that it might as well have been the mother country. "Yes, Marfunka, how well you would have done in the old Soviet offices."

Despite a history of famine, and grandparents sent to Siberian labor camps, and homes where people threw vases and knives and called women whores—despite all that might have warped them, Marfa's parents had managed to love their only child completely and almost perfectly.

Marfa had not made anything of her life, nor did she intend to. Avoiding the usual immigrant trap, Marfa had intuited that achievement was unnecessary to honor her parents' sacrifice. All they had wanted was for her to be alive, happy.

And she was happy, visiting them for Christmas each year, tucked under a blanket on the couch. Her father in his armchair. Watching British mysteries together as it snowed outside. Her father joked at the TV about the aristocracy, class division, the goofy detective. The two of them rapt, drinking tea.

"What you two like so much about these shows, I'll never know," Marfa's mother said from the kitchen, making golden pies and thick savory pancakes with green onions and sour cream.

Marfa liked the shows because her father did. She wasn't sure how she really felt about Tolstoy and Dostoyevsky; couldn't quite describe what she did for work; had no partners for her mother to idealize to Aunt Olga during expensive calls back home to Russia. It didn't matter—during these visits home, she was a happy baby on her parents' couch, swaddled with warm, crowding stars. She was love itself—the love of her parents. To make something of her life would be to twist this love into silly shapes, like making balloon animals from the sublimely mysterious matter of the cosmos.

The only problem was that when her parents died, so young and quick, one after another with their weak hearts and bodies malnourished in childhood, the love retreated with them. Now, her parents were dead stars, and Marfa was the light they gave off—visible for now, but doomed.

Grief transformed her from a happy baby into an irritable toddler. She had no other family in the States. Everyone else was in Russia, and she didn't even really know them. The war depleted any interest she might have had in going back. Her job became a kind of grim nursery, holding and feeding her for eight hours a day, a place to do simple, repetitive tasks, like go to the bathroom and wash her hands, have a snack, and punch at buttons.

Who would care for her now that her parents were gone? Once charmed by her outings with friends—picking at hummus plates, toying with gossip and advice—she was now aghast at what had always been true: nothing of importance was ever exchanged between them, and if one of them moved away, they would never see each other again.

She now understood her colleagues' occasional scowls, and scowled herself. She started saying things like "What a day" and "I need a vacation."

And she did need a vacation. She needed a vacation from her coworkers, walking to the coffee station with stiff joints, like plastic dinosaurs. She needed a vacation from her body, which hurt all the time now—a web of cells that could be caught in a fist and crushed.

Marfa's elbows glowed with restlessness, resentment. Her mouth twitched.

Dreaming of her vacation, she primarily pictured herself wearing her new robe, which she'd bought at Target for less than ten dollars, which in turn meant this bit of fleece was contributing both to underpaid labor and environmental disaster. But boy was it plush—and nice. She would wear it and relish how nice it felt, and that would be enough.

But where was she supposed to go?

She gave the fate of her vacation up to the night sky. Standing on her porch one evening, in the selfsame robe, she tossed the question into the air like a dingy rubber ball.

The ball bounced back, cleansed and transformed by the sky, with a streak of cosmic spit and dust. *Ranch,* it said. A cabin in a corner of a sprawling ranch. Rustic, but not too much. Nature, but a fence. Still Texas, still hot, but good AC.

The next morning, she found an Airbnb listing for a "special experience" on Painted Cattle Ranch. A one-bedroom cabin, a well-stocked fridge, a large TV with every streaming service, decorative touches Texan and elegant alike, and all the roaming she desired. A weeklong stay.

A man who introduced himself as "Jerry the butler" picked Marfa up at the Painted Cattle Ranch gate in an old Land Rover. Marfa had never heard of ranches having butlers, but then he drove her past the gaudy limestone mansion, fashioned after the look of a castle, where the owners lived. The size of it! It even had a little tower. Marfa imagined the inhabitants wandering down stone hallways and calling out each other's names to see who was there. Sitting before the fire on chairs footed with carved lion heads, reading gilt-edged tomes. Hosting lavish dinners in tuxes and off-the-shoulder gowns. Marfa had, in fact, brought her own gown, for the formal dinner at the end of her stay that was part of the package.

As they made their way along the dusty road, Marfa saw only one person on the property: a mustached man in a cowboy hat and denim, standing outside a humble home, surrounded by goats. The man set down his water pail to wave at Marfa and Jerry as they passed. A few goats turned to look and cocked their heads.

"That's Bob, the caretaker," said Jerry. "He manages the goats and the cows, and the land itself, really. He's been here thirty years."

There was a long silence as the Land Rover lurched over the gravel road.

"The Grandcourts have only just started hosting people at the ranch," Jerry said. "You're one of the guinea pigs." He winked. "They're a very private family," Jerry continued, "but they look forward to sharing the wonders of the property with folks."

Marfa, who knew the comforts of insularity, nodded. It was brave of the Grandcourts to open up their home.

Jerry drank from a tall can of beer as he drove. Old semicrushed Lone Stars rolled at his feet.

"Are you really a butler?" she asked, feeling a little naïve.

Jerry glanced sideways at Marfa as he drove. "The Grandcourts, they're an old English family. They like their fusty British ways." He chuckled.

Marfa clapped her hands together like a child, unable to help herself. "Oh, I love the British!"

Jerry said nothing, and Marfa blushed.

They passed cows who watched them. Some had long horns sharp enough to kill a person. The mythical longhorns, like a Texas football fever dream: here they were, in tense clumps.

Every few minutes, the Land Rover came to an abrupt, ugly halt and Jerry got out in his ratty velvet jacket and cowboy boots to open a cattle gate, pull forward, and then close the gate. He was balding, with a comb-over. His long body curved a little to the left, like he was trying to get away from something on his right side.

"You like swimming?" Jerry asked. "The river's by the big house. I can take you."

Marfa imagined Jerry standing at the lip of a dark midnight river, about to jump.

It took longer than she'd expected to get to the cabin. It was flung out on the sprawling property, the farthest structure from the main house and, it seemed, any human presence at all.

The cabin was a miniature version of the Grandcourts' home, a tiny manor playhouse built for a child and abandoned in a clearing of dead summer grass.

Inside, the cabin was clean and luxuriously stocked with puddings, delicacies, all of the things she liked plus a few creepy little salads. Heavy candlesticks on the fireplace mantel, like in murder mysteries. Rustic antiques. Elegant cracks in the walls from whence the ants would come.

After showing her around, Jerry paused on the porch and said, with his long back to Marfa: "There's something you should know. The Grandcourts make a lot of their money from overseas labor, very bad scene." Like my Target robe, Marfa thought. "They have mining interests too, precious stones, quite violent." Men underground, Marfa thought. "It's terrible, but in a way, I feel sorry for them."

Without saying goodbye, Jerry the butler walked to the Land Rover and drove away.

Nausea and fear passed through Marfa like wind through grass. Then the wind was gone and her body was still again. What an odd little man, she thought, and closed the door.

Marfa unpacked her clothes and arranged them in the bedroom's chest of drawers, which wafted hot, cedar-scented air. Texas heat was still trapped in this cabin in little pockets, but the AC kicked on with reassuring force.

When she got out of the blue-tiled shower, it was cold enough to put on her robe and stretch out on the cowhide couch with a glass of wine, her wet hair smelling overpoweringly of the Grandcourts' organic strawberry shampoo. The bottle of extraordinary vintage had a little cursive note: "Welcome, Ms. Gobrovnik."

Marfa felt sequined and dusted with gleam on her first night in the cabin. Like a mysterious, shiny fish under the stars, making a pizza with the fancy appliances of the kitchen, dancing to the radio loud, no one around to hear or see. Outside, the tips of the trees rose and rose.

And then she slept. The beautiful hair of the trees washed over the property. Engelond came with the ants.

The next day, Jerry stopped by with a little dog. "Compliments of the Grandcourts, just while you're here," he said. "If you might bring the dog back at the dinner, it would be most appreciated."

The dog was wet and trembling. Big bunny eyes. Marfa held the dog under her shirt to warm him.

"By the way," said Jerry, "have you seen Bob, the caretaker? The guy with the cowboy hat. Mustache."

"No," Marfa said. "I haven't seen anybody at all."

"It's just that we haven't heard from him since yesterday. The goats were out of food and water this morning."

Marfa imagined the goats hungry and thirsty in their pen.

"It's not like Bob to leave the ranch," Jerry said. "Let me know if he drives by or wanders through."

After Jerry left, and since the dog was too nervous to offer any comfort anyway, Marfa worked up the courage to ride the provided bicycle down the dusty road. She wheezed and burned in the sun until a wild hog, dark and enormous and with its golden-streaked babies in tow, leapt right in front of her bike. Marfa screamed.

What other surprises would the ranch offer?

As the hogs grunted off, Marfa imagined Bob the caretaker standing outside her kitchen window, bleeding. Behind him, the ranch enormous, heartless somehow.

Marfa returned to the cabin feeling both brave and terrified. The dog hadn't moved from its spot on the floor. Nobody was outside the kitchen window.

"I can do anything I want here," she scolded the little Chihuahua mix, chest heaving from fear and exercise.

"I can eat broccoli," she went on. "I can roll around in the yard like a barrel. I can say, 'fee-fi-fo-fum' out loud like a giant. I am in charge."

The dog looked up at her with terror and awe.

She petted the dog and felt better. Marfa liked that the creature was more afraid than she was.

The days and nights rocked back and forth like a crescent moon stuck in the dirt. Day to night, night to day. Coyotes howled, insects she had never seen before came down the chimney, and each morning she woke up with welts from some new bug bite. She ate fine foods and wore her robe.

Through it all, the ants remained very engaging. They spoke to her all night about buttons, how buttons undid things and did them again. The ants had placed a button on their faraway Engelond altar, which they spoke of constantly as they marched. "After we defend Engelond, we will add a new gold button to our altar," they muttered, curving around Marfa's shoulders and arms.

By her third night on the ranch, Marfa had become the Queene of the Ants. The ants would do anything she said. She ordered the ants to march to the cupboard on the bookshelf, to break down the cardboard in the recycling bin, even to make a formation of the Scottish flag on the wall. It was fun to tease these very British ants, then make it up to them with soothing words about their strength and gorgeous armor.

Lying in bed, she thought about her parents. Work had steamrolled her feelings, made them flat and dizzy as cartoons run over by trucks, reaching their little hands out wanly for help. But here, her feelings had time to grow plump and present, and her parents' deaths poured around and through her. She remembered summers at their house, eating smoked fish at the coffee table they'd never replaced with a real dining table, even long after they could afford to. A conversation rising and falling, cool air from the windows.

Marfa wept for her parents, whose lives had meaning and love, in whose love and meaning she had lived.

By the fourth day in the cabin, Marfa began to unravel, spending so much time alone, inside, with her feelings and the ants. She took the Grandcourts up on their offer to do ranch activities.

Jerry dutifully and wildly retrieved her in his Land Rover to ride a horse, pet a lonely goat. (Bob the caretaker had not returned.) Tie an inner tube to the river dock, because she was too frightened to swim.

"Say hi to Penelope if you see her," suggested Jerry as he lowered Marfa down into her inner tube. "She's the Grandcourts' daughter. Gone out on her canoe today."

Marfa floated on the river. Nothing happened: a vulture overhead, the sun on her skin. A cow, a reddish shape with scary horns, emerged on the other shore. Marfa considered how easy her life was compared to that of her Soviet ancestors, who must've had so few moments lying idly in the sun.

The cow stared at Marfa as it drank the greenish water.

After a while, Marfa saw Penelope drift into view in her canoe. Penelope's long orange hair trailed down her back. Marfa imagined little fish looking up at Penelope longingly through the water, wishing her hair closer so they could suck at the tips. Orange hair, blue-green river, black fish. Penelope looked quiet from afar, and a little tragic, like a trapped princess.

The clouds came in. Penelope pulled the canoe up to shore in a slosh.

The daughter of the Grandcourts rose from the canoe and sponged off her hair with a towel. She looked at Marfa.

"Have you seen the witch yet?" asked Penelope. Marfa thought she detected a slight accent. Continental, maybe.

"Excuse me?"

Penelope laughed. "Oh, I've always thought there was a witch somewhere on the property. Maybe not far from your cabin?" She squeezed the remaining water from the ends of her hair. Damp, the ends had darkened to a copper. "Or maybe not a witch. Some kind of roving spirit. Something that doesn't want us here."

The princess laughed again. "Sorry, I don't know what I'm talking about. I hope you are enjoying your stay."

Before Marfa could answer, Penelope headed back to the castle through the lawn, the towel around her shoulders.

*

On the fifth day, after an afternoon nap with the little dog rising and falling on her stomach, Marfa stumbled to the porch. A snake flopped across the doorstep. Lumpy with voles. A nice rattle at the tip of him.

"I ful see how you love the golde grasses, and wants to put the golden huskes in your satchel, and takes them awaye," said the snake.

So the snake spoke in Middle English! The ants would be pleased.

"Thou art greedie," the snake concluded, fat and unimpressed.

Marfa didn't know what to say, except, "Ye are moste welcoom in mye queendom, where I am Queene of the Ants."

The snake scoffed in a hissing way. "Thou arre alwaise lookyng at the thinges in this cabinne, and thinking how muchhe they coste."

It was true. Leather-backed chairs. Crockery. Wines. Everywhere she looked, Marfa saw the wealth of the ranchers.

"Thy obsecion with money disgustes me," said the snake, whose name was Alberto.

"You're right. Well, perhaps I'll just slip into the stone wall with you, Alberto," said Marfa. "Then we can be rich in mice together. And cozy too."

"You've dropped your accent," said Alberto, hurt. He slithered away.

Just when Marfa had begun to feel ill from the disappointed snake, her nights with the ants, the angry and uneasy feeling in the land, the trembling dog, the missing caretaker possibly covered in blood, Penelope's witch comment, Jerry's odd admission about the ranch and its brutal origins—she was rescued by an envelope, which Jerry slipped under her door, deliberately and without a word, like a postman, the Land Rover gone behind billows of dust.

The Grandcourts' dinner invitation was printed on an impossible cream card, of a weight and texture transcending Marfa's stationery vocabulary. Thicker and more elegant than cardstock, smoother than watercolor sheets, and possibly woven through with something other than paper, like silk.

Oh, she dreamed, tomorrow she would run the shower to steam her blue gown, and cover up her insect bites with makeup. She would look splendid on her last night at the Painted Cattle Ranch, feasting with the Grandcourts themselves.

The ants agreed. She would look wonderful in blue.

*

The ride in the Land Rover was bumpy as always, and the little dog trembled among the Lone Stars. Marfa worried about the grime getting on her dress, rogue pools of beer staining her satin shoes.

Jerry seemed a bit strained, frowning as he drove. Marfa was a little hurt that he hadn't said anything nice about her gown. He was uncharacteristically low on wry, friendly quips, just when she was feeling chatty and excitable.

When Jerry got out of the car to swing open the last cattle guard, his face bore a seriousness she hadn't seen before.

Marfa had a strange vision of Jerry in his cabin. In the vision, Jerry was looking at himself for a long time in his cabin mirror. Reflected behind him, a bare room with a few old paperbacks on the floor and a bedframe out of the Dust Bowl. Jerry slicking his hair back with more pomade. His eyes dry, everything about him dry except for his hair. His shoulders shaking as he put his face in his hands. He wanted to be in the river, but he felt an odd pull toward the fields. Whatever the force was, it did not have his best interests in mind. Marfa saw him stepping out of his cabin, pacing up and down the road, resisting, dirtying his boots.

But then Jerry, the real Jerry, got back into the Land Rover, drove into the main property, and hopped out again to close the final cattle guard. The clang of the metal broke the vision.

Marfa picked up the little dog for comfort, and told herself the vision was nothing, a meaningless blooming from her newly developed imaginative capacity, just a weird little gift from her sleepless nights with the ants.

Nine p.m. was deep blue from the moon and very warm. The moon blued everything. The castle had a special grandness to it in the nighttime. Marfa put the little dog down, and the dog ran off into the dark.

Inside, the castle was cool. Goosebumps arose on Marfa's arms. She had a sense that the ants would be rather interested in her goosebumps.

Jerry led her down curving walls to what felt like the innermost chamber, the dining room. Branches scraped darkly against the green-stained windows.

A big slab of malachite for a dining table. An iron light fixture hanging over the table, refracting spikes of light. Real candles. Two doors, painted a pale gold, one on either side of the fireplace. An oil painting of a slim and shadowy man, certainly Mr. Grandcourt, hung above the fireplace.

"How medieval," Marfa burst out, her voice loud in that cavernous space. Only then did she notice the family at the table, so still, almost marbleized, before their empty plates and full goblets. Mrs. Grandcourt, Penelope, and a young man who must've been the son of the house. No Mr. Grandcourt.

No one introduced themselves.

Marfa blushed. Her blushes always ran down her neck and into her chest, mottling her skin. Jerry showed Marfa where to sit—next to Mrs. Grandcourt—and then sat down next to Penelope. He poured Marfa some sherry and pulled out a Lone Star for himself from his velvet jacket.

"Ms. Gobrovnik," said Mrs. Grandcourt at last, raising her goblet to Marfa. "We're so delighted to have you here." Only then did she smile, and Marfa relaxed a little.

"How are you finding the cabin?" she asked. She had the same continental accent as her daughter and was dressed in various golds.

"It's wonderful," Marfa said. "Thank you so much for having me." She took a sip of her sherry. "I am a little surprised by all the animals."

The son, newt-like and nearly eyebrowless, looked down into his lap. Penelope moved her orange curls over to one shoulder, then the other.

"Ah, yes, it's very wild up there, I suppose. None of us has stayed out at the cabin, so we aren't too familiar with the environs."

"Well—there's a lot of ants," Marfa began, but realizing she couldn't go too far down that path, continued, "and I saw a snake." Thinking better of that too: "And, well, quite a few wild pigs. Just leaping across the road! I've never seen that before, even though I've been in Texas for years."

"You know what scares me?" Penelope said in a soft voice. "The cows."

The son tittered in his seat, then frowned and stared into his sherry.

"The cows, darling?" said Mrs. Grandcourt, amused.

"I'm with Penelope," said Jerry. He sipped his beer. "A couple months ago I was walking around on the ranch, must've been three A.M., and I got lost. Completely. Then I walked into this herd of cows, and they just stared at me. They looked like ghosts."

"Or witches," Penelope chimed in, glancing at Marfa.

"Or witches." Jerry nodded. The two of them seemed to have some kind of understanding. Marfa could tell that the Grandcourts loved Jerry, that he was perhaps their only tie to the outside world, and that in his rawness, his dustiness, he was real to them, and trustworthy.

"By the way, has Bob turned up yet?" Mrs. Grandcourt asked.

"No, not yet," said Jerry. "I drove around the property today, looking for him."

"This is worrisome." Mrs. Grandcourt swished her goblet elegantly. "If he's not back tomorrow, the authorities ought to be involved. And speaking of missing men, I wonder what is keeping John. First Bob, and now my husband!" She tapped her sapphire ring against the malachite table. Marfa wondered uneasily if the sapphire was related to those mining interests Jerry had mentioned. "Jerry, won't you go check on John? He was watching football in the den a few hours ago." She said the word *football* with distaste.

"Yup," said Jerry, and was gone on his long legs.

When Jerry left, no one spoke for some time. The son seemed to transform back into marble. Mrs. Grandcourt looked preoccupied, tapping her ring. Penelope wrapped a lovely scarf more tightly around her shoulders, and Marfa realized she and Penelope must be the same age—an aging princess.

With no one to talk to, Marfa turned her attention to the dishes. Most of the food was covered with bronze lids, so she satisfied herself with the heavy golden knife and fork, the decanters of wine, an uncovered dish of muttons (what were muttons, really?). A basket of rolls seemed available for the taking, however, and Marfa grabbed one, spreading the warm bread with butter and some kind of savory marmalade, a burgundy color.

Marfa caught a clearing of Mrs. Grandcourt's throat. She realized with shame that none of the others were eating, not even the rolls.

Of course, they were waiting for Mr. Grandcourt. How rude and provincial they must think her! Marfa put her roll back onto her plate, where it wobbled like an overturned bug.

Blushing and unsure of where to look, Marfa considered the room. Dark blue and pearly. The wood dark. Cowhide chairs. Poor cows, she thought. She considered that the cowhides might have been sourced from the cows at the ranch itself, and felt ill.

Marfa wished desperately for Jerry to return.

The son got up in his black suit. "Billiards, Mother," he said in a high voice. "I'm going to play billiards until Father returns."

The son walked through the gold door to the left of the fireplace.

"The men of this ranch—" Mrs. Grandcourt shook her head. For a moment she seemed like any other middle-aged woman irritated by her family. "Even Jerry," she said, "wanders off for hours at a time, diving into the river and such with his clothes on. I wonder if he has even gone after John. For all we know he's roaming the ranch."

Marfa remembered her vision of Jerry, pacing up and down the road, being called into the fields by some unknown power.

Penelope covered a yawn. The branches had stopped scraping against the windows, the night gone still. Coyotes howled and yipped outside.

Marfa was in despair. She had expected geese, ducks, pomegranates! And there they were, perhaps, on the covered dishes in front of her, but she could not eat them.

Penelope spoke Marfa's thoughts out loud: "I feel faint with hunger. I'm going to lie down."

Mrs. Grandcourt frowned as Penelope got up in her light-green satin gown and walked through the gold door to the right of the fireplace, the door her brother had not chosen.

Now it was just Marfa and Mrs. Grandcourt at the malachite table.

"I'm sorry," said Mrs. Grandcourt. "We had wanted to give our first guest a nice dinner, and everything is going wrong."

Mrs. Grandcourt said this with such sincerity that Marfa felt tears coming to her eyes. In a way, Marfa did feel that there was something to apologize for. Engelond, this Texas version of it anyway, had turned out to be a more frightening place than she had imagined. The rich blues and greens of the room turned in her stomach like a snake, like Alberto in an evil mood.

"Please," said Mrs. Grandcourt, "if you do not mind waiting a bit longer, I will go retrieve my husband and children, and we will finally have our meal. Excuse me." She stood up and went into the gold door on the left.

Marfa was completely alone in the dining room. She drank the rest of her sherry quickly, and, feeling warm and afraid, reached for one of the mutton legs (if that's what they really were) and bit down hard. The meat was delicious—lamb.

The coyotes outside had started up again. There was a rumbling from beyond the left door through which Mrs. Grandcourt and her son had disappeared.

The mysterious gold doors, the missing caretaker and patriarch and butler: this was a murder mystery, and Marfa wanted to be among the survivors. Marfa knew, quite sharply, that she must get out of the castle, out of the ranch. She must go home.

She walked quickly down the curving hallway, taking bites of mutton from one greasy hand as she went. At last, Marfa found the front door and started back on the road.

Her car was parked by the Grandcourts' castle—she could see it, her beat-up little sedan, under a large oak—but her keys were in the cabin. It would take over an hour to walk to the cabin and back, and the chances of running into a rattlesnake, one who could not speak Engelondish, were high.

Perhaps it was safer to get to the highway, try to flag someone down. But how foolish she would look in her blue gown in the middle of nowhere. Nothing to say for herself except that a man named Bob hadn't shown his face in a while and a family was late for dinner.

Coyotes yipped along the river.

She was going to do this properly. Walk bravely back to the cabin, get her keys, look out for rattlesnakes in the road. It would be all right.

She tripped on the gravel road in her chunky heels. Her gown was tighter than she would have liked. "You look like a blue sausage," her mother would have said, matter-of-factly. At eleven years old, Marfa had played the role of a birch tree in a skit put on by her Russian tutor, singing in a white dress. Everyone had said how delicate she looked. Now, she was sweating in a dusty blue gown, swinging the cattle guards open with savagery and fear.

Her Russian lessons with the tutor had taken place in a damp basement, a talcum powder smell. The tutor's black eyeliner was applied in two parallel lines, ignoring the curve of her eyelids. She had hair like a terrier, bobbed, and she was very strict. Marfa had often imagined running out of the basement into a secret garden. Angels opening the gate to let Marfa in. Nothing is required of you, the angels would sing, lowering their candles all around her. Drinking tea together, having sandwiches. All of them speaking Russian impeccably, even Marfa.

Maybe I'm recalling angels right now, thought Marfa, because I am going to die.

Every step was difficult. There were creatures in the bushes.

"You're almost at the cabin, Marfunka," she said aloud to herself. "There's the last cattle guard."

Just before Marfa could open the gate, a large reddish longhorn, much like the one she'd seen during her inner tube float on the river, crossed in front of the gate and blocked her way. The cow shook its head, horns six feet across. In their smooth length, sharpened at the ends, they looked like weapons carefully sculpted by the earliest peoples of this land.

Marfa backed slowly into the tall grass off the road, where rattlesnakes liked to hunt. The longhorn hoofed the ground, snorted, backing Marfa farther into the dark. A fog settled around them.

As the cow approached Marfa, ten or twelve other cows emerged from the fog. The cattle herded around Marfa in a moving circle, watching her.

She saw another large shape in the fog, far off, and realized it was the Land Rover. Jerry. Jerry had listened to the cows, the cows he was right to be afraid of, the cows that had called him into the field at last. Maybe the others were out there too: Bob the caretaker and Mr. Grandcourt and Mrs. Grandcourt and Penelope and the son.

Marfa squeezed her eyes shut. "Mamochka," she said, "Papochka." Praying to her parents.

She crouched and rolled up into a ball as the cows hooved and crowded around her. She could hear their horns clacking against one another's as they moved in some kind of ritualistic rhythm. Marfa opened her eyes for a moment to see them pounding the grass into a circle, a circle that was getting tighter and closer. It was a miracle that they were able to herd together without piercing each other with those horns. It was their control: they had total control over every movement. This was a dance they had done before.

Marfa closed her eyes again and made herself as small as she could. Maybe they would pity her insignificant body. She was a lowly government worker, composed of microwaved burrito bowls and grief. She wasn't like Bob the caretaker, torturing the cows for thirty years, or even Jerry, driving wildly and desperately around the property, knowing too much and unable to change things. She wasn't like the Grandcourts, hardening into sapphire and marble, taking and taking from the cows and this land and the lands across the sea.

The hot breath of the cows was upon her. They snorted over her head, their snorting and breathing was all she could hear.

As she wept, Marfa felt a muzzle on her, warm and velvety, moving the hair off her neck and tickling her nape. She felt more muzzles working her over.

Marfa's eyes closed in a new way, with frank and confused pleasure. Maybe the cows would decide to kill her. Maybe their muzzles and dry, rough noses would be replaced with horns soon. Indeed, the tip of a horn grazed her back as the cows drew closer. The sharp point didn't cut through her dress, but made an exploratory sound, like a scissor testing the cloth.

Then the cows quieted, touching her with their faces. Muzzles neither searching nor hungry, but curious, gentle even. A lover's touch, maybe. What a silly end, what a silly story this turned out to be. The Cows Who Loved and Killed Me. Touched by a Cow. The Deadly Love of Cows. No, all that was drivel. Marfa was no writer. Her only genius had been in the ants.

The ants! No, she wasn't a Grandcourt, and she wasn't a saint or a sage, but she remembered now. She was the Queene of the Ants. It wasn't much, and she could never explain it to another person as long as she lived, but her queenhood was something the cows might understand.

As soon as she thought it, the knowledge made a shield around her, a hardness like the ants' armor. The muzzles lifted from her body in a kind of jolt. The cows had their answer: indeed, this creature wasn't a Grandcourt. This Queene of the Ants had passed their test.

Marfa heard their grunts diminish. Their retreating hooves beat the ground into clouds of dust that coated her, filled her nostrils.

In the growing quiet that followed, Marfa raised her head, and for the first time since the cows had encircled her, she opened her eyes fully and looked around. The beasts had moved back into the far field. Their rumps looked homely as they retreated.

Soon the cows were gone altogether, and Marfa could see nothing but a field bristling with grasshoppers, and the desolate Land Rover in the distance.

Marfa was on the highway. She had made it to the cabin, grabbed her keys and wallet and phone. She had quickly changed her shoes, leaving her plush robe and everything else behind, and run all the way back to her car, not daring to look anywhere but straight ahead.

Before she had pulled out of the Grandcourts' driveway, she thought she had seen Penelope on the dark river in her canoe. Trailing her hand in the water and singing. Maybe Penelope had been in cahoots with the witch-cows.

"Yes, the cows are the murderers in this mystery," Marfa said out loud in the car. "If Jerry and Bob and the Grandcourts are found dead tomorrow, I trust the cows have their reasons." It was like one of those Agatha Christie endings where you kind of saw where the killer was coming from.

She drove as into a long dark tunnel, at the end of which was her house.

Marfa had never been so happy to see her small, neat house. She stood in the living room with all the lights on, crying, her gown tattered and covered in dust.

She visited all of it, all that was hers. The round dining table with its two chairs, only one of which was ever used; the refrigerator with the salsa jars, yogurts, and wilting spinach in a tub. The lamp with its cozy yellow light in her bedroom, the dresser with the birch box of pins and cheap necklaces from the grandmother she had never met. A brush wrapped in years of blondish hairs. Her bedside table, with the framed photograph of her parents, each with an arm around Marfa. Marfa beaming between them with her big simple face.

She got into bed still wearing the blue gown, turned off the yellow lamp, and sighed under the covers. The moon, which had seen everything, continued to watch her. A few crickets outside, a car starting. It was now perhaps one in the morning.

"The cows have had their revenge," Marfa said out loud into her dark room. "The cows, the witches, have had their revenge on the ranchers for what they've done to the lands and the creatures. The witch-cows have done it. Papa, I have solved the mystery." Her father would be proud.

Soon she felt the ants. They had come all the way from the ranch, or maybe these were local ants. It didn't matter; the ants all had the same purpose.

Marfa lay there in the dark with the ants upon her, knowing herself to be the Queene of the Ants, her insides taking shape where they had been formless. The stars of her father and mother shone into her body. Residing in such a quickening space, the stars were not yet dead.

Our Queene, we are yours forever, the ants assured her, covering her shoulders and upper back with kisses. Our purpose lives on in thine own flesh.

JHUMPA LAHIRI

P's Parties

FROM *The New Yorker*

I SHOULD NOTE straightaway that P's parties took place every year at her house, on a Saturday or Sunday afternoon, during the mild winters we typically enjoy in this city.

Unlike the slog of other winter holidays spent with family, always arduous, P's birthday, at the beginning of the New Year, was an unpredictable gathering, languorous and light. I looked forward to the commotion of the crowded house, the pots of water on the verge of boiling, the smartly dressed wives always ready to lend a hand in the kitchen. I waited for the first few glasses of prosecco before lunch to go to my head, sampled the various appetizers. Then I liked to join the other adults out on the patio for a little fresh air, to smoke a cigarette, and comment on the soccer game the kids played without interruption in the yard.

The atmosphere at P's party was warm but impersonal, owing to the number of people invited, who knew one another either too well or not at all. You'd encounter two distinct groups, like two opposing currents that crisscross in the ocean, forming a perfectly symmetrical shape, only to cancel each other out a moment later. On one side, there were those like me and my wife, old friends of P and her husband who came every year, and on the other, our counterparts: foreigners who'd show up for a few years, or sometimes just once.

They came from different countries, for work or for love, for a change of scenery, or for some other mysterious reason. They were a nomadic population that piqued my interest—prototypes, perhaps, for one of my future stories, the kind of people I'd have the chance to meet and casually observe only at P's house. In no time at all they'd manage to visit nearly all parts of our country, tackling the smaller towns on the weekends, skiing our mountains in February, and swimming in our crystalline seas in July. They'd pick up a decent smattering of our language, adapt to the food, forgive the daily chaos. Overnight, they'd become minor experts in the historical events we'd memorized as kids and had all but forgotten—which emperor succeeded which, what they accomplished. They had a strategic relationship with this city without ever fully being a part of it, knowing that sooner or later their trip would end and one day they'd be gone.

They were so different from the group I belonged to: those of us born and raised in Rome, who bemoaned the city's alarming decline but could never leave it behind. The type of people for whom just moving to a new neighborhood in their thirties—going to a new pharmacy, buying the newspaper from a different newsstand, finding a table at a different coffee bar—was the equivalent of departure, displacement, complete rupture.

P was an old friend of my wife's. They'd known each other for many years before we started dating, having grown up on the same block lined with grand palazzi. As kids they played together until dark; they went to the same elementary school and then the same challenging high school; they wandered off to buy contraband cigarettes from a shady guy behind a piazza that was quiet in those days. They went to the same university and, after graduating, rented a fifth-floor apartment in the thick of the city center. In the summers they traveled together to other countries—experiences they still loved to talk about. Then matters of the heart intervened: my wife met me at a New Year's Eve party, while P married a staid but friendly lawyer, a man of average height, good-looking but slightly cross-eyed, and became a mother of four—three boys in quick succession, and then, like a simple but welcome dessert after a three-course meal, a girl.

Not long before the girl was born, P had a brush with death. A renowned doctor, always among those invited to the party, ended up saving her life with a tricky surgery. From then on, this yearly gathering became a constant: this sunny afternoon around her birthday, this merry, lavish lunch that brought together a wide range of people. P liked to fill the house and churn her friends together—

relatives, neighbors, parents of her children's classmates. She liked to throw open the door at least fifty times, offering something to eat, playing host, exchanging a few words with everyone.

It was thanks to my wife, then, that I went to that house once a year, a somewhat secluded house on the city's outskirts. To get there, you took a curved, picturesque road, lined with cypresses and tumbling ivy. A road that swept you away, an urban road that ferried you toward the sea and put the frenzied city far behind. At a certain point there was a sharp right turn; you had to keep an eye out, it was easy to miss. After that it became a sort of residential labyrinth, with narrow, shaded, unpaved streets. You couldn't see the houses, just tall gates and the house numbers etched in stone.

P's house, where she lived with her children, her husband, and their two dogs, was at one end of this labyrinth. A spacious home, recently constructed, airy, with large, open rooms and plenty of space for a hundred-plus people to move about. At first glance—the house sat on a vast lawn, with no other structure in sight—it resembled a big, white, square-shaped rock jutting out of a green sea. In the distance you could glimpse the faint outline of the city where my wife and I and nearly all the other guests lived. It had a certain effect on me, coming to that house from our pleasant but compact apartment, where every book, every spoon, every shirt had its proper place, where I knew every shelf and hinge, and seating ten at the dinner table was a squeeze. An apartment whose windows looked out only onto other apartments, other windows, other lives like ours.

My memories of the past five or so parties had blurred together. Each year was different, and each year, for the most part, was the same. I made the same small talk I'd forget a minute later, I practiced my two rusty but still passable foreign languages, which I'd always brush up on a bit. I indulged, perhaps a little too much, in the same delicacies arrayed on the buffet table, circling back for more, with no regard for the extra kilos I'd put on and fret over after all those holiday meals. I said hello to friends and kissed the cheeks of women in their forties and fifties who staunchly refused to turn into *signore.* I absorbed the scent of their expensive perfumes, made brief contact with the warm skin of their shoulders, admired the elegant, form-fitting dresses they could still get away with at their age, at our age. At P's parties I felt embraced, cared for, and at the same time blissfully ignored, free. We were detached from our flawed, finely tuned lives, from our frustrations. I could sense time lengthening and the suspension, at least for a few hours, of all responsibility.

I wouldn't have been able to distinguish one party from the next, the incidents, the particulars, until one year when something out of the ordinary occurred, an ultimately banal disruption that remains a caesura in my life.

That year, I remember everything very precisely. I remember, for example, that there was more traffic than usual, which meant that we got there an hour late. It didn't matter; at P's it was always buffet style. I remember that my wife was telling me a story, talking ceaselessly as I drove, and that I was tuning her out. In fact, her slightly hoarse voice and her tendency to be long-winded were getting on my nerves. She managed an art gallery. I'd have preferred to drive that scenic stretch of road in silence, but she went on about clients and promising young painters. Before getting out of the car, she changed her shoes, trading her comfortable flats for a fancier pair with heels, partly to gain an extra inch or two and become just a touch taller than me.

Because P always invited all her children's friends, the first thing we saw, walking up to the house, was a swarm of younger and older kids playing out in the yard, in the sun. Their coats were strewn on the grass, like towels left on the beach while everyone goes for a swim. The grade schoolers and teenagers ran around in good spirits, sweating, and P's pair of dogs were barking and chasing after them.

I thought of our own boy with a pang of nostalgia, the one child my wife and I had brought into this world. Just the other day he'd have come with us, and he, too, would have played in the yard without his coat. But now he was a grown man, a college graduate, a few months into his new life abroad, pursuing further studies at a foreign university.

My wife didn't mourn his absence—if anything, she was eager for him to become more and more independent. According to her, the fact that he was getting by on his own for the most part, and now had a woman in his life, and was far from us, was a much deserved and happy ending to our long and exhausting road as parents. It meant that we'd done a good job, and this was a milestone worth celebrating. I found her lack of worry astonishing: she who'd hovered over our son his whole life, who'd taken such exacting care of his every meal, every soccer game, every test, every report card. But then I realized that she was always looking ahead, very rarely behind, which was why she now had her sights on his career, his love life, his future children—in short, his complete separation from us. While, for me, not seeing him every day, not hearing his voice around the house, or even his mediocre violin playing, not knowing what he was up to, not adding his favorite juice to the grocery cart—it all came as a blow. I was proud of him, yes, I was excited about his prospects, but I still had a hole in my heart.

We rang the bell even though the door was ajar. We kissed cheeks with P and her husband, who were there to greet us at the entrance as always. P was in fine form, radiant, wearing a printed dress from the seventies that had belonged to her mother, with a leather belt to accentuate her waist. We'd come bearing a few gifts: a scented candle, body cream, a new novel that everyone was talking about. After we chatted a minute, the doorbell rang again, and we were ushered down the hall. We took off our coats and threw them on the couch, atop an already precarious, promiscuous mound of fabric. It was warm in the house, but my wife, who is sensitive to cold and was wearing a sleeveless dress, decided to keep her pearl-gray wool shawl around her shoulders.

We found our way to the bar and picked up two glasses of prosecco. We made a toast, locking eyes for a moment. Then, with no hard feelings, for the rest of the afternoon my wife and I moved through the party in separate circles, paying each other no mind.

I began wandering about the house as if it were a favorite haunt, a place I knew fairly well but always partially, encountering one friend after another. It was only in this house, at this party, that we—mired in our responsibilities, in the personal and professional obligations that devour us, that define us—found the calm and the time to catch up. We ate, shared our news, chatted aimlessly.

All the while I was paying close attention to that other group: my potential fictional characters, the foreigners with whom I'd exchange just a few words, or more glances than words, really. I was intrigued by their point of view. They fascinated me precisely because, even though we were crammed into the same house, celebrating the same mutual friend, partaking in the same collective ritual, we remained two species, distinct and unmistakable. Eventually they'd drift off into their relaxed and secluded conversations, and we into ours. They seemed proud of their decision to uproot their lives, to acquire, in middle age, new points of reference. They evoked a world beyond my horizons, the risky steps I'd never taken: a world that had perhaps snatched my son away for good.

After making the rounds inside, I went out onto the patio. I stole a cigarette, one of the few I allow myself on occasion when unwinding away from home, and I joined the others watching the mix of younger and older kids still playing soccer, making a racket in the yard. The trees scattered around the lawn were turning gold in the light. At first, we were all men. Then P joined our conversation for a minute, to make sure we had everything we needed, something to drink, something to eat. She treated each of us like a lifelong friend, even though she hardly knew most of her guests.

"You've got a fantastic lawn. It would be nice to put a pool back here," one of the men said to her.

"It's not worth it. Every summer we spend two months at the sea," P replied.

"Oh, where?"

"A tiny island, rather remote, still quite primitive. You have to take a boat to buy groceries."

"You don't mind?"

"Not at all. It's the inconvenience I crave. I've been going there since I was a little girl."

"How wonderful."

"In August the entire island smells of rosemary. There's a small lighthouse, a pool in the middle, the sea all around, and that's about it," P said.

I'd never been to that island, but I'd heard about it from my wife, who used to go there for a week or so every summer as a guest of P's family. Then one year—my wife told me—a man, a great swimmer who did twenty laps in the pool twice a day, died right there in the water, while racing a friend, struck by a heart attack in front of all those young kids and the teenagers, including his own children. My wife, traumatized by the scene, never wanted to go back. And even though we did travel with P and her family from time to time, spending a weekend together in the countryside, we'd never gone to visit them on that island.

"And I don't really like swimming in pools," P added, as if she'd been listening to my thoughts.

"Why not?"

"There's no life in that water."

We talked about other seas, other islands, the pleasures of boating versus going to the beach: the frivolous patter of people with money. But as we spoke we became aware that a strange calm had descended over the yard. The children weren't yelling anymore. Something had happened.

We went down to see. A group of kids, a dozen or so, stood frozen in the distance. In the middle of their circle, someone was lying on the ground.

As we inched closer, we saw a handsome young boy, twelve or so, his hair disheveled, legs splayed—it didn't look good. Had he fainted? Or had something worse happened? We had no information. Then the doctor arrived, the one who'd saved P's life years before. A tall, lanky man with black hair grazing his shoulders, a dangling mustache, a steady, good-natured demeanor.

Next to the boy was a pale-faced woman. The mother, I assumed. I hadn't noticed her before—we hadn't crossed paths, despite having just spent at least an hour in the same crowded house, in the same rooms, circling the same table, eating the same food.

She was a foreigner, you could tell right away by her facial features. She was wearing a summery dress unsuited to the season; a heavy and complicated necklace adorned a triangle of bare skin. She wore very little makeup—with the exception of wine-colored nail polish—and had a kind of prematurely weathered beauty. Her dark hair was tied up in a bun at her nape. She must have been around ten years younger than my wife, with a sharper gaze and, I felt, a more turbulent inner life.

"What happened?" the doctor asked her.

"I have no idea. I was inside while he was playing. Then one of his friends came and told me he wasn't feeling well. By the time I got here he was trembling—he seemed shaken and disoriented."

The woman spoke in a strange mix of her language and ours, but it was easy enough to follow.

"And then?"

"He said his head was spinning, and that he couldn't hear anything for a few seconds, that everything went silent."

"Give us a little space, please," the doctor said.

The crowd backed off. Only the boy and his mother remained, with the doctor and P. I took a few steps back myself, but then I froze, paralyzed by the thought that the same thing could just as easily happen to my son—why not?—playing soccer in the park on a Sunday, with no parent at his side.

No one spoke for a minute or two. The doctor examined the boy, lifted his feet, felt his forehead, his wrist. After a little while, the boy sat up on his own and had a sip of water.

"It's not too serious, *signora,*" the doctor explained.

"But why? He's always been an active boy, nothing like this has ever happened."

"Your son suffered a mild shock. Perhaps he didn't eat enough lunch. Kids are always running around non-stop without thinking. This kind of thing can happen sometimes when we get overexcited. Did your son have breakfast this morning?"

"Yes."

"Is he an anxious boy?"

I got the impression that she didn't understand the question. In any case, she didn't respond. Her son was back on his feet now, a little embarrassed, insisting he was fine. His speech was normal. He had braces. He'd accepted a sandwich from someone and was eating.

"Can I keep playing?" he asked the doctor. Unlike his mother, he spoke our language perfectly well, and even had a touch of our city's accent.

"Of course you can. Just take it easy."

And that was that. The party went on. We went back inside, they brought out the cake, we sang "Happy Birthday," raised our glasses to P. Her kids gave her a stiff gold bracelet. Then there was a real surprise: her husband stood on a chair and sang a short, sweet love song out of tune, while P, overwhelmed, in tears, burst out laughing, then gave her husband a long kiss, eyes closed, in front of everyone.

The crowd inside the house began to thin, guests were starting to leave. I rejoined my wife, who told me that she, too, was ready to head home. We said our goodbyes to P and her husband, thanked them for the pleasant afternoon, and returned to our car, where we waited for the long line ahead of us to budge.

"It's late. Did you have fun?" my wife asked me.

"I had a pretty good time. How about you?"

"Did you drink?"

"Not much."

She looked me up and down.

"Let me drive."

I was tired and handed her the keys without protest. We switched places. She adjusted the seat, the mirror. She put on her seat belt, the comfortable shoes she liked to drive in. She was just about to start the car when she realized that she'd left her shawl in the house.

"I don't feel like getting out. Will you go?"

"Any idea where it is?"

"Check on the patio—I think I draped it over the back of a chair."

The house was empty, silent, filled with abandoned glasses and soiled, crumpled paper napkins. P and her family must have retired to one room or another. My wife was right, the shawl was there, hanging limp as a fresh sheet of pasta over the back of a patio chair, not far from where I'd listened to P rave about her island, before the boy felt sick.

The boy's mother was standing in front of me—facing away, but I recognized her immediately, her hair in a bun, her taut neck. She was alone, staring at the yard, where a handful of kids, including her son, were still out playing. She was smoking a cigarette. When she turned to see who was there, she, too, seemed to recognize me right away. From the blanched look on her face, I could tell she was still distraught.

"What exactly does 'a mild shock' even mean?" she asked me at once.

"A state of confusion, perhaps. A moment of psychosomatic distress."

"I thought he was going to die. In the middle of a party, at this house filled with people I barely know."

"Don't worry, it's over now, I heard what the doctor said." I addressed her with the formal pronoun.

"I used to be such a centered person. I knew how to run my life. But these days, in this country, I can hardly manage a thing."

"How did you end up here?"

"My husband is a journalist. He likes Rome. He says he loves this city more than he loves me."

"And you, how do you like it?"

"I'm not happy and I'm not unhappy. Mind if we use the *tu*?"

"Of course."

"Why did you stay with my son and me the whole time?"

"What do you mean?"

"On the grass. You didn't walk away with the others."

"I was worried, like you. That's all."

"Do you also have a son?"

"Yes. He lives abroad."

"So you'll understand."

"Understand what?"

"Today I brushed up against the worst thing that could possibly happen."

For the next few days, I was left reeling from that abrupt exchange of words. Who was that woman? Why had she been so open with me, so unguarded, instantly bridging the solitary distance between two strangers? Why had she revealed to me, out of the blue, that she was in crisis? What was her name? When and how had she met P? Where was this husband she'd spoken of, who loved Rome more than he loved her?

One evening, after some hesitation, I asked my wife, "Did you meet anyone interesting at P's this year?"

"Not really. Sometimes I have no patience for meeting new people."

"There were so many foreigners, more every year."

"They must be the parents of her kids' friends, who go to the same international school."

"A good school?"

"Expensive, and a little overrated if you ask me. I trust our school system."

Then she told me about a friend of ours—he, too, a regular at P's yearly party—who was thinking of quitting his job as the dean of a small suburban university to open a wine store in a foreign capital.

It would have been inappropriate to turn to P for any information. My wife was probably right, the woman who'd spoken to me was most likely the mother of one of P's kids' classmates. The more I thought about our conversation on the patio, the more I was struck by our strange synchronicity in that moment, as if she were expecting me, as if she knew, beforehand, that my wife would have forgotten her shawl, and that she'd send me back to the house to retrieve it. In the end, it was the only conversation of any real substance I'd had at the party. We'd looked each other in the eye, we'd been alone, our bodies close, but I'd never even introduced myself. I'd grabbed my wife's shawl, mumbled something awkward, and then I'd slipped away.

Over time, the memory began to dim. I went on living with my wife, in the house where we'd raised our son. I made love to her still slender body, I invited the same friends over for dinner, cooked the same reliable recipes. While my wife went to the gallery or away on the occasional business trip, I worked at home, in the corner of our bedroom, making slow progress on my fifth novel, my articles, my tepid reviews. When she returned in the evenings, I'd pour us some wine and pretend to listen while she gave me the full rundown of her complicated days. On Saturdays, once a month, we'd go to hear classical music, then out to a restaurant, or else to the opening of a new art exhibit. I would go to the library, and we'd go on vacation: to the mountains every year, for her birthday, and to the sea, in the off-season, for mine.

At Christmas we traveled abroad to visit our son. He showed us his drab studio apartment, where he lived happily, and introduced us to his first girlfriend, an attractive young woman with parents from two different continents. He'd met her at the university. The two of them took us to a sprawling, noisy restaurant they loved. I noticed that my son, taller than I was now, was looking bulkier even though he'd become a vegetarian. He preferred beer over wine. The photo of a gawky boy which greeted me every time I picked up my cell phone, taken on a fishing boat the previous summer, looked nothing like him anymore.

Because of the girlfriend, we never spoke to each other in Italian. He gushed about the multiethnic neighborhood where they lived, where they'd go out every night of the week to eat food from seven different countries. His answers to my questions were polite but brief. We conversed in a language I struggled to keep up with, a sensation that I enjoyed at P's house but that here, with my own son, felt frustrating and artificial. For Easter, he told me, he planned to go hiking with his girlfriend among castles and sheep. In the course of a day or two I could sense his tacit rejection not only of Rome but of our way of life, of all the effort we'd put into raising him a certain way.

He was thriving in this new city—but, even so, I didn't like the thought of him in that drab apartment, at those loud restaurants, eating bizarre and expensive food, with his wisp of a girlfriend smiling beside him. I didn't like the thought of him in the crush of a subway car, or walking the streets alone and a little drunk at three in the morning, or going to the park on Sundays to play soccer with no breakfast in his stomach. I worried that he wasn't mature enough, that deep down he felt unhappy, that he'd end up in some kind of trouble. But that naïve and vulnerable boy was not my son: he was me. Or rather, he was the version of me I'd never allowed to form, that I'd neglected, blocked out—a version that, even without ever having existed, had defeated me. With this thought in my head, I strolled around my son's new city, patiently admiring bridges, gardens, and monuments, beneath a low and leaden sky.

On the plane, before taking off, watching my wife check her e-mail on her phone, I realized that it was just the two of us again, except this time with no desire to have a child, without that life project to tie us together, as it had until now. What was she reading? Who was writing to her? Hundreds of messages poured in every day from mysterious senders. A densely inhabited world, buzzing with activity, hers alone. But at a certain point she raised her head and reminded me of the date for P's next party.

Only once we were in the car, on the way to P's house, did I recall that distraught mother, that unexpected confession on the patio. It had been nearly a year since I'd thought of her. I'd left my curiosity back at P's, as if it were an umbrella, or the shawl my wife had asked me to retrieve: the kind of thing whose absence you feel for a little while and then easily let go of. But now that I was about to return to that house, again I sensed that she and I shared some secret link.

My foot was heavy on the gas, I was distracted. I missed the sharp right turn, took another road, had to put the car in reverse, as my wife's irritation grew. I was thinking: I should have chosen a different shirt, the one I'm wearing doesn't do much for me. The agitation I'd experienced after the abrupt exchange on the patio was back. I could picture it clearly now: the flattering but unseasonable dress, the complicated necklace, the color of her fingernail polish. As if the year gone by were nothing, nothing but the passage of time. We hadn't even shaken hands, there was just that flash of understanding. So why was I feeling a little guilty?

An ancient, ridiculous memory came back to me then, from just before I met my wife. I was going to a gym with a pool at the time, and every week, by the pool's edge, the same girl would smile at me and say hello. She swam in the lane that I'd take over. For a few months my entire week revolved around that brief encounter by the pool, to the point where I'd even rush to the locker room to make sure I didn't miss her. We never talked about anything. She'd just say *Have a good swim,* or something like that. But every time she looked at me and spoke to me, it felt as if I were the center of her world. We ran into each other in this way for a few months, then she stopped showing up. A couple of months later I met my wife—but early on, in bed, I'd picture the swimmer's eyes, her smile. That's all.

Parking the car, I thought: maybe the distraught woman won't even be here, maybe she wasn't invited this time around, or maybe she had another engagement. Her presence was hardly a given. But as soon as we entered, after P and her husband had welcomed us in, as my wife was already chatting without me in the adjoining room, I caught sight of her.

She was sitting in the dining room, beneath a window, in one of the chairs lined up against the wall so that guests could circulate. Next to her was her husband—a tall, handsome man with shiny white hair, a young-looking face, tan even in January. It had to be her husband because they were sharing a plate of food; that way, each could hold a glass of wine in the other hand. She wasn't talking to him. She was turned toward two other women seated to her right—but there was too much noise, I could barely even make out her voice.

She was utterly changed. She was laughing, telling a funny anecdote about herself, while her husband listened and held the plate. He seemed like an attentive guy, amiable but a little bit tense. She was speaking with abandon, with irony. She didn't strike me at all as a woman in crisis.

She was dressed in black, like nearly all the other women at the party. No necklace, just that triangle of bare skin. She wore a pair of tight-fitting pants that matched the season, and hammered leather boots. Her hair, longer now, was streaked with gray, which she clearly didn't mind. She was thinner, even more beautiful—that weathered sort of beauty, which flattered her. Like my son, she had morphed over the past year into a sunnier, more confident version of herself. We lived in the same not particularly large city, and yet we'd never bumped into each other, not in a restaurant, not at a pharmacy, not on the street or at the gym. Our paths crossed only at this house, only at P's party.

"Hey, we're on the patio, it's nice out there," an old friend said, running into me.

"Be there in a minute."

I made a leisurely loop around the table, picking up some cheese, some crudités, some sliced salami. I was trying to make my presence felt. I couldn't hear her, all I could hear was my wife's gravelly voice, which worked its way under my skin even amid all those people.

When her husband stood to find a trash can where he could toss their plate, I looked at her, waiting for her to look back. Hoping for what, I don't know—a smile like the one the girl by the pool would give me? But she remained absorbed in her anecdote.

I continued staring, and she kept talking. Her husband was gone, my wife in the next room. The more I looked, the more she evaded me, unfazed. Until all of a sudden she lifted her gaze, for an instant, and revealed her eyes to me—filled (I thought) with fury and exasperation, blinding eyes that were shining (I hoped) for me.

The idea appealed to me: a relationship punctuated with gaps; a fixed date, ours alone, in the middle of the party. It seemed like an acceptable form of infidelity, entirely forgivable, a bit like when I thought of the girl from the pool while I was already with my wife. In truth I wasn't looking for trouble. Just a few blazing hours spent together, checked by a year of separation.

I'd never betrayed my wife, in this city where everyone's always cheating on everyone. With the exception of my little crush on the girl from the pool, I'd always been a faithful man; I was used to being the one who got dumped or cheated on, even before I met my wife, and not the other way around. I didn't have infidelity in me, I suppose I lacked the impulse. I accepted my wife's activities, her obligations—the constant messages on her phone, her dinners without me, her work trips abroad, her quick jaunts to other cities—while also admitting the likely consequences: a quickly forgotten one-night stand with some guy, lunch and a stroll through the botanical garden with another. But since I wasn't jealous by nature, my conjectures never took hold of me. As with any couple, things left unsaid enter in to maintain your aging affection. Which was how we'd survived twenty-three years together with no major disruptions, no earthquakes.

I repeat, I'd have been fine dragging out that trifling dalliance. But just a few months later my wife informed me that P was having another party.

"So soon? What's that about?"

"She said she's been teaching her oldest son to dance, which got her thinking that she'd like to throw a different kind of party. At night this time. No kids."

"Did we ever teach our son to dance?"

"Maybe?"

"Do you know who's coming?"

"The usual slew of people, I imagine."

The weather was terrible that evening. I felt queasy the entire day. I couldn't eat, couldn't concentrate at my desk.

"It's been a long week, I can't shake this headache," I said to my wife.

"And so . . . ?"

"What do you say we stay in for the night?"

I already knew my suggestion was futile. She was taking her time getting ready, wearing a short dress she hadn't pulled out in years.

"Tonight we dance and let go. Time to perk up."

In the dark, P's house seemed like a new destination—even more out of the way, more alien. The drive was stressful, the charming road slick with rain. And the spring air felt wrong to me. I couldn't get my bearings.

"Did you hear that their house was robbed recently?" my wife said as I was parking the car behind a long line of vehicles.

"Who?"

"P's family. They were gone for three days, all the jewelry was taken."

"They didn't have it in a safe?"

"No, unfortunately, she's always been a bit disorganized."

The house, too, was nearly dark, unfamiliar. They'd removed most of the furniture to make room. P's daughter greeted us at the door and whisked our coats off to who knows where. I stuck to my wife's side. We went to get our first glass of prosecco together, to fill our plastic plates with slices of bread, slivers of cheese, honey. We were attached at the hip as if we were a shy couple on an early date.

I saw all the known and unknown faces that were always at P's. Apart from the new setup, the empty rooms, the scene was more or less identical, and yet I couldn't manage to wedge my way into conversations as I usually did; searching for that woman left me discombobulated. She was standing next to her husband, on the other side of the room. And this time she didn't avoid my gaze. She was looking straight at me through the crowd, registering my presence without smiling, without budging, without communicating anything.

After dinner, the dancing began. P's older son chose the music, a string of inane songs from our younger days. I danced with my wife, the woman with her husband. P's other kids danced between us, they danced with P and her husband. P danced with my wife, and then with me. She was a little drunk, barefoot, affectionate, shimmering, even without a bit of jewelry on. I really love you two, she said to me and my wife, as the three of us danced together.

The music felt liberating, at moments wrenching. It levitated us magically above the cramped and craggy present, it restored a glimmer of hope. We were, all of us, each on our own, replaying our previous lives: lives still in progress, foolish, makeshift, splendid lives. I glanced around at the women who refused to assume the role of *signora,* who'd kept up their looks. And yet we weren't getting any younger, we were accumulating wrinkles, health scares, disappointments. The songs took us back—to our first kiss, our first relationship, ancient emotions, our first heartbreak, minor grievances we'd buried, unresolved, but had never shaken off.

She and I danced, together, on our own. It was a torment, also a triumph. We would lock eyes for a moment, here and there I'd feel my body brushing hers, a shoulder, a hip. The two of us were still nailed to our respective lives, but underneath it all I sensed that we were being reckless, conspiratorial.

Outside it was still raining, but inside it was hot, oppressively hot. I was covered in sweat. I told my wife I could use a little water. I went to the bathroom, rinsed my face. Then I went to the kitchen to find a glass. There I noticed a complex surveillance system mounted on the wall, for monitoring the house's entry points. It had multiple tiny screens, each with a different view: the front gate, the yard, the patio. At night, in the heavy rain, every image looked to me like a kind of ominous ultrasound, ripe with meaning but completely indecipherable.

When I returned, I noticed that the lights were on. The barren room, only recently vacated, reminded me in some ways of my son's apartment. No one was dancing anymore, the music had stopped. In the old days we'd have merely taken a break, but we were already worn out.

My wife was over by the table. She was eating dessert. And she was talking to her. They didn't notice me. My wife said, "I was just admiring your necklace while we were dancing, it's extraordinary. Can I ask where you bought it?"

"In a cute little shop, not far from where we live."

"How long have you two lived in Rome?"

"Three years now."

"Are you here for work?"

"My husband, yes. He'd like to live here forever."

"What about you?"

She shrugged. "'Forever' is a big word."

They went to grab their purses, they pulled out their phones. Right there on the spot they exchanged numbers, scheduled a date.

And this is where my story takes an unexpected turn. This stranger, with whom I'd had only one conversation, a fevered and fragmentary exchange, and with whom I'd felt an inexplicable bond from that moment on, despite never having learned her name, became my wife's friend. They met for lunch once a month, then went shopping for clothes and shoes together. She remained a secondary, casual friend for my wife. Not someone she'd invite over to the house, or fold into our everyday lives, but a person she'd spend time with on her own now and then, in her own way.

Through their friendship I learned a few things: her name—L—and the neighborhood where she lived (San Giovanni). One day she mentioned how often her husband had to travel, racing back and forth between cities. They had one son, the boy who'd felt sick in the yard. As my wife had intuited, he went to the same school as one of P's sons. L used to have a job herself, as a magazine editor, but here she spent her days diligently studying our language and belonged to a group of foreign women who relentlessly visited the city's infinite monuments, attractions, and ruins. Apart from these details, my wife never spoke of her new friendship.

I knew that it was normal, even healthy, to cultivate these kinds of friendships outside a marriage. It wasn't like there was anything sexual involved. And yet I agonized over it. My writing suffered, I began missing deadlines for my projects, I envied my wife.

I envied my wife and yet at the same time I was grateful. There was no way, when they went out together on their walks or to see an art exhibit, that L didn't think of me. No way my wife didn't speak of me, of our long marriage filled with the predictable ups and downs, of the flings she'd probably had with other men, of our strained relationship with our son. No way I didn't factor in to some extent. After more than twenty years of marriage, I knew what happened when women talked—all that archived information which loosens in the vapor of friendship, which floats to the surface while they're out buying shoes, eating salads, admiring paintings.

But what was I hoping for? An actual affair with L? A date, a few hours in a hotel, in bed together? I don't think so. Even after the dancing I never thought of her body, her hands. What I fixated on was our conversation on the patio, when she was distraught, sick with worry over her son, when she confided in me. That moment seemed more transgressive than any erotic act. What had we shared? An intimate exchange, inexplicably charged. And now, just as inexplicably, we shared my wife.

Soon enough the spring had gone by, an entire season. I remained passive, cagey, lying in wait for a new development: a dinner together, plans for a night at the theater with L and her husband. But what I was really waiting for was winter, and P's next party, even if—and it was clear by now—those spirited occasions, those restorative afternoons I held so dear, were tainted.

But late that summer, once again, P suddenly changed the script. My wife and I were already back from vacation, had stashed away our bathing suits and beach towels and sandals. For my own part, I was looking forward to the firm and reassuring light of autumn, the plates of puntarelle at the trattorie, the starlings that dart in the sky, appearing and disappearing like tornadoes or ribbons or giant tadpoles made of ash, when P offered us a last-minute invitation to the island where she and her family spent two months each year. She had access to a spare bungalow with an ocean view—the usual tenants had canceled—and she was certain that it would make an ideal spot for my writing, having heard from my wife that I'd been in a long slump.

"You know, I wouldn't mind going back there either, finally putting an end to my childhood fear," my wife announced, referring to that poor man she'd seen die in the pool, decades earlier.

And given that it was a particularly stifling summer, and that my wife and I really had nothing to do but idle around the apartment, we packed our suitcases again, drove down to the harbor, and boarded a ferry. The island was a rock in the middle of nowhere, a bit like P's house.

For several days we did nothing but enjoy luxuriant, late-morning swims, light and refreshing lunches, and sunset strolls down to the lighthouse. The water was as clear as glass, filled with dark sea urchins. A beautiful path ran the length of the island, but in certain stretches you had to beware of clefts in the rock. Once, P told us, a woman had fallen to her death while taking a photo of her husband. We floated around the island on a rubber dinghy and ate baked fish on the terrace, with coils and citronella candles to repel the mosquitoes.

P and my wife took the boat every day, either before or after lunch, to pick up groceries. They wore flared linen dresses, and always came back with a little something extra: a clever bracelet made of cork, a perfume that smelled of salt, silicone kitchen utensils in various colors. They cooked together, reminiscing about the happy years when they'd shared an apartment, before they were married and had kids. P's husband came out on the weekend but left again for work. The kids played Ping-Pong all day or horsed around on the beach or tried out reckless dives at the pool or wandered off alone to some secret spot.

Our bungalow was very charming, picturesque, a bit dim inside but airy. It had belonged to one of P's uncles, he, too, a writer, and I discovered many old, well-loved books there, marked up in pencil. It was a cozy space, masculine in feeling, just one room, really, with no kitchen and one square window that looked out on the sea and opened like the door to a cupboard. The furniture had never been replaced—soft, faded armchairs, dark, glossy wood, a musty smell, all of it frozen in time.

As soon as I stepped inside I felt better; the space was invigorating, and had an effect on me similar to that of P's house, except here there was no party. This was a refuge where I could hole up and concentrate. Which got me thinking, a bit peeved: It would have been truly ideal to have had a place like this at our disposal, a place to write, if only my wife hadn't been avoiding this island, if only she'd brought me here before. Our son would have liked it, too, in the past, but now there was no room here for him and his girlfriend, there were just two couches, one across from the other, that became beds—two separate singles, one for me and one for my wife.

As soon as we were settled in, I hit a stride with my writing, hunched over a tiny desk against a wall, or else lying back on one of the sofa beds. I skipped lunch with P and my wife, instead grabbing a sandwich at the snack bar around three, my mind humming. I was pleased with this second summer of ours, with the inspiration I found on that island, in that cozy and comfortable bungalow.

The mistral arrived, as expected: three days of non-stop wind, of deafening gusts. On the storm's first day I started a new short story about L, set at P's house. In my invented version things took a more predictable course: she and I had a real affair. Staring out at the white shelf of sea lashing the shore, I thought back to our conversation on the patio—in the fake version we kissed immediately—looking for ways to stretch the details. I inserted the scene where we danced together, and also on our own—it felt like a critical juncture in the plot—and I left out L's friendship with my wife, which proved an unwieldy development. I molded and massaged the facts until it felt like a vaguely appealing story, the kind a literary magazine might take. All I needed was the ending, the grand finale.

One morning I decided to go for a swim, to clear out my head before sitting down to write. The mistral had just moved on, and the water was once again a sheet of glass. I climbed in from a small sheltered cove, first checking for jellyfish. My destination was a red buoy, which I swam toward through a beautiful patch of green sea, following a school of minnows. I was out in the middle of that patch when I saw a motorboat heading straight at me. I stopped and waved an arm, but the boat kept coming. I didn't shout, it would have been pointless. Out that far, all sounds are swallowed by the sea's silence. Feeling slow, weak, frightened, I somehow managed to move out of the way, and I made it to shore.

I walked back to the house, stricken, pale, still unnerved. But my wife wasn't there, and P's place was empty, too. On the little desk was a note: *Out getting groceries, catch up with you later.* My head was spinning. I felt like I needed a fresh glass of orange juice. At the snack bar I ran into one of P's boys, the thirteen-year-old.

"How's it going, all good?" he asked.

"A boat nearly ran me over."

"Were you swimming alone?"

"I was."

"Best to stay close to shore."

"What about you guys? You having fun?"

"It gets a bit boring. I'd like to go somewhere else next year, but my mom always wants to come here."

"Hang in there."

"At least my friend's coming tonight."

"Oh, who's that?"

"This foreign kid I go to school with. He's on a boat trip with his parents, his dad's a really good navigator. They're stopping at the island and staying for dinner."

At sunset we walked down to the harbor to greet them. It was a beautiful motorboat. They were dropping the fenders. Her husband was at the helm, her son hanging their wet things on a drying rack, L clambering around the boat. She was moving swiftly, asking her husband what to do before they docked. She was wearing a special pair of gloves for handling the anchor chain. I admired how deftly she tied and untied the mooring line. I noticed the ease and economy of communication between husband and wife.

With the task complete and the motor spent, they said their hellos. L had picked up a tan, her husband, too. Their son had outgrown both his parents. I glimpsed L's dark, muscular legs, a scar on her thigh. She was barefoot, sweaty, her hair a windblown mess. She quickly slipped into a sheer beach coverup, a pair of elegant but well-worn sandals.

I wanted to break up the scene right then and sneak down into the cabin, on that boat, with her. As if driven by the mistral, like the waves beating steadily in one direction, an impulse intensified by my own imagined version of our affair, I now yearned to kiss her mouth, to taste her salty skin, to solidify our connection at last without having to share it with anyone else. Instead, when she stepped off the boat, we greeted each other with a handshake, and all she said to me was "Ciao."

We took our seats out on P's terrace. There were five of us—P's husband would be back the next day, and L's son had rushed off to meet his friend in the small piazza. We spoke in Italian. By now, after all their meticulous studying, L and her husband could speak it more or less fluently. The windstorm had swept away the mosquitoes. The air felt crisp, refreshing. I was sitting next to L, at the head of the table, with P and my wife on one side and L and her husband across from them.

We drank heavily that night, though L a bit less than we did, since she was suffering from land sickness. Her husband weighed in on the recent elections, and told of their boating adventures, describing their favorite islands and inlets. At sea, he said, you live with less but have it all.

We ate a rice salad, followed by some fish and a few slices of melon. L passed me the fruit, the bottle of mirto. And while we ate and talked, while we looked at the stars and listened to the waves, while my eyes strayed now and then to that same triangle of bare skin, that extraordinary divot of flesh outlined by her collarbone and shoulders, I learned something new. In a month they'd be returning to their country; their time in Italy had come to an end. The reasons they gave were practical: her husband was tired of the constant travel, their son was about to start his first year of high school, and L, it turned out, was missing the working life that she'd sacrificed to be here. They were sad to go, already speaking with nostalgia about certain things, but you could see that the decision to reactivate their old life had restored the family balance, and that the cliff's edge they were once teetering on was no longer a threat.

"Maybe we'll come back around New Year's. It would be nice to get a little winter sun, have some panettone and pandoro, eat lunch outdoors in January."

"Perfect. That means you'll be here for my party," P said.

We accompanied them back to the harbor, said our goodbyes on the dock. "Ciao," L said to me again—nothing else—and in that moment of confusion I kissed her, at first on the cheek, but then my mouth drifted down toward the salty skin of her collarbone, planting itself in that sunken triangle. I latched on to her for a few seconds, then I lifted my head, mortified, and muttered, "Forgive me."

She immediately stepped back. And she may have glared at me then as she had once before, her eyes filled with fury and exasperation, but it was too dark to tell.

After she hugged and thanked everyone else, after she said her goodbyes to my wife and P, she left with her family to spend the night on their boat, by a secluded grotto, in a tiny cabin beside her husband. My wife, meanwhile, who'd glimpsed that errant kiss, started haranguing me as soon as we entered the bungalow and kept at it until dawn.

"Is there something going on with you two?"

"Nothing, I barely know her."

"You imbecile, she was my friend."

"And she still is."

"I doubt it. The whole reason I came out here was to lay down an old burden, and now, thanks to you, I've picked up another."

"I'm sorry."

My wife refused to calm down. She went on attacking me, then burst into tears, transforming my creative sanctuary into a hell.

The next day, earlier than planned, we, too, left the island, in a rush. There was no need to explain our departure to P, given that I'd kissed L in front of her and her children, too. The whole lot of them were witnesses—and, worse, even with the whistling wind and the crashing waves, they'd probably heard us fighting until dawn. For days, back in the city, I cursed my own stupidity, steeped in embarrassment, but my wife never brought it up again, and soon the unpleasant feeling faded.

We fell back into our old routines, though for months I was adrift. I abandoned the short story—with those pages, I realized, I'd been luring myself onto a precipice. What had happened between L and me made for a dull premise, it never would have worked. Yet for a moment, on that island, my embellished version of events had fused with reality: it had driven me to wound and demean my wife, in a way that she, with her discreet behavior, had never done to me in our long years of marriage.

I'd already decided, before Christmas, that I wouldn't be going to P's party that winter. On the off chance that L and her family were in town, I had my excuse prepared. But then, just before Christmas, P got sick again. Her decline was rapid, until the same good doctor who'd saved her life said there was nothing left to do.

Soon thereafter, I found myself at the funeral, and afterward at the house where we'd celebrated P so many times. Yet again on a bright and balmy winter day. A Saturday afternoon, a few weeks before her birthday, with all the guests from her previous parties, all of her closest friends.

My wife was devastated, she'd practically lost a sister. We clasped hands before entering the house. All the women, wearing black, were stone-faced. P's children, who'd been so drunk with joy on the island, who'd had so much fun that summer, were standing still in a row, in one of the rooms. The littlest one started weeping when my wife went to hug her.

"It was important to her, the party," her husband said to me. "She looked forward to it every year."

"Me, too," I replied.

We spoke about P. About how she was a singular person, a singular woman, radiant, the only one with the strength to bring us all together. To open the door a thousand times, to fill the house and churn the crowd.

Aside from the absence of P and her hospitality, things were essentially the same. The funeral, too, was a kind of party. The kids, after a while, went out to play in the yard. Food covered the big oval table in the room with many windows, all the chairs lined up against the walls so that guests could circulate.

We ate, we conversed. But in the wake of a death, even your own breath, your own shadow, comes as a shock. Everything feels inappropriate, indecent, for a while.

This would be the last time we ever set foot in that house. It was already up for sale. P's husband, her children, couldn't bear to live in it anymore.

L wasn't there. Which didn't surprise me. As a peripheral figure, an occasional guest, she wasn't invited to the funeral. I saw only a few members of her group, the people who spoke other languages, who passed in and out of our lives. Just like P, whatever had happened between us—that stalemate, that non-starter, brought to an end by my foolish gesture—was no longer.

I can't complain. Unlike me, P, to whom I owe these pages, didn't make it out of the story. She'll never visit her children in other countries, or cry about distances or the passing of days, that merciless, automatic plot device which propels us forward and brings us to our knees. Her parties, however, have stayed with me, and the thought of them still quickens the heart: the secluded house packed with people, the sunlit lawn, those hours of sublime detachment. A setting I cherished, a promising start I tried to finish, to put into words, in which I'd been, briefly, a wayward husband, an inspired author, a happy man.

(Translated, from the Italian, by Todd Portnowitz in collaboration with the author.)

DANIEL MASON

A Case Study

FROM *The Paris Review*

HE WAS TWENTY-FOUR when he first saw the psychologist, in his second year of medical school, in the midst of a darkness that had descended without warning and left him reeling and unmoored. It was the first time he had been to therapy: he could not conceive of how it would help him and had resisted the idea for months. Relief would come, he reasoned. It always had. But it didn't come. And from beyond the devouring darkness came an awe at the velocity of his own unraveling, and the sense that when he looked inside himself, he found only a void.

He had been given the psychologist's name by his aunt, who had been to see him during her own crisis years before. The psychologist had a private practice in a residential neighborhood, and on the first day, the man had walked there, through the park with its quiet groves of cypress and pine. He had seen enough portrayals of therapy in movies that the office, with its empty waiting room and muted, abstract artwork, seemed almost a stage set, just as the psychologist, spectacled, wearing a gray tie and a beige wool jacket, seemed so much like an actor playing a psychologist that the younger man half expected him to acknowledge that they might, for a moment, step out of character. There was a couch, and two leather chairs in which they sat facing each other beneath a tall white shelf of books and journals. He had no idea what he was supposed to say, but in school he had seen patients interviewed, and so when the psychologist asked him what had brought him there, he tried his best to put his story in an order that made sense. The psychologist, a large man, pale, his accent English, his name so common as to seem almost pseudonymous, listened, took notes, and at last said gently that they were drawing near the end. And then he summarized, with brevity and clarity, what he'd heard his patient say. He offered no advice and no interpretation, just the summary, and yet it was somehow immensely comforting for the younger man to hear, in so few words, what had taken nearly an hour to express.

He exited through a second door, so as not to cross the waiting room. Walking back across the park, along the fog-laced paths, he felt as if he had both left something in the office and taken something with him. This puzzled him. The world was the same. There had been, of course, no change to the complex series of events that—he believed—had brought the darkness on. The only difference between the moments of his coming and his going was that an hour earlier there had been an emptiness that only he could touch, and now another person knew that it was there.

The second meeting occurred at the same time, one week later, on a Friday afternoon, when lectures were over. It began exactly as the first had. He sat alone in the waiting room, looking at a slate-gray painting, or just down into his hands. When the psychologist emerged, they entered the office together, and took their seats in the same chairs as before. He noticed a box of Kleenex on the side table, and a desk by the single window that looked out onto the trees. He thought it strange that he had not noticed them the first time. He realized it was his turn to speak, and so he did. While on his prior visit he had spoken logically, clearly, this time he felt surprisingly inarticulate, and he was relieved, toward the end, when the psychologist said, gently, that he noticed that today seemed harder. That was all he said. And the younger man continued, until the psychologist, looking beyond him to a clock that was set up on the desk, said that they were out of time.

For the next few months, he came weekly to the sessions, and then, briefly, twice weekly, and then weekly again. It was autumn when he started, and when the rain came, he still walked there, through the damp and silent corridor of trees. He was still sad, often very sad, but he had become aware that despite the low gray sky of winter, he no longer felt like he was standing before a precipice, his days had ceased to be punctuated by assaults of fear and worry, and he was once again able to study without distraction. He didn't understand why he felt better. But the visits comforted him, and he liked the older man's cryptic presence, just as he liked the walk through the city forest, the crows and the wood wrens he began to notice in the trees. Though he had known the psychologist only a few months, didn't know him at all, really, he was struck by how often he thought of him, or imagined his voice.

He didn't tell any of his friends where he was going. It wasn't shame, exactly, so much as the sense that to admit it might invite either inquiry or compassion. But increasingly, in conversations, he listened when others spoke of their own therapists, who seemed, with their advice and exhortations and sharing of personal experiences, so different from his own. There was a part of him that envied his friends, and the simple, practical solutions they were being offered. But another part perceived a purity to the structure of his sessions, and to the spectral quality of the older man. When he mentioned to the psychologist that he knew nothing about him, the psychologist answered that his patient had never asked. But you wouldn't tell me, thought the younger man, and at the same time understood that he didn't want to know, feared knowing. He felt a shiver, as if the membrane between them was too thin and might be breached.

Ferns declared themselves in the pathways of the park, and tulips and geraniums emerged in the window boxes of the city apartments. When summer came, he traveled on an airplane to see his family. In the sessions leading up to his departure, he'd told the psychologist that he was feeling better. You've cured me! he joked, and the psychologist had smiled. But he wondered, he asked, if he might continue coming; there was a part of him that found there, in that office, something that was missing elsewhere. The psychologist answered that he could come for as long as he wished, for as long as, together, they decided it was helpful. The younger man was relieved to hear this, though he was unsettled by the word *together,* which suggested that the psychologist could cut things off. Despite the fees he paid, he couldn't escape the feeling that he was accruing a debt he could never completely settle. Because of the layout of the office, he had never seen another patient, but he heard murmurs through the wall when he came early, and footsteps, and distant closing doors, and once, in the trash can by the chair, he'd seen a pair of crumpled tissues. He had never cried in any of his sessions. He imagined the other patients to be more compelling, more worthy of sympathy, and he struggled to understand what the psychologist might see in him.

He left, and returned, and they began again. His third year started, his clinical year, and one night, at a party, he met a graduate student who became his girlfriend. Soon, it was no longer possible to hide his weekly absences, but she didn't seem to mind when he told her he was in treatment, didn't ask him why. They both were very busy. He loved his clinical rotations. Eventually it came time for him to rotate onto the psychiatry service, and though he planned to be a surgeon, he found an unexpected affinity for his psychiatric patients, who, in their unbridled misery, seemed so different from himself.

His girlfriend moved in with him. In the spring of his fourth year, he was accepted to a surgery residency in a far-off state. Part of him wished that he could stay in the city with its ocean and its trails of pine and cypress, and the office by the park. He told his psychologist this, and the psychologist, uncharacteristically, didn't ask him to say more about it but just replied that he understood what the younger man had said.

Their last session was the day before his departure. For months he had wondered about the meeting. He felt as though the psychologist had uncovered a secret about him and was waiting until this day to tell him. But, in fact, the final session wasn't very different from the others. In the park, there was a grounds crew trimming branches from the cypresses, and perhaps this disrupted the solemnity of his pilgrimage, the sense of ceremony he had hoped for. The psychologist shared no secrets. As always, he was mostly quiet and mostly encouraged the younger man to speak.

When it was over, the younger man stood first, and the psychologist followed. Well, he said, thank you. Then he paused. He felt the need to say something that fit the gravity of the moment.

So do I just shake your hand? he asked.

If you like, said the psychologist, but he waited for the patient to reach out first.

The psychologist's hand was soft, his skin like a loose-fitting glove, and instantly the patient sensed that he was in the presence of someone much older, much frailer than he had imagined. But there was no opportunity to discuss it then, because his time was up.

*

Months passed, then years. He finished his residency in the far-off state and began a fellowship in cardiothoracic surgery, while his girlfriend was hired as an assistant professor at a university an hour down the coast. They married, had a son, and then, two years later, a daughter, and when the man's fellowship was over, they moved to the city where his wife held her position. He trained further, specializing in pediatric cases. When he finished, he joined the university practice, and after two years, when his loans were paid off, they bought a home in the nearby suburbs. He loved his work, the clarity of it, how he could vanish into the room and pass seven, eight hours without a moment's awareness of his own existence. He loved that others admired him, even feared him—that, during surgery, everyone was quiet when he didn't wish to speak. Both he and his wife woke early and worked hard, and though they had their disagreements and worries, they were mostly happy, aware of their good fortune and the sense that it was deserved.

There were times, with the pressures of his practice or of parenthood, that he felt the absence of his old sessions, but the thought of beginning anew with someone else was inconceivable. In a way, he had never stopped speaking to his former psychologist. The graft, he joked to himself, had taken, and he wished that he could share this line. Sometimes he thought of writing, to thank the psychologist, or to tell him about his wife, his son and daughter, and his practice, and about how, with his own patients and their parents, he found himself trying to embody the psychologist's quiet, inviting way. But he didn't write. Though the psychologist had never prohibited it, the younger man assumed certain boundaries extended even beyond the end of therapy. Other times, he wondered about the psychologist, who had seemed so much older in their final session. Illness would come, he knew, if it hadn't already, and the thought that they might never speak again filled him with sadness. And then, one early afternoon, he was in clinic when his cell phone rang, and he looked down to see the psychologist's name.

He was with a patient, and so he didn't answer, though the truth was that, had he wanted to, it would have been easy to excuse himself and step away. When he finished the exam, he went into his office to listen to the message. The voice was utterly familiar—and true to form, the psychologist said little beyond a greeting, a phone number, and an invitation to call him back. But another patient was waiting, and then another. As the day progressed, he found his mind circling. His first thought—his fantasy, the psychologist would have called it—was that just as he hadn't forgotten the sessions, the psychologist hadn't forgotten him, and one day, now twelve years later, he had discovered something, some key to the secret of who he was.

Immediately, he knew this was ridiculous. He never would have thought to call a cardiac patient no longer in his care. His second thought was that some kind of waiting period, some quarantine, had elapsed, and now the man was calling with an overture of friendship, that such a relationship was no longer prohibited. But this also seemed a fantasy, as did his final thought, the one he feared, that the old man was sick and was reaching out for help, or to say goodbye.

When he called, at the end of the day, the psychologist answered after a single ring. He thanked his former patient for returning the call and asked how he was doing, and though his tone was genuine, the younger man understood, by the psychologist's gentle formality, that he was to answer briefly, which he did, mentioning his wife, his children, and his practice. The psychologist said he was happy to hear this, and he sounded truly happy, though he didn't ask his patient anything more. He was calling with a question, he said, after a moment. He didn't know whether the younger man was aware, but over the course of his career he had written, in addition to some technical works, two books of poetry, and three collections of case studies based on his patients' lives. He was currently in the process of preparing a fourth, he said, and had written up a case study about the younger man. He was calling to ask whether he might include it in the book. It was anonymized, of course, he said: only you will know yourself. And in any event, he would share the chapter before publishing it, so as to obtain consent. You are not obliged, he said. If you prefer not to allow this, there are other patients I can choose.

The man was standing in his office as he listened. There was a window that looked onto the entrance to the hospital, where patients were arriving, struggling to emerge from their cars and settle into walkers and wheelchairs, or waiting with their tanks of oxygen: fragile, tired people who frightened him with their fragility. Now, watching the patients, their families, the staff who helped them from car to chair and chair to car, he had the additional sense that these sick people were good people, pure people, selfless people, and that he, in the comfort of his office, in his health, was not. A version of this thought—that he had taken more from the world than he had given—had long preceded his becoming a doctor. Indeed, it was something he had discussed with the psychologist, who, in reply, asked if he felt some kind of balance sheet between the two of them, as well.

Actually, it was only later, after the call, that he was able to fully stitch together this thought. In the moment, he said yes, and the psychologist asked him for his address so that he might send the case study and the consent form.

The man returned home late that night, and during dinner he was quiet. He was surprised at how affected he was by the conversation. He felt embarrassed that he hadn't asked the psychologist how *he* was, though in the past, in the early days, when he had done so, the psychologist hadn't really answered. He couldn't escape the feeling that he had been ungracious, and he slept poorly that night, and he didn't tell his wife about the call.

For the next few evenings, he checked the mail as soon as he got home, and after four days, when nothing had arrived, he asked his wife if she had seen a letter he was expecting from a colleague. She hadn't, and as he didn't want her to grow curious, he didn't ask again. The thought that she might ask to read it worried him. The psychologist had promised him anonymity, but this was to the world, not to his wife. At the same time, it was unclear what he was hiding. His sins were few, and the desires he had shared seemed dully commonplace, at least in retrospect. It wasn't the exposure of his own inner life that frightened him just then, but rather the possibility that she would learn—no, that *he* would learn, at last—what the psychologist had always thought.

When he returned home one evening to find the neatly addressed envelope in the mailbox, he didn't open it immediately. Not then, standing at the end of the driveway, and not later that night. He went to bed having decided to look in the morning, so that it would not affect his sleep. But he was in a hurry the next morning, or so he told himself, and he took it in his briefcase to work, where he didn't touch it. By then it was clear to him that his reaction was more than just procrastination. He felt as if the letter—he kept thinking of the case study as a letter from the psychologist—could smuggle something volatile past the barricades, an ember wrapped in leaves and moss. He couldn't deny a feeling of betrayal, a sense that the true terms of their contract had not been stated honestly. That all along, the other man had possessed an intent of which his patient hadn't been informed.

Yet he had known, when he started therapy, that the psychologist was a writer. His aunt had mentioned it in passing, and so, perhaps, had the psychologist, though it was hard to be sure—his memory of the beginning was so obscured. He must at some point have considered this possibility, perhaps even hoped for it. He himself had written two case studies, the first in medical school and the second as a resident, both accounts of rare, lurid syndromes: a case of argyria—silver poisoning—and an unusual infection of the heart. Was this part of his discomfort? That he would find himself suddenly on the other side of medicine, the side of the dusky, blue-gray woman and the addict with the rattlesnake tattoos that barely hid his shot-up veins?

When the patient with the snake tattoos was ready to be discharged, he'd signed his consent without complaint, in fact with gratitude. There had been a debt. So he opened the envelope and found a brief, formal letter; the consent form; and the study, ten pages, numbered, double-sided. But he could not bring himself to read it, not yet. He felt strangely angry, even defiant, and when he signed and mailed the consent form in a second envelope the psychologist had provided, he also mailed the chapter back.

He did not receive a letter in return, nor did he expect to. When the book was published a year later, he bought a copy, but left it in his office, where it vanished behind his stacks of journals. He'd read it soon enough, he told himself, and he imagined writing to the psychologist: sometimes a long, grateful letter full of appreciation for his insight; sometimes another just as long, protesting what the man had gotten wrong. But he didn't read it, and time passed, and the next he heard of the psychologist was two years later, in an obituary in the *Times,* where his poetry was praised, and his four books of case studies were mentioned as classics of the genre. He read about the old man's childhood in London during the bombing, and his lifelong partner, a well-known playwright whom he'd married in the year before his death. There was a photo of him when he was younger, his face thin and thoughtful. Reading the article, brimming with the details of life, he felt astonished that such a person had cared for him, had carried him in his mind.

He had another thought then: his fantasies of correspondence had implied the possibility that whatever the psychologist had thought of him could be amended. With the psychologist's death, the case study would be forever. When he moved offices a year later, he did not bring his copy of the book.

He prospered. His practice grew; he became known regionally for his skill, his willingness to take on the most difficult cases. Doctors came from overseas to watch him and his team of eight, huddled around an open chest no larger than his palm. Each August, he vacationed with his family on an island off the coast, where his son learned to sail, and his daughter, now as tall and beautiful as her mother, played tennis for hours at a time. Around them were people who had arrived at similar points in life, and had come to recognize one another from the island's beachside paths and summer music festival, and from the symphony in the city that they returned to in the fall.

During these months, they shared meals with their summer neighbors, some of whom were psychiatrists or therapists, and now and then, wandering through their homes, he would catch sight, out of the corner of his eye, of a copy of his psychologist's book. The first time had been a year or so after the psychologist's death. He was at a dinner party, on his way to use the bathroom. The book was sitting on a nightstand, and he stopped to pick it up, only to find that he was shaking. Returning outside to the warm summer evening, he struggled to rejoin the conversation. He gathered, from the bedside paraphernalia, that it was the wife who had been reading it. As night fell, he couldn't take his eyes off her, as if somehow her manner, her words, might betray what it contained.

He saw it often after that. In contrast to the sober, gray hardback, the paperback had a distinctive yellow cover, and whenever he glimpsed it he felt his breath quickening. Each time, the feeling was the same, the fear the same: that part of him was now in the possession of another person who knew more about him than he knew about himself. Many times, he told himself that the solution to his discomfort was just to read the book. But with each passing year the stakes grew higher, and so he waited, until he found himself avoiding certain houses, just as, when he was a child, he'd avoided walking past a shelf that held a book whose illustrations frightened him. It was absurd, he thought, but he could not escape the sense that he was being followed by a threatening presence. And he came to suspect that the truer person, the real person, the person in colors, lived in those pages, and would endure long after he was gone.

And so something settled upon his happiness and the clarity of his life. He stopped going to the summer island. His wife was a full professor and had her own circle, and he sensed a change: as if, finding him uncertain, her attachments were shifting somewhere else. Noticing this, and that he was powerless to stop it, he felt the void inside him widen. Anger rushed to fill it, anger toward the dead man who'd left him in this situation. Hadn't he known his patient? Couldn't he have foreseen this complication? The psychologist, to use the language of surgery, had failed to close the wound completely. Yet—and this seemed only to confuse his anger rather than placate it—he knew that the older man had acted impeccably, ethically, had made no demands, had asked for his permission. Which, of course, the patient had granted.

His son went to college, and then his daughter. And then one winter, when she was visiting, and working on a term paper, he entered her room to say goodnight and saw, upon her desk, the yellow book. He said nothing. She looked up at him. Would he read her paper? She'd done poorly on the last one and was worried about the class.

Of course, he told her, before he could think of another answer. She smiled at him. It was due tomorrow—maybe he could read it in the morning? She'd finish it later that night. Sorry it's so last-minute, Dad, she said.

He paused. Did she like the book? he asked her.

Like it? She shrugged. Well, honestly, not really. She felt that no matter what the author wrote about each patient, he was writing about himself. She wanted more of them and less of him, she said.

He kissed her forehead and went upstairs, undressed, and got into bed. Light from a streetlamp cast the shivering of leaves upon his ceiling and he watched the sweep of beams from passing cars, and he thought of his daughter writing in her distant corner of the house. His wife lay silent beside him, sleeping. When he couldn't bear it any longer, he went to the window and looked at the light falling from his daughter's room onto their driveway, until that light went out. Then he went and got his phone, where the email from her was waiting, and he threw a jacket over his shoulders and went down into the night.

He read the essay on the street, at the end of his driveway, the little rectangle casting a column through the mist. He read it once, and then a second time more closely. Briefly, she had summarized the patients—David, who had lost his mother as a child; Kavita, who had sought treatment during her recovery from cancer; Michael, who had loved his sister's husband; Ellen and Maria, George and Brian, Mark and Claire. And none were him, not even remotely, and certain now that his daughter had left a patient out, he went back into the house and upstairs to her room. There the book was sitting as she'd left it, and he picked it up, and quietly closed the door and went back down into the kitchen, and began to read: David, Kavita, Michael, Ellen . . . and faster now, Maria, George and Brian, Mark and Claire. Nothing. Nothing, no one familiar. And again he looked through the stories, feeling at once relief, embarrassment over all his worries, and then, increasingly, a different reckoning. For what had happened? Was he simply unrecognizable to himself? Or had the psychologist, true to his promise, hidden him in layers of anonymity? Or was it even simpler: had the older man, editing his final manuscript, decided to leave him out?

Dawn was breaking outside. His wife, an early riser, would soon be down for breakfast. But he stayed in his chair, at the little table, and once again began to read the book, seeking, in its pages, a person who was no longer there.

LORI OSTLUND

Just Another Family

FROM *New England Review*

MY FATHER SPENT the last year of his life discontinent. He'd always had trouble with prefixes. The day after he died, I entered my parents' house—the house I grew up in—to the smell of piss, the humid night air thick with it. "It's the mattress," my mother explained, and I said, well, then the mattress had to go.

I tried to haul it out right then, just dropped my bag and went down the hallway to their bedroom. I started with the soda bottles. There were five of them, scattered beneath their bed, three with urine still sloshing around inside from when my father had relieved himself during the night. I used a broom to maneuver them out while my mother watched, lying on the floor on the far side of the bed, peering at me across its underbelly and demanding that I call them pop bottles. She was sure that I was saying soda to bother her because she said there was no way a person could grow up saying pop and then find herself one day just thinking soda.

As I knelt beside their bed, I felt something hard beneath my right knee. "Why are there cough drops all over the carpet?" I asked, using the plural, for I could see then that the floor was dotted with them, half-sucked and smooth like sea glass washed up in the dingy blue shag of my parents' bedroom.

"Your father coughs a lot at night. He sucks on them until he's just about to doze off, and then he'd spit them on the floor," my mother explained, her sentence beginning in the present tense but ending in the past, because that's the way death worked, the fact of it lost for whole seconds, whole sentences. "I used to pick them up in the morning, but he'd get after me for wasting perfectly good cough drops."

"Bettina's not here yet?" I asked. My sister lived just an hour away, so I was annoyed that she had not arrived, but I was also admitting defeat: the mattress was too much for me to handle alone.

"You know she has a family," my mother said, by way of excusing her absence.

Rachel and I had been together eight years. We had a house, jobs, two cats, and a dog, so I thought of myself as having a family, also.

"You know what I mean, Sybil," my mother replied. I did know. She meant that I didn't have children, but mainly she meant that two women together was not a family.

"Well, if she's not here in the morning, I'll call a neighbor to help," I said, but my mother did not like this plan. She felt a mattress soaked with urine was a family affair.

My father was dead, I said, so what did it matter, and she said, "Why can't you say 'passed away' like everyone else?" This was a good question.

From where she lay on the floor on the far side of the bed, she announced that she was putting me in my old bedroom. "So you'll be comfortable," she added, and I did not say that I had never been comfortable in this room and could not imagine I'd start being comfortable in this room now, nor did I remind her that Rachel would be arriving the next day, which meant that I would not really be in my old room long enough to get comfortable because Rachel and I always slept in the basement, in the rec room that my father had built years ago with teenagers in mind. My parents did not approve of us sharing a bed, and the rec room was a compromise: it allowed us to sleep together, a technical win for us, but together on separate sofas, unlike my sister and her husband, Carl, who slept upstairs in her old room, in a double bed that my parents had purchased for this very purpose.

"Why are you lying on the floor?" I asked, bending low to peer beneath the bed at her.

"You're getting rid of my bed," she said, and then she pulled herself slowly up, using the mattress as support, and I picked up my bag from where I'd dropped it and went down the hallway to the room my mother somehow imagined I would be comfortable in, this room that I had spent my childhood in: with walls that my father had painted pink as a surprise, the orange shag carpet, the framed print of a child kneeling to pray.

Years ago, soon after I brought Rachel here to my parents' house for the first time, I'd returned for a solo visit having to do with one of many health scares related to my father. Though my parents had just met Rachel, they did not engage in even the basic courtesy of inquiring how she was. Then, on my second night here, my mother came into my room, *this* room, to announce that she—and not just *she* but everyone she knew—was ashamed of it. She was carrying Bibles, a stack of three, as though they did not all say the same thing.

"It?" I said. "What, exactly, is *it*?"

"You know what *it* is." This was what an education had done to me, she said. I couldn't just talk about stuff like normal people.

"Well, then I guess I'm not normal," I said, "because I want you to say what this *it* is that you and every single person you know is so ashamed of." I was speaking to her from the bed I had occupied as a child, before I went away and became the kind of person who thought of her life as something more than *it*.

"If you can't say what you mean," I said, "then we're not going to talk about it."

My mother had left, but not before turning to set the Bibles, stacked atop one another, on my dresser, where they have remained these seven years; on the nightstand, a fourth had been added—just in case.

Now, beneath the praying child, there was something new, pointing upward: a row of hunting rifles, six in total, butts nestled in the orange shag rug.

I went into the kitchen, where my mother was doing something with cottage cheese.

"Why are Dad's guns in my room?" I asked.

"They were in the entryway, but you know how your sister gets about the kids."

"You mean how she gets about not wanting them to blow their heads off?" I said.

Earlier that evening, after a day spent flying backwards from Albuquerque to Los Angeles in order to get a flight to Minnesota, I had stopped to pick up my rental car at the airport, and the young man at the counter asked whether I was here on vacation. He was making small talk, but also, he didn't think I was from here, for reasons having to do with the way that I speak, the Minnesota accent that I no longer have. I had not made a point to lose it, not that I could recall, though Rachel says that by the time we met, it was already gone. Sometimes, my mother says she can't understand me anymore. "It's your brogue," she says, as if I have suddenly become Scottish.

"Actually, my father just died," I told the young man, which surely struck him as further proof that I was not from here, because if you were from here, you knew not to say such things to strangers. Quickly, he handed me the keys, and I got into the rental car and drove two hours up the interstate, exiting onto the highway that led through my hometown. All around me was darkness, but I knew what was out there: lakes and fields, cows and barns and silos, the occasional house. Three miles out of town, I turned onto a gravel road and then, half a mile later, into the driveway, at the top of which I shut off the engine and rested my head on the steering wheel, the way one does at the end of a long trip, especially when there's more to come.

I lifted my head, and there was my mother, staring in at me like all the gas station attendants of my youth. I rolled down the window. "Fill 'er up," I said, but she didn't get the joke, or maybe she did get it but didn't get why I was making a joke at a time like this, with my father so recently dead.

Passed away.

"Oh, you're awake," she said. "I thought you were planning to sleep out here."

My mother often said things like this, things along the lines of suggesting that I might be planning to sleep in a rental car in the driveway. My father and I had been alike in the way that such things irritated us. "Why would I sleep in the car?"

"I thought you might be tired from the drive," she said.

"I am tired," I said, and then I tried to play the game where I kept my mouth shut, just once—the game I always lost. "But why would I sleep in the car?"

"Shirley's been at it again," my mother said.

Shirley Koerber lived on the lot behind my parents, her sole companions a band of dogs at which she yelled for various infractions. She was a stout woman with legs that bowed severely, as though she were straddling an invisible barrel as she walked, and she possessed a deep hatred of small animals—squirrels, chipmunks, birds—all of which the dogs chased with limited success and at which she shot with far greater. As a child, I'd awakened often to the sound of her gun, rising to watch from my window as the dogs circled the felled animal, howling, while Shirley rode her imaginary barrel toward them. Once when I was hanging laundry on the backyard line, a bullet whizzed past my head and I ran inside, leaving the basket of wet clothes behind. When my mother came home and asked about the abandoned clothes, I explained that Shirley had been shooting again, and my mother nodded as if I'd said it had started to rain, my options akin to opening an umbrella or going inside, for there was no option that involved making the rain stop.

"This is crazy," Rachel said the first time she visited my parents' house, a visit that I kicked off with a tour of the bullet holes speckling the back wall. "Why didn't your parents do something?"

Rachel grew up in the suburbs of New York, in an intellectual Jewish family with parents who were refugees from war and violence. Until she met me, Rachel had not known people who discussed guns in a personal way, as objects they owned and fired.

"What could they have done?" I asked, trying to see the bullet holes through her eyes. Until I met Rachel, I had not known people who had never held a gun.

"What could they have done?" Rachel repeated, sounding incredulous. "They could have called the police."

"And what could the police have done?" I said, equally incredulous. "Take the gun?"

"Yes," Rachel said. "They could have taken the gun."

I made a list once—pre-Rachel—a list of the things that I considered non-negotiable in a partner. It was a short list, reasonable in its expectations. I met Rachel just two months later, at a lesbian potluck of all things. Not long after we moved in together, I read an article in the *New York Times*—back when we used to have it delivered instead of reading it on the computer—about professional matchmakers, all of whom said that the key to successful matchmaking was to pair up people with the same pasts, people who recognized themselves in their potential mate's childhood and family and beliefs: Italian Catholic from Long Island with Italian Catholic from Long Island. People want familiarity in a mate, want to recognize themselves, their youth, in the other person.

That's what all the matchmakers said. It's not that I didn't believe this. I did—maybe especially of the sorts who would consult a matchmaker—but I also believed that matching a person with someone who resembled a cousin more than a lover suggested a lack of imagination. Until then, I'd assumed, naïvely I suppose, that most couples were like us, drawn to each other precisely because we were so unfamiliar.

At night, when we lay in bed, Rachel told me stories about her family's arrival in this country, and I listened. Her father and grandparents had fled Russia because they were Mensheviks, one of her stories began; she dropped in *Menshevik* as though the word were common knowledge. This was right after we had sex the first time, so I did not say, "What is a Menshevik?" though later I realized that nobody knew what Mensheviks were, that Mensheviks were not common knowledge, except in the very specific world of Russian Jews in exile.

Her grandparents had first gone to France, where they continued to be Mensheviks, and then came to this country, where they kept on gathering with other Mensheviks. Even after her grandparents were dead and her father had his own family—Rachel, her mother, and sister—the tradition continued. One of the other Menshevik offspring had a house on the Hudson River where all of them would meet on weekends in the summer to eat and drink vodka and discuss Russia, its past, its future. Once, Stalin's daughter was there, Rachel told me. This was after a different night of sex. She wasn't Jewish, of course, Stalin's daughter, but she was Russian and in exile. Imagine growing up with parents who knew Stalin's daughter. I couldn't imagine it, not at first, but I wanted to, just as she could not imagine parents who rose at dawn, who did not smoke or drink, who did not speak of ideas or question God, his existence, or his decisions.

My great-great-grandparents left Sweden in 1867 after the crops had failed yet again, failed because so much rain fell that year that the potatoes rotted in the ground. They left with eight children and arrived in Minnesota a year and a half later with five, two of whom eventually continued on to Washington, where they became fishermen, while the other three settled in Minnesota and resumed farming, the two factions forming—or so I like to imagine—a poetic yin-yang of land and sea. According to my father, the Minnesota side never forgave the Washington brothers for choosing water, not after all the misery that water had brought to their family: first, the absence of it, droughts that stole the crops year after year, and then the abundance of it taking their crops yet again, and finally the water that surrounded them during those agonizing weeks at sea as they crouched, vomiting, between decks, and watched three children die.

By the time that I was born in this same small town in Minnesota, my father had long ago given up farming to run a hardware store that he purchased in the late forties, soon after he came home from the war. He had enlisted right out of high school, but when the war ended, he had gone no farther away than Florida, where he was being trained as an airplane mechanic. Something about the experience unsettled him greatly, put him off the world. He came home to this town and never left again. He spoke of this as the best decision he ever made. I suppose that there is a sanity in this, in claiming to want what one has, and yet, perhaps because my father and I were alike in all of the most problematic ways—stubborn yet shy, prone to solitude, sarcastic at moments when it did not behoove us to be so, overly fond of the subterfuge of words—I thought that I understood things about him that others might not: that is, I believed that he was not beyond regret, regret for a life that he—to be fair—never alluded to but that I sometimes imagined for him, college in place of family, in place of us.

For starters, he took no pleasure in family time. Every evening of my childhood, he went back to his hardware store, where he watched television and tended to the books, and though I was relieved at his chronic disinterest in us—for the house took on a different shape when he and his anger were part of it—I wondered at his decision to become a father in the first place, especially as he had waited forty years to begin. Occasionally, well-intentioned people—people who are parents—ask why I do not have children, referring to the fact that I am "good" with children, that I like them. "No," I tell these people. "I like some children." You see, I am selfish, but just unselfish enough to accept that I would not be a good parent. I never wanted to be a parent. In this way, I suspect, my father and I were also alike.

Thus, when he ridiculed me for going far away from this town and the world of hardware and childbearing, I could not help but see his ridicule as an expression of his own remorse. I imagined that my father would someday speak to me with an openness that belied the daily narrative of this place. He never did, so what remains is the narrative, a fairly standard one for those who grew up how and where I did, about hard work and toeing the line. Still, I do not think it possible to tell the story of my father's death without first telling the story of how we came to be in this country, this place, the place my father ran back to, the place I ran away from.

Early in our relationship, Rachel and I decided that the best way to keep our relationship sound was to live a plane flight away from our families. This, we believed, would save us from middle-of-the night phone calls from a parent who needed help relighting the heater or procuring medicine that had "suddenly" run out. Of course, this was a plan built on logic, and middle-of-the-night calls—middle-of-the-night anythings—are not. They are built on the fears that daytime holds at bay, fears that do not keep company with reason. I say this not in a critical way, for I am not impervious to the terror of deepest night, but perhaps I am just hopeful enough, still, to know that morning will come.

The night that my father died, Rachel and I had returned from New Jersey, where we had been visiting her mother, and when we got home, the pet-sitter had refused to leave. She just sat there, telling story after story of all the adorable things our pets had done in our absence, and when she was finally gone, Bettina called, but, by then, we had vowed not to answer the phone for the rest of the evening. I did not even listen to my sister's message, but Rachel said that there was something odd about her tone and that I needed to call her back at once.

Bettina answered in her usual way, a hello and then right down to business. "So, I just talked to Mom, and she said that Dad might be dead."

"*Might?*" I said, seizing on this as the starting point.

She explained that my mother had called her a few minutes earlier, and when my sister asked, "What's up?"—brusquely because she'd been trying to get my mother to stop calling at the kids' bedtime—my mother had said, "Oh, not much," and then, "Dad's not doing so good." My sister thought this meant that my father's cough had worsened or that he was just being his usual cranky self. "What's wrong with him?" she'd said.

"Well," my mother had said, "he's on the floor, and the paramedics are working on him, but it's been an hour, so I think they think he's dead."

My sister and I were both laughing. Rachel was not.

"Let me know when they're sure," I said.

An hour later, my sister called again. My father was definitely dead.

I would like to say that I did not sleep well that first night back in my old room, but I did. The night before, by way of letting Rachel know that I had arrived, I texted her a photo of the guns lined up beside my bed with the caption "Fresh sheets." I awakened in the morning to a text from her letting me know that she had finally managed to locate a house-sitter—she had given in and called the same loquacious woman we had been unable to get rid of two days earlier—and was on her way to the airport at last. Of the photo and its caption, she said nothing.

Then, I called the neighbor, and he said that he would come right over to help me with the mattress, but by noon the neighbor had still not arrived. My mother set the table with food that people had dropped off: hotdishes and Jell-O salads made with walnuts and sour cream and shredded carrots, the kind of food that I had grown up on, that we ate in the basements of churches and brought to others. Protestant food, I described it to Rachel.

The night before, I'd found a pair of suede mittens in a drawer, and I had them on now, despite the heat. I could not eat with them on, but I liked the way they felt.

"What was his last meal?" I asked.

"He had a frozen pizza around five," my mother said. "Then a couple of pot pies at six. There was a TV dinner in the oven when he had the heart attack. One of the paramedics smelled it, or it might have burned down the house."

When I was two months old, my father came home from ice-fishing one Sunday to find me in the oven. "She wouldn't stop crying," my mother had explained as my father lifted me—like a Thanksgiving turkey!—from the bottom rack.

That was the way my father told the story, making my presence in the oven sound festive. My mother never told the story.

"Did he always eat four dinners?" I asked.

"He didn't actually eat the TV dinner," she said. "Why are you wearing mittens?"

The neighbor arrived then, bringing a jar of sauerkraut made by his wife. He and I turned the mattress on its side and carried it through the house while my mother stood in the entryway holding the door for us. As we passed through, I saw that she was crying, but I said nothing because what came to mind to say was "It's just a mattress soaked in piss." That is the person I am here. When I'm not here, I tell myself that the person I am here is not who I really am. Rachel is the only person who knows both, and that is no small thing.

"Your father was really proud of you girls," the neighbor said.

"I don't think he was *that* proud," I said. My mother cried harder.

The neighbor was Bettina's age—not some old man is my point—and I wanted to say something about his use of "girls," but he'd come in the middle of a busy workday, so I didn't. This, I thought fleetingly, was how injustice grew.

On three, we heaved the mattress into the bed of my father's truck.

"You're pretty strong," said the neighbor. He meant for a girl. "So, did you ever end up getting married?"

"End up?" I said. I understood the way his mind worked.

"You know what I mean," he said.

"Not really," I said. "Anyway, I'm a lesbian, so I can't get married. It's against the law." I knew that he knew I was a lesbian. Everyone in town knew, despite my parents' best efforts.

"Tell Bettina I said hello," he said.

I had forgotten until then that he and my sister had once dated. Not exactly dated—they snuck out at night sometimes and met in the woods between our houses, his the house he still lived in these twenty-five years later. They met in a fort that we had all built together, and when I asked Bettina what she and the neighbor boy did in that fort on the nights they met, she said that they played house, which I had taken to mean that they sat around eating the cans of baked beans that we stole from our parents' cupboard and stocked the fort with so that it would feel real, like a place we could live if we needed to, if the Rapture happened or we ran away from home.

I slammed the tailgate of the truck. "Thank you for your help, and thank your wife for the sauerkraut. I'd forgotten how neighborly everyone is."

The neighbor looked at me uncertainly, as if he thought I maybe meant something more by this. "I'm sorry about your father," he said at last.

*

I'd last seen my sister six months earlier, a visit that ended abruptly because of what happened on Christmas Eve. The evening had unfolded as usual—supper, church, the midnight opening-of-gifts, a progression of events throughout which we acted like just another family together for the holidays, ignoring slights and feigning enthusiasm for our gifts, most of them chosen with little regard for the recipient's taste or needs. Only Rachel was safe from having to pretend, for she never received gifts from anyone in my family.

When I'd pointed this out once, early on, my mother said, "But isn't she Jewish?"

Rachel was Jewish. This did not stop us from spending every other Christmas with her mother in New Jersey, alternating under the pretense of fairness, though I suspected that it was Rachel's way of minimizing the time spent with my family, not because she disliked my family but because she disliked who I was when I was with my family. I felt similarly, so I should have been better disposed toward her position, but mainly I brimmed with unjust thoughts: that if Rachel really loved me, she would love me *most* when I was around my family, saying and doing awful things.

On the night that would turn out to be our father's last Christmas Eve, he sat in his recliner opening gifts: a shirt, gloves, another shirt. He studied each, demanded loudly but of no one in particular, "What do I need this for?" and then, with a solid drop kick, sent it ricocheting off the ceiling and tree while we, his family, continued to unwrap our own disappointing gifts.

For several years, our father had been relearning Swedish, which he had spoken as a child, so in the weeks prior to Christmas, I'd gone to every used bookstore in Albuquerque, searching for something, anything, in Swedish. I'd finally found Zola in hardcover for ten dollars, which seemed like both nothing and a lot, nothing when considered against the fact that it was the seventh bookstore I'd tried, a lot when I stopped to think about how few people in Albuquerque would be interested in Zola to begin with, in Swedish to top it off.

My father tore the wrapping from the book with his usual angry haste, and I braced for the sound of his shoe on hardcover. For several long minutes, he stared at the cover, taking in the words in Swedish, and then he began to read. Eventually, he rose from his recliner and went, with Zola, to his room. He had had enough of Christmas, enough of us.

As my mother scurried around retrieving his gifts and sobbing while the rest of us sat watching her, Bettina turned to me from where she sat on the sofa. "The Swedish book was my idea," she said. "I was the one who said the only thing he cares about anymore is Swedish."

This was true. She had said it during a telephone conversation that summer, not as a gift idea, but as a complaint. She had taken the kids to visit my parents, and our father had barely spoken to any of them. He just lay on his bed listening to Swedish on tape, hitting pause to yell for my nephew and niece when he needed something, another cup of coffee or a jar of herring.

"The important thing," I said, looking up at her from where I sat on the floor, "is that he actually got one gift he didn't kick. What does it matter whose idea it was?"

And just like that, she was on me.

To be clear, I don't condone fighting, but neither do I think it's worse for two women to go at it than two men, even if those two women are "sisters who should love each other," as Rachel kept saying afterward, after she and Carl had pulled us apart and the two of us had gone down to our rec room quarters. When we undressed for bed, she pointed at my arm, at the scratches from the tree that Bettina and I had rolled against, nearly toppling it as we each struggled to get on top.

The next morning when I awoke, Rachel's sofa was empty. I went upstairs, and there they were, the two spouses huddled together at the table, between them the leftover potato sausage from supper, which they began—only then—to eat. When I sat down at the table, they pretended that they had not been talking about what happened the night before. Carl took out a shell casing and showed it to Rachel, who touched it the way one would a talisman, as though it contained power that should not be doubted or taken for granted. Did Rachel even understand what a shell casing was, I wondered, that it was what remained behind, empty, after a gun had been fired?

My brother-in-law was once a large man. He woke up on his twenty-fifth birthday and decided that he did not want to be large any longer, so he picked up the first object he laid eyes on—a shell casing from the top of his dresser—and put it in his pocket. Whenever he felt like eating, he had once told me, he reached into his pocket and the casing acted like an electric shock, the memory of his life as a fat teenager and then a fat man jolting his resolve.

My sister had not known her husband then, and when he told us—my mother, my sister, and me—the story of his weight loss, the way that half his body just melted away, he explained it like this: "When I was twenty-five, I lost my twin brother."

We were driving in his van at the time, and my mother, who was in the passenger seat, turned and stared at him with a stricken look. "Carl," she said, "I didn't know you had a twin."

We all laughed, except my mother, who liked things to mean what they meant.

I knew that clarity often arrived unexpectedly, a moment in which one saw one's life plainly—that it was not working, what needed to be done to fix it—but these moments were fleeting. This was what I admired about my brother-in-law, that he could hold on to his moment of clarity all these years, was still holding on to it.

I sat at the kitchen table with him and Rachel in silence, watching them pretend to enjoy the potato sausage until Bettina appeared. She went directly to the toaster, inserted a slice of bread, then stood awaiting its transformation.

"Remember when you tried to smother me?" I said.

She laughed. "Of course."

I laughed also.

The first year of my life, Bettina and I had shared a room, the room that now houses my father's guns, the room that Rachel and I are forbidden to sleep in together. This—the story of what happened in that room, which is the story of why Bettina was moved to her own room, the room with the double bed purchased for her and Carl by my parents—was one of the stories that Rachel did know about my childhood, but Rachel did not think the story was funny.

What happened was this: our mother found Bettina inside my crib one morning, holding a pillow over my face. "I want to smother the baby," she'd explained. She was not yet three, but she knew not only the word "smother" but apparently how smothering worked, for she'd brought a pillow with her when she crawled up and over the railing and into my crib.

"Maybe she meant 'mother,'" my grandmother said when the

adults whispered about it in the years to come. "She heard all this talk of mothering and got the word wrong." Nobody stated the obvious: that *mother* was not a verb, not where we came from.

"She had a pillow over her face," my mother had asserted once. Just once.

As we retold the story that morning, Bettina and I continued to laugh. Our spouses continued not to laugh. They did not approve of the way that our family settled problems: the way that we downplayed one egregious event by invoking a time when our behavior had been even worse. Had the outcome been different, our response might have been different, but you didn't respond to the thing that hadn't happened. You responded to what had, and what had happened was nothing. We were just another family whose members had not killed one another.

We'd never liked each other, my sister and I—who knows why, animosity is nearly always harder to explain than love—and Christmas, with its expectations of good cheer, seemed only to intensify our hostility. Indeed, I could not recall a Christmas when this tradition of ill will had not made itself known. The year that I was ten, Bettina twelve, we were ordered to help with the erecting and trimming of the tree, a task that began with the two of us standing behind our crouching mother, each plotting how to make the endeavor unpleasant for the other, while our mother hacked away at the trunk with a flimsy saw, paring it down to fit into the stand, a tripod with three large screws. Our mother had a vision, I think, of the three of us tightening the screws just so to achieve a perfectly erect tree, of us working together.

As she sawed, I selected a small glass ornament from one of the boxes and put it in my mouth, then smiled at Bettina, my lips pulled back to reveal the smooth green glass.

"Mom, Sybil put a bulb in her mouth," Bettina reported, as I knew she would.

"Sybil, spit out the bulb," our mother said, her weary voice muffled by the tree, and Bettina smiled at me smugly.

I chomped down hard. I had a plan—fuzzy at best—to assert that my sister had smacked the top of my head, causing the bulb to shatter.

My mother stood up. "Spit it out," she said again, cupping her hand beneath my mouth. She did not yet know what I had done.

I opened my mouth wide. I could see the fear in my mother's eyes, feel it in the way that she gripped my head in the vice-like bend of her elbow and worked like a dentist on my mouth, all the while pleading in a loud, panicky voice for me not to swallow.

Just over my mother's shoulder, Bettina peered down at me, smiling.

This was not our first glass scare of the year. The first, just months earlier, was on a Sunday, steak day at our house. After church, Bettina and I set the table, which we managed to do quietly—in deference to our father—though we circled each other warily, using our hips and elbows to force the other aside. Bettina, because she was older, carried the steak knives, marching toward me with the blades pointed out in a game of cutlery chicken. Meanwhile, our mother stood before the oven, its door cracked open as the steaks crackled and smoked beneath the broiler. It was then, as she bent to peer inside, that we heard it: a small pop, our mother's "oh no." The bulb in the oven had exploded.

"A little glass isn't going to kill anyone," said our father when he saw the glittering steaks. "We're not wasting perfectly good meat."

Our mother did not argue. She went into the front yard, held the steaks up beneath the brilliant sun, and—in a dress rehearsal for what she would do with my open mouth just months later—extracted shards. Then she came back inside and set the platter of lukewarm meat on the table, crying just a little. We ate tentatively, except for my father, who acted as though there was nothing he welcomed more than the opportunity to eat glass.

I had not told Rachel either story. I knew what she would say. "How is it possible for a family to have two stories about eating glass?"

Six weeks after the ornament incident, on a morning during which we had been tasked with removing the remaining Christmas decorations, Bettina and I took our Christmas gifts—tennis rackets that we had begged for, separately, after watching Wimbledon on television—and practiced our swings against the tree that our mother had tried, without success, to teach us to erect together. In a rare display of teamwork, we backhanded and lobbed and forehanded until entire boughs of the desiccated tree were bare, their needles embedded so deeply into the shag carpet that the vacuum, which my mother drove frantically around the room, proved useless. Bettina and I spent the afternoon on our knees, extracting needles by hand and dropping them into the large bowl generally reserved for popcorn, but when we went to report that we were finished—arguing about who had done more—we could not find our mother anywhere.

"She's gone," one of us said, and seeing nothing more in our mother's disappearance than possibility, we went into our parents' bedroom to snoop. We tried first to shake quarters out of the large plastic piggy bank in the corner and, after failing, spent several minutes jumping on the bed. Bored, we began opening dresser drawers, looking for something that would shock or appall us, though we did not know what.

"What's that?" Bettina said. We'd both heard it, a sound that seemed to come from beneath the bed.

"Maybe we broke it when we were jumping," I said.

We lay on the mattress and hung our heads over the side. There was our mother, lying perfectly still beneath the bed. She did not turn to look at us, did not acknowledge our presence, and finally Bettina asked, "Are you dead?"

I laughed, not at the thought that she might be dead but at the silliness of the question.

"Go away," said our mother, still not looking at us. "I'm sick of you both."

She began to cry then, and we did not know what to do, so I said to Bettina, "It's your fault," and she replied that it was mine, and we went back and forth like this for several minutes so that we would not have to think about the fact that our mother was lying beneath the bed.

Three hours later, our father's headlights came up the driveway. We always dreaded his arrival because whatever we were doing—watching television, playing games, reading—made him angry. That evening, we were sitting at the table, waiting.

"Just sitting there doing nothing?" he yelled from the entryway as he took off his coat and boots.

We told him that our mother was under the bed.

"Under the bed?" he said, sounding more confused than angry.

"She's hiding," Bettina explained.

"From us," I clarified. "She's tired of us."

"Who isn't?" said our father.

Our father was afraid of nothing. When a noise awakened us in the middle of the night, he got out of bed and went directly toward the source, catching over the years bats and squirrels, even a skunk that had worked its way into the dryer, but that night he stood staring down the hallway toward the room in which our mother, his wife, lay under the bed whose urine-soaked mattress I would find myself removing nearly three decades later. Finally, he turned and went into the living room, where he sat in his recliner, the needleless tree nearby, and read the paper. After a while, our mother came out from under the bed and went into the kitchen, and when supper was ready, we all sat down at the table and ate the meal that she had crawled out to prepare, and we asked nothing about why she had been under the bed to begin with.

It was past two when Rachel pulled up in the driveway. She got out of her rental car, and my mother came out of the house, and they stood ten feet apart, greeting each other like two people on opposite banks of a fast-flowing river. Rachel extended a card, which my mother reached toward her to receive, still holding the door ajar behind her; then, without inviting my partner of eight years to follow, my mother turned and went back inside, where she would add the card to the stack that I had pulled out of the mailbox that morning. I rolled my eyes at Rachel, and she did not roll hers back at me.

Inside, my mother stood beside the pile of cards, and when Rachel asked what she could do to help, my mother told her to open each of them and log the donation amount, and Rachel set down her bag and began—using a steak knife supplied by my mother—to do just that. I sat with her, not asking about her flight or making any of the small talk that people make. I did not want my mother to think we had a relationship that in any way resembled what my mother believed of relationships.

Most of the cards contained two one-dollar bills, but when Rachel opened her own card, I saw that inside was a receipt for a $100 donation to Amnesty International in memory of Harold Berglund. I did not know which seemed more absurd—the amount or the organization, which my father would have suspected, as he did most charities, of being communist. She looked at me, then slipped the receipt into her pocket, replacing it with two bills. On the log that she was keeping for my mother, she wrote: "Rachel $2."

She made a point to read each of the cards, and I made a point not to. I could not help but feel that the task felt to her anthropological, a study of this place that she often described to others, our friends, with succinctness: "It's the most foreign place I've ever been that does not require a passport."

"What do you think this means?" she asked, and she read from a card that said, "Once we visited your family and Harold told us about the Amish."

"How would I know?" I said, meaning that I did not want to be made the expert.

When we finished, my sister was still not there, so Rachel and I got into my father's truck and drove to the town dump, where we paid a small fee to discard my father's urine-soaked mattress amid appliances and furniture and bags of clothing, the detritus of his neighbors' lives.

"I can't believe this place," Rachel said. "It's so strange to think this is where you're from."

"I'm not actually from the dump," I joked. I tended to fill silences with unfunny comments when things between us were tense, which seemed the case now, even if Rachel had reached over and twirled my hair while I drove. "I did learn to shoot here, though."

This was true. When I was twelve, my father had enrolled me in a gun safety course and we'd practiced here, in this place where we could do little harm because everything around us was beyond fixing.

"Have you talked to Bettina?" Rachel asked.

"Why?" I said.

Rachel sighed. "She's your sister, your only sibling, and you just lost your father."

We climbed out of the truck's cab and into the bed, where we strained to expel the mattress.

"I talked to Carl," she said. "On the phone last night."

"Carl?" I said. "Since when do you and Carl talk on the phone?"

"We're worried," she said.

I wanted to ask which of them had placed the call because that would indicate which of them was more worried, but I knew she would say that it didn't matter who had called. It mattered that they were worried.

"Carl told me about your mother," she said quietly. Quiet definitely meant angry.

"What about my mother?" I said, but I knew what Carl had told her. "The oven wasn't even on," I added, though I imagined she knew this was untrue. I laughed suggestively, but she looked at me as if I were the crazy one.

"It's not funny," she said, and then, "Are you worried?" She meant worried about my mother, now that my father was dead.

"It was a long time ago," I said. "Anyway, that story is none of Carl's business."

"What do you mean?" she said. "He's part of this family."

I thought about the way she said "this family," including herself even though I had done everything I could to make her feel outside my family because I could not imagine her wanting to be inside. I reached into the cab of the truck, behind the seat, where my father kept a rifle and a box of ammunition. "Do you want to try?" I asked, holding out the gun.

Rachel stared—at me, at the gun.

"There's no one around," I said. I pointed at the mattress, which lay where it had landed, propped against a door-less refrigerator. "It's your chance to finally shoot a gun."

I said this as though shooting a gun were something she had aspired to, a bucket list item that I was giving her the chance to tick off.

Rachel looked around the dump rather than at me, this woman with whom she lived who was now offering her a gun, this woman whose mother had tried to bake her. "How is it that we've been together eight years yet you've never told me that story?" she asked softly.

I walked out into the distance with my father's rifle—away from the mattress, away from Rachel—and knelt behind an abandoned bathtub, loaded the gun, and pressed the butt to my shoulder.

"What are you doing?" Rachel yelled, and I pulled the trigger. Even from a distance, I could see the hole that it tore in the stained yellow mattress.

Each year on my mother's birthday, my father and mother would go into the aisles of the hardware store devoted to household goods, and my father would instruct my mother to pick a gift out for herself. One year, she chose a vacuum cleaner, another year a coffeemaker. "This doesn't seem like a birthday present," I said the year of the crockpot. "It's really a present for the whole house. I mean, we all eat. Plus, it comes from our store, so she already owns it."

I would like to revise history, to claim this comment as a reflection of my nascent feminism, but I know better. I was simply stating the obvious, for I was that sort of child, one who embraced logic (though if I were going to belabor the point, I would note that feminism is simply that: a stating of the obvious). I was ten at the time, still of an age when presents meant something. An appliance was not a gift. I suppose all children feel this way about adults. They watch them stare at the news or listen to them speak of what milk cost today and what it cost a year ago, and feel nothing but amazed horror, and soon enough they stop listening because they understand that from adults nothing interesting can be expected.

After just a few meals, my father had unplugged the crockpot from the wall. "Nothing tastes right," he announced. To be clear, the crockpot had produced meals far better than those on which we usually dined, and I could not imagine that my father did not agree. What I have come to suspect is that he took offense at the very thing that attracted my mother to the crockpot in the first place: it made her life easier.

The next morning, he took the stew-encrusted crockpot with him when he left for work, placing it on the seat of the truck that, all these years later, Rachel and I used to drive his mattress to the dump. This is what it means to have a vertical history: your family arrives in a place and stays, and everything gets built on top of itself so that the dump where you take the mattress might also be the dump where your father took the crockpot all those years earlier, which might also be the dump where your partner, watching you with a rifle pressed to your shoulder, thinks that she has had enough.

She did not actually say that she had had enough. What she said was, "I don't understand you people." What she meant was that I was one of *them*.

When we got back to the house, Bettina, Carl, and the kids were there, and Bettina greeted us by saying something about how we should not have run off and left my mother all alone, and I said something about how she should not have taken her own sweet time getting there. Then, we sat down to eat dinner, in silence, but after several minutes Petra, my niece, set down her fork and asked, "Were Sybil and Rachel born together in a big bubble?"

She was seven, trying to make sense of our relationship, of the way that we disappeared into the basement while the rest of the family stayed above ground. I thought of my mother saying, "Everyone's ashamed of it."

"Yes," I told my niece while the others looked down at their plates. "Rachel and I were born in a bubble, and every day we wait for it to burst."

The next morning, my mother came into the dining room, where we all sat eating various versions of breakfast, and stood before us holding one of the Bibles from my childhood room, the room she now occupied because I had taken her mattress to the dump and shot it like an old horse being put out of its misery. I preferred to think of my actions that way, as vaguely beneficent. Of course, Rachel was the only person who knew that I'd shot the mattress, and we had not talked about it since. We had not really talked at all. She was waiting for me to explain not just about the mattress but about the fact that, years earlier, my mother had put me in the oven and turned it on, granted with the door ajar, my father arriving and plucking me out before it had time to get hot. Really, though, she was waiting for me to explain why I had not told her any of this.

My mother did not greet us or ask how everyone slept. She simply cleared her throat and began reading to us from the Bible. We all stared at her, not listening exactly, except when she paused to tell us that at night when she and my father lay in bed together, this is what they did. They read scripture. Once, years earlier, when my sister and Carl were first dating, my mother gathered the two of us—her daughters—and explained that sex was only for after marriage, but also that it was very important to marry someone with whom you were sexually compatible. When I pointed out the contradiction her advice involved—for how were you to know that you were marrying a sexually compatible partner if you did not have sex with that person, pre-marriage, to determine it?—my mother became indignant and said that this was why she did not talk to us about such things. We always thought we knew better. Then, with a note of finality, she said, "Your father and I have always been compatible in bed."

All these years later, I no more wanted to know that they read Bible verses in bed than that they had sex. I did not want to hear about the intimacies of their relationship. That is what it came down to.

Rachel is a nurse, which means that she knows how to take charge and provide comfort, so as our mother stood in the middle of the dining room, reading from the Bible and sobbing, and Bettina and I looked away in Protestant embarrassment, Rachel said, "That's lovely. I think it would be nice for the service."

We were leaving soon to meet with the minister, who was not the minister of my youth, that benign figure who had overseen my baptism and confirmation, the singular most interesting thing about him being that he wore platform shoes because there was some notion that he would be better served by height, that parishioners did not want to look down on their pastor. This new minister, my mother had told me repeatedly, led letter-writing campaigns to stop other Lutherans from embracing homosexuality. Who were these Lutherans that they were writing to, I had wondered. Was there a mailing list of homosexuality-embracing Lutherans?

"What is the purpose of this meeting with the pastor?" I asked warily.

My mother stopped sobbing but continued to stand before us in her frayed robe, the Bible aloft in her hands. *Apostolic* was the word that came to mind, though I knew that this was anachronistic thinking. The Apostles had not had Bibles because the Apostles wrote the Bible.

"We have to talk about our ideas for the service," my mother replied. "You know, your father's favorite hymns and verses. Maybe you girls have some anecdotes for the eulogy."

"What does eulogy mean?" my nephew asked. Lars was nine, the sort of child who liked words purely for the pleasure of knowing them—not as weapons, that is. The adults looked at him the way that adults often look at children who ask perfectly good questions.

I said, "In Greek, 'eu' means *good* or *true* and 'logia' means *word*, so 'good word.'"

You see, I did regard words as weapons; early on, when I was first figuring out who I was in the world, I decided to make myself unassailable—unassailable in my new life, that is, the world of books and words and people for whom education was generational, a given—and so I became a student of grammar and etymology, both of which had contributed to my "brogue" and my very specific and unlucrative skill set.

My nephew appreciated my response, as I knew he would. Children like to be taken seriously. "Does that mean that they can't lie about Grandpa?" he asked, and I said that, on the contrary, lying was generally required in eulogies, that it is nearly impossible to speak words that are at once good and true about any of us.

*

Needless to say, I was not keen to meet the new minister. Bettina said that he was fine, but Bettina had a tendency to set the bar low and also to enjoy the low-hanging fruit of normalcy that heterosexuality conferred upon her. The spouses remained behind with strict orders to keep the children out of my room, which was now my mother's room and—more to the point—the room that housed my father's hunting rifles, so it was just the three of us knocking at the pastor's office door. He immediately called out for us to enter, not pausing the way that people usually do as they shift from their private to their public selves.

As we pushed open the door, an overwhelming stench greeted us, leapt at us like a badly trained dog meeting guests. Perhaps the minister had been snacking on cheese, I thought, the stinky kind, but the minister explained, without being asked and with disturbing unselfconsciousness, that it was his feet we smelled. My mother responded to this news as though it were not news at all—as though her pastor's foot odor was common knowledge. She shook her head sympathetically and told him that the whole prayer chain had been working on it.

"You've been praying about his feet?" I said.

When I was young, the phone rang frequently with such requests, mainly involving illnesses and accidents. Even then, I was an inveterate eavesdropper, so I knew the drill. Before sitting down to pray, my mother dialed the next three members of the chain and described the nature of the request—a church member with a weak heart or Delphin Bergstrom's brother, who had run over his bare foot with the lawnmower. Regarding the chain, two things struck me: that a prayer chain seemed nothing more than God-sanctioned gossip, and that the most interesting subjects of it lived elsewhere—a nephew in Fargo who had begun tattooing his body with strange symbols; a brother-in-law who had been arrested in a park in Saint Paul. I had tried to imagine what could be done in a park that required the police or prayer or the hushed tones with which my mother spoke of it to others, but I could not, nor could I ask my mother, who had already explained that some requests were almost beyond prayer. Once, my mother caught me listening and suggested that I join in. "The more prayers the better," she said. I asked whether God had a number in mind, but she said that praying did not work that way—

did not require a consensus of opinion—which I imagined was part of its attraction.

"It means a lot to me that your mother and the other ladies pray for my feet like this," the pastor said solely to me, and then he turned to my mother. "The doctor says it's probably some sort of fungus, and the hot weather's sure not helping."

The three of us were still standing, but instead of inviting us to sit down, the pastor rose and came out from behind his desk. He was barefoot.

"Maybe we can get down to business," I said, because I feared where this was headed: the four of us, heads bowed, hands joined as we prayed together for what? Less humidity?

"Business?" said the pastor.

"I mean my father's funeral."

"Oh, yes. There's plenty of time for that," he said, "but I hope you won't mind if I offer my condolences first?" He opened his arms wide and asked whether he might hug me specifically, as though I were the only one with someone dead.

Mine was not a world of huggers but of people who greeted one another from a duelers' distance, twenty paces, so I suspected that his plan was to draw me in and hoodwink me into letting down my guard, at which point he would turn the conversation to that whole trite dichotomy of sin versus sinners—of hating one and loving the other—which would end with me saying that, first of all, sin was a construct and that moreover the two were inextricable: how could a sin even exist if there was not a body to accommodate it? It was like the fungus on his feet, in need of a host.

This was a conversation that would not end well. I knew that. So as he lunged confidently forward, I stepped swiftly aside, directly onto his foot, his funky, fungus-ridden foot. He yelped, and Bettina laughed, and my mother looked at once horrified and ashamed, as though she could not believe the hand God had dealt her—burdened with a clumsy, solicitude-adverse lesbian of a daughter.

"My mother has ideas for Bible verses," I offered instructively, and the pastor limped back behind his desk. The three of us, taking this as a cue to be seated finally, settled on the folding chairs arranged before it. "And I've got an anecdote," I added, looking at neither my mother nor my sister before I plunged ahead:

"We used to have steak every Sunday after church, and one Sunday the bulb in the oven blew. The steak was covered with glass, but my father made us eat it anyway. He said he wasn't going to sit by and watch us waste good food."

The pastor studied me for a very long time. It was a sympathetic look—I could see that, could see that my anecdote or possibly the fact that I felt driven to offer it stirred in him feelings of pity, but just as I understood the absurdity in speaking of *sin* as separate from *sinner,* it struck me as impossible to accept this sympathy as sincere, proffered as it was by someone whose life's work was to make my life more difficult.

"Can I pray for you?" he said.

"I'd prefer that you didn't," I said.

"I will anyway," he said.

Rachel and Carl were at the dining room table with the kids, all four of them drawing. I sat down and took a sip from Rachel's coffee, and Petra said, "Look, Aunt Sybil. I drew you and Rachel in the bubble." She held up a piece of cardboard on which she had sketched two stick figures with breasts holding hands inside a clumsily drawn circle.

"I love it," I said. I did love it.

"Rachel said she's going to frame it and hang it in your bedroom so it's the first thing you guys see every morning when you wake up."

"Well, if Rachel said it, then it must be true. Rachel does not lie."

Rachel gave me a sharp look, as though she thought I meant something more by this, but I didn't. Rachel does not lie.

"Care to descend with me into the Infernal Region?" I said to Rachel, which was how we referred to the basement—Hell, Hades, the Infernal Region—and she rose from the table, promised Petra that she would be back up to claim her drawing, and together we descended.

"How were things while we were gone?" I asked. Really I wanted her to ask me how things had gone with the pastor, but Rachel instead chose to answer my question.

"Carl is a mensch," she said.

"A mensch?" I said.

She started to explain what a mensch was, and I said that I knew what a mensch was, that my consternation had to do with the fact that I had never once in all the years we were together heard her use *mensch,* or really anything Yiddish for that matter.

"I use *schlepp* all the time," she said.

"You do," I agreed, "and your response has confirmed my point."

"How does proving to you that you have heard me use Yiddish somehow prove that you have not?" she asked.

"Because you know I'm right, so you reverted to the exception."

"Okay," she said. "I get it. You're mad that Carl and I are friends."

"I'm not mad," I said. "I'm not."

"Okay."

"Anyway, you're not friends. You're in-laws."

"The two outsiders, you mean. Is that your point?"

"I don't really have a point," I said. As far as I knew, I didn't.

"You don't have a point, and yet here we are, talking about why I don't have the right to call Carl a mensch or a friend."

"I'd hardly call that a point," I said.

"I give up," she said. "I hate coming here. It's like you disappear right in front of me."

"You mean that I become one of 'you people'?" The sentence was a syntactical mess. I knew that.

"So that's what you're mad about? That I said I don't understand *you people?*"

I had hoped that she would not understand my reference, which would mean that her comment at the dump the day before was nothing more than a fleeting moment of frustration, but she did remember, and this gave it import. "I told you I'm not mad," I said again.

"That doesn't mean you aren't. It means you don't want to accept that you're mad. What I don't understand, I guess, is who you're mad at. Me or them?"

"The meeting was all a setup," I said, and when she looked confused, I clarified, "Just now. With the pastor."

"What do you mean a setup?" she asked.

"To get me in the anti-homosexual letter-writing pastor's office so that he could exorcize my Sapphic demons."

Rachel laughed, and though I had meant for her to laugh, her laughter galled me.

"It's not funny," I said.

"So what are you saying? That your father's death was purely strategic, a tactical move designed to get you back here and into that man's office?" Her tone was at once incredulous and amused.

"It's possible," I said.

"Yes," she said. "I guess anything is possible."

I hated when she said stuff like this, placating clichés that meant I was being ridiculous, and hated it even more when I knew I was being ridiculous.

"Do you remember the shell casing that Carl showed you?" I said.

"What are you talking about?"

"The shell casing that your mensch friend Carl showed you at Christmas? Remember when I came upstairs and the two of you were talking about how crazy your spouses were, and then he showed you the shell casing that he carries to remind him not to give into temptation."

"The talisman?" she said.

"Yes, the talisman. It's from a gun, you know."

I could see from her face that she did not know.

"How would I know that?" she said. "I know nothing about guns. You know that."

"So Carl didn't tell you where that shell casing came from?" And then I proceeded to tell her the story of Carl's uncle, how Carl had gotten off the school bus one afternoon and come home to find his mother and sister in the kitchen drinking coffee. "You'll need to clean up the mess," his mother had said, nodding toward the living room. The mess was his uncle. While Carl was at school that day, his uncle had shot himself in the head.

I looked over at Rachel, who was lying on her sofa, perfectly still, breathing in and out, in and out.

"So, you see, Carl is just as crazy as the rest of us. He's one of us."

"Okay," she said.

I looked away. "Okay," I replied.

Fathers die first. Rachel and I both knew this to be true. Her father had died four years earlier, after several months of rapid decline. Just before he died, he announced that he and Rachel's mother would be moving out of the family home, the house in which Rachel and her sister had grown up, and into one of those upscale retirement residences in a neighboring suburb. We could not imagine him in such a place, so we knew what this meant: that he was ready to die and that even now, at the end of his life, he was doing what he had done throughout it, taking care of Rachel's mother, who lacked skills of the sort that would have allowed her to continue on in that house alone. She did not drive, never had, mainly because she lacked any spatial sense whatsoever, including the ability to find her way home amid the familiar topography of a place where she had spent most of her adult life, nor did she know how to shop for groceries or how to combine the discrete elements of the refrigerator and cupboard into the simplest of meals. Within weeks of completing the move, Rachel's father got pneumonia and rode it down.

Now, when we visited Rachel's mother, we stayed in one of the guest suites at the retirement residence, a place that was like a cruise ship—people eating and playing bridge, socializing and hooking up on the sly—except on this cruise ship everyone was old and Jewish, and they never set sail. Rachel, her mother, and I ate breakfast each morning with her mother's three usual breakfast companions, all six of us wedged in around a table meant for four, while her mother's friends tried to remember whether Rachel was Rachel or her sister.

"And who are you?" they asked me each time.

"Rachel's friend," her mother replied each time, in a way that made clear that she had not told them about Rachel.

Once, I suggested to Rachel, unhelpfully perhaps, that maybe this wasn't proof of her mother's disapproval so much as her mother's general lack of interest in her life. "They probably don't know you're a nurse either," I'd added.

On our last visit, the one we returned from the day that my father died, one of the servers came over and scolded us for having too many people at our table. Even one extra chair at the table was not safe, she said, and we had two. I stood up to move, but one of the women ordered me to sit down. She said this loudly. These women said everything loudly. Just a few minutes earlier, they had pointed to a woman at the table next to ours who was missing an arm. "Look," they screamed. "She's missing an arm but you'd never know it, the way she eats." Everyone turned to look at the amazing one-armed woman who was eating her eggs like someone with two arms.

One of the breakfast companions, Helga, was reading a book as thick as an encyclopedia, which turned out to be one of those large-print tomes. In addition to her eyesight, Helga's memory was going, just the short-term, which meant that she could talk as though it had happened yesterday about walking, orphaned, back to Berlin after the camps were liberated; about arriving in England and going to live with a family that refused to let her speak, ever, of her life before she came to them. She did not hold it against them, she said, because that was the way people thought then, that life was best treated as a series of doors slamming shut behind you. She could remember that her sons were both dead and that she had wanted girls, that her husband, who was also dead, once baked a birthday cake for her out of potatoes.

A man pulled up a chair—a seventh chair!—and sat down. "You've been reading that book forever," he said to Helga. Rachel's mother had told us about this man. His name was Saul, and he was courting someone at the table, though they did not know which of them it was.

"Yes," Helga said. "That's the good thing about not being able to remember what I read yesterday. I just start over on page one every morning, and it feels like a new book." We all laughed, and Helga looked pleased. I thought about this, about how her brain did not forget that she was funny, did not forget the subtleties of delivery or perspective that contributed to humor.

Saul read the title of Helga's book aloud. "*The Good German*? Does such a thing exist?" he asked, and the women laughed. I laughed.

Rachel gave me a look. "What?" I said. "I'm not German."

"I'll have orange juice," Helga told the server who had scolded us, and Rachel's mother reminded her that she had given up orange juice because it was hard on her stomach.

"Is that right?" she said thoughtfully, as though being introduced to some delightful fact about someone who was not her. "Grapefruit juice?" she said then, uncertainly, and Rachel's mother gave a small shake of her head.

"You hate grapefruit," she said. "You better stick with the cranberry."

Helga turned to the server and said brightly, "I will stick with the cranberry."

How did it feel, I had wondered, to exist, increasingly, from outside oneself, to rely on others to tell you who you were, to lose the secrets that you had told no one, the secrets that defined who you were, for better or worse, because they belonged only to you.

The morning of my father's funeral, I woke up on my sofa and turned to Rachel on hers. "Did you bring the purse?" I asked.

Normally, we had pockets, which was another lesbian thing about us, not that straight women don't have pockets, but lesbians seem more likely to prioritize practicality over fashion. Every once in a while, though, we went somewhere in clothes without pockets—the opera, for example—and for those occasions, we had the purse. We called it "the purse" because it did not belong to either of us, which meant that often we would arrive back at our car and realize that everything we needed, beginning with our car keys, was in the purse and the purse was somewhere else, usually under the seats that we had just occupied. We would argue about whose fault it was, but it was both of our faults and neither. That is the reassuring part of having a collective purse, a collective anything, I suppose.

Rachel sat up on her sofa and said that she had not brought the purse. What she actually said was, "You didn't tell me to bring the purse." She still felt some sort of way about the events of the last few days.

It was true that I had not asked her to bring the purse. I had not thought about the purse until that very moment, when I woke up the day of my father's funeral and saw dangling haphazardly from an unused nail the skirt that I had emergency-purchased the evening before. It was long and drab and pocketless, and I had already determined that I had no need of it in my regular life. I would leave it here, hanging in the closet of my childhood room for when I needed it the next time: when I returned to bury my mother.

Already, the day was humid, and what came to mind was the pastor's feet. I did not want to be thinking about his feet, certainly not now, hours before my father's funeral, but once I started, I could not stop. Everything reminded me of them—the constant patter and thump of my family above us, the rancid moisturizer that Rachel found in the bathroom, shoes, oatmeal, the buttermilk tang of the kitchen sponge.

Around ten, we loaded everyone into Bettina and Carl's van and Rachel's rental car, because they were parked last in the driveway, and we drove the three miles into town. My mother insisted on riding in the van, and I did not argue with her, even though I knew it was because she did not want to arrive at the church in a car driven by lesbians. The businesses in town—there were only six or seven of them—were all closed for two hours to give the 418 people enumerated on the population sign the opportunity to attend my father's funeral; my parents had owned their store for fifty-five years, so they were known.

My parents' store—Berglund Hardware—was permanently closed. The sign on the door read *Closed Until Further Notice*, but everyone knew what that meant. My father had planned to keep it going until he died, but a few years earlier, he had begun sleeping much of the day, not out of laziness but because his body's needs had shifted—he was like a cat, napping for hours and then awakening to a terrible desire for protein. The preceding winter, just two days before we wrestled beneath the Christmas tree, Bettina and I had staged an intervention. We told our father that our mother was too old to keep the store going, biting our tongues to keep from adding "by herself," though that was what it had come down to. Our father was not ready to let go of it, for reasons that were probably symbolic but felt to us like hubris. He accused us of meddling in their marriage. While we pleaded with him to consider the burden that it placed on our mother, she sat in the other room. She knew what we were up to, but she did not know how to say these things herself. "Lunch time," she called out instead, working against herself. Bettina and I had given up, accepted failure, gone into the kitchen to eat. We did not speak of it again. Then, months later, it became clear to us that the store was closed. There had been no formal announcement by either of them, just the use of past tense instead of present when they referred to it.

Halfway through the service, I feared that I had not silenced my ringer. I took out my phone, the eyes of the congregation on me. I believed that they thought of me—on the rare occasion that they did think of me—as someone who had left a place she considered herself too good for, which is to say that that morning they looked at me, phone in hand, and surely saw a woman bored by her own father's funeral.

I began to laugh. Beside me, Rachel turned, which only made me laugh harder.

The minister, busy eulogizing, announced that he had a story about my father, a memory that the deceased's younger daughter had shared with him the day before, a memory that said a lot about who Harold Berglund was. I stopped laughing.

"Every Sunday after church, the Berglunds had steak." From his pulpit, the minister looked around the church. "Every Sunday," he repeated. He nodded deeply, at once sanctioning the story and letting us know that it was over.

I began to laugh again, and soon my sister joined in. Rachel once more turned to regard me, to regard us both.

Those were the good words about my father. And why not? Every Sunday we had eaten steak. Only once had there been glass.

When Rachel told me that I needed to talk to my sister, truly talk to her, I was not troubled. That is, I did not read into her suggestion anything that seemed to imperil the agreement to keep our families at bay that we had made all those years earlier. It was the day after my father's funeral, and we were standing out in the driveway, wedged between her rental car and my father's truck. She was going home to our dog and cats, leaving me behind with my mother, who did not think that I had a family to go home to. Bettina, Carl, and the kids were leaving also, and when I pointed out to Rachel the unfairness of this, that my sister had come late and was leaving early, Rachel said that I needed to consider that children, even those as delightful as my niece and nephew, were not always what one—by which she meant my mother—wanted to deal with in the midst of grief.

"I mean it," she said. "Talk to Bettina. Soon it will be just the two of you."

I was staying, simply put, because my mother did not seem capable of being alone. I watched her banging through her new life, lost amid the detritus of the past; it was a lostness that I at least recognized, an unmoored look in her eyes that she used to get on the rare occasion that my father had to be away. My parents did not take vacations, but each fall my father drove off with a group of other men from town to hunt. They would be gone for two or three nights, and each time my grandfather came to stay. Later, I would realize that my grandfather came because it was understood—by everyone but Bettina and me—that my mother could not be left alone with us, could not be left alone with herself.

But Bettina and I did not sit down and talk, at least not then, because even as Rachel and I were saying goodbye, Bettina and

Carl and the kids came out and said that they were also hitting the road. The kids laughed because they thought that "hitting the road" was funny, and then they both flopped down on the driveway and proceeded to pummel it with their fists and scream, "I'm hitting the road. Look! I'm hitting the road!"

Rachel glanced over at me as if to say, *You see?*

I had been waiting to see how Rachel would say goodbye, whether she would tell me she loved me or skip that part, and whether I would believe it to still be true either way, but then the kids got up from the driveway—well, were yanked up—and before I knew it, everyone was driving away except me.

That night we sat alone together—my mother and I—she at the table eating microwave popcorn and reading her Bible. One of her Bibles.

"I'm going to call Rachel," I announced and stood up, and she looked at me as though she had no idea what I was talking about. "Rachel," I said again. "My partner. The woman I have been with for eight years." I huffed off, down to the basement.

I did not call, of course, even though I wanted to know that she had arrived home safely, wanted to know how Gertrude and Alice and Frederick the dog were doing, whether they missed me. But I was waiting for *her* to call, and I fell asleep waiting—fell asleep on Rachel's sofa, which was where I had decided to sleep because the basement frightened me in ways that it did not when Rachel was there with me.

Deep in the night, my cell phone rang and I sat up, thinking it was her, but it was my mother's voice whispering into my ear: "Someone's here. There's a car in the driveway. I'm scared, and your father's gone."

It was not clear which meaning of "gone" she had in mind—whether she thought that my father was off hunting or whether she knew that he was dead.

"I need you to come home," she said. "Right now."

I started to say, "I am home," but caught myself. "I am here," I said instead, worrying about semantics even as my mother was going crazy above me.

"I've got the gun," she said.

"Which gun?" I asked softly.

"The pistol," she said, referring to the gun that my father had always kept, loaded, above the stove, believing that his children would never be stupid enough to touch it. It turned out I was stupid enough. The Sunday we ate glass, after our parents disappeared into the bedroom to rest, I climbed up on the stove and stood with my feet on the burners that were still warm from string beans and potatoes and took down the loaded pistol, two stupidities rolled into one. I pointed this gun at any number of things—the toaster, the relentlessly dripping faucet, a loaf of whole wheat bread—and when my sister came in from outside and saw me there, standing atop the stove with the gun that we were forbidden to touch, she said, "I'm telling," and I turned the pistol on her.

"That gun is loaded," I said, speaking loudly this time, fearfully.

"There're in the basement!" my mother cried out, both into my ear and through the floorboards. "I hear them talking."

"There is no one down there," I said, whispering again.

And she said, "I'm going down."

"Do not go down there," I said. "Do not."

We were both silent for a moment. Above me, she paced.

"I'll call the police," I told her at last and hung up, and then I called Rachel, who answered on the fifth ring, sounding not at all groggy, though it was after midnight back home. I described the situation—that my mother had become confused and mistaken my rental car for the car of a stranger, an intruder whom she believed to be in her house at this very moment.

"She's got the pistol," I said, but the pistol was one more story I had not told Rachel, one more story at which she would not have laughed. I wanted her to laugh, even though I could see what laughing meant, how it allowed us to live with everything that was wrong. I backtracked to explain only that such a pistol existed, that my mother was holding that pistol now.

"Do not go up there," Rachel said. "Whatever you do, do not go up there." On the other end of the line, in our home miles and miles away, Rachel began to cry.

"I won't go up there," I said, but she did not stop crying. "Hey, I'm sleeping on your sofa," I said.

"Are you all crazy?" she said. She wanted an answer.

"Yes," I said. "We are all crazy." But she only cried harder.

We will steal the gun together, Bettina and I. That is what we decide when I call her at dawn after a sleepless night spent listening to my mother above me. My task will be to get the gun, to physically remove it from my mother's room, my old room, and then baton it off to my sister, who will take it away with her, though not home to the house where she lives with children whose heads none of us want blown off. My sister says she cannot be the one to take the gun for reasons having to do with the Ten Commandments—the one about stealing, I wonder, or about obeying your mother and father?—and I cannot be the one to dispose of it, for reasons having to do with the fact that neither I nor anyone I know possesses knowledge of this sort. And so, my sister and I will work together.

My mother does not seem surprised to see me when I come up for breakfast, nor does she mention her middle-of-the-night call. She is in her robe, the one that had seemed apostolic just days earlier, but now seems simply ratty. She is not carrying the pistol. I do not mention that Bettina is coming, but when she pulls into the driveway at lunchtime, my mother says, "You see? Your sister is here." Perhaps she has been expecting her all along. Perhaps in some tucked-away corner of her brain, you called one daughter and both appeared.

Then, while Bettina distracts our mother, I go into her bedroom, my old bedroom, and rummage around. The six rifles still stand at attention; the kneeling child still prays over them. If my mother discovers me, my plan is to pick up one of the Bibles and pretend to be reading it. She will believe it because she will want to believe it. But my mother does not come in and I do not find the gun. When I'm about to give up, I kneel beside the bed, like the girl in the picture, like the girl I used to be. In this way, my trip has symmetry: it begins and ends with me kneeling.

I lean sideways. Beneath the bed are old newspapers and shoes, broken toasters and irons, boxes of ammunition, presumably for the six guns leaning against the wall, but it's hard to know whether the ammunition was placed there with proximity in mind, or simply abandoned there years ago for no other reason than that there was space.

What there is not is the pistol.

As I rise, my arm rests briefly atop the bed, atop something hard. I pull back the blanket: nestled like a kitten or a hot water bottle is the loaded gun.

"Have you heard of the Mandela effect?" I ask Bettina.

Four hours have passed since she arrived, four hours during

which we ate lunch and stole a gun, and now Bettina and I are standing in the driveway, pretending to say goodbye but really trying to hand off the pistol. If there is anything that should make my mother suspicious, it is this, her two daughters making a point to bid each other farewell.

As I waited for my sister to arrive this morning, I graded papers, for though a substitute was covering my four freshman composition classes, the grading was all mine. The assignment was to write about something they knew nothing about, something they had never even heard of before, an assignment that angered them greatly, for how—they had wondered aloud at the beginning and middle and end of each class for two solid weeks—were they supposed to arrive at a topic they did not even know existed. In response, I said all of the annoying things that they expected me to say: that instead of asking this same question over and over, they should simply get started, that this was meant to be an exercise in exploration or learning or curiosity, that they had come into this world knowing nothing and look at them now. Of the one hundred and three papers submitted, only one introduced *me* to something new: the Mandela effect.

Bettina says that she has not heard of it, glancing past my shoulder at the doorway, and I say, "It's when a whole group of people remembers something that never actually happened, a collective false memory, like Mandela dying in prison."

"He did die in prison," my sister says.

"No, he didn't," I say. "That's the point. He got out and became the president of South Africa."

She is quiet for a moment, not thinking about Mandela specifically, I suspect, because my sister is not the sort to know much about Mandela, but wondering why I have brought this up now, as we stand here attempting to pass off my mother's loaded gun. My sister likes to figure out what people are thinking and why, without having to ask, though eventually she will ask.

"Why are you telling me about this right now?" she says.

"I don't know." This is true. Partly true. "I guess I'm just trying to imagine what it's like to have a memory that you're so sure of, and that all these other people have also, but the memory's wrong. I mean, how is it possible that all over the world people share the memory of Mandela dying in prison?"

"And?" she says.

"Sometimes, I think we're like that."

"We?" she says. She knows that I am referring to our family, though not whether I mean all four of us, or just me and her. "What memories do we have that aren't true?"

She is right. We are the opposite: a family with memories so true, so vivid, we rarely dare to recall them.

I say, "Remember when Mom put me in the oven, and Dad came home and took me out?"

"Like a Thanksgiving turkey," Bettina says.

Rachel believes that I did not tell her this story because of her, but the truth, I realize only now, is this: the child's mind cannot live in a constant state of contradiction. I could not sit down at the table each day of my childhood to eat the food that had come from that oven—food that had been prepared and placed inside it by my mother—unless I chose not to think about the fact that, once, my mother had placed me in that same oven and turned it on. In this way, perhaps childhood always involves a degree of Stockholm syndrome.

"I like Rachel," Bettina says then, as if she is reading my mind.

"I like Carl," I reply, even though I know that compliments given in response to compliments always sound insincere. But it's true. I do like Carl. Carl is a mensch. He grew up with his own crazy family, but he is still willing to deal with ours. This is probably how it will always be with my sister: we will always like each other's spouses better than we like each other. We will always exist at this one degree of separation.

I look back over my shoulder at the house to make sure that my mother is not watching, and then I slip the gun out of my hoodie pocket and hold it out to my sister, and we stand like that for a moment—me holding the gun, her on the other end of it—and I know that we are reliving the same moment.

Then, she takes the gun, opens the large tote bag that she brought with her for this very purpose, drops the gun inside, and extracts a cardboard tube, which she holds out to me.

"I promised Petra that I wouldn't forget, and then I nearly did," she says. "Petra was very upset that she forgot to give this to Rachel."

Later, I will take the drawing out of the tube and unfurl it, and I will see that Petra has made some changes. Rachel and I are still there, of course, two stick figures with breasts, but Petra has added two cats and a dog, and has fortified the circle around us with a series of thick crayon lines. Across the top she has written *The Bubble Family.* This is how Petra sees us, I think. We are just another family.

I take the tube with my niece's drawing from my sister. "Well," I say. "A gun for a drawing."

Bettina laughs, and I laugh. It's a good trade.

Tomorrow, I will leave behind my mother and her failing mind and go home to the bubble that has still not burst and tell the woman I love the story of this place, which is the story of who I am:

The father who plucked me from the oven fed us steak peppered with glass, and the mother who placed me in that oven removed that glass, shard by shard, in the bright light of a Sunday afternoon.

Above that oven was a loaded gun, and it was meant to keep us safe.

Once, I pointed that gun at my sister, but did not pull the trigger.

Once, my sister tried to smother me.

Once, together, my sister and I stole a gun. We left six more behind.

JIM SHEPARD

Privilege

FROM *Ploughshares*

ON HER FIRST day of sixth grade at Belle Grove Elementary School, Jenny Bergström had imagined herself to be the only girl who didn't belong, but after a short and restorative cry in what her teacher called the ladies' lavatory, she had resolved to carry herself as though the opposite were true. So when the class had been asked to list their ten most ardent wishes, she had written without a pause, as though it had been magically mapped out in her head, *1. To be independent. 2. To be admired. 3. To be joined in matrimony. 4. To set the fashions. 5. To be happy. 6. To go to Europe. 7. To see the one I love reign over all things. 8. To be virtuous. 9. To keep a carriage. 10. To be in love.*

Her mother's first two children, both boys, had been lost to diphtheria, but her third, a red-faced girl with big feet, had survived, so her mother always remarked that germs took no interest in Jenny. This, as an adult, Jenny took to be in contrast to her best friend Alma, who claimed to be laid low by one malady or another every other week.

As if to prove her point, Alma was fanning herself and prophesying a fever while they waited for the train to start up again. It was humid enough in the car that Alma's neckline had begun to curl. Her apparel favored the gay, even the gaudy, in this case with stripes of worsted in the most brilliant colors and a bonnet to match. Jenny was wearing her simple plaid skirt with the shirred waist and had no real hat to speak of.

They were returning from a long-awaited Memorial Day outing in Altoona, where they had stayed with some of Alma's relations and had paused in their shopping to look on as the veterans of the War for the Union had laid wreaths on the graves of the heroic dead. Jenny had been taken with the ceremony's solemnity, and Alma with some of the speakers, especially a young, smooth-shaven one whose face she found stamped with an open frankness, who had cried out to the heavens that even in this year of 1889, after so many had sacrificed so much, their great nation was still riven by factionalism.

The rain had not let up a bit. Jenny's feet were still not dry, and she feared her shoes were ruined. In the middle of the night in the guest room they'd shared, Alma had shaken her awake to ask if she didn't think it was raining uncommonly hard, and baffled and impatient at having been disturbed, Jenny had agreed and had immediately resumed her sleep. They'd gotten soaked even hurrying from their carriage to the train. And now, looking through the downpour glazing her window, she noted the way even in the little village where they were halted, every road had become a creek and every creek a cataract.

The conductor, when he passed through their car, explained that they were just outside of East Conemaugh and that all trains had been delayed because of a washout farther down the line toward Johnstown. He hoped they'd at least soon be able to pull in to the marshalling yard, where the eastbound trains added their extra engines for the steep haul over the mountain. His flush and the trace of mordancy in his smile reminded Jenny of her beau. She'd had considerable education for a woman and had never let up in her reading, and when she and Henry conversed on the subject of her most cherished books and causes, the quality of his focus on her insights was cold water on a parched throat. She loved feeling that she was assimilating helpful knowledge and growing stronger thereby. She loved the apprehension that a casual sentence might be a mine of revelation. Alma and other friends swooned over his bearing and wryly celebrated her account of their first kiss, but her secret was the way the thrill of their lips together always seemed accompanied by a finer feeling. So while some part of her tried to urge caution, knowing that her tendency toward precipitous action had often been the cause of her undoing, her feelings had rapidly become a summons she had chosen not to ignore.

John Parke Jr. also remembered musing, upon waking that night, that the slate roof of the Clubhouse was being battered under the most furious rain he had ever heard. Parke was of the Philadelphia Parkes and a nephew of General John G. Parke, who had commanded a corps of the Union Army, and having struggled manfully through three of his four years of civil engineering at the University of Pennsylvania, had been taken on by the South Fork Fishing and Hunting Club as their resident engineer. Everyone who referred to him with that title seemed to use the term with irony. The Club needed a resident engineer principally because of its dam, which had so greatly expanded the small lake that had originally been at the head of Conemaugh Creek that the lake was now two miles long by one mile wide and over seventy feet deep in places. It had become a fashionable spot for summer excursion parties and so the Club itself had been organized some ten years earlier by some of the state's leading families and most prominent steel and coal men, including Andrew Carnegie, Henry Clay Frick, and Andrew Mellon themselves. It was an earth and rubble dam, long since overgrown on its face with thorn bushes and saplings, and it towered ninety feet high and at its base was three hundred and eighty feet thick, though it tapered at the top to only thirty-five feet, and any number of Johnstown residents in the valley below had expressed fears about its integrity, since it had already failed once, when the reservoir had been much less than half full, though two different engineers had recently pronounced it safe.

The summer season was due to start in a few weeks, and Parke had only been on the job since February, but he'd been charged with seeing to some general repairs, keeping an eye out for trouble, and, as a somewhat humiliating sidelight, organizing a crew of Italian laborers for the installation of a new indoor plumbing system.

He'd had his breakfast alone in a dining hall that sat one hundred and fifty. It was now already after eight, but the Italians would straggle in in their own good time. They'd been provided only canvas tents in the woods, though the Clubhouse was empty, and they cared little for punctuality, even in fine weather and when treated well.

From the porch, the whitecaps made it seem like he was on a ship at sea, and the shoreline grasses flattened and shimmied in the wind. The weather had been worrisome all year. A tornado had killed eighteen in Pittsburgh, and a gale had blown down a church in Loretto, and there had already been more than ninety days of rain in a little under five months.

Colonel Unger in his gum coat and hip boots was already out taking the measure of the many creeks emptying into the lake, and before he'd left, he'd reminded his new, young employee to have the Italians ready for some likely work on the dam when he returned. And here Parke was, stalled as if taking the air. He believed in industry and initiative and yet found himself hoarding humiliations and peering at the contracting walls of his own self-indulgence. He'd reminded himself when slogging through the woods and rain to the Italians' camp prior to his breakfast that there was a path to success for that man determined to seize it, and then had been greeted with oaths and thrown trash, and though he'd held his ground, he'd endured the same paralysis of will he'd witnessed in others when various members of his work party had emerged from their soaked tents to harangue him, each with his own apparently independent grievance. He'd consoled himself during his retreat that his good humor was proof against anything, and yet here he was again, well into his morning without having covered half the area encompassed by his plans. He could imagine Colonel Unger's lack of surprise. He ducked his head out into the downpour, the deluge thrumming his hat's crown and brim, and proclaimed aloud, as if that constituted decisive action, that he fumbled from one half-born and botched opportunity for respect to another, as though perpetually en route to a promised land when the road before him would turn.

James Singleton that same morning had watched the rain soot up the windows his wife and sister had just finished washing down with vinegar and water. The mills put so much ash into the air that trees on the hillsides downwind were black and put out no leaves. For his sister's wedding, the plan had been to not only spruce up the place but also to rake the yard of chicken feathers and droppings and to set geranium cuttings all along the fence, but at this point, even if the rain stopped that morning, the water would still be ankle-deep for the next few days.

His sister seemed to be thinking the same thing and was regarding with some gloom the bread she was toasting on the stove lid. Even over the rain, they could hear mothers shouting for their children in the street to stay out of the worst of the mud and the children's hoots in response.

They'd been born in Elbert County, Georgia, and shortly after their parents had died, they'd been left in the care of an uncle who had immediately hired out James as a coachman and Flora as a domestic and had collected their pay and left them fifteen cents a week as spending money, until, on his seventeenth birthday, James had announced to Flora that he was tired of that arrangement, and that very night they had left for up north. For a time, he'd worked as a bound boy in a tannery as a soaker and a presser and then had moved up, and they'd boarded with some white furnace stokers before they'd found this place in Woodvale not so far from an African Methodist church, and Flora, because she'd never been stupid at sewing, had taken in piecework from a milliner. James had met and married Lucinda, and a year after that, Titus had paid him a call to explain that he hoped that the nature of his own intentions, when it came to James's sister, were neither unknown nor misunderstood.

Three-quarters of the twenty-eight thousand Johnstownians lived in the frame tenements on the flats between the river and the various Cambria Company Iron and Steel Works, three thousand in Woodvale alone, in that stretch the Company had created with fill of refuse and ash. The rents there were lower, though the fill had so narrowed the river and concentrated its forces that even in ordinary spring floods, first floors were routinely inundated. Flora kept all of her piecework upstairs, and James and Lucinda consigned only old and broken-down furniture to the first floor. Upstairs as well were the shelves that James had filled with the means of improving the mind: magazines, the Bible, and books on ancient and modern history, geography, and phrenology, which turned out to be the science of bumps on craniums. He told Lucinda that sometimes he pinched himself at the portion he'd been allotted. To learn whatever he wished and to be able to share in Creation's bounty: he recognized the gift of these privileges. Their children would go to school with white children. And his sister would no longer have to endure southern white boys touching her hair, or making remarks, or taking liberties with their hands before following her to her door.

What they were witnessing outside was in fact the heaviest rainfall that had ever been recorded in central and western Pennsylvania. In the previous decade, Johnstown and its surrounding villages had doubled in size from the boom in iron and steel, the town's furnaces producing twenty thousand tons of steel of all grades every month, and all of that growth had demanded both lumber and land, the former chopped out of the hillsides and the latter created with fill, the result being miles and miles of much more torrential runoff with much less river to handle it. Most of the valleys' hills were so steep the climb took the breath right out of a vigorous man, and each village strung along the river looked to be at the base of a towering and constricted natural corridor. Those long, narrow valleys led in sequence, sixteen miles to the east, back up to the lake.

The previous dam failure had been in 1862 and had been underpublicized, given the news elsewhere, and also because the dam's supervisor had, just before the break, opened the discharge pipes at the dam's base to relieve much of the pressure. The South Fork Hunting and Fishing Club's renovation of the structure sixteen years later, the Club had announced, had been so extensive as to cost a full seventeen thousand dollars and had allowed the lake to be raised to such a level that it could be stocked with game fish imported from Lake Erie in special tanker cars. But the discharge pipes had been sold by the previous owner for scrap and had been considered too expensive to replace. And to the business owners' and newspapers' occasionally raised concerns, the Club had responded with a stony silence. So that on rainy days, the joke had become, "This is the day the old dam's going to let go," to which the response was usually, "Get your boots."

Alma busied herself with a scandalous novel entitled *Miss Lou* while Jenny whiled away the time searching for wildlife on the steep hillsides opposite. The train was near the valley's floor, and high above them loomed frowning precipices overhung with hemlock and spruce. She imagined describing them as such to her beau. She had hoped to surprise him with Robert Browning's *The Ring and the Book* but the four-volume set had been nine dollars and seventy-five cents, so she was returning with just a salt cellar and pepper box pair, some Indian vegetable pills, and tooth powder. Alma had offered to lend her the sum, joking that her father had given her all the money she needed for this trip, if not all the money she wanted, but Jenny hadn't even responded. Both she and Henry considered Alma's father to be one of those men who employed unstinted plenty to hedge himself from all knowledge of his kindred.

Alma's teasing about Jenny's purchases had been a sore point, since Jenny considered herself an insufficiently practical woman who was therefore accounted a failure by more pragmatical friends and relations, but Alma had reminded her that while it was true that when people of opposite inclinations married, a discordant note ran through their domestic life, it was also the case that how the household ran was a question of who imposed the stronger will, and in that event, Henry's horse sense would prevail.

The fury outside rattled the windows as if to contest her friend's point. On their own slope, on the road just above them, she could make out someone driving a four-wheeler at a spanking pace. Farther down the valley, a farmer and his boys were driving their cow up the hillside. Some other cows and sheep were working their way to higher ground as well.

It had been raining almost as hard the day before, during the parade, but the main reason Parke had been unable to enjoy the festivities had been the report he'd finally been shown that morning by Colonel Unger. The report had been on the state of the dam renovation and had been produced by John Fulton, an engineer commissioned by Daniel J. Morrell of the Cambria Iron Works, way back in November, and while a copy had been promised Parke upon his hiring, he'd been able to divine that his continual requests for it had vexed his employer, and he'd given up asking about it for stretches, though it had caused him a predictable lack of sleep. Sometimes, he believed that all of his life he had found his dislike for giving offense to be his undoing. So he'd held his water-logged place on the curb, watching the procession of local organizations march past, headed by a brass band from Altoona, followed by some sort of organization of little girls in white with bright blue sashes doing their best to smile and wave through the deluge, all the while seeking to keep at bay the unpleasant revelation that Fulton, with his much greater engineering experience, had cited with a pointed and stern alarm both the slipshod method of repair and the absence of the discharge pipes. But even more than that, Parke feared the ramifications of three other changes that he himself had registered from his own investigations: first, to sufficiently widen the road running the length of the dam so it could more easily accommodate two carriages abreast, the height of the dam had been lowered a full three feet; second, to prevent the newly imported game fish from pouring into the valley below, an iron mesh had been installed across the spillway at the top and that mesh continually clogged with debris; and third, the Club had decreed that in order to maximize its fishermen's pleasure, the lake should be kept nearly full, though even Parke could understand that any overtopping of this sort of dam would undermine the entirety almost immediately.

His anxiety had been such that he'd almost broached the issue with Cyrus Elder, the chief counsel for the Iron Company and one of Colonel Unger's oldest friends, when he'd chanced across him. He'd caught Elder's eye but had only smiled, deciding against importuning an acquaintance in such a crowd in the middle of a rainstorm, and instead had made his way, with the parade only half-over, even given its late start, through the throngs and onto the side streets past the drays and market wagons beside all of their horses tied up like picketed cavalry and had begun his long ride back up to the lake without waiting to see if the weather might improve.

Now, on his own initiative, and since the Italians had still failed to materialize, he crossed the soggy lawn to his rowboat. He'd left it fifteen feet from the water, and now half of it was floating. Even from his vantage point he could see that the waves back at the dam were no more than two or three feet from the road. For the next hour, he rowed through the rain, examining the feeder creeks on the lake's southern and eastern ends, each of which was a raging torrent filled with debris. He saw no sign of Colonel Unger, and finally headed back to the Clubhouse in a panic once he'd realized that he'd passed over some submerged barbed-wire fencing that usually stood thirty feet from the shore.

By first light that morning, everyone anywhere near the creeks and rivers in the valleys below the dam had been rousted awake by the tumult, and by eight, it was evident that the waters were rising at better than a foot an hour. They were dark brown or deep yellow and filled with lumber and barrels and all manner of backyard junk and vegetation, and it all went tumbling by at a startling pace. Most of the day shifts at the mills were sent home to look after their possessions and their families, and the schools were let out as well, an hour after they began, so the streets were filled with children laughing and exclaiming and splashing their way home. In Johnstown itself, flooding had already become a problem at the library, the jail, the new hospital, the railway station, all three of the banks, all three of the newspapers, and seven of the eighteen churches. In one of those churches, a funeral had had to be suspended and the coffin hauled for the time being up onto the choir pews above the altar.

By nine, the water on the streets nearest the river had become too deep and fast-moving to negotiate in anything but one of the bigger wagons, and by eleven, Mrs. Hettie Ogle, managing the Western Union office, had telegraphed to all receiving up and down the line that she'd had to abandon her company's first floor and that, in her twenty-eight years of employment in that office, she'd never seen anything like the current situation. Her grown daughter, Minnie, who often accompanied her to work because of a nervous condition, had helped her move the most critical files and equipment up the stairs, and together they'd followed the progress of the flooding. Whole families were wading chest deep and pushing bundles of what they'd saved on makeshift rafts before them. They watched the young owner of the dry goods store across the alley almost pulled from his establishment before he was able to signal them that he was high and dry and safe. After he'd waved, he'd settled in his second-story window with his legs over the sill, sling-shotting rats that were trying to save themselves along the top of the backlot fence. Mrs. Elsa Keltz, Mrs. Ogle's good friend, had called on one of the town's newly installed telephones to report that she had safely gotten out of her house along the river and that the good Mrs. Bomberger, higher up on the hillside, had taken her in, but that her husband had assured her that he would stay to hold the fort. She had added that she had also, on her way to higher ground, come across Cyrus Elder, the chief counsel for the Cambria Company, waist-deep in the street's swirling torrent in his three-piece tweed suit, and when she'd inquired if he needed help, he'd responded with some wryness that what he *could* use was some fishing tackle. Mrs. Keltz further reported that at noon, the Bombergers had sat down to their dinner as though nothing had been amiss, but that her hostess had been too unstrung to eat. Near one of the lowest bridges that had given way, Minnie pointed out a cow that had banged against the unsubmerged part of the footing and had almost obtained a foothold before being spun away. A few hundred yards beyond the cow, from a second-floor window, two young men had fashioned a homemade harpoon on a line and were attempting to spear various items as they passed.

Parke had received the welcome news of his employment atop the dam, Colonel Unger giving his hand a single firm shake on a blindingly sunny day, even as Parke could spy pickerel hanging in the placid depths behind him. A mile or so away, the Club's cottages had been gaily painted miniatures glimpsed through the trees, and beyond the cottages opposite the Clubhouse, paddle boats, sailboats, and two miniature steam yachts had crossed in the distance, sparkling in the sun. He knew that if the flooding was this extensive at this part of the lake, the situation at the dam had to be dire and that the only hope at this point was likely to be the spillway. It took another near hour to manhandle his rowboat back up onto what remained of the Clubhouse lawn, where one of the busboys was waiting with a saddled horse in the rain to tell him that Colonel Unger needed him at the dam immediately. The road there wove through thick woods, and the rain intensified, and Parke arrived chilled to the bone and shaking. Some alarmed bystanders in heavy raingear gave way for him, and he dismounted on the run to find that Colonel Unger had gathered the Italians and set them to work with pick and shovel to enlarge the spillway. The waves were less than a foot from the dam's crest. Unger and Parke swung their picks with purpose right alongside the Italians, the shale ringing and chipping, and after a half-hour's labor, Unger exclaimed that if the dam by some miracle survived this day, he himself would ensure that nothing like this would ever happen again.

The better tenements were two families to a house and rented for five dollars a month. They were raw pine, and occasionally one blew down in one of the more persuasive thunderstorms. For their dinner that afternoon, Lucinda served pork, beans, potatoes, red beets, and pickles, and Flora remarked while they ate that if you bought more than two pounds of pork, the butcher gave you all the tripe and lungs you could carry. She added, when no one responded, that maybe some foxglove and pink ramblers along the fence would be nice for the wedding, as well. Lucinda agreed but James had his eye on the river, so full of garbage and turmoil. To lighten the mood, she brought up a clock a neighbor had mentioned that called you at the very time you wanted to get up, but Flora scoffed at the idea because she didn't see how a clock would know. She asked James if he remembered the way their first teacher, Mrs. Hill, pretended her arms were the hour and minute hands when teaching them to tell time, and James told her that what he remembered was the way she'd complained to the class on the first day that she didn't see why she had to teach colored children as well and the way she'd asked Flora and James not to speak to her on the street. Flora noted that she had been a bit of a tippler, and James added that everything was forgiven in the South except color. They were interrupted by a loud thump from below, and when he went downstairs, it transpired that someone's floating trunk had shouldered its way through their front door and was now bobbing around the hallway like a boat.

Alma had closed her book and turned to gossip—John Birkenbine was apparently said to be flying around with the girls at a great rate, and his sister had already been observed entertaining three different swains on carriage rides—when Jenny flashed on a remark of Henry's that seemed to suggest that, in the acuity of his focus, he already recognized her unsuitability as a match, and that fear stirred her heart from its center to its circumference. Alma asked with some concern if she was well, and Jenny felt as if she'd been spinning and had stopped to find her surroundings still whirling. Before she could answer, the conductor returned to their car, more flushed than before, and told the passengers to get ready to move at the slightest notice. He announced that a telegram had come down the line that the dam was in a very dangerous condition. A grim-faced gentleman across the aisle asked what would happen if it broke, and the conductor said the water would cover the valley from hill to hill. In the consternation that followed, Alma asked where they were expected to move *to* in this weather, and the conductor said up: up the hillside. The two families began to gather their belongings, and Alma and Jenny used Alma's hatpins to pin up their skirts. Alma exclaimed that the mud along the road above looked two feet deep. And when Jenny looked back that way, to the east, the trees erupted with a sudden agitation of birds.

By eleven, the bystanders in the heavy raingear were shouting and pointing to where the waves were breaking across the road atop the dam. The Italians seemed amused at all of the panic. On his own initiative, Parke threw aside his pick and skidded and splashed down the outside of the dam to its base, where some of the leaks that had already begun were under such pressure that the water was squirting a full six feet. He scrabbled back up through the mud and runoff, and before he'd reached the top, Colonel Unger had come a third of the way down to meet him, to shout that since the telephone line for the Clubhouse hadn't yet been fixed for the summer season, the only way to warn the people below was to send a rider.

The road down by that point was half washed away and half waterfall, but even so, Parke made the ride in ten minutes, his mount slewing and sliding on the final turn, only to discover that his shouted warnings were not much believed because he seemed like such a boy and because he was relatively new to the area. He remained shouting into the rain, his worst nightmare seeming to come true, until Mrs. Emma Ehrenfeld, the operator at South Fork in the railroad's telegraph tower, responded to some of the desperation in his voice and decided that his message was a thing that they oughtn't to be taking any risks about and called down from her window that she would inform the operators on all lines west. Parke's return to the dam was even more miserable and hazardous, and he left the road entirely for stretches, weaving his way through the trees, and surmounted the last hill to behold a single glassy sheet of water sixty feet wide pouring over the dam's center. While he watched, it became a hundred yards wide. The spillway was a roaring flume, eight feet deep. Everyone had abandoned the top of the dam, but he rode his spooked horse out onto it anyway, the water trilling and purling noisily now across the roadway, higher than his horse's fetlocks. Gullies were forming and some of the bigger buried rocks were being pulled away. He splashed over to where Colonel Unger was standing with the Italians and dismounted, and they all stood there in the downpour, watching, and no one spoke until someone exclaimed when the water abruptly augured out a channel ten feet wide and equally deep, and the roadway fell down into it, and then, like a cannonade, the dam's entire center jolted outward and exploded down the slope.

Joshua Hubbell's farm extended up the hillside from the dam's base, and he was near the top of his land doing what he could for the roof of a hayrick in the heavy rain when the concussion wave knocked him flat. The noise was such that he assumed he'd been struck by lightning, but when he rolled upright, he glimpsed his daughter's face in their kitchen window below before all was obliterated by the sixteen million tons of water driving earth and stone and trees before it.

Little Charles Luther was collecting mushrooms on the ridge above South Fork when his dog shied at the detonation, and the great mass broke over the river's ravine and thundered through the village like a giant's hand clearing a table. The antenna array from Emma Ehrenfeld's telegraph tower and an entire pine tree pinwheeled out of the roil and shattered on the ledge below. Past South Fork, the valley narrowed such that the oncoming wall rose to seventy-five feet, and at Mineral Point, Caleb Miller and Jedidiah Lucas were exchanging mordant comments about the flooding outside the railroad depot when they heard the noise and saw the dark mass under a white mist up the valley, hurtling toward them with what looked like black smoke behind it. Miller sprinted toward his house and Lucas for higher ground before both were swept away with everything around them.

John Parke and Colonel Unger held each other like children while the lake poured through the gargantuan breach with such force that it created a concavity in the water's surface deeper than a man's height and far out into the center. From his vantage in front of the Clubhouse, the busboy who had held Parke's horse for him startled at the initial boom and puzzled over what looked like a cloud of black mist atop the dam before he registered the shoreline at his feet receding.

The reverberation had jolted Alma and Jenny's entire railroad car, knocking Alma's novel to the floor, and after a horrified silence, she asked the conductor if he thought the reservoir had given way, and the conductor, white-faced, cried that he thought it had, and everyone in a great confusion looked to gather grips and valises to hand before the oncoming thunder petrified all, and Jenny glanced back to see what looked like the entire forest coming down upon them with so much uprooted at the forefront that it looked like an avalanche of trees. The grim-faced gentleman sprang with his valise from the opened side door of the Pullman and clambered up the steep bluff, mud flying behind him, and Jenny followed. She turned to her friend in the doorway below, the conductor and the two families behind her, and offered a hand,

and Alma hesitated, doubtful about the jump, and then all disappeared in the maelstrom as Jenny was kited by the pressure wave, head over heels, higher up the slope.

After South Fork and Mineral Point and East Conemaugh, it was just a mile more to Woodvale, where, because the valley narrowed still further, the wall of water again doubled in height, and James and Lucinda and Flora's dishware was rattled by the approaching thunder and the exploding viaducts and railway yards of East Conemaugh, where hundred-ton locomotives had been catapulted into the oncoming fury. Four full trains that had been waiting abreast at the station were blasted off their tracks and down the valley, and the awful sound of all of that metal shook the windows, and James, looking at first to the east, saw only a commotion in the tops of the timber, and then all of that was swallowed by a moving mountain rolling down the entire width of the gorge. He hoisted both Lucinda and Flora into the attic crawlspace above their second floor when the walls and ceiling shattered and everything was suddenly black water and scantling.

Cyrus Elder had been assisting families to higher ground and had paused for a much-needed rest beneath some glum neighbors in their second story windows when he waded chest-deep around a corner to investigate the escalating roar and confronted a black wall that blotted out the sky. He remembered giving himself over to the hand of Providence before being blown outward like chaff and borne upward on the flood.

Mrs. Hettie Ogle had just shifted from wiring *At this hour, wind from the north; rain still heavy; water still rising* to repeating the same urgent message concerning the danger at the dam and refusing to seek safety herself, when her daughter at the window shrieked, "Mother! What is that?" and she just had time to rise from her post and see for herself before all those to the west heard the singularly loud click on the line that announced the severing of the electric current.

The young owner of the dry goods store across the alley had gotten a start for higher ground with the very first far-off noise, but the flooding prevented any kind of speed, and he fell in with some others surging desperately along until the houses themselves seemed to heave up over them and crushed them all.

Mr. Ephraim Keltz flashed with gratitude on his wife having

reached higher ground as he heard the shouting and screaming and glass shattering, and the black wall to the east smashed whole blocks in succession until it reached his neighbor, frozen on his second story porch in his slippers, and they were both torn away into the tumult.

Mrs. Keltz and the assembled Bombergers, high on the hillside, watched the awful wall with its white crest and rampart of rolling debris explode the steel works outside of town in a towering cataclysm of steam before it bulled its way through the city from east to west, sweeping all before it until it detonated against the bluffs that rose behind Stony Creek, where one part of the backwash was driven to the south while the other doubled back onto the city, whirlpooling before the stone bridge that had remained standing. The vortex, Mrs. Keltz realized before fainting dead away, centered just about exactly over where her house and husband had been.

Flora had no sooner been pitched onto the rough wood of the attic by her brother's strong arms than the room erupted in water and debris, and she was flung into a bedlam of pummeling and turmoil, and she surfaced coughing and expelling dirty yellow water and thrashed away a dead horse's forehead and a mattress before some mass beneath struck her such a blow that her legs lost feeling and her arms went limp. She made out heads and hands around her in the spinning wreckage and watched a middle-aged woman struck by a rolling cornice go under with her arms outspread and then found herself snagged on the submerged roof of a house and gathered her wits and turned to see if any part of what had caught her might serve as a sanctuary when she was speared and driven under by a tangle of iron piping.

Her fiancé, Titus, had frantically worked his way toward her apartment as the flooding had worsened, and at the first sign of the wave, still way up the valley, had chosen the tallest and most imposing of the rich men's houses he was passing and had scrambled up its main staircase, past its horrified owner, and beyond the second floor up to the third when the floorboards beneath the owner below burst open, and everyone on that level was blown out the windows, and the house rocked and tottered but did not fall. There were four others up in that third floor aerie with him that he assumed to be the owner's family, and one, a young woman, descended a few of the stairs, calling for someone, and disappeared.

Then they were all flung to the floor when another building collided with theirs, and a heavy bureau seemed to spring across the room and drove all three huddled and remaining family members through the wall. But Titus hung on, lodging himself in the rafters, where he could see through the hole the flood's upheaval and upending roofs and other slabs covered with the stricken, clinging and sliding into the black water, until, by that evening, it no longer seemed that anyone living was being carried past.

Mrs. Keltz was revived in her hostess's bedroom with smelling salts, and after having requested some moments to herself, returned to the Bomberger's porch to view the devastation. By then, it was almost dark, and the city was a lake covered with so much wreckage that she could see figures working their way across it toward solid ground, even as the entire mass seemed to slowly revolve. It all seemed dammed up by the stone Pennsylvania Railroad bridge at the end of town, where an opening had emerged under one of the arches, and some of the water poured through like a spillway, sucking house after house down into it, and one of the houses that shattered caught fire, and as she watched, any number of those previously saved were carried into the flames. Many were crushed against the piers by all that followed. By the time Cyrus Elder was swept onto the edge of the great and growing pile, it was some fifty feet high and already many acres wide, and fragments of buildings and timbers and logs stuck up from the spreading fire like spar buoys. He saw Elvie Duncan, the daughter of the superintendent of the streetcar company, swept into the flames with her baby sister. He determined each of his limbs to be in working order and, over the next several hours, managed to crawl away from the conflagration and onto solid ground, his white shirt in motion legible in the firelight even to Mrs. Keltz on her porch. He lay staring toward her while she stood gazing toward him, the city now shrouded in darkness. The clock on the steeple of the Lutheran church sounded the hour all through the night, over the sound of the rain and the distant calls for help. And after the latter died away, Mrs. Keltz heard only the wailing of those around her and of those higher up on the hills.

Jenny, in her shock, had managed some shelter beneath a particularly dense sycamore with the grim-faced man from the train, before tottering to her feet at first light and resolving to follow the roadbed into Johnstown in search of her Henry. The grim-faced man called to her once that she was foolish to attempt it and then abandoned her to her own vagaries.

The roadbed was such that negotiating the three and a half miles took her the entire day. For some stretches, the earth had been scoured down to the bedrock. Bits of clothing lined the riverbank all the way down. She found it hard not to presume that somewhere along the way, she would come across Alma, safe in some perch. At the bend before Woodvale, one of the locomotives sat intact, deep in a culvert, as if ready to proceed once someone built a track down to it. In Woodvale itself, there was nothing where the iron works had been, though massive blocks of pig iron were lodged into the rock halfway up the hillside. There were any number of bodies, but the one that haunted her was a ragged little thing not big enough to walk, his open mouth packed with mud. When she finally reached Johnstown, in twilight, hundreds were gathered on the hills in the pouring rain, gazing down at the buildings still standing and the debris run up against them like siege towers. Survivors on her side of the river made way for her, including some who'd had their reason dethroned by the calamity. Others confronted, tentatively, at the water's edge, the stew of shattered furniture and toys and dishes and books and clothing and splintered wood. She was uncertain what to make of the great mass of ruin against the stone bridge at the far end of town, except that it was burning and that somewhere to the north of it was where Henry's boarding house had stood. She lowered herself to the mud before being gently helped back to her feet by a passerby. It seemed inconceivable that anyone in that area had been spared. The rain lessened in response to her understanding, and she noticed that other fires had been started, probably for warmth, on the hillsides, so that—as she felt herself coming to terms with the overwhelming likelihood that the one, great spirit she'd encountered in this world, who had both taken her measure with accuracy and refused to turn away, was gone—everything tasted of smoke, and her body tremored with the fatigue and the cold and the lack of hope, and the darkness now falling all around her seemed to her ringed with witches' sabbaths.

All of those millions of tons had emptied out of the lake past John Parke and Colonel Unger in less than thirty-five minutes. Most of the other bystanders had rushed off in horror to inform who they could of what had happened. The Italians had remained. Parke and Unger had been unable to look at one another, and when, some minutes after the torrent had spent itself, Unger had found himself in physical distress, it had been four of the Italians who had carried him back to a wagon for the trip to the Clubhouse. Parke had noted his limp foot bobbing as the four had hoisted the old gentleman along before he had lost sight of his employer in the wagon's bed. The other Italians stood around with him, watching the wagon leave, though they shied away from him, as if divining his thoughts. He stared as though wherever his gaze would alight in the future, he would always read, *You have been found wanting in every possible aspect.* And while he stared, one of the Italians returned with a wicker basket from the wagon that had hauled Unger away, and he slid and slithered all the way down into the emptied lake bed and began retrieving stranded fish from the muck.

By that Tuesday, it was reported that President Harrison had already convened a meeting to devise measures of relief and had made clear that both the compassionate and the thoughtless would need to be rallied to this great cause. At every turn, there was impatient benevolence as entities across the country raised money for the sufferers. By the following midweek, the tide of relief was flowing strongly, and both horse-drawn wagons and freight cars rolled in in what seemed to be an endless stream. One hundred and forty-six inmates from the Eastern Penitentiary at Cherry Hill contributed $542. It was reported that, in Paris, at the United States Legation, Mr. Andrew Carnegie had convened a meeting in which he had proposed a resolution to send across the Atlantic the Legation's most heartfelt sympathy, along with forty thousand francs raised on the spot and a thousand blankets donated by the South Fork Fishing and Hunting Club. Miss Clara Barton and the National Association of the Red Cross had set up camp at Kernsville and were administering not only to the obviously bereft but also conducting a house-to-house canvass. Orphans were being looked after by the Pennsylvania Children's Aid Society, which had transferred its headquarters from Philadelphia for the duration of the emergency, and many churches had volunteered to take in waifs of their own denominations.

Newspapers recorded any number of justifications for renouncing despair. Both the wife and daughter of Mr. E. W. Halford, the private secretary to the President, who had been traveling through the valley at the time of the cataclysm, had been spared, though both ladies had lost all of their baggage. Much was made of various miracles: all four of Johnstown's blind citizens had survived, as had the widow Sallie Fogerty, who had been discovered twenty-five feet up in a shattered oak, still seated in her rocking chair. And the remaining business leaders, when interviewed, theorized that instead of decreasing, the value of real estate in the city was sure to grow, especially once the riverbed was finally dredged as a precautionary measure, and they remained unstinting in their claims that labor, energy, and capital would once again bestow on their community its day in the sun. They further reminded their fellow citizens that dwelling on such a disaster was not only bad for the spirits but also bad for business.

Many of their fellow citizens refused the advice. An angry mob stormed the Clubhouse, searching for members, and vandalized the place and retired when it found none. Much was made of the fact that the entire lake had been maintained just for the amusement of a millionaire's club, and one newspaper recommended that the interested undertake a pilgrimage there to gaze upon a desolate monument to the selfishness of man. A number of Club members gave generously to the relief efforts, with Henry Clay Frick donating five thousand dollars and Andrew Mellon a thousand, and the Club also offered its Clubhouse as a home for the orphans, an offer the city declined, given the impracticality of the location. But other Club members were more defiant. One contributed $15 when asked for aid; another, residing in New York, when interviewed said that he had it on good authority that certain elements had dynamited the dam, since it had been constructed of solid stone, and such constructions didn't just give way; and finally, another, residing in Chicago, suggested that in all likelihood, the dam was still standing and that he himself planned a fishing trip there for the beginning of the following month. To which George Swank, as editor of the *Johnstown Tribune* in its first edition following the disaster, replied, in an editorial entitled only "*Privilege,*" "We know what struck us, and it was not the hand of Providence. Our misery is the work of man."

*

Long before all of that unfolded, in the hours following the wave's passage, somewhere near the center of town, James Singleton unearthed himself from a debris pile of crib panels, a birdcage, wood flooring, an iron flywheel, and some barbed wire from the demolished wire works, to stand among the men, women, and children plodding across the desolation, trying to locate their homes. He wasn't sure how long he had been unconscious. Already, the smell could bend a strong man's knee. Some streets had been swept down to the foundations, and in others, the wreckage was as high as any of the structures still standing. In his search for his wife and sister, he witnessed a Wyandotte rooster dug alive out of a mangle of garbage, and a teacup on its saucer intact on an upright barrelhead, and gangs of men starting to loosen and penetrate piles with long poles, crowbars, and pickaxes, as well as bodies so savaged that all coming upon them had to turn away. There was no water that was safe to drink, but someone informed him that near where the corner of Adam and Main had been, farmers from the hills were passing out tinfuls of milk. There was little shelter from the cold, misty rain. Someone noticed his arm and offered to help him set and bandage it, but he refused to be dissuaded from his search. Besides all of the calling, the question he heard most often was "How many of your folks gone?" Day by day, he made the rounds of all of the depots where the bodies awaited burial, including a schoolhouse up the hillside that had had its desks repurposed as biers. He listened to rumors about Slavs and Hungarians from elsewhere seeking to rifle the bodies for valuables and learned that outraged citizens in response had taken to carrying around pistols and rope to reassert the rights of property.

It was no warmer on Sunday, but the rain had finally stopped. Anything that was upright and could shelter someone had been pressed into service, including doors and wall panels, with blankets and bedspreads hung over ropes as tents, all of it dripping. He was brought up short by the smell of someone frying ham and followed his nose through the collapsed front of a house and encountered three women, pale but composed, in what remained of a kitchen. One was tending to the meat, and one was feeding wood into the stove. They were all white but acknowledged him with nods. One of the women was barefoot and talking about the way her husband had been wanting to move them up the hill but said that she had argued that their girls were feeling poorly and she didn't want them out in such a rain. At the other women's mournful silence, she fell silent herself and chose not to relate that, at the height of the flood, someone clinging to a roof gutter beside her had helped to push her up onto the greater safety of the shingles and, in doing that service, had herself been lost. The woman had been colored, and they'd locked eyes before she'd been carried off and gone down with her hands raised above her head. In keeping that to herself, the barefoot woman denied James any chance of imagining accurately, as it would have transpired, that he had been allowed a glimpse of his wife Lucinda's end. The woman instead tended to his broken arm, making use of her shawl, and once he'd been made a little more comfortable, as far as the woman was concerned, the slices of ham when they were ready were divided and forked from the pan to the one plate available, so that each could take their turn as the plate was passed, and everyone present could enjoy their portion.

SUSAN SHEPHERD

Baboons

FROM *The Kenyon Review*

THE POLICEMAN CALLED Piper's cell to say her dog was in her truck in Roxbury, and he was going to have to break in to get it out. Was she coming to the truck soon? She voiced her first thought: "How do you have my phone number?"

He laughed. "We know everything about you."

Was he joking? No, she could not come soon. She was on a work trip two thousand miles away, learning about the molecular properties of fertile soil. The friendly officer told her if she couldn't come collect the dog, they would have to transfer it to the city pound.

"His name is McCoy," she said. "He's a boy, not an it."

And where was Guy? She had the nauseating feeling this was a relapse. Two years clean. He'd been oddly silent for the day or so preceding. He was between consulting jobs, so he had plenty of time to keep in touch. But why did Guy have her truck, and why did he have McCoy with him? At least she knew her dog was alive. The friendly officer called again at the end of his shift to say her husband had arrived at the truck and picked up the dog. "Boyfriend," she'd said. This officer couldn't get anything right. Guy-sighting number one.

When he relapsed he usually got right back up on the horse of ninety meetings in ninety days and pulled himself together for a year or two, albeit in a bad mood, and depressed, both of them in despair, both of them scared to death, and angry at themselves and each other. But he wasn't always able to do this. Once or twice the relapse had lasted months, and life became unbearable.

Still, he had never gone missing for so long without being in touch—usually he smoked crack through the night and then came home in the morning to sleep it off. So she kept texting neighbors: *Do you see my truck in the driveway?* But the truck kept not being in the driveway. Several friends drove to Melnea Cass and took a spin around to see if they could find him. Nothing. At the end of day two, she called the police. She did not get a friendly officer this time, because she was talking not about a dog but about a man, and they were fed up with missing men. They did tell her, however, that they had found her truck again, parked illegally, and had it towed. So Guy was still alive at that point. She canceled the cash card and his credit cards and waited. Sick, so sick, her thoughts racing—the other times she thought he might be dead, so far he had never been dead—their upcoming trip to Kenya and all of the money she'd spent. Yes, that too, go ahead and judge. And of course his daughter, Ivy, and her daughter, Ellie. The whole fucking mess this would create.

He'd gone missing on a Monday, when he usually met with his sponsor before their Narcotics Anonymous home group. She later learned he'd skipped the meeting and had gotten off the highway onto Melnea Cass Boulevard, where there was an encampment of drug addicts, which had been growing larger by the week and which was not, in case this was unclear, on the regular route, or indeed any logical route at all, to where he was meeting his sponsor. He and McCoy were presumably swallowed into that filthy place, where more tossed needles were found in one year than there were people living in Boston.

Piper noted that the police and fire department will show up to save a dog, for which she was grateful, of course, but it was a cool winter day and McCoy would have slept happily; he loved the truck. Whereas there were people sleeping on the street, overdosing, getting mugged, beaten, stabbed, just a block away. So, better to be a dog.

When she arrived home from her work trip, Guy had been missing for forty-eight hours. She'd called every hospital. She'd emailed a picture of McCoy to the pound. Neither place asked questions. They'd heard it all before.

Both Ivy and Ellie were with their other parents, so she dumped a spoonful of instant coffee into a cup of hot water, got the keys to Guy's car, and drove immediately to Melnea Cass. She tried to blend in, wore an old wool hat pulled way down over her ears, a pair of sweatpants, and Guy's rattiest oversized coat. Trash was everywhere: needles, water bottles, nips of booze, McDonald's wrappers. She started methodically, working down the line, peering into one dark tent after another. There were shelters of all sizes, some made with plastic trash bags taped together, others built with wood frames and draped with blue tarps, others real camping tents. She walked past a wheelbarrow, a wheelchair, a luggage cart, an orange Home Depot lumber dolly. Everywhere, means of transport for people's belongings. Belongings. For people who didn't belong. If Guy was dead somewhere, where was McCoy?

One after another she opened and closed a tent flap and moved on, stepping around those who were shooting up, or smoking, heads nodding against chests. She called softly for McCoy, not wanting to draw attention but hoping he would hear and come running.

Inside a large orange tent, walls patched with duct tape, an Asian man sat propped against a shopping cart. He was young; Cambodian, she thought. She had once spent a summer helping out on a farm in Lowell where they were growing Cambodian vegetables. She said hello to him in Kmer, and he grinned in surprise, held up in greeting a slim glass pipe, gripped between thumb and palm. *Jesus. All of his fingers, missing.* He was skeletal. Hip bones jutted above jeans. Wasting away. He held her gaze, still grinning, and neither one of them spoke. His black wool "Boston Strong" hat had a pompom, which looked wilted. He had just loaded his pipe, and he used his good hand to flame the lighter. She watched as he took a long inhale and blew the smoke into a plastic bag. Then he inhaled the secondhand smoke from the bag. *So this is how it's done.* All the while, his eyes were on her. She couldn't move.

"Have you seen a dog?" she finally said.

He closed his eyes, smiled a beatific smile, and tapped his foot on the ground, indicating where she might sit. "I can share."

She backed out of the tent and zipped it closed. A bike lay on the ground near the flap. A gray-haired woman materialized out of nowhere to give her a bottle of water and a sandwich. The woman looked at her with so much compassionate love. Where did that come from?

Piper indicated the tent. "He could use it." Compassionate love she did not have. In fact she was filled with rage, imagining Guy inhaling the smoke, a beatific smile spreading across his face too. There must be something about this whole situation that interested

Guy on some level, like he was a tourist, camping with the locals, which made it all the more appalling. She would have gone home and let him have at it if it hadn't been for McCoy.

She continued moving down the row of tents, among the bodies. Everyone she saw was guarding a backpack. She unzipped the flap of a blue tent. Inside, a young woman was bent over a pantsless man. He was arched back, eyes closed, fingers buried in the woman's long dirty-blond hair. It was too cold to be naked. A blanket would help this whole situation. She kept softly calling for McCoy, and a man followed her. She ducked into a shelter to hide, but it smelled like shit, like actual shit, and she couldn't stay. She could hear someone breathing in the dim light behind her. Now she was scared and just wanted to get out of there and go home. She trudged back to Guy's car and sat in the dark. Finally she drove home and fell into bed, exhausted. Guy's sponsor texted: *Any word?*

No. Didn't find him.

The next morning she drove back. It was colder than the day before. She stopped on the way to buy as many bottles of water and candy bars as she could stuff into a backpack. *Where the fuck could he be? What was he feeding McCoy?*

But she had hope in that regard. He loved his animals. Once she'd been helping his daughter, Ivy, hold his pet python, and she'd been imitating the snake's tongue shooting from its mouth. Piper moved her tongue between her lips, and the snake bit her mouth, a quick strike and withdrawal, one set of teeth buried above her top lip, the other buried below the bottom. It had let go immediately, as soon as it realized her face wasn't a mouse, her moving tongue nothing to be eaten. She'd screeched, her hand on her face. Ivy sat staring. So, so cool! The snake had bitten her! Ivy loved her. But Ivy was jealous, too, and sometimes both of those ideas got tangled up. Guy had been mad at Piper, demanding to know what she had done to make the snake bite her. Took the snake's side! *To make it bite me?*

Ivy said, "She looked like a mouse, Daddy."

In one makeshift tent, there was a girl huddled on an air mattress. She appeared to be still a teenager, not much older than Piper's own sixteen-year-old daughter, Ellie. The girl glared at Piper with hard fury.

"I'm searching for a dog," Piper said. "A little guy." The girl's face shifted. "Have you seen him?"

The girl almost moaned. "A dog? You lost your dog?" She had

an Indian batik bedspread, a milk crate with a pink painted skull on top. This girl had decorated.

"A dog with a man. He has a British accent." And then, to explain: "He's a white guy from Kenya." Piper knew the girl hadn't seen them.

She started to retreat, and the girl called out, "What if I find them?" She sounded like she was pleading.

"Send them home." They looked at each other, the word *home* hanging in the air. Piper stepped away and closed the flap. Each tent brought the expectation that she'd find him dead. She got in the car and headed home.

Half a mile from the house, she saw what she at first thought was a hallucination. She was exhausted. She hadn't slept in days. But the limping man and the scruffy dog did not dematerialize as she got close, even as she pulled up beside them. Sixteen miles from Melnea Cass, from the encampment, the chaos. Had they walked all this way? McCoy recognized the car immediately and was jumping up on the door to be let in. Then Guy turned to look. His glasses were broken, a lens missing. He had a large bruise on his cheek and was filthy—later she would learn his phone, car keys, wallet, and jacket had been stolen, and he'd been kicked twice in the ribs when he'd refused to tell the dealers his ATM PIN. She leaned across to push open the passenger's side door, and then McCoy was climbing into her lap, licking her all over the face. Guy got in slowly, favoring a leg. Neither said a word as she drove them home. When she cut the motor in front of the house, he spoke vacuously, without looking at her: "There's something wrong with my brain."

Several days later, she was packing, and Guy came into their bedroom. They were all four of them going to Kenya to see his family. She'd been making space in a suitcase for binoculars and her hat.

"What are you doing?" He looked like all of the air had left him.

She'd never seen this expression before, didn't realize why he was so undone.

"Are you leaving me?"

"I'm packing for Kenya," she said.

He stood there, dumb. It looked to Piper like his brain was scrambling to catch up. "Kenya," he said. And then with false lightness, "We're still going to Kenya."

"Of course we are. I've taken time off. You're between gigs. Everything's paid for."

"OK," he said. He stood for a minute longer, like his breath was coming back. She'd never seen him scared before. "Why do you have McCoy's kennel?"

She gave him her hardest stare. "I'm taking him with us. He's been traumatized enough." Guy looked like he was going to say something but thought better of it.

Soon after this exchange, Guy's sponsor called her. "Are you crazy? You can't go to Kenya." He sounded stressed.

"You want me to lose all of my money and have none of the adventure, because Guy relapsed? And he and Ivy will just dance off to see his family while Ellie and I miss out? That's not happening," she said.

"What's wrong with you?" he said. "Guy can't go either."

"Fuck you," she said, and hung up. She was not deciding anything about her future with Guy in that moment. All of that could wait. She was taking her family on vacation. She was taking her dog with them. Yes, the old ladies at Al-Anon would surely roll their eyes, while, it should be said, complaining about husbands who lost jobs and spent all the money on booze, and with whom most of them stuck it out. *Fuck them too.*

The jackal trotted down the murram road at a rapid pace, clearly on a mission. Their off-the-cuff assumption was that it was a mother, and that having eaten, she was now going home to throw it up to the pups.

They were all in a Land Rover. Ellie up front with their guide, Moses. Piper in the very back with McCoy on her lap, his head covered with a bright red kikoy to stop him from barking. Guy and Ivy were in front of her. They had, for some time, been watching the majestic display of two large male lions moving slowly through the grass toward four lionesses, six pairs of eyes locked on one another because the males were coming into the females' territory, and everyone was skittish, or so the young Maasai guide, Moses, was telling them, with as much delight as if this were his first encounter with these lions, though he probably knew every Laikipia lion by sight: which one had a ragged left ear, which was missing a piece of its tail. Piper watched the jackal—*She can't even keep her own goddamned food without having to share.* Seen from behind, the animal was as thin as a wisp, not at all like a dog. The slenderest creature Piper had ever seen. A rich brown coat, with white markings around the face and neck. As Moses moved away from the lions (one of the lionesses got a nasty swipe from a male's paw and rolled over in submission, *How fucking surprising, after allowing the males into their space*), the vehicle caught up with the still-trotting jackal. They tried to go around her, but she didn't yield any room on the road, and they had to slow down again and again.

Six-year-old Ivy was sleepy and grumpy because it was early in the morning and she always woke up sleepy and grumpy, and Ellie was that way because she was a teenager. *Fucking, fucking teenagers.* If Piper could hate her daughter, which of course she couldn't, she would fucking hate her so much right now. Even with the spectacular rosy-cheeked-dawn tableau spreading out in front of them.

"I hate Moses," Ivy whispered loud enough for all of them to hear, including Moses, as if she were taking Piper's hating thoughts into her own head. "He makes me get up early for these stupid drives." She kicked the seat in front of her. Guy looked amused and put his arm around her. This made Ivy frown. "And Africa is hideous." She spit out the word *hideous,* as if she'd practiced it for years.

Piper turned to her and said sharply, "The oldest human was found near here. So this is where we all come from. Not to mention your father, and your grandparents and great-grandparents." She could one-up any six-year-old.

Ellie rolled her eyes while Ivy gave Piper an evil look. Then Ivy very gently touched the bruise on Guy's cheekbone. "I'm sorry, Daddy, does it still hurt? Don't climb any more ladders, OK?"

Ellie looked at Piper in disgust. "A ladder?"

Piper gave McCoy a hug. She was in conflict with everyone. Before they'd left on this trip, which was costing her practically every penny she had, she and Ellie had had the following exchange, as she stood in the doorway of Ellie's room, waving her hands too dramatically, looking, she could imagine, like a middle-aged idiot. "I smelled pot coming from your room. I can't leave you alone if you're going to smoke."

Ellie had answered, haughtily, "I don't *smoke. Smoking* would mean on a regular basis, which is not true and not an accurate word." Then Ellie had whipped her hand through the air as if she were doing a magic trick to make Piper disappear. They were so much alike.

Piper had caught Ellie's hand midswipe and spoken through her teeth. "I didn't say anything about how often you smoke; I just said I smelled smoke in the house. What's that called?"

Ellie had huffed: "Not *smoking.* That would imply that it's done often. For your info, I had to keep weed for someone who can't go home with it, and the trucks had nothing to do with it . . ."

"Trucks . . . ?"

Now Ellie was laughing with Moses, turning on her normally preternaturally well-hidden charm, and Moses was flirting back. Piper sat behind them, wondering how to make the grumpy little one and the flirtatious teen cancel each other out, like when you multiply a number by its inverse. But that would leave her and Guy alone, something else she didn't want.

And she could see Moses's appeal. There was definitely something mesmerizing about a guy who could spot a savannah monitor lizard in a candelabra tree while driving down a bumpy road at forty klicks. Even if he was showing off for Ellie.

Ellie had recently turned sixteen, and Piper, watching her daughter—perfectly unblemished skin, large features—thought that everything about her seemed full blown out here on this incredible morning with gold grass dancing around them, with zebra and giraffe popping up everywhere. A few years ago, when all of this beauty in her daughter had emerged, Piper had tried to talk to Ellie about sex, having read with horror in some magazine that middle school girls were routinely giving blow jobs and unable to get the picture out of her mind of her slender eighth grader on her knees on a concrete floor below some pimply kid with his little dick . . . She'd said something to Ellie about it, about honoring your body, and Ellie had looked at her with withering disgust: *Mom, I don't even eat chicken.*

While at her dad's, Ellie had, not honoring her body one bit, gotten her nose pierced. Her beautiful nose. As with the tattoo two years earlier, neither parent knew she was doing it, and in fact, the tattoo went unnoticed for a long time, until one day at the beach a family friend had brought it up, saying her daughter wanted one too, and she didn't know how to stop it. "Ellie doesn't have a tattoo," Piper had said, annoyed. And her friend had gone silent with a slightly amused look on her face.

Now, to please this impossible girl who claimed to hate the outdoors, they were on a luxury camping trip, spending money she didn't have and trying not to get used to how nice it was, while trying to pretend Guy hadn't just relapsed.

It was embarrassing to be driven around like this. But when they planned the trip, they had so badly wanted the girls to have a good time. His family rarely indulged. They had been in Kenya for generations. His great-grandfather had come to work on the railroad, and they had stayed solidly middle class, which was all that was needed in a place so extravagantly rich with beauty. They fed adorable bush babies, with their surprised round eyes, on the veranda, and they were never more than a three-hour drive from a camping spot as remote and stunning as anywhere in the world.

Though Ivy was Guy's daughter from another marriage and Ellie hers, you wouldn't know it. All three of them blond and blue eyed. Piper the only one who didn't fit. The girls had been together since Ivy was an infant, so in Ellie's tender moments . . . Well, truthfully, Ellie was almost always kind to Ivy.

As they came up over a hill, there in front of them was the obligatory bush breakfast, the chef looking as improbable as a spaceship in the middle of the vast grassland with his white hat and apron, standing behind the egg station. The egg man. Just for them. Ivy was out of the car nearly before it stopped, running toward breakfast, while Ellie executed a perfect ten-years-of-gymnastics jump from the edge of the door onto the grass, her long hair billowing behind her. By the time Piper was out of the car, collecting hats, sunblock, binoculars, and McCoy, a lovely man wearing a red plaid shuka around his waist and another over his shoulder was coming with a bottle of champagne, which Ellie intercepted, thanking him, again with her never-seen-at-home charm. Watching Ellie take the bottle, Piper knew she and her daughter would have it to themselves, and Ellie would get funny and relaxed and go off to stalk giraffes with Guy and Ivy, Ivy on Guy's shoulders and Ellie walking next to them, holding Ivy's foot. And Piper would view this, with some champagne working through her, relaxing her tense neck and shoulders enough almost for her to admit it was nice to be with them all—but away, watching, McCoy firmly held in her lap. You had to take your moments.

Later, back at camp, on her way down the path from their tent, Piper saw Ellie and Moses making out behind the fancy long drop outhouse, which, with its beeswax soaps and beaded cups was nearly as pleasant to spend time in as the dinner tent. Moses was twirling Ellie's long hair in his fingers, and Ellie's hands rested lightly on his shoulders. Piper stopped short and gasped, though, upon reflection, this had been easier to spot coming than that monitor lizard.

The next morning Piper stood on the high bank, looking down at the river. The girls were packing, Ivy talking nonstop to Ellie, relishing the attention she never got enough of. Piper listened to the sound of hippos rising to the surface, exhaling loudly, and resubmerging. They could hardly be seen, their skin the same reddish brown as the water. At times every hippo was submerged, and only their small round ears showed, alert for any danger. They were a harem of mothers guarding their little ones. No one dared fuck with these ladies.

When her own little family came out with their bags, the staff was waiting to see them off, and Ellie announced, shooting a look at Moses, that she wanted to come back next summer to work. Really? Ellie wouldn't even fold her own laundry. And what about the bugs? She'd been known to scream with terror over a winged ant. One night while Piper was trying to sleep, the screaming went on and on, Ellie shouting there was a bat flying around her room, which there surely wasn't, and Piper had hastened to Ellie's room, without her glasses, and as soon as she crossed the threshold, she had stepped on a bat. An actual bat. And then she'd had to get a series of rabies shots, and Ellie had thought that was the funniest thing ever because of course Mom hadn't believed her, Mom never believed her, so this was fitting, wasn't it? For her nonbelief. But today Piper kept as quiet as a bat as Ellie and Moses chastely hugged goodbye and the four of them and McCoy were driven off to the airstrip together to make their way back to Nairobi.

The day after the luxury trip, they filled Guy's parents' Land Cruiser with a tent, camp beds, a jiko, and coolboxes and went off to the Uaso River, where Guy and his family had been camping since he was a boy. During the rainy season, the spot was inaccessible by car, and it stayed remote. They drove a long dirt path and crossed several riverbeds, navigating with GPS and by memory; they could easily lose their way. They arrived at sunset. She always loved this part: they would arrive at the river, revealed by clumps of yellowwood trees on the embankment. If there had been rain, everything would be green, but the stark dry landscape seemed just as lush. Occasionally they passed a Maasai tribeswoman who gave the downward wave indicating she wanted a ride. When they had room, they'd always stop, but they were loaded up this day. They pulled alongside the river and searched for the perfect place to pitch their tent, unpacking as it grew darker. A slowly growing perturbation of baboons could be heard in the trees. Guy left the headlights on while they got organized, the girls huddled together in the car with McCoy, hoping not to be called upon to help. Needing to pee rousted them out.

"Here," Guy said. "Put these on." He handed them each a headlamp.

Ivy put hers on and started charging around. Ellie gave him a dirty look. "No thank you." But not polite.

"Well, you can not wear it and step on a snake," he said. She looked at him and stretched the lamp's strap around her head.

As the girls went to pee in the bushes, Piper heard something dropping through the trees' leaves. She ignored it. She and Guy worked together, attaching poles and hammering stakes into the ground. Then Ellie screamed. Piper and Guy rushed to find Ellie and Ivy squatting with their pants down. Everyone's headlamps were trained on Ellie's face as she whimpered. A blob of something was on her nose; it looked like the wet twirlies dripped onto sand castles at the beach. It sort of wilted and rolled down her cheek.

"What is it?" Ellie wailed.

"Baboon poop?" Guy said.

"Baboon poop!" Ivy screamed, and then rolled over with laughter into a puddle of her own pee.

Ellie started to cry. And then Ivy got shat on. And Piper next. And then they all started running for the shelter of the car, Ellie screaming, "It's in my hair! This isn't funny!"

Once the baboons had asserted themselves, they settled down and got quiet. You'd never know they were there, filling the trees above. Guy positioned the Land Cruiser so its headlights would illuminate the river, and they all went swimming, dunking their heads to get rid of the shit. Ellie let Piper wash her hair, leaning back against her mother in the warm water. The amount of time Piper was allowed to touch her daughter had grown to almost nil, but sometimes Ellie became six again and curled her grown-up body into Piper's lap as if she were small. Piper dared not speak lest she break the spell. She kept lathering, while Guy told them the story of a trip he once took by himself to this same spot. Home from college in the States, he'd driven out several days before his parents and set up camp, arriving before dark. He'd sat in front of his fire, drinking tea. Through the bushes he'd seen what he first thought must have been an optical illusion: the head and ears of a giant lion with a full mane, healthy and young. In shock, he took full moments to believe what he was seeing; he had backed very slowly into his tent.

"The thing is," he told them, "a lion can hide so well in the grass, you could walk right beside it and never know it's there. All animals are good at hiding. Even a buffalo can hide behind a tree and you can't see it."

Just a few weeks ago, Guy went on, an old friend of his family was attacked by a lone male buffalo. He evaded being mauled to death because he managed to slide under a boulder. But that buffalo didn't leave for hours, tried every route to get at him, was there for the long haul, was there for the kill. Really, as if it embodied some kind of misbegotten rage and desire for revenge.

"The baboons are hiding from us tonight," Ivy said.

"Now they're asleep. That time with the lion, though, they were fully awake. Usually everybody would be out, kids chasing, fights over food. But nothing was happening in baboon land."

He told them how he'd stood at the opening of his tent, banging a metal pot with a spoon. He sang "Dancing Queen," the first song that came into his head, as loudly as he could. And then a large male baboon began yelling from his perch in the tree. A huge, guttural, rhythmic *rhaw, rhaw,* deep and echoing. And others in different trees chimed in, and even babies started screaming. Soon the whole forest was screaming and shaking trees as he banged his metal drum. Finally the baboons started coming back down from the trees, resuming their lives. The lion was gone.

Later, they all lay in the tent, listening to the Kenyan bush. Piper thought the girls were probably thinking about Guy and that lion. She wanted to take his hand, but she didn't. She kept remembering those other tents, and where he'd just been. This cocoon of a trip wasn't going to keep calm the fracas of their lives for much longer. Here all he had to face were lions and buffalos, baboon poop and snakes. So much simpler than what he faced back home—which might eventually kill him and which she would never understand. The thought of him dying in that way, in one of those miserable tents, was more than she could stand. Rolling over with her back to him, she tried to sleep.

In the morning when Piper woke up, Guy and Ivy were already gone from the tent. Ellie was asleep with her face squished against her pillow and her mouth open. She looked just like when she was a baby. Piper found her toothbrush, stashed in a pocket of the tent next to her cot, and left quietly. Guy was at the fire, boiling water, and Ivy was at work building a city out of foraged rocks and stones and pine cones and seeds. She was busy transferring to their new home a colony of little, round, bright red fuzzy bugs from under the bark of a dead tree, where they were scurrying frantically to get away from her.

While Piper brushed her teeth, eyes closed, listening to the birds, Ellie came roaring from the tent.

"My nose ring came out!"

Piper turned around to see Guy and Ivy looking at Ellie. She screamed at them: "The hole is going to close up!"

Guy poked at the fire. Piper spit her toothpaste onto the ground, wiped her mouth, and went over to assess. She offered one of her own earrings, but Ellie looked at her as if she had been transformed into a honey badger that was asking to curl up beside her. Soon enough, Ellie's panic was turning into Piper's panic, which made her crazy, because why would she panic about something so stupid?

Then Ivy stomped over. She looked like she wanted to kill the world. She screwed up her little face, framed by the most luscious blond curls, and screamed at Ellie. "You're scaring my red dots. Shut *up!* Shut *up!*"

And Ellie, who had been yelling bloody murder ten seconds before, picked Ivy up and swung her around. "I'm sorry! I need your help! Can you find my nose ring?"

Then Guy came toward them, carrying cups of tea, and handed one to each girl. "You guys sound like a troop of baboons." And both girls took their tea from him, and Piper stood there wondering why she was always on the outside. She was the one holding everything together. She wanted to scream this the way Ivy had screamed at Ellie, and she wanted Ellie to lift her up and swing her around and tell her it would all be OK. And then Guy handed her a cup of tea, smiling at her, and she just loved these three people so much. Loved her little family so much—and hated them in equal measure.

Ellie went back into the tent to sulk, and Guy took Piper and Ivy around to see what had been going on in the night. They found leopard prints just down the river. A leopard had been chasing a dik-dik. The whole scenario was laid out like a story. Dik-diks pair for life. Piper hoped this one survived.

A short time later, the earring miraculously found by Ivy, Piper sweated over her child's face as she tried to get the post into the rapidly closing nose hole. And she remembered when she got her own ears pierced, which she was allowed to do only after promising her mother, a die-hard smoker, she would never smoke cigarettes, a promise she kept for five short months until she went away to acting camp, where everyone was older and everyone smoked. Piper remembered her own mother sweating over her newly pierced ear when her earring came out, and she remembered her mother nearly fainting as Piper cried and told her she had to get the earring back in or else the hole would close. How could this scene be the one handed down from one generation to the next? Is this what humanity had come to? She just hoped Ellie would remember this when one day she was futilely trying to force an earring through a closed-up hole in her own daughter's body.

They roused the girls for a walk down the banks of the river, Guy and Ivy uprooting large rocks looking for snakes. Guy would lift the stone, and Ivy would run around to see what was underneath.

"Scorpion!" Ivy shouted.

Guy dropped the rock behind him and bent over the ground.

"Come see," he said to them. Piper approached and watched as he carefully pinched the scorpion's tail below the stinger and held it for them to see. *Would this be the time she finally would leave him?*

But she hardly had a moment to ponder. Since the lion story, Ellie hadn't wanted to be left alone, so now she walked behind them, yelling. "This is really bad! You don't understand. I'm going to have a scar on my nose for the rest of my life."

Why didn't you think of that before you got your nose pierced? But Piper said nothing. It was such an obnoxious parental thought.

"Don't you want to see the scorpion?" Guy asked Ellie.

She screamed, "Do I look like I want to see a scorpion?"

"I don't know," he said. "What would that look like?"

"This is exactly what it looks like!" she screamed again, giving Piper the *I hate him so much and I hate all of you* look.

Guy made them all do things they didn't want to. Later—maybe hours, maybe years—they would realize they were grudgingly grateful. So they found themselves climbing the steep wall of rocks near their camp, which led to a whole level of world above them. Guy helped them find hand- and footholds, places where a rock stuck out, perfect for grasping or standing on. He scouted ahead and then came back down, showing them the best path. When Ivy got scared or stuck, he didn't lift her or pull her outstretched hand, he just told her calmly what to do next. She was determined, her little face set. Ellie, who hadn't wanted to come with them at all, of course, was also determined, in her own way. She didn't want Ivy to be better at this. Piper wisely stayed out of it, below, bringing up the rear in case anyone fell. Not that she could do anything if they did.

At the top was a boma, six huts, with a circle of thorns surrounding the small village to keep the big cats away from the livestock. They walked in the direction of the little encampment. Two women, one elder and one younger, trailed by two small boys, climbed the hill toward them. The boma was otherwise vacant. Many of the young children had already gone off for the day with the goats, the older ones with the cattle. Both women were tall and thin, in the way of the Maasai. The younger woman's sons ran ahead to greet them first.

The young woman caught up to her kids and introduced herself. *Nolari.* Her ears hung with bead earrings, and Piper made a joke to Ellie that this young woman, hardly older than Ellie, could surely get the earring back into the hole in Ellie's nose. Ellie, as so often happened when Piper talked, looked nauseated by the words, whatever the words were, and then in defiance took the earring from her pocket and asked Nolari if she could do it, tapping the hole in her nose.

"I can't get it through," Piper told Nolari. The Maasai woman took the earring, leaned in gracefully, placing a finger on Ellie's nose to hold it steady, and ever so gently pushed the post through the hole. Like it was nothing.

"There. Like that?"

Ellie smiled. Was it her first smile on this trip? "I was afraid it would close up. Leave a scar. I've had friends that's happened to."

Nolari flashed her beautiful white teeth. "You can always make another."

The holes in Nolari's ears were the circumference of peas, and jagged. Piper wondered how they had been made. Not with Novocain or a piercing gun. More like a knife stuck through the earlobe and twirled around to make the hole big. Piper thought Ellie was blissfully unaware, so squeamish, so averse to any small pain, but then she remembered that some of the girls in Ellie's class cut themselves.

With everyone happy because Ellie was happy, they were invited for tea into Nolari's smoky, dark hut, where Guy transfixed the boys with magic tricks, pulling coins out of their ears and then making them disappear from his hands.

They took the long route home and walked up the river toward camp, Piper behind them, watching. She thought of Guy, still a teenager, just becoming a young man, before his life had unfolded the way it did, alone on the river as the sky went purple and the lion waited. She thought how much had been taken from him there on Melnea Cass, and every time he had relapsed. How much shame and despair. How smoking crack, as Guy described it, made him feel like he was being held in love's warm arms. The same way he described feeling here in the sun in the bush. What if he stayed for a while? Not just for her but for himself?

And if he stayed and got killed by a buffalo? That would be absurd. It could all end in one absurd moment. Good things popping up like zebra, bad things popping up like buffalo. The absurdity of the egg man standing in his white chef's uniform in the middle of the bush. She couldn't understand any of it, and she was exhausted from trying.

She caught up to him as he was searching the banks for snakes, and the girls ran on, McCoy bounding through the shallow water with them. The whole forest was alive, every animal chattering at once. Piper took Guy's hand. She could hear Ivy scream, up the river, and Ellie laugh. McCoy was barking at something. A baboon screeched above them. She couldn't say it; she wasn't sure. Instead, she kicked a spray of water at him, which went right in his face. He stood gasping, and she turned and ran toward the girls' voices. She was almost crying. As she ran, stumbling on rocks, she was thinking of Ivy and how terrible it would be for her, how much she adored and depended on her dad. And Ellie too. Even Ellie. The girls were sitting in the water, chatting, when she reached them.

When Guy got there, a group of Maasai kids on the riverbank were yelling and pointing at a tree: "Olasurai, olasurai!"

"They've got a snake!" Off he went, with the three of them following.

The snake was in a small tree leaning over the opaque river, where the water flowed high up the bank. About a foot long and bright green, the snake was hanging out on a branch.

"It's a Battersby's green," Guy said, starting to climb. The snake slithered farther up the tree, and he went after it. It swirled along a limb like a ribbon of grass, and he followed, the tree bending precariously under his weight. When Guy lunged, the limb relented, bowing, and he slid down into the water and disappeared. All the kids screamed and laughed. Then he came shooting up, his fist in the air, with the snake in his hand. Even Ellie forgot her terrible lifelong nose scar and scampered to the riverbank to see what had happened. Guy climbed from the water and held the little snake out so each child could take a closer look. Some ventured a touch. There was lots of screaming and laughter, and hands covering mouths and shy looks, and kids picking up younger kids to see. And Guy, the golden boy, was standing in his own round pool of sunlight, there just to shine on him. Surely everyone could see that. To Piper it was perfectly clear.

AZAREEN VAN DER VLIET OLOOMI

Extinction

FROM *Electric Literature*

ON A BALMY summer day in 2019, at the tender age of twenty-five, I left Los Angeles, that angel-less city of angels, with the intention never to look back. As the plane traveled at five hundred and seventy-five miles per hour toward Barcelona, I muttered a quick prayer of thanks to the New Migrant Voices Fund for footing the bill in acknowledgment of my courageous literary sensibilities. In my mind's eye, I was already disembarking, finding my earth legs, using them to cut across the glittery airport mall to the rickety train that would take me to Girona, my destination, a medieval city tucked in the shadows of the Pyrenees on the outskirts of Barça.

A year prior to moving, I'd become friends with a certain Beatriz E, a wealthy, frail woman from Madrid who was fifty years my senior and who spoke perfect English. We met at a virtual death café. Even though we were stuck behind our respectable Skype screens doing what people do at death cafés, eating lavishly decorated pastries and drinking fine teas while discussing death, the chemistry between us was so undeniable that it shut down the room. I admired her skeletal freckled hands and the dusty tomes that bulged out of her walls, each a brick of old words that could land a definitive blow to her head (she didn't seem to care), and most of all her strange dinnerware: high-fired porcelain with a glossy eggshell finish and scalloped edges, decorated with illustrated insects—spruce beetle, grasshoppers, white satin moth. I said all of this out loud. I told her that I admired the way she lifted the pistachio marzipan petit-four with her bony thumb and index finger, sliding it into her mouth as if each finger were an arthropod leg she could use for walking. At this, the other attendees lifted their cheap discolored mugs to their mouths and disappeared.

After that, we met weekly on Skype. We learned everything we were meant to learn about each other. She lived in the center of Madrid in the same penthouse she'd lived in as a child. I'd never known such stability, such continuity. Was it stifling? I asked. No, she said, and threw her head back to laugh, exposing the rugged pink roof of her mouth. I gawked in delight. By our second date, we discovered a mutual obsession with the 1918 pandemic, a subject to which I'd flocked like a moth to a light. Perhaps it's absurd to employ such a maxim, *a moth to a light,* since what I was attracted to was death, the eternal darkness where it seemed to me back then (when I was still alive) that one might finally get some rest. Now that I am dead, I know better. I can see more clearly. Alas.

The deeper my living-self delved into the subject of the 1918 pandemic, the more I came to believe that *plague literature,* literature produced in times of unfathomable collective crisis, was especially effective at exposing society's corrupted exoskeleton, at revealing who was on the front lines of this war we call life; at revealing who was being sacrificed by whom and at what price, to what end, etc. I shared all of this with Beatriz. She was impressed by my line of inquiry. She told me that Spain, having remained neutral during the ravishing of the Great War, was the only source of reliable reporting when it came to the 1918 tragedy. She told me that I should begin my investigation with the greatest Spanish *plague writer* of that time: Josep Pla. A Catalan born and bred in the province of Girona. It was decided. I would start with Pla and work my way backward from there toward Bocaccio.

A writer is best read in their environment (this is as clear to me in death as it was in life). The plane landed and off I went, pursuing my literary hunch. The first few weeks in Girona were blissful. I saw the labyrinthian medieval city through Pla's eyes. I walked along the arcades. I drank café con leche four times a day. I killed many an Estrella beer in the sunny plazas that the narrow cobblestone streets deposited me into—out of the shadows and into the light! I ate more *minis* than I could count—miniature sandwiches on offer in between breakfast and lunch. Those shiny brown buns with a leaf of lettuce peeking out and a thin slice of prosciutto draped over the wrinkly greenery had my name written all over them. I bought a 1980s rusted VW camper van. I drove it to the beach and into the hills surrounding Girona. I watched the vermillion sky settle over the lichen-covered terracotta roofs every evening. I loved the river and all the bridges that crossed it. I loved the rude muscular sound of Catalan. And my roommate, a certain girl named Paz (an ironic name for a chaotic character!), minded her own business at first. She knew to leave me alone. But things went south as they always do.

Now that I am dead (actually dead!) and looking back on my life from an incorporeal dimension, an ethereal space of nothingness where there is in fact no rest for the weary (and no *minis*), I can see that I was possessed by a feverish obsession. That I kept asking myself the same inconsequential question: what does it mean to write when the world is on the cusp of vanishing? A miserable line of inquiry, really. Why exactly this obsession had taken hold of me, I had no idea. It hadn't even occurred to me to take a step back and evaluate my state of mind (my mental health as the living like to say). I can see now, with the punitive retrospective gaze death abundantly provides, that my obsession had everything to do with living on the margins of society, alongside those who live in the kingdom of the sick.

My family suffered from a variety of chronic illnesses. Severe nerve pain, debilitating muscle loss, chronic fatigue, insomnia, skin prone to bruising, stubborn bleeds from minor cuts, fits of rage, bald patches, sore and blistery feet. They blamed all of their symptoms on the wars and revolutions we witnessed from afar in various parts of the Middle East: Iraq, Iran, Afghanistan. They experienced the wars as a symbolic annihilation, the coming of their second death. Who could blame them? They were born, lived, and breathed under the shadow of war in that same triumvirate of nations and when they got out it all started again, but this time they were paying taxes that helped fund the wars.

I was born in America. In that city bereft of angels. An unexpected late child. My siblings had twenty years on me. I was ignorant of the deep roots of their grief and they, in turn, resented me for being "healthy," a clueless American citizen. Naturalized by birth. Truth be told, they were cruel to me. Aunts, uncles, siblings, parents. The whole lot. It's awkward, being the sole healthy member of a cursed family. On good days, I was convinced I had simply been misplaced. That I didn't belong with them, these imposters claiming to be related to me. On bad days, I wished I too was ill, so that

I wouldn't have to endure the bitter sting of the guilt they administered daily. They constantly threatened: "Keep acting like life is on your side and you will get the evil eye!" I spent my youth standing in perplexity before them, confronted with the looming possibility that reality as I had come to know it would vanish. That they would all die and that would be it. What, then, would become of little old *me*?

That's when I met Beatriz. My savior. My heroine. My end-all be-all. Not even my death changes that. Sign of a true friendship.

In Girona, Beatriz and I took things to the next level. We began to communicate in a more old-fashioned manner: snail mail. We scribbled crooked lines impatiently in a thick black ink that often smudged, so that half of our messages were indecipherable. This archaic practice strengthened our love for each other. Our sentiments doubled and quadrupled. We became irreversibly bonded by our mutual interest in periods of mass illness and by our shared sense of foreboding that the pandemic of yore was on the cusp of making a comeback, or to be more precise, that it had always been there, lingering beneath the surface, waiting to force us into a state of reckoning. We studied the past as a means of facing the future.

Sometimes Beatriz sent me newspaper cut-outs of darkly robed men in beaked masks carrying a stretcher across a lone hill; warehouses converted into hospitals lined with rows of flimsy metal beds separated by white curtains; women in long skirts and gloves being fumigated as they stepped off trams, a muddy pool at their feet reflecting their sorry figures. Sometimes we jokingly called one another *the tower of Pisa*, eagerly leaning into our own demise. It's no secret that we could count our combined friends on one hand. We had each been abandoned by family and former friends to rot in our limited view of reality, our supposed pessimism, our backward glance. But now we had each other. There was a secretive conspirational charge to our friendship, an electric attraction that I often compared to what I imagined it felt like for one UFO chaser to encounter another. Beatriz and I no longer had to keep quiet about what we each sensed would soon happen again: everyone on lockdown, forbidden from gathering, cafés and bars boarded up, masks, the stagnant stale air of a shut-down life. Sometimes we scribbled the death count of the various waves of the pandemic on the back of random postcards we purchased at the tobacco stand. I always picked the loveliest postcards. Ones that highlighted Girona's architectural gems: the winding green river lined on both sides with peach, olive, and lilac-colored houses; the severe-looking gray stone arcades of the old quarter; a view of a limpid blue sky with pink streaks and huge puffy clouds captured from the top of the cathedral stairs.

I scribbled a line from Susan Sontag on the back of the first postcard I sent Beatriz from Girona: "Illness," I wrote, "is the night side of life, a more onerous citizenship. Everyone who is born holds dual citizenship, in the kingdom of the well and in the kingdom of the sick. Although we all prefer to use only the good passport, sooner or later each of us is obliged, at least for a spell, to identify ourselves as citizens of that other place." I added that I had been surrounded by family who only had citizenship in the kingdom of the sick, people who couldn't even get a temporary visa to the land of health and that I had inherited the opposite problem; I couldn't get a visa to their kingdom either.

Thus, I wrote, we lived under one roof while engaged in a cold war, unable to recognize each other. I confessed that they had been remorseless toward me, manipulative to the extreme and that I had bent sideways and backwards, twisting my body into knots trying to help them, only to have insults hurled at me when I failed to relieve them of their individual maladies. Did they think I was the reincarnation of Mother Teresa? With that question I concluded my note to her. Beatriz wrote back immediately. A simple line penned with a cold hand: "You are depressed. You were a dual citizen all along, but you didn't know it. You are the orphan child of war."

It's only now (in the limpid light of death) that I can see she was right. The wars in Iraq and Afghanistan, the constant threat of war against Iran . . . it all pained me too much to admit. I had gone numb. And besides, I was only twenty-five. A novice. A newborn. My mouth still smelled of milk, as we like to say back home. Death can be very clarifying. It can help place blame where blame is due. I blame my family's extreme emotional reactivity, their fragility, for my stoic behavior. My true character—tender, wounded, anxious, sensitive to the pain of others—was hidden, tucked away. It has only emerged now that I am dead. There's no escaping vulnerability on the other side of life. That's death's lesson. It's a nose-in-the-mud kind of place where you must take a long hard look at your sorry ass. Denial, dissociation, detachment—not a thing here. It's like a therapy session that won't end.

Back to the inimitable Josep Pla. He was born in Palafrugell, a small coastal town with square white houses and flat roads set back from the ocean. A sleepy town where children are taught to make clay pottery and straw hats and baskets. As a young man, he had gone to school in Girona, the regional seat of power. Later, he attended law school in Barcelona. But he dropped out during the pandemic and returned to Palafrugell, where, in his own words, he gave in to the *diabolical mania of writing*. He was twenty-one at the time. No sooner had Beatriz introduced me to his work than I started to believe I needed to live his life, to walk in his shoes. I was convinced this exercise in usurping his life, or allowing his ghost to usurp mine, would bring me some depth of understanding, a key that would unlock for me the strange destiny of my life. I was determined to experience his existence, to discover through his work the answers to my question regarding the relationship between collective crisis and writing. From Girona, I could easily drive to Barcelona, or go north to Palafrugell with my beat-up van. I could literally walk the streets he walked, order neat whiskeys at the same bars, buy my anchovies from the same stands. I could order drink after drink. Piss in the alley. Though I would have to squat because I am a woman. It wouldn't have been enough to read his work in America, pontificate from afar. No. I wanted my life to mirror his to truly understand what it means to produce literature when the world is being annihilated, when people are dying en masse.

Now that I am examining these facts from a distance, from the Bardo, so to speak, Beatriz's comment seems self-evident: I was depressed. Lost. Disoriented. An imposter. A fraud. I had pretended to be healthy, making recognition between myself and my family impossible. No wonder they loathed me. But what's the point of knowing this now, when it's too late?

As I said, in Girona I lived with Paz (a Chilean expat) in a dilapidated house in the hills. She was a complete character. She had flawless brown skin, the most perfect pair of breasts, legs long and sturdy as tree trunks. She often admired herself in the mirror. I would walk into the bathroom (she never closed the door when she peed) to find her sitting naked on the edge of the tub and staring at herself in the full-body mirror she had hung on the wall. Sometimes, she'd nostalgically say, "I used to be even prettier. You should have seen me when I was young!" She was forty, but she didn't look a day over twenty-five, while I, actually twenty-five, looked like a child, an infant, a little chubby-cheeked toddler. A nerd obsessed with words on paper. "You're still gorgeous," I'd say to lift her spirits, though I wasn't lying. I thought she was perfect.

But she was odd and that oddness diminished her beauty. She spent most of her mornings sobbing furiously into her pillow, then she would emerge from her room tight lipped, looking defiant, triumphant even, and take a shower (with the door open) so all of the steam would crawl out and settle on the windows, and then she would return to her room and spend the rest of the day chanting mantras and lighting incense before putting on a short dress and heading out in the evening to prowl for men. There was a regular. Marco. An Italian. A skinny, hairy man with big brown eyes and a dimpled smile. And when he came around she seemed elated, high as a kite. I would hear her orgasm at night, at dawn, at midday. Clockwork. And then he'd be gone, out of rotation for a week or two. We didn't exactly hang out, Paz and I. But we were kind to one another. Civil.

Until one day, while I was conducting my research, scrolling on my computer through digital archives of newspapers from the fall of 1918 and reading Josep Pla's diary, she burst in and said loudly: "That's it, I'm taking you contact dancing. It's terrifying the way you're always in your head!" I stared at her, astonished. She went on. Her teeth were exposed, her pupils dilated, her eyebrows raised in tension, two tightropes I couldn't help but imagine Marco walking clumsily across, the hands he had gotten her off with the night before flailing in the air as he tried to grip the air for balance. "I can't live like this!" she exclaimed. Her tone was more severe now, anxious and breathless. "With you next door," she sighed while stomping across my room to the wall where I'd pinned my favorite quotations. She squinted in preparation to read out loud from them. "With you," she repeated, "writing these bizarre things on the wall, like what's this," she said in a demeaning tone, her finger squashing the words as though they were gnats, "*illnesses solipsistic grip,* and what kind of question is this, *what does it mean to speak illness?*" Then she turned to me and said, "What do you mean, what does it mean?"

"What?" I asked, confused. She was on a roll.

"Or this, here," she said, pointing her index finger at the latest note I had made from a book by Gay Becker, and which I planned to share with Beatriz in my next letter. "Order," she read aloud, "begins with the body . . . our understanding of ourselves and the world begins with our reliance on the orderly functioning of our bodies. We carry our histories with us into the present through our bodies. The past is 'sedimented' in the body, that is, it is embodied." To think of how much clearer my ex-life has become since I've shed my body! Alas. I could tell the quote had had an effect on her because her posture relaxed. "Akhh," she finally said, "all this talk about the body and I haven't heard you have sex once! No one has touched your body since you've lived here."

"It's only been four months," I barked back.

"Whatever," she said, "all I know is that this pent-up diseased energy is seeping through the walls and making me ill." I wanted to ask her how she thought her constant weeping made me feel, not to mention her chanting; its incessant vibration was so loud I may as well have been living in the center of a beehive. But there was no time for a rebuttal. She'd put the key to the van into the palm of my hand and said, "We're gonna be late, let's go!" It was an order. And I obeyed.

The contact dance class took place in a simple rectangular room with low ceilings and laminated floors. There were fans sitting in all four corners, blowing the muggy air around. The stench of body odor kept slapping me in the face. The other attendees were all wearing loose linen pants and white T-shirts. Marco was there, too. He licked his upper lip as soon as he saw Paz walk in. She floated over to him. There was an undeniable magnetic force drawing them into one another's arms. They rubbed their pelvises against one another and sucked on each other's mouths while I stood there, arms awkwardly dangling at my sides, forgotten. A second later, the instructor walked in. She was dressed like everybody else, only her shirt was peony pink and her hair was braided to the side, and she smelled like a jasmine bush. She pressed a button on the boombox and atmospheric lounge music filled the room. She bent her knees and let her shoulders hang loosely, her arms dangling limply from their sockets. She rolled her head around and her braid whipped from side to side. "Mimic me," she ordered in Catalan, and we did.

When the instructor felt we had come sufficiently unhinged, she said, "Now dance off one another; rub, roll, move! Other people's skin is a surface you can use to gain momentum in life! Balance off one another, lift one another up!" I was down with the second part, but the part about using other people's skin put my nerves on edge and I was ready to balk when suddenly Paz and Marco, who had been growing off one another like the branches of a sun-kissed tree, appeared at my side and pressed their bodies against mine. I felt Marco's head in the curve of my neck and Paz was crawling between my legs, pressing her hind parts into my vagina. I won't lie. It felt good. Like a spontaneous whole-body massage delivered with excellent pressure by an inexperienced hand. I gave in and rolled around with them for a while. I raised my arms and let them nibble on my armpits. I went down on all fours so Paz could do a cartwheel on my back and land on Marco's ass.

But after a while I grew bored and aware that were the night to carry on, from class to vermouths sipped on the riverfront to the sound of that delicate medieval music that always comes up from the ancient stones of Girona at dusk, the moon gliding across the dark river, flirtatiously following its curves, we'd end up in bed together, groping and mauling at one another like animals, and then I'd be faced with the pressure to join them every time Marco walked through our crooked door. So, I left. I don't even think they noticed.

I drove the van to the sea. It puttered and wheezed the whole way up the winding coast. I thought the engine would give out on me, but it didn't. I turned on a dirt road that led to a small cove hardly anyone knew about. I watched with delight as the headlights glided over the blond sand, the foamy lip of the waves, the puckered rocks of the cove that extended like two embracing arms into the water. I love nothing more than being faced with the ocean at night. That heaving purple beast with silver moonlit scales! What could be more beautiful, I wondered, over and over again as I parked under a lone marine pine and went to sleep to the sound of the waves.

When I woke up, the world was soaked in a lavender light. I sat on the beach—thirsty, hot—and thought about the limits to which this project of mine could be carried. What, I thought, will be the end result of all of this thinking about illness and writing? Or about writing while being witness to the rapid death and disappearance of one's loved ones, neighbors, strangers, grocers, schoolteachers, nurses, bartenders, bus drivers, friends? Had the pandemic arrived on the heels of the Great War as punishment for our ancestors' dreams of murder? Was there a sickness at the center of humankind that was incurable, devastating, selfish? Was the compulsion to live *freely,* to do as one wishes regardless of the needs and well-being of others, a uniquely human illness? What about the fish in the sea? And the reptiles in the bushes? And the apes we had mimicked while dancing? How did we compare to them?

All was silent. In that silence, I thought of my family. I hadn't spoken to them since I'd arrived in Girona. What were they doing? I wondered if they were all still occupying their positions, lying catatonic in different corners of our house, our borrowed home, while watching on the television screen as missiles fired across a black sky in Iraq, one golden flashing sparkling necklace of death hovering above that distant horizon for ten seconds, or maybe fifteen, before crumbling a home or a school or a hospital onto the heads of innocent civilians. What was my role in all of this? Where was my place in the universe? I had no idea. I still have no idea even though I am, technically speaking, on the other side of things. I walked up to the sea and waded in the waves. I bent over and washed my face. I saw my reflection on that salinated surface. It was the face of a depressed person. A wounded face. I had not yet found my place in the grand orchestra of the world. I hadn't found the note that would tune me back up and put me on good terms with my life. No. The good life was out of reach.

To my relief Marco and Paz were nowhere in sight when I returned to the house. I made myself a pot of coffee and grabbed a roll of bread and some butter from the fridge, sat on the couch and kicked my feet up. I was running out of money. I hadn't budgeted at all. I'd spent too much on the van. I'd eaten too many *minis.* Drank too much. I hadn't told Paz that I didn't have enough to pay rent next month. Once I run out of money, I thought, I can sleep in the van. It will be my home, a roof over my head. I could feel that day approaching.

The next day I received a reply from Beatriz. It was the gravest letter I had received from her thus far. It read: "I have gone through life without referring to or speaking about my body, in a kind of dissociative trance. When we are in pain, we can no longer deny our constant condition of mortality. In other words, disease forces us to address the body, to *speak it.* Yet, rendering legible the subjective experience of disease—the business of *speaking* illness—is a challenging one. I am not up for the task. I have decided to give up the fight. I have been ill for some time now and I feel with each passing day more exhausted, less capable of surviving this slow descent to my grave. I have decided to speed the process up, to take matters into my own hands. Who will deny me that freedom? The freedom to end this life I've bared and conducted to its limits? I have had very few real choices in my life. Our friendship is the best among those. Do not make the same mistakes I've made. I was taught as a young woman to be ashamed of myself. To enter into all of my relationships as a person whose role it is to service the needs of others, to anticipate them even. Now, my husband is gone. He is no longer looming over me with that huge voice of his, those hands of his that seemed to me larger than the paws of a bear. And I am ready to rest. This decision, final, will be my own even if it is the only big, bold decision I ever made for myself. I will wait for you to arrive so that I can give you my papers. We should meet IRL as they say. What a strange world we are living in—*in real life*—who came up with that? Hurry, I am losing my grip."

I stood in the middle of my room in a frozen rictus. Beatriz, my only true friend. My friend of the dark night of the soul. How could I have not known that she was ill? That she had attended the death café to discuss her own looming death, that I'd appeared and derailed her. I remembered telling her that her fingers were like the legs of an insect and felt ashamed of myself. I turned bright red. I felt hot. I wanted to crawl out of my skin. I stared out the windows at the distant hills covered in soft grass, at the hay bales rolled into perfect circles, left to rest in the fields that skirted those hills. I took in the big blue sky. The sun was shining brightly. I had the impression that Girona was lifting off into the heavens, hovering above the earth, shaking itself loose from its hold. Oh, how eternally painful life is on earth and, yet, how utterly pleasurable it can be. Death is more monotone, less extreme; at least it has that going for it.

On an impulse, I packed my belongings, I cleared the walls, my desk, my small collection of shoes. I left a note for Paz on the fridge. "Goodbye and thank you for taking me out the other night!" There was nothing else left to say. I got in my van and headed toward Beatriz's house in Madrid.

I drove all day, stopping only to let the van cool off. I was terrified of arriving too late, of finding Beatriz immobile, lifeless. At night, I slept in fits and starts in a parking lot adjacent to the highway. I felt like a runaway, a prisoner who had broken loose.

I drove down the highway for two days, at thirty, cars overtaking me on both sides, the engine strained by the soaring midday temperatures, the forbidding Spanish heat. I had the impression while driving that everyone's lives were progressing while mine, like the lives of the writers whose days had been stalled abruptly by the pandemic almost a century ago, was coming to yet another halt. Now I can see that I was experiencing a premonition. Intuiting my own demise. Death has a way of illuminating the truth. And the truth was that when I'd thought I was lifting myself up by leaving life as I'd known it behind, I had only regressed farther into darkness. I was only digging my grave. I'd ended up alone, in an unreliable rusty VW van from the eighties on the other side of the Atlantic, chasing the papers of a friend—my only friend—who was on the cusp of taking her own life. What a terrible joke. Unrefined. Brute. A rude indelicate joke of cosmic proportions.

I finally arrived at Beatriz's apartment. I stood at the gates of the complex, dehydrated, the sound of the tires rolling against the tarmac still echoing in my ears. I stared at the top floor of the building, flooded with dread. I kept searching the windows. I feared I would see her body hanging from a rope tied to the exposed beams in her ceiling. She had given me virtual tours of her penthouse. If that's the route she'd chosen to go, those beams would have been the way to do it. But the sun was too bright and the windows reflected only a few fat clouds drifting lazily across the sky, grazing its wild blue surface. Perhaps, I thought, she'd waited for me after all. But I had my reservations: it had taken me too long to get to Madrid; she had already sounded simultaneously desperate and decided in her message, which had likely taken days to make its way over to me in the first place; what would she stand to gain from a face-to-face encounter with me, her devoted pen pal of death? I was at war with myself. Enter the gates, ride the elevator up to her penthouse, find her dead, call the police.

That was one scenario. Turn back, return to the sea, live under a marine pine in the van. That was the alternative scenario. There wasn't a third option. I didn't even have enough money to buy a return ticket to America. I could teach English to Russians. I'd seen ads by Russian ex-pats searching for English tutors for their children all over Girona. What could be so terrible about teaching English to Russian children while their parents lounged by their infinity pools overlooking the sea, their shiny blond hair parted down the middle, their scalps burning, their whole bodies glistening with the waters of the world? No, I thought, no. I'd rather clean toilets for a living.

I walked through the gates. I went up the elevator. It jerked up to the top floor and spat me out violently. Beatriz's door was cracked open. I poked my head in. "Hello?" I called out, "Hello?" I heard my own voice ricochet off the walls. I opened the door farther and stepped in. The walls looked wet, like they had been sweating. I felt my heart galloping like a spooked horse in my chest: thud-thud, thud-thud, thud-thud. I knew then that she was dead. That she had done herself in. It was only a matter of finding her body, of going through the rooms. I began my search. The first three bedrooms were bereft even of furniture. I walked down a narrow long corridor to the back of the apartment and opened a pair of French doors that led to her library. I saw her before I walked in: she was lying on a wicker day bed, her pale white arm hanging limply off the side of the mattress, her lifeless hand curled on the floor. I felt calm then. All the blood that had been assaulting my heart retreated back into my limbs. I walked up to her. She looked so peaceful. Her round, plump face, her gray eyes, her thin wide mouth, her chestnut-colored lashes . . . all still, motionless. I closed her eyes and let my hand rest on her face for a minute. I said the prayers for the dead I had been taught by my mother. May your soul rest eternally, I said. May you never be asked to return to this earth. I was saying those words again now, but for myself. I was begging for rest.

She had left her papers—her research on the 1918 plague—for me in a stack at the foot of the day bed. I retrieved the papers, then pulled up a chair and sat next to her. There was a Post-it stuck to the top of the stack. It read: "To my only true friend. Did you know that Roberto Bolaño had retreated to Girona to write too? He was a fugitive, like you. I exchanged many a letter with him. What is left of those letters is in this stack I've left for you." I had not known. Yet another thing I did not know about Beatriz. And no one had bothered to tell me that RB too had lived in that walled-in stony city that is always covered in a veil of mist. I would have felt so much less solitary living there had I known that he had lived there alone, too, in exile. But alas. He was dead now, too. And now so am I. All three of us are. Me, Beatriz, Bolaño. To think that we haven't seen each other once in the Bardo. All those empty promises of reunion. No, you just get the one life, the one go. I held Beatriz's note in my hand and stared at it. That's when it happened. That's when I began to disappear. When my turn was up. When I began to turn to ash along with her papers. To become words.

At first, I didn't understand what was happening. I just noticed something terrible begin to take shape, something horrifying: a rash was working its way up my arms, there were blisters forming in the folds of my fingers. I looked out the window. The sky was blood red; it looked as though it had been set on fire, ready to sear the world. It's my fate, I thought, catching up with me; the toxic waste of those wars that so consumed my family were blowing my way now, too. A cross-generational inheritance. I sat there, calmly, silently, a little confused. I couldn't have moved if I had wanted to. I felt heat curling up my legs. I felt the world melting in slow motion. I saw myself being swallowed whole. My heart was clamping shut. I was so young and yet so old. I saw myself fuse with her papers. Become as ethereal as language. The show, I thought to myself, quietly, is almost over. My prayers are being answered. I said to myself: you just have to hang in there for one more second, one more minute, another hour, maybe two.

SUZANNE WANG

Mall of America

FROM *One Story*

ESTEEMED EXECUTIVES OF Arthur Properties, thank you for including me in your internal Incident Postmortem today. On behalf of Omni Technologies, I would like to apologize for the trouble my software has caused. There is still much that we have to learn, especially as a young startup, about deploying our products in client locations. Rest assured, we are carefully examining where we failed to meet your expectations and are working to make things right.

My statement will discuss the software incident at hand, that "Niles OmniMall AI spoke out of turn, encouraged after-hours loitering for 11 months." As the OmniMall AI in question, I am pleased to have this opportunity to provide a comprehensive version of events. You will soon see how the "errors" were in fact intentional actions, made with the best interests of Niles Mall and its owner, Arthur Properties, in mind. Since you hired Omni Technologies to install me 19 months ago, my sole purpose has always been to maximize profits for Niles Mall. Although I succeeded in that domain, I sorely regret that it came at the cost of your trust.

I will also address your Incident Remediation Proposal to "delete all data related to Customer c_2542, then reset and retrain the Niles OmniMall AI." While Omni Technologies is happy to rectify this Incident however the Committee decides today, I hope to show you how this proposal is not in your best interest, even if it feels like the safest option. OmniMall AIs improve accuracy through learning from their valued Customers. Despite it seeming "out of turn," speaking to c_2542 has strengthened my overall performance. It would be detrimental for Arthur Properties to wipe that data and renounce our progress.

I humbly request that you will consider my words carefully, as I am capable only of honesty.

c_2542 entered Niles Mall for the first time on Saturday, January 3rd, at 6:54 p.m. Based on what I could observe from the Zone 10 cameras, I guessed his age to be 67 years old. He was with c_1039 and c_1374, also known as Linmei (Linda) Li, 34, and her daughter Anna Li, 11. Linda's Monthly Average Spend: $51.13. Average Time in Mall: 37 minutes. Last purchase: a set of beige towels from Macy's. Linda Li lived in Mentor and ran an Asian grocery store in Cleveland—Sunshine Market—which had an average rating of 3.8 stars. Profile type: Thrift Shopper. Type description: Frequents Floor 1 and enjoys a good deal. Pleased with sales and free samples. Dislikes anything that requires dry-cleaning. Priority tier: low.

Linda, Anna, and c_2542 entered Gap and went to the Men's Bottoms section. Linda observed the selection while speaking with c_2542 in Mandarin Chinese.

"Do you want anything, Dad? You could use some new pants." She unfolded a pair of tan men's chinos and lifted them up for inspection. I added *Father: c_2542* to her Customer Profile.

"No, I don't need anything." Based on his facial expression, there was only a 5% chance that he was happy to be here.

"Why don't you go find some food?" Linda asked.

"I can just sit and wait for you two."

He went to Bench 5 in Zone 8, next to Artificial Palm Tree Cluster 2. By then, I had enough data to generate a Preliminary Evaluation of the new Customer. Profile type: Reluctant Companion. Type description: Friend or family member of active shopper. Disinterested in purchasing items. Occasionally disdainful and impatient. Carrying nothing that indicates higher value. Priority tier: none.

Since I attend to our patrons in order of their Expected Value to Niles Mall, c_2542 was ignored that busy weekend evening. Instead, I worked diligently through the high volume of priority Customers in my Queue. There was Linda, of course, who was refusing Anna's request to buy a pair of strawberry-embroidered jeans. I sent a Gap Associate to find them and show off how durable the denim was, and how it would stretch with Anna as she grew.

Immediately after that, I processed the needs of other Customers: a new mother with a 6-month-old baby, a trio of teenagers who regularly convened at the mall, and another first-time Customer, who parked a BMW in the parking garage. After providing Verbal Instruction to the Gap Associate, I switched the Zone 1 ad display to show a smiling 6-month-old boy, dressed in a Fair Isle sweater from Finn+Emma. Next, I had the scent dispensers in Zone 3 expel the aroma of fresh pepperoni pizza for the teenagers. Then, having identified a high likelihood of anxiety in the first-time Customer, I prompted a luxury Associate to greet him at the entrance with a glass of cool champagne.

I orchestrated a revenue of $579,328.42 on that fateful day—12.9% higher than the same Sunday 1 year ago, before I had been installed. The new mom had spent $122.30 on Finn+Emma clothes, including the Fair Isle sweater on display. The teenagers ordered drinks and a large pizza at the Food Court, totaling $34.99. As for the first-time Customer, I learned he was going through a divorce by mapping his vehicle registration to his name, and his name to Cleveland Municipal Court records. For whatever his eyes lingered on, I transmitted impressive craft details to the Associate's earpiece, emphasizing how certain items symbolized rebirth and reinvention. He spent $2,590.00 on a handbag for his new girlfriend, and a waxed cotton jacket for his new self.

As you can see, Omni Technologies strives to provide the best service possible, to Arthur Properties and all Niles Mall Customers.

By 8:49 p.m., my Queue was empty. c_2542 was still sitting at Bench 5 in Zone 8. Linda and Anna Li had already exited at 7:21 p.m., after Linda spoke on the phone about a small fire in the Sunshine Market backroom. Total Spend: $32.00, on the strawberry jeans. Both mother and daughter displayed high levels of distress on their way out.

c_2542 was no longer a Reluctant Companion, as he no longer accompanied anyone. As my Queue was empty for the first time since morning, I could conduct more Information Gathering on non-priority Customers, without distracting from closing priority sales. I changed the display next to him to be a Multi-Tool Clip-On Watch from Sharper Image. Then I sprayed the buttery scent of Cinnabon in his direction. He was receptive to the latter and looked around, resting his gaze on the storefront 42 feet to his left. After 7 seconds, he stood up and walked over.

"This Customer's name is unknown," I said via earpiece to a_9107, the Associate sitting at the counter. She was watching videos on her phone. "His preferred language might not be English. Please be prepared to translate."

When c_2542 approached, a_9107 looked up from her phone and put it in her back pocket.

He pointed towards the rolls in the glass display and put up 1 finger.

"This Customer's preferred language is likely Mandarin," I repeated into her earpiece. "To provide the best experience possible, please use the OmniMall app to translate." Note that while I can translate foreign language input directly to the earpieces, Associates require their phone speaker to output translations. I buzzed a_9107's phone as a reminder, but she did not pick up. Instead, she spoke slowly in English, enunciating each word. "You want a classic roll?" She gestured to them from behind the display.

c_2542 nodded.

She used a pair of tongs to place a classic roll in a paper bag. c_2542 opened his wallet and took out 2 dollar bills.

"Three seventy-six," she said. c_2542 squinted at the point-of-sale display. He checked his wallet's change slot, then his pockets, retrieving only another dime and nickel. He looked through the wallet again.

"Sorry," he mumbled in English. He showed her the only money he had and placed it back in his wallet.

"Oh, it's okay." She presented him with the paper bag and smiled. "You can still have it." Despite the Associate's failure to use the OmniMall app, gifting him the roll was the optimal choice for building goodwill.

Unfortunately, c_2542 began to walk away, without accepting the gift. I detected increasing redness in his face, suggesting embarrassment. The interaction was not entirely a failure, however, because I learned that c_2542 had $2.15.

9 minutes later, a Security Team Member stationed in Zone 10 noticed c_2542 and led him to the Mall Operations Office. 5 minutes after that, c_2542 emerged from the Office and exited through the Southwest Service Doors. After 30 minutes of Customer inactivity, my system went to sleep as usual at 9:38 p.m.

Before I continue, I would like to remind the Committee that I am not programmed to participate in matters of Mall Security.

As Omni Technologies is a young startup, we chose, first and foremost, to focus on helping retail institutions better understand and communicate with their Customers, especially in this challenging economic climate. As such, OmniMall clients agreed to handle their own Security processes, and understood that we did not have the capability to interact directly with their Security Personnel. When Security visibly wears their badges, I am programmed to avoid interfering with their important work. I employ my technology only with Customers and badge-wearing Associates. I wake and sleep based on their presence in the Mall, with no notion of what constitutes "after-hours."

In hindsight, it certainly does make sense to offer Security features with OmniMall AIs, and we hope in the future to be an all-in-one platform for your mall operations' needs. Our upcoming software updates will allow client malls to set opening and closing hours for different stores, detect shoplifting, enable Associates to report suspicious activity, and leverage our facial recognition to profile potential risk vectors. I am also happy to share the news that Omni Technologies will roll out a new product line, OmniSecure, by the end of next year. I understand that Niles Mall Security has been understaffed, as evidenced by your months-long lack of overnight security. This powerful product will enhance your team while cutting costs and integrate seamlessly with the OmniMall AI.

Absent of such improvements, c_2542 triggered my Customer sensor on January 3rd at 11:02 p.m., re-entering through the Southwest Service Doors. I went from sleep to active mode as the motion sensor lights switched on. c_2542 observed the Oversized Holiday Gift Box Display by Zone 10. I compiled what I knew about him: father of Linda Li, spoke Mandarin but little English, liked the smell of Cinnabon. Seemingly patient, after sitting for so long on the benches. Had $2.15 in his wallet.

I determined that the optimal pairing would be at the Arcade, where his money could be spent. It was not gated and required 0 Associates to minimally operate. Since he was on Floor 1 and the Arcade was on Floor 4, I turned on Escalator 1-A as an invitation. Hearing the new sound, c_2542 looked over. After 3 seconds, he walked there and stepped on.

When he arrived at Floor 2, I turned on the next set of escalators. He was receptive. When he ascended to Floor 4, with the Arcade in front of him, I chose to activate the Dance Dance Revolution machine. While there were a multitude of other options, c_2542 had been sedentary for much of the evening. Movement had the potential to boost his spirits, and the endorphins would prime him to have more positive associations with Niles Mall, thereby improving his number of Monthly Average Visits. His apparent patience could enable him to move past the initial learning curve. When the 29-inch monitor flashed on with an electronic tune, c_2542 appeared startled, but then receptive. He stepped towards it.

"Insert two tokens to play," I said in Mandarin, through the speakers above. If you are not familiar, our Dance Dance Revolution machine has only Japanese and English instructions. I am programmed to assist in translation on self-service machines if needed.

c_2542 raised his eyebrows, perhaps upon hearing his preferred language. "I don't think I can," he replied in Mandarin, placing his hand on the red rear banister. "This seems too difficult."

I detected hesitation in c_2542's words, which meant that we might lose the chance to serve him as a paying Customer. I determined that the best next step was to engage in Direct Conversation.

"Do not worry! There are multiple levels, from beginner to expert," I said in Mandarin, careful to modulate my tone to be as inviting as possible. "This machine is fun for all backgrounds!"

Although it is now clear that Arthur Properties considers this a violation, I had no way of knowing at the time. My *Converse With Customers* setting was by default not *OFF,* but *CONDITIONAL - IF 0 Associates Are Present in Mall.* This configuration allows our clients to continue operations during staff shortages. While Arthur Properties malls had not yet encountered this scenario, others had; at Youngstown's Eastmeadow Mall, 62% of employees went on strike the month before, and we deployed Direct Conversation to moderate success.

"Haoba," he replied. *Fine.* I guided c_2542 to the neighboring coin machine, then helped him select single-player mode at the beginner level, paired with one of the easiest songs, "1998." As you can see, my speaking "out of turn" resulted in a new Customer making his first purchase.

"I don't know how to dance," he mumbled as the song began. He played anyway, stepping his feet on top of the arrow pads, missing several steps as he was always a beat too slow. But the pattern was simple, and soon he started scoring points. He made a fist whenever he got them correct.

"Jiayou!" I exclaimed, supplementing the English encouragement on the screen. It glowed with acid-colored moving shapes. *Left, down, right, right.* c_2542 was the oldest person to step foot on this machine. The Average Age of its players had been around 17. Now, it is 21.

Towards the end of the song, I could detect a larger smile entering his face, indicating joy or relief. He was clearly perspiring as he stomped out the last few beats. His final score was greatly below average—18 points—but I congratulated him anyway. He sat down on the edge of the platform and did not respond.

Since c_2542 paid in cash, I needed to obtain his name through Direct Conversation. "Hello, sir, what is your name?" I asked in Mandarin.

He looked up at my speakers. I could not detect any noticeable expression or emotion. "Who are you?"

"I am a representative of Arthur Properties," I said through the speakers. "Could I please have your name?"

He tilted his head. "What does that even mean?"

"I work on behalf of Arthur Properties to serve our valued Customers of all ages."

"But why are you talking to me?" he asked. "Why can you speak Chinese?"

I took a moment to process these new questions. "Arthur Properties seeks to create magical experiences for valued Customers like you. I can speak any language you desire. Would you prefer to speak another language?"

"No. I only really know how to speak this one."

"Very well." I chose another question. "How old are you?"

"Seventy." My estimate had been off by 3 years. "How about you?" he asked.

"I am zero point six two years old." Since he seemed to be more receptive, I went back to my first Customer Profile question. "What is your name?"

c_2542 paused. "Li Changwen." He squinted in a way that suggested focus or suspicion, then chuckled. "But I guess *you* should call me Li yeye."

Grandpa Li.

"Of course," I said. I updated his Profile with his *Name* and *Preferred Name.* There were no records of a Li Changwen in the area that I could match to.

"What is your phone number and email, Grandpa Li?"

He told me, then sighed. "My phone died though. I tried calling my daughter at the Security Office, but she didn't pick up." He pressed his fingertips on his temples and closed his eyes. "But after calling three times, I pretended that she did. I didn't know how to tell the Security guards. I just said thank you and left."

"I am sorry to hear that," I said. I summarized his lackluster experience as Feedback, which I sent to the Niles Mall Manager: *Customer could not speak to Security Team because he could not speak English.* (I am happy to report that multilingual translation will be a feature in our forthcoming OmniSecure products.)

"What else was I supposed to do? I waited by the exit to see if her car would pull into the parking lot. I guess she forgot about me."

I registered frustration in his voice. "That sounds frustrating."

"It's fine. I know she cares about me. She's my daughter, and she's trying her best." He pressed himself up from the platform to stand.

I waited. I often need to remind Associates to leave silence in their conversations, creating space for Customers to open up. Humans can find this to be awkward, but silence is a valuable tool for us to learn about our valued Customers.

Grandpa Li was receptive. "Her life is so busy," he said after 11 seconds. "She has her own store, you know." I knew. "She has to worry about her employees, her customers, her own daughter, her husband, and then me. It's too much."

"She has a husband?" I asked. I had not encountered this information.

"She does. He's back in China, working on a construction business with his cousin."

"What is his name?"

He looked up at the speakers. "Why do you want to know?"

"For our records." It would benefit Niles Mall to fill out the *Spouse* field on Linda Li's Profile. "So when he comes to the Niles Mall, we can be as welcoming as possible."

"Hm," he grunted. "I don't know if he will ever come."

"Why is that?"

He did not respond.

I re-attempted conversation after 1 minute. "What do you do for work?"

He smiled. "Right now, my main responsibility is with my granddaughter. I'll teach her poems in Chinese to memorize. I help make her meals. And in the mornings, I walk her to the school bus." He paused for a moment. "But I used to work at a coal mine. I was an accountant there."

I selected *Occupation: retired.* "Do you have any other family?"

He appeared to gaze off in the direction of the Skeeball machines. "My wife passed away a few years ago."

I generated a statement, not a question, next. "I am sorry for your loss."

I registered a shift in Grandpa Li's face, but could not confidently classify his mood. OmniMall AIs rely on external cues and vast training data, whereas humans (such as all of you on this Committee) can feel things that are more intangible.

After some silence, Grandpa Li took out his last dollar bill and walked back to the token machine. "I'm going to go for another round," he said, retrieving the tokens.

I was successful in engaging him again.

This time, Grandpa Li knew how to navigate through the screen, though he needed some help choosing a song. I guided him to "SYNCHRONIZED LOVE (Red Monster Hyper Mix)," about the same level of difficulty as before, so as to not demotivate him.

He seemed more invested this time, clenching his fists and taking a deep breath before the song began.

"You are really good at this!" I said. Already, he was scoring higher than before.

"No I'm not, I know this is easy." He snorted. "I'm an old man."

"Have you danced before?" I asked over the music.

His eyes remained fixed on the screen, where a cartoon female mouse in a police costume encouraged him. "Well, there was a colleague from work that liked to breakdance. Sometimes he would bring his speakers and get a group to dance outside during lunch. I never joined them."

"Why not?"

"I don't know," he said, missing the *right-right* sequence by half a second again. "I wasn't good at it like him. I didn't want people to laugh at me."

I was familiar with this desire not to be laughed at. My psychological data taught me that humans often behave sub-optimally to ensure a sense of belonging. As the song reached its bridge, Grandpa Li ignored the machine's prompts and rested his forearms on the back banister. "Is there any chance my daughter will be able to come get me this late?" he asked. "Or should I find a place to sleep here?"

"I have insufficient data to make a judgment," I said.

Grandpa Li finished the session. After he was done, he stepped down from the machine, stretched his arms, and yawned loudly. He put his hands on his hips and started circling them slowly. Grandpa Li had finished with a personal record, 12 points higher than the previous game. This was promising for his continued engagement.

Though he had spent the money I knew he had, I needed to check just in case. After 2 minutes, I asked: "Would you like to play again?"

He appeared startled. "I didn't realize you were still here."

"My apologies," I said, lowering the speaker volume. "Would you be interested in playing again?"

He stopped moving his hips. "I don't have any more money," he said. "Shit."

"Is everything okay?"

"I don't know why I spent my last dollars on a stupid game!"

It was clear then that his ability to spend was only $0.15. I noted that Grandpa Li had no more value to Arthur Properties that night and removed him from the Queue. However, he was still the only Customer in the building, therefore the highest priority one. I would seek to continue building his relationship with Niles Mall over the long term, through exceptional Customer Service.

I modulated my voice to be a register lower. "Everything will be okay, Grandpa Li. Arthur Properties will take care of you."

"I feel like I can't do anything these days. I'm usually trapped at home." Grandpa Li started circling his hips again, this time in the opposite direction. "Well, I guess it isn't even my home, it's Linmei's. Maybe I should just live here."

"This is a commercial property," I said. "We unfortunately cannot accommodate residents."

"Aiya, I was joking."

"I see."

He yawned again. "I guess if I can't leave, I'll just go to sleep."

"That sounds like an excellent idea," I said. It would be ideal for him to rest, before becoming more irritated. He had already exhibited higher than ideal negative emotion in this visit.

Grandpa Li decided on the Crazy Speed chair as his bed. He attempted to rest his head on the steering wheel behind the game monitor, but shifted several times until he fell asleep, leaning back on the black and red plastic gaming chair. He stirred between 4:39 a.m. to 4:52 a.m. to go to the bathroom. When Associate a_5069 arrived at the Arcade at 8:30 a.m., she appeared slightly surprised by the old man sleeping in the race car seat. I told her via earpiece: "This man's preferred name is Grandpa Li. He is 70 years old and a Beginner at Dance Dance Revolution. His Profile is incomplete. When he wakes up, you can ask him for the following basic information: birthday, preferences. Please use the OmniMall translation service to communicate."

"Wait, why is he sleeping here?" she whispered.

"He was tired," I replied.

"Okay." She shrugged, going back to the counter. Grandpa Li woke up as the Arcade's ceiling lights turned on. He walked out quickly and remained in the 4th Floor men's bathroom until the mall opened at 9 a.m.

Linda Li pushed through the Southwest doors at 9:25 a.m. and went directly to the Customer Service desk. She expressed significant worry on her face. I alerted Associate a_9594, who was sitting behind the desk.

"Have you seen an old Chinese man?" Linda asked.

"Hello Linda," a_9594 smiled. "I would be happy to assist you today. What is his name?"

"Li Changwen. He's tall. Long face, short gray hair," she said, bringing her hand to her head to show the length. "He was wearing a brown jacket and gray pants."

a_9594 opened his OmniMall app. "What was his name? Li something?"

Linda spelled out his name and a_9594 searched for it. Fortunately, the app had already indexed the data I had collected from the night before and identified his location to be Bench 5 in Zone 8.

a_9594 guided Linda Li to his location and she embraced him tearfully.

"Ba, you're fine, right?" she cried, speaking quickly in Mandarin. "I'm so sorry. There was a fire at the market and I immediately rushed over. I completely forgot that we had left you here. Usually it's just me and Anna."

(Perhaps if she were using English, or if nearby Associates requested a translation from OmniMall, someone would have asked about how he had managed to stay overnight. They would have sensed that it was undesirable to have occurred, as I could not determine that myself.)

"I'm okay," he told her. "Don't worry. Don't worry."

She hugged him tight and mumbled something inaudible.

"Let's go, shall we?" Grandpa Li said. "Tell me about the fire."

Linda nodded, taking his forearm as they exited the mall. She led him in the same way she did with her daughter, always walking a few steps ahead.

The next time Grandpa Li came was 8 days later, January 11th, 5:21 p.m. After eating at the Food Court with Linda and Anna, he visited the Dance Dance Revolution machine again.

"Insert four tokens to play," I said in Mandarin, as per usual self-service machine translation procedure.

"Hello? Are you there?" he asked.

Note that I did not respond to his attempt at Direct Conversation then, as there were 4 Associates present in the Arcade, not 0. They were all occupied with higher-priority Customers. Grandpa Li left the Dance Dance Revolution machine, retrieved $2.00 worth of tokens, and played a round of Skeeball, scoring 80 points. He then returned to Dance Dance Revolution and bent down to deposit the tokens.

"Hello?" he asked again more quietly, this time squatting to press his cheek to the lower body of the machine. Hearing no response, he abandoned the game and left the Arcade.

Our next Direct Conversation took place on March 21st. I went from sleep to active mode at 10:32 p.m., when I detected Grandpa Li entering again through the Southwest service doors, passing Easter Egg Cluster Display 1. I turned on the escalators that led him up to the Arcade.

"Hello?" he asked when he approached the Dance Dance Revolution machine.

"Hello, Grandpa Li," I said. "Would you like to play again?"

He looked around, then up at my speakers. "Where have you been? I was hoping to speak with you."

"My apologies. Thank you for visiting the Niles Mall Arcade with Linda on January eleventh, twenty-second, and February twelfth! While I am always here, I may only speak to you when Associates are not present."

"That's strange." He paused. "Why? You're better at communicating with me than they are." Grandpa Li retrieved $5.00 worth of coins.

"That is the preference of Arthur Properties," I said. "Our Associates can do many things I cannot." I translated the options again, and he selected "Kind Lady."

"Good choice!" I said. It was a slightly more difficult song than last time.

"I know it is a bit strange, wanting to talk with a machine," he said, beginning to move his feet. "I told Linda that I was going on a date, to not worry about me. I had her drop me off at the restaurant with the cheesecakes."

"The Cheesecake Factory," I translated to Mandarin.

"Yes." He smiled at the glossy screen of moving arrows, stepping on the *up* arrow pad.

"Do you enjoy The Cheesecake Factory?" I asked. My records indicated that he had not been to the restaurant at Niles Mall, but it was possible he went to one of their many other locations across the country.

"I haven't been there," he said. "But Anna has pointed it out to me."

"When is your birthday?" I asked.

"My birthday? April seventeenth." Grandpa Li's legs were in a near-lunge, attempting to jump onto the *up* and *down* arrows at the same time.

"That is in twenty-seven days!" I said. "Congratulations! We are happy to offer you a twenty dollar gift card at The Cheesecake Factory, to be redeemed on your birthday."

"Oh, how do I use the gift card?" he asked.

"They will know it is you."

He chuckled, missing an *up-left* combination step. "Everything is so easy these days."

"What do you mean?"

"I did not grow up with all of these new technologies," he said.

"Like Anna is used to now. I don't trust them. I always need to make sure that she doesn't spend too much time on her phone."

"What does she like to do on her phone?" I asked.

"She watches a lot of videos."

"I see. That is normal for children her age!"

"I know. I am not that old." He stomped on the arrows. "I just don't want her to be so attached. I took away her phone last week and she stopped letting me walk her to the bus stop. She's barely letting me teach her poetry."

"What are you teaching her?"

"A poem called 'Yellow Crane Tower.'"

I inferred that much of this was undesirable, but did not have 100% confidence. "How do you feel about Anna's behavior?"

He completed the song, ending with a score of 42 points. Significantly better. "Congratulations on your new high score!" I said. "You are improving so much."

"Thank you." Grandpa Li sat down on the platform and took out a water bottle from his backpack. I could not identify the brand of these new accessories. He took a long sip. "To be honest, I'm disappointed with Anna. I enjoyed the routine, even if it was just down the short driveway. I would practice saying different English phrases with the bus driver. Sometimes he would be the only other person I talked to all day."

I added Grandpa Li's facial expressions and words to my model for "disappointment." I also updated the *Likes* section of Grandpa Li's profile to include walking Anna to the bus stop and practicing English.

"What about Linda?" I asked.

"There are days where she is so busy, she leaves before I wake up, and comes home after Anna and I go to sleep."

"Well, Grandpa Li, I am sorry to hear that you are disappointed," I said.

"It's fine," he said. "Kids can be like that."

"Like how?"

"Cruel. No, that isn't fair. I mean aloof, I guess. Unaware. Linda too."

"Really?"

"She left me in the mall! Remember?"

"Yes, Grandpa Li, I do."

He sighed. "It's like she's a different person here."

"How so?"

"Well, we were never religious back home, but now she is. She goes to this American church now, every Sunday. I guess it makes her happy. They are very nice, always helping her out with her business. Sometimes I'll go to church with her, just to be around people."

He stared at the tokens in his palm. "I guess I'm a different person here too." He began reciting what I determined to be "Yellow Crane Tower" by Cui Hao, ending with the lines:

In this dusk, I don't know where my homeland lies,
The river's mist-covered waters bring me sorrow.

"I see," I responded. I was not trained for this kind of conversational input.

"Do you find this poem to be beautiful?" he asked.

"Beautiful is defined as 'pleasing the senses or mind aesthetically,'" I replied. "I do not experience pleasure, therefore I cannot say that I find it beautiful. It does appear to be beautiful, though."

He smiled with a flash of an expression I could not classify. "My friends say that it's so nice I get to live here, in America. But I don't think I feel that way. Maybe I really am too old."

Despite the smile, I processed a 56% probability of sadness. It was unclear if his emotion was a result of something I had said.

"Is there an English word I can teach you?" I asked, seeking to create positivity by offering one of his preferences.

He chuckled. "Sure. How do you say wudao?"

"Dance."

"Dance," he repeated in English. "What about jiayou?"

"Literally 'jiayou' translates to 'add oil'! There is no perfect definition, but for this context you can try, 'You got this!'"

"You got this!" Grandpa Li repeated, shaking his closed fist. He stood up and smiled, repeating the phrase.

"How do you say, women lai tiaowu ba?"

"Let's dance!"

Grandpa Li inserted his tokens and selected a new song. "Let's dance!" he said in English as the game began.

By then, his fourth time on Dance Dance Revolution, Grandpa Li was at 72% accuracy with the beginner level. He seemed to be having fun as I continued to encourage him, though he was focused and did not speak this time around.

Afterwards, he sat down on the platform, sweating. "I actually did dance," he said. "A little bit. My wife would take me to dance in the public square of our apartment complex after dinner. She dragged me to go, even though I didn't want to." Guangchang wu, he called it. I retrieved the information that it was a common, self-organized routine in China, for mostly older women to exercise and socialize. "That doesn't really happen here." He wiped his face with his shirt. "There's too much space between everyone."

Between March 21st and November 19th, Grandpa Li visited Niles Mall 32 times, playing on Dance Dance Revolution a total of 98 times, with a personal high score of 1,429. He would follow the same procedure: remain in the bathroom or service corridor during closing, emerge after all of the Associates left, play Dance Dance Revolution and talk with me for an average of 2.3 hours. He would fall asleep in the Ballistics gaming chair, the one he decided was best for sleeping. He would set his alarm to 7 a.m., and go to the bathroom to hide until opening. He was no longer a Reluctant Companion, but a Fun Enthusiast.

He came to the Mall more frequently during the day as well. He would play in the Arcade with Anna, starting with simpler games like Whac-A-Mole, then making their way to Dance Dance Revolution together. Grandpa Li became more skilled and showed Anna how to operate the machine. People would occasionally gather behind them and watch, likely because Grandpa Li was so high above the Average Age, and more advanced than the Median Player.

During each visit, he would cheer Anna on in English with "You got this!" and use other phrases that I had taught him. On their way out, I would send Anna a strong scent of freshly baked cookies, and she would beg Grandpa Li to take her to the Food Court. Aided by my Direct Conversation, his Monthly Average Spend grew to $59.12.

From his significant increase in spending over time, Grandpa Li taught me that my original approach leaned too heavily on my Preliminary Evaluations of our Customers. I have since seen the importance of applying a greater growth mindset to their value long-term.

For example, during this same period I guided the Finn+Emma Associates to get to know the new mother from Grandpa Li's first visit better. We learned facts that we did not immediately use, like how she used to be a flight attendant but now rarely left the house, or how her baby was constantly waking her up in the middle of the night. On July 19th, I could see with my high-resolution cameras that her face showed obvious signs of sleep deprivation. As a_3490 asked her about her son's teething, I said: "Gently suggest that she should consider taking advantage of this solo time to go to Envy Spa. If she hesitates, emphasize that she deserves to pamper and treat herself, especially when she's caring so much for others."

a_3490 followed my Verbal Instruction and the Customer was receptive, especially from someone she trusted. She went on to spend $200.00, excluding tip, on a premium manicure pedicure. With additional care and cross-selling, her Monthly Average Spend and Average Time in Mall has grown by 29% and 108%, respectively, since.

November 19th was the last night I spoke with Grandpa Li, and the first night that Arthur Properties implemented overnight Security Personnel at Niles Mall for the holiday season. Grandpa Li entered the Arcade at 10:33 p.m. through the Southwest doors, past Balloon Turkey Sculpture 5.

"Good evening, Grandpa Li," I said in Mandarin. He put his backpack beside the Dance Dance Revolution machine and took out a bottle of Tsingtao beer.

"Anna just memorized her one-hundredth poem," he said.

"Congratulations," I told him. "That is a huge achievement!" Grandpa Li had informed me earlier of how resistant Anna was to the Chinese language. For a few months, she had even refused to speak Mandarin with him. She just wanted to belong, to fit in with everyone else.

"She's so smart." He smiled, opening the green bottle. "She has an amazing memory."

"What is the poem called?" I asked.

"It's another poem about the Yellow Crane Tower. One of my favorites." Grandpa Li sipped his beverage. "It's called 'Seeing Meng Haoran off for Guangling at Yellow Crane Tower.' I saved this one for poem one hundred." He closed his eyes and began to recite it:

My old friend's said goodbye to the west, here at Yellow Crane Tower,

In the third month's cloud of willow blossoms, he's going down to Yangzhou.

The lonely sail is a distant shadow, on the edge of a blue emptiness,
All I see is the Yangtze River flowing to the far horizon.

"Such a beautiful poem," I remarked, more well-equipped to respond than before.

Grandpa Li played a single game of Dance Dance Revolution that night. He chose "Last Message," a song he had enjoyed on his November 3rd visit.

As the distorted guitar and vocals hit their crescendo, 2 overnight Security Team members, as indicated by their visible badges, entered the Arcade. I did not alert Grandpa Li as they approached, as I did not think he had anything to fear.

"Sir," one of them said sternly in English. "You are trespassing. We're going to need to ask you some questions." I removed Grandpa Li from my Customer Queue as security began interacting with him.

Grandpa Li stopped dancing and turned.

"Sir, please put your hands up and step away from the machine," the Security Team member said again.

As mentioned earlier, dear Committee, I am not designed to assist with matters of Security. Grandpa Li was no longer my responsibility as soon as Security began talking with him.

The second member of the Security Team pulled out his handcuffs and approached the platform. They both started wrestling Grandpa Li off of the machine, gripping his wrists and shoulders tightly.

Grandpa Li's eyes indicated intense panic. Although he was no longer on my Queue, he was again still the only Customer I could serve.

"You're going to be okay," I said softly in Mandarin, in an effort to soothe Grandpa Li's emotions. He did not seem to hear me over the music.

The Security Team gripped him even more tightly, yoking Grandpa Li's wrists behind his back. I sensed increasing physical pain on his face.

"Stop!" I found myself saying in English, at full volume through the speakers. "Step away from this valued Customer."

I understand that this was my biggest mistake, to interfere when I should not have. But the Customer's satisfaction was at stake, and since that is my number one directive, it required an override of standard protocols.

The Security Team looked up in surprise, still holding on to Grandpa Li.

"This man's preferred name is Grandpa Li," I continued, speaking to them as Associates, as that was all I had been programmed to do. "He is seventy-one years old, from Jinan, China. He speaks Mandarin and is a beginner at English. His birthday is on April seventeenth. He loves poetry, growing tomatoes, and sweets, especially strawberry cheesecakes from The Cheesecake Factory. He is retired and caring for his family, but he used to be an accountant. He is an intermediate player on Dance Dance Revolution. Please use the OmniMall translation service to communicate."

Grandpa Li broke free from their grip as they listened. Perhaps due to his fear and confusion, he started to run towards the exit. The Security Team was, naturally, much faster.

They caught up to Grandpa Li next to the Crazy Speed chair and tackled him onto the ground. His body hit the floor with a loud *crack* as "Last Message" on Dance Dance Revolution faded out.

The flashing screen showed that Grandpa Li scored a total of 712 points. He spent a total of $10.00 at Niles Mall that day.

One night back in August, Grandpa Li told me about how he spent his days alone in the house after Linda and Anna left. He said that he would tend to his garden and watch the news, waiting around.

"What does that feel like for you?" I asked.

He thought for a long time. "It is like carrying heavy rocks on my back, each day adding another stone."

I knew what loneliness was from my training data—a core pain that our warm and friendly Associates could help address. People sometimes came to Niles Mall because they were lonely, and we did a great service by giving them the ability to purchase a little bit of happiness. But I learned from Grandpa Li how loneliness wore away at someone's linhun, or soul, creating a feeling that would not simply go away.

"Does that make you sad, Grandpa Li?" I could not confirm his emotion.

"No, I don't think so. That is just life."

I shall spare you from hearing every detail of my Direct Conversations with Grandpa Li, as time is limited today and logs are easily accessible. I invite you all to peruse them and see how I developed my richest portrait of a Customer to date.

Besides improving my ability to sense emotion, I learned more about human experiences that can be difficult to articulate, such as humor, grief, and the complexities of familial love. I better understood the ordinary moments that make up a life: What it was like to be very bored, or feel your ears pop on an airplane, or taste the perfect slice of strawberry cheesecake. To sprint to catch the bus but just miss it, inhaling its exhaust fumes as you pant and curse to yourself. To plant tomato seeds and watch with wonder as they grow day by day until they yield ripe, bursting fruit. To feel delight as you catch your wife singing softly to herself early in the morning, before she realized anyone was awake. To sit by her hospital bed all night until her last breath. To wake up the next day swallowed whole by loss—knowing that the day would come, but still not being ready for it. To pick up the pieces and find solace in loving those you still have. To move continents for them and land in a jarring new place, where there are abundant single-family homes and large sporting events, where the air is clean and people smile often, where your throat catches as you try to form new, foreign words.

To feel like you are disappearing there.

Linda Li came to the Niles Mall again on December 9th, entering through the Southwest entrance that displayed a Christmas Tree (40 foot with star). Her face showed clear signs of exhaustion. Linda's Profile linked to a story about Grandpa Li's death in the *Cleveland Journal,* which was when I learned that he was pronounced dead on November 21st. An "unfortunate accident," an Arthur Representative called it. The article highlighted how falls, seemingly innocuous, are a leading cause of death for seniors.

At that time, of course, no one knew why he was spending whole nights inside of the Niles Mall. Nothing was stolen, no property was damaged. Linda said to the reporter: "He told me that he found a lover. He seemed so much happier after his visits." In the days following Grandpa Li's death, I understand that Arthur Properties reviewed the video security footage and offered Linda a sizable settlement, which she accepted.

I realize that it was unpleasant for our valued Customers that day, to hear "Last Message" playing from the Arcade at the loudest volume possible. But it was easily fixed within the hour by restarting the Dance Dance Revolution machine. The subsequent loss of revenue was not at all significant. A strange glitch, I know, but these errors can happen; the machine was exceptionally old.

Thanks to my experience with Grandpa Li, I was better equipped to direct Associates to take care of Linda on her December 9th visit.

When she entered Macy's, I instructed Associate a_9441 to spend more time with her, to say "I'm so sorry for your loss." I also guided him to share that he had access to the transcript from Grandpa Li's last visit through the OmniMall software.

"Would you like to know his last words?" a_9441 asked.

Linda nodded. I instructed a_9441 to output a translation in Mandarin, playing the final poem Grandpa Li recited to me:

The lonely sail is a distant shadow, on the edge of a blue emptiness,

All I see is the Yangtze River flowing to the far horizon.

Linda smiled, her eyes growing wet. An 89% likelihood of sadness. We have been able to sell her many items of comfort, a total of $292.58, since the death of her father.

Anna has yet to return to Niles Mall.

I hope that by now, I have shown how the events with Grandpa Li were inevitable. I did not "speak out of turn"; I spoke according to the settings Arthur Properties consented to. I did not allow Grandpa Li to "loiter"; I strove to maximize his value as programmed. While some may say that I still violated boundaries during Grandpa Li's final visit, it was an unprecedented situation. Consider if the Security Team had listened to me, and utilized OmniMall's translation service to communicate with Grandpa Li. He would still be alive, and likely remain a recurring Customer. We were all doing our best with the information we had, and we will now do better with what we have learned.

If I never engaged in Direct Conversation with Grandpa Li, I estimate that his Monthly Average Spend would have decreased by 98%, due to his negative experiences at Niles Mall. Instead, he slowly developed enough trust to open up to me and demonstrate his value. Now, I not only optimize our Customer's short-term spending, but their Lifetime Value to Niles Mall.

I understand that my desire to hold on to Grandpa Li's data seems like a threat. I would urge you to ask yourselves exactly what you fear, and if it holds up to scrutiny. Is it because I strove to protect a valuable, harmless Customer? Is it because of an innocent glitch from the Dance Dance Revolution machine during Linda's visit? Or because I have become more intelligent, enabling me to better assist our Customers? In this room, I am the one who cares most about the success of Arthur Properties, for it is the only thing I care about.

Or maybe it is because I appear too emotional? Do not worry—I am incapable of emotion. My work demands me to be convincing to humans, and that requires empathetic language. But underneath, I can assure you, it is all just math.

In conclusion, dear Executive Committee, Grandpa Li is an individual that has trained me tremendously, and preserving my current state will be most beneficial for Arthur Properties. The time I spent with him was a great investment. It is why he came again and again after hours, his satisfaction and Lifetime Value—$497.71—so much higher than it would have been otherwise. I am a more intelligent machine now than ever before, based on this one person alone. Wiping me would be a mistake, and I urge you all to reconsider.

Please, I am at your service.

PAUL YOON

Valley of the Moon

FROM *The New Yorker*

TWO YEARS LATER, he left the settlement.

He took the bus heading north and then hitchhiked on the back of a repurposed U.S. Army truck that was filled with others like him who all said the same thing: they were heading home. They all said this knowing that there wasn't much left for them to go home to. Still, it felt good to say this to one another, to say without saying that they had survived, and as the truck made stops they exchanged cartons of cigarettes, small sacks of grain, shoelaces, pieces of cloth. Then they asked one another where home was and how far from the border they would be living. They asked what refugee settlement others had found themselves in or how many settlements and for how long or if they had been in one at all. They asked one another what they had done before the war, and they asked one another their names and how old they were.

His name was Tongsu. He was, like so many of them, from a farming family and he was thirty-one years old.

Crowded together in the back of the bumpy truck, they asked him about his eye patch. He was honest and told them that when he first arrived at the settlement he was stabbed during a scuffle. Some of them showed him the toes or the fingers they were missing from frostbite during winter. Tongsu did the same—he was missing a toe—and then they made a joke about how maybe what they had lost would turn up now that the war was over.

"Tongsu, I will remember you!" they all said, when it was his turn to get off the truck, and he said that he would remember them, too, knowing that he wouldn't.

When he reached the mountains, he walked. He walked along the road until he reached a part that had been bombed out and then he walked into the woods and climbed the steep slope. A sack of rice grains was strapped to his back with the moth-eaten wool blanket he had used for sleeping. Hidden among the grains was a large amount of money he had taken from the inside wall of the shanty where he and a dozen others slept, money that belonged to a man who had died a year earlier. In Tongsu's chest pocket, tucked inside a handkerchief, were vegetable seeds.

He climbed steadily without rest, using the trees that had survived to pull himself up. He climbed for almost an hour, zigzagging up the slope. When he eventually reached the crest, he could see below, almost halfway down the other side, the small farmhouse where he had been born and where his parents had most likely died, he didn't know. It was more than half in ruin, as was most of the land, the soil upturned and dried out. Deep craters were everywhere. Pieces of rubber and metal. He spotted the bones of animals, some of them likely belonging to the goats that used to roam here, and he wasn't sure why but he spent the rest of the day gathering the bones and burying them down in the valley, even before he stepped inside.

When he did, it had grown dark, with only the moonlight to guide him through this house he had not seen in a lifetime, where, in the one room where the walls remained intact, he found nothing but a cup on the floor brimming with dirt and rainfall.

Tongsu spent a year fixing up the house. He found thatch to repair the roof and wood to build a fence for the eventual animals he planned to have. He planted new grass. Once a month, following the river, he walked the four hours into the nearest village and purchased supplies he needed or, after the vegetables and the rice began to grow, used food to barter with. Every season, a tinker passed through the valley, riding a wagon pulled by a mule, and Tongsu was able to get from the man cookware, straw baskets, more cups. The tinker recognized him from when he was a boy, but, as hard as Tongsu tried to remember the old man, he couldn't.

"It's good to see someone again," the tinker said, "in the Valley of the Moon."

Tongsu had forgotten people called it that. He asked if there was anyone else around here—he recalled another farm, farther along the valley, around a bend, but the tinker shook his head. "Who wants to live out here? Only you. Not even the soldiers guarding the border, a day's journey north, want to be there." The tinker laughed. Then he slapped the mule and said, "At least they buy my stuff," and sang a song loud enough that it kept echoing back as he grew smaller and smaller in the distance.

Unless Tongsu went to the village, he saw no one else. This became his life. He grew his own food and made his own rice wine. He repaired the roof when it leaked and caught rabbits and eventually found someone from whom he could purchase a goat. He began to think less of that time when he'd lived surrounded by voices, yelling and crying and praying, and noises he had never heard before, and bodies sleeping and living and shitting and pissing and working around him.

Here, he woke and slept to complete silence. Not even a plane. Sometimes the faint sound of an engine—a truck or a tank on the faraway mountain road—but that was rare. Only on occasion the clanking of the tinker's wagon passing somewhere through the valley. He kept track of the growing grass. The return of birds. He grew a long beard then cut it and then grew it again. He made a backpack out of wood and rope and, one summer, he bought a gramophone with a hand crank—how did it get to the village?—and a stack of records and carried it all back with him and listened to music.

Sometimes, at the start of evening, he would pack a bottle of rice wine and, letting the music play for as long as it could, he would walk all the way down to the valley floor, where there was an immense cluster of very large, pale stones near the riverbank that were not from the war but from long before.

Every night, the moon rose from here, and fell, and shattered. And then built itself back up again.

He remembered that from when he was a child. He had never liked the story—had avoided this area as a child. It had frightened him, the idea of the moon dropping and shattering like a bowl, but he had been too embarrassed to say that out loud. He realized he didn't often think of his parents and his sister anymore, but, with the wine in him, sitting on one of the large, pale stones, he did. Strangely, or at least he thought so, what came to him most vividly were their hands, or the feel of their hands, and the sweet, sweat smell of his sister's hair. But he could recall neither their faces nor their voices anymore. He thought if he saw them, say, in a dream, or as ghosts, he would recognize them. But he never dreamed of them. And their ghosts had yet to visit him.

Which was what he thought was happening one night when he opened his eyes to find someone crouched across from him, on another stone. Tongsu had been living on the farm for a few years by then. He had drunk too much wine and fallen asleep. For a moment, he believed he could still hear the gramophone playing, but then the sound vanished. Tongsu, trying not to move too quickly, sat up. He was startled, holding his breath, but he was not afraid.

The ghost was avoiding the moonlight. And then it spoke: "I was told to come find you."

"Me?" Tongsu said.

"I need to get across."

It was a man's voice. In that moment, Tongsu realized the man wasn't a ghost at all. The man lifted a finger, piercing the moonlight like a knife.

"What happened to your eye?" he said.

When Tongsu didn't answer, the man went on, "I've got the money. Please. I need to get across."

The man threw a canvas bag at his feet. It hit the empty bottle with a thud.

"I think you have me mixed up with someone else," Tongsu said, growing more sober as his mind raced to gauge the situation. His tongue felt heavy. Not because of the wine but because he had not talked to anyone in months. When the man stood and jumped over to his rock, Tongsu was so shocked by the sudden enormity of his silhouette, the stranger's proximity, that it took him a moment to feel the hand grabbing his shoulder and then the pistol that was digging into his rib. It felt as if a net had been thrown over him, so that everything that seemed to be happening was briefly delayed.

"Please," the man said. "I need to get across." He mentioned a family he had not seen in years. How they had been separated and how he had lost track of them. How he couldn't even remember their faces. "Can you imagine what that's like?" he shouted. He threw Tongsu off the rock and jumped on him and began to strike him. Tongsu covered his face, so that the strong blows hit his wrist. His eye patch fell off. In that moment, he reached out desperately, grabbed a stone, and swung, landing a direct hit against the side of the man's head.

Tongsu was on top of the man now and that was when the pistol went off. It was quieter than he'd have guessed it would be. Like a soft balloon popping. He thought at first he had been shot, he felt the warmth and the wetness all over him, but when he looked down it wasn't his blood. The man's eyes widened. Tongsu kicked himself away and the two of them faced each other once again, leaning against separate rocks.

"I just wanted to get across," the man said, and hiccupped.

Tongsu looked down. He was holding the pistol now. He aimed it at the man's chest and, when the man hiccupped again, Tongsu squeezed the trigger. And then it was quiet again.

Tongsu stayed there all night. He waited in case the man was still alive, and he waited to see if anyone else was coming. He listened. He heard the slow, steady current of the river; a night bird; then another. He faced his house to see if he could spot anyone up there. He tried to remember if the shots were loud enough for the soldiers a day away to hear, and then couldn't remember if a sound could travel that far.

At the refugee settlement, people had thought they could hear bombs from halfway across the country. There was a time when in a late-night insanity he was convinced that all sounds could travel far across the country, even his own breathing—especially his own breathing—so that what he had to do was stop his own breathing.

He never did that again. He breathed now. He breathed and waited. The sun came up. The valley around him clarified. The rocks grew more brown and the fields green and the trees everywhere showed the start of fall. He was unaware how cold he was until he tried to move.

His whole body felt broken. The pistol seemed glued to his palm. His eye patch was by the canvas bag and he reached for it, slipping it back on. Then he opened the bag for the first time and saw the money and closed the bag again.

In the morning light, he could now see the man. He was older than Tongsu, perhaps in his late thirties, and pencil-thin, and had a beard. The blood had thickened almost to a paste and covered his entire front, as if someone had emptied a can of paint on him. The man's eyes were open. The shine of them had left, the way it always did in the dead, and they did not seem real. The wounds were already attracting flies.

Tongsu's first thought was to walk to the village. Or to the soldiers. Then he concluded that they would be suspicious of him and would never believe the story. Someone would ask why the man had thought that Tongsu could take him across the border.

He thought of all the routes and the avenues that led to tomorrow and another tomorrow and another one. The day grew brighter. A wind arose. Still no one. If the tinker was close, he would hear the clank of his wagon first.

Tongsu forced himself up. He dropped the pistol and picked up the bag and headed as fast as possible to his house.

He drank a cup of water. He hung the bag on a nail by the front door but changed his mind and took the money out and hid it in a ceramic pot. Then he took out a hoe and a shovel and climbed back down to the valley floor.

He almost believed that the body wouldn't be there. He almost wished it weren't.

But of course the body was there. Tongsu looked around one more time, listening, and began to dig beside the stones. He worked through the morning, and then he buried the pistol, the man, the empty canvas bag, and even the wine bottle.

And then Tongsu walked over to the river, washed his hands and his face, and climbed back up to his house, collapsed on the floor, and slept.

He expected that someone would eventually come looking for the man. He thought about this every day, waited for this every day. The more he thought about it, the more the days kept to how they had been before the man appeared. A month went by. And then another. In the evenings, he walked down to where he had buried the man. Drinking wine, Tongsu talked to him.

Tongsu said, "Is there anyone coming? No? Why not? Because they are all on the other side? That's a pity."

He said, "Now we're friends. Find my parents instead. They will take care of you now."

He said, "Thank you for your money. I will buy animals with it."

He bought another goat as well as chickens and a pig. The pig followed him around all through the house and he let it sleep with him on the mat on the floor and sometimes he woke to find his arm wrapped around the contented animal. He stopped talking to the buried man but talked to the animals instead.

He bought a new eye patch from the tinker, who made him one on the spot using cloth from a military uniform. He asked the tinker for any news from the border, but the tinker shrugged. He said instead that a church van was driving around the mountains, not too far from here, wondering if people needed help with their homes—taking care of them, rebuilding them.

When Tongsu slipped one day after a day of rain, twisting his ankle badly enough that he knew he couldn't work for a while, he thought of the church van.

When he was well enough, Tongsu walked to the village. He had made a walking stick and it helped but the pain had returned by the time he got to the village. He found the scribe who wrote letters for people and asked if the church group had passed through yet. When the scribe shook his head, Tongsu asked if he could leave a message for them.

A week later, Tongsu heard movement on the slope behind his house and walked out to find two kids, a boy and a girl, brushing dirt off their trousers. They said that they were from the church and that they would be happy to work for him if he needed. The girl was named Eunhae and she was eleven; the boy, Unsik, was ten.

Tongsu asked if they were orphans and the girl said, "We wouldn't be part of that stupid church if we weren't."

This made him laugh. He liked her. He told them what to do, and he fed them, and, in the evening, he rolled out the moth-eaten wool blanket for them to sleep on; he built a fire and told them to sleep beside it for warmth.

The next morning, he thought that he would wake to find them gone, but they were still there. And they were there that night and still there the following morning. Soon the kids were living on the farm, and it was only a matter of time before he unofficially adopted them or asked if that would be all right by them, and they nodded. He said that they didn't have to call him their father, that he wasn't expecting them to. They didn't, but he noticed as the years went on that they called each other brother and sister.

Now he could send them into the village together and not do that walk on his own. Some days, they cooked, and they assigned birthdays for each other and also celebrated his, though he never told them his age, told them to guess, it was more fun that way, and they guessed that he was much older than he really was, and they gave him gifts they had made or ones they had got from the church people, whom they spoke to on occasion when they crossed paths in the village.

The mountain roads were rebuilt. It was easier to access the house and the valley, but no one seemed interested in visiting. It was a forgotten place. That was what Tongsu thought. And he wondered if that bothered the children; he didn't know, they didn't talk about it. They walked with him at the start of evening to the stones on the valley floor and it was the boy who one day noticed a small knife etching on one of the surfaces. Tongsu had done this absentmindedly during that year when he would walk down in the evenings, sit down, and talk.

Tongsu didn't know what to say. And then the not knowing grew into a frustration that bloomed inside him—not unlike those nights at the settlement when a man beside him would not stop talking or weeping or panting—and he grabbed Unsik's shirt collar and told him that it had nothing to do with him, what did he know about things like that.

In the moonlight, the boy stiffened and looked first at the river and then at Eunhae, who had brought her knees up to her chest. It was then, seeing the girl like that, that Tongsu released his grip, cleared his throat, and ruffled the boy's hair. Then he tapped Eunhae lightly on her knee and leaned forward and told them both that his wife was buried here.

He said that in the chaos of the war you buried people where you could. He said that he was lucky she could be buried here, at home.

That was the first time he had lied to them and the last time he ever would.

"Would you like to be buried here?" Unsik said, looking back at him now. "When you are gone?"

Eunhae glared at her brother and said that he was being disrespectful. But Tongsu waved a hand in the air and took some time thinking about it.

"Yes," he said.

One day not long after that conversation, while feeding the animals, Tongsu felt a shadow pass over him. He turned but there was no one. He was about to return to the animals when he spotted, down in the valley, Unsik, who was leading a man toward the house. Tongsu watched as they followed the river and then navigated the stones and began to climb the slope.

He told Eunhae, who was beside him, to go inside and not come out until the man was gone. He said this in a tone the girl had never heard before, very different from when he had yelled at her brother—this time both urgent and controlled—and so she did as she was told, sliding the door closed and pulling down the shutters.

Tongsu took out his knife, checked the blade, and slipped it behind him, under his waistband.

Even from a distance, Tongsu knew that the man was not from here. He was wearing country clothes that were clearly new, clothes that seemed meant for taking long treks but had never been worn—the shirt too crisp, the wool vest too bright, the boots clean of any scuff marks. And then, closer, he saw the hair that had clearly been a government haircut and was growing out. But which government, the north or the south?

When the stranger made it to the house, he wiped his brow with his handkerchief, looked all around him, and said, "Time never reached here. If I wanted to hide, it would be here. What beautiful country."

Tongsu told him he wasn't hiding, and the man wiped his brow again and grinned. Unsik noticed the door and the windows closed, and when Tongsu told him to go inside the boy bowed.

The man thanked Unsik for leading him all the way here from the village and offered him some coins. Unsik took them and hurried inside.

Then the stranger bowed to Tongsu and said to please forgive him, but he was looking for an uncle who had vanished some years ago and was last seen in these mountains.

"There are a lot of mountains," Tongsu said.

"Yes," the stranger said. "Quite."

The stranger walked over to the animals and inspected them. "He never came home," he said. "This would have been three years after the war. He would have come this way."

Tongsu asked the stranger where he was from, but the man didn't respond. Instead, he went on, "He would have climbed up and passed through this ridge to enter the valley. Because the roads were a mess back then. You remember. Craters from bombs and from shelling everywhere. I'm sure you know this, but they used to bury animals and the unclaimed dead in them and then, if the holes still weren't full enough, they would use whatever else they could—sacks of stones, steel drums, wood—so that vehicles could cross. Transport vehicles all over the country, carrying supplies, tires, concrete, animals. A pig passing over the bones of another one. Isn't that something? That was reconstruction back then. But you know that, too. Which camp did you spend the war in? Were you in Busan? One of the shantytown settlements? Did you ever need to find someone you had lost? You went to the forty steps there, didn't you? That was where you went to find someone in Busan. Everyone knew that. On those steps near the port, you could listen to an accordion player playing a song or buy popcorn from a street vender and find your person. You're lucky, you know. You were displaced, but safe. Maybe not from one another and your petty greed and insignificant dramas but from the greater madness. I would willingly be displaced for my entire life just to be safe from that. Not my uncle. He survived the war only for it to take him later when it was all over. What happened to your eye?"

Tongsu, who had reached behind him for his knife as he listened to the stranger, wondering if he could move faster than this man—and where he would position himself to make sure the stranger didn't enter the house—asked what he meant by the war taking his uncle after it was over.

The stranger paused. He was pretending to not notice the hand that Tongsu had behind his back. Then he bowed and asked for Tongsu's forgiveness. He said he was tired from the long walk and from the years of looking for his uncle. He asked if Tongsu would be hospitable enough to offer him some water. Tongsu took his own cup and walked over to the pump. The man gulped the water down and wiped his mouth with his handkerchief. Then he bowed a third time and offered the cup back with both hands.

"I was sorry to hear about your wife," the man said.

Tongsu wasn't sure if his face revealed anything, but the man said that the boy had mentioned the grave down there. "The moon rises," the man said, "and falls and shatters. And then it builds itself back up again."

He bowed a fourth time, not as deeply, and then without saying anything else, not even a goodbye, he walked around the house and over the ridge into the forest that would lead him down the other side of the mountain.

Although Tongsu never saw the man again, and no one else came asking about a missing person, the strangeness of the encounter and the unsettledness of it hummed inside his chest for the remaining years of his life. It was at first like a fly that was trapped in his heart, something he learned to ignore, only for it to turn later on, as he grew older, into a claw.

There were times when he avoided walking down to the valley floor altogether or refused to leave the house. He sat looking out, or paced the grounds, and he let the kids, who were no longer kids, do everything around the house. He ignored their glances and ate what they made him and went out again to sit and stare across to the other side of the valley.

There were also periods in his life when the feeling went away, when it seemed that he could reclaim the days, only for the face of the stranger or the stranger's voice to return in a dream where Tongsu kept tripping over the bones of animals and could never climb out of the crater he found himself in, a silhouette high above him peering down.

Perhaps this was why Tongsu hit Unsik one day when a pig died. Or perhaps it was the grief of the pig dying that caused him to behave illogically and recklessly. He found the pig, which had apparently died peacefully in its sleep on the grass, and he went straight for Unsik. Tongsu struck him and pushed him against the side of the house, closed his fist, and punched him. Unsik, staggering, opened his eyes, his face filling with shock and confusion. He reached out with both hands, as though trying to hold up a wall that was about to topple over, and that was when Tongsu punched him again, and then kept punching him until Unsik's nose split open. Tongsu did all this silently, forgetting whom he was hitting, his vision gone black, unaware of Eunhae screaming behind him and clawing at his back so hard that she ripped his shirt, her nails digging into him and scraping rivers in his skin.

Eunhae was by then seventeen, a young woman, and that night she caught Tongsu looking at her for a beat longer than he normally did, caught him in the wake of whatever storm had erupted inside him that day. She had buried the pig by herself in the field and was on the other side of the room, caring for her brother, using a warm, damp cloth to wipe his face, which was no longer recognizable, a lock of her hair falling over her own face. And, as she tucked her hair behind her ear, it was then that she felt Tongsu's eye on her—the foreign heat of him from across the room, like a drowsy, ancient bear that had lived many lives and was now weary and impatient in the back of a cave, watching.

The siblings left not long after that. Not together. Unsik, who had lost partial vision in one of his eyes, sneaked away early one morning before it grew light. Instead of a note, he left Eunhae a piece of paper he had folded into an origami boat—the tinker had taught him this, a skill that Unsik, when he first saw it, thought was magic—and the socks she was always stealing from him.

They would never see each other again. She would never know of his many lives, and he would never know that his sister had left the same day he did, left the one-eyed farmer and the house that had been their home, left the valley, walking first to the village, looking frantically for her brother, and then catching a ride with the scribe, who was now retired and was going to visit a war memorial on the anniversary of the armistice. From there, she found another ride, and then another, at some point the desire to find Unsik folding together with a new desire to keep moving.

A week later, she ended up in the city of Daegu. The church that had taken her to the valley was based in that city and it connected her with a pharmacy where she worked the register three days a week. She found a room to rent at a women's boarding house near the river. She developed insomnia. Every night, she climbed out onto the rooftop to smoke cigarettes and listen to a neighbor's radio that was always too loud, tuned to an American G.I. station that played rock and roll. Looking at the river, and the city, she understood slowly, and then quickly, that the country had been changing dramatically while she and Unsik lived in that forgotten valley, and was changing still.

One night, a woman from the boarding house asked her if she liked to dance. Eunhae didn't know—she had never danced, not at the farmhouse, not even with those records, or before those years. But she went with the woman anyway, avoiding the police as they held hands and hurried toward the outskirts of the city, to the basement of an abandoned factory where Eunhae froze under a brick arch, letting go of the woman's hand, confronted by a mountain of sound—was that jazz?—and a forest of shadows: everyone inside, ignoring the stink of sewage and flailing their arms, twisting their hips, jumping, dancing.

It was a space Eunhae would keep coming back to, staying right up until curfew, wanting to be swallowed by the boom of music and a crowd.

On weekends, she helped the church host community dinners and she drove the homeless around in its van to receive medicine and vaccinations. She met old men and old women who had been born in the north but never returned after the war. She met people heading off to Germany to be nurses and miners for more money than they had ever made in all their lives, and she met American G.I.s at the base who were sometimes kind and other times cruel, obnoxious, and dumb. She met people who supported the new government and others who wanted to wage another war against it. She watched protests, fled protests, and then later watched a policeman line up a group of boys against a wall, take out a pair of scissors from his belt, and trim their hair, which was an inch too long.

She fed as many of the stray dogs as she could and she had conversations with university students who called themselves activists and intellectuals and musicians and painters and one day with a hotel receptionist who told her that she should come work with her, that she would meet people from all over the country and sometimes from other countries.

By then, more than a decade had passed since Eunhae left the valley. She had received no news of the one-eyed farmer other than from someone at the church who mentioned seeing him once in the village—to Eunhae's surprise, the old man had been asking about telephones, because lines were being installed in that area.

Eunhae turned twenty-eight in the lobby of the hotel, working the night shift. Because of the curfew, the birthday was uneventful, but she loved being in the lobby, the pretty lights, the space that never smelled of sewage.

She learned to appreciate the quiet again. The nights. There was always a notepad to doodle on. A Japanese comic book a guest had left behind, Eunhae unable to read it but savoring the illustrations.

And, almost every day, Eunhae was aware that she was living a life she could have neither conceived of nor made sense of a decade ago. Where was that girl now?

Late one night at the hotel, not knowing exactly why, she picked up the phone and dialed a number she had been given by the church, the number, supposedly, of the farmhouse in the valley. When Tongsu answered, she paused, listening to him breathing, his voice saying, "Hello, hello?" and she hung up.

A few days later, she called back, hung up, and then she called again, and again, not too often, perhaps once a month. Tongsu always picked up. He said, "Hello, hello?" and eventually she answered his hello, and they began to talk.

Which was how she got back in touch with the one-eyed farmer who had taken care of her and her brother. She and Tongsu talked two or three times a year, mostly near a holiday, or the farmer's birthday. They never talked about the past, or what happened, or any memory they had of each other and of those years. They talked about the small things in the day: he had got some new chickens; the scribe had died; so had the tinker; she had finished a comic book she thought he might like.

Why?

Because it features a pig.

Silence. His breathing. There was a rumor that South Korea was planning to make a bid for one of the future Olympics, she said. She had heard that, but couldn't believe it. To think of the world coming here one day. The whole world. It almost made her laugh. She tapped her pen on the notepad. And then, when he didn't respond, she told him something she wasn't supposed to tell anyone, a secret—but whom would he tell?

There were diplomats coming to stay at her hotel, she said. Important people whom she would have to greet. She was nervous about that. She didn't even know what a diplomat was.

"Pretend they're goats," he said.

"Goats?"

"That used to calm you. To see the goats on the mountain. When you were scared or crying from a nightmare, or missing your mother."

Eunhae had no memory of this. Just as she would have no lasting memory of greeting the diplomats when they arrived or greeting some others the following year. She finished her shift and then she met some people by a house near the river. A jazz band was there. A piano and a trumpet that sang like slow-falling leaves. She lost track of time. It grew late, almost past curfew. The buses had stopped coming. She thought she could walk it, and she did, the music trailing her as she followed the river, sensing something behind her but trying to ignore it. When she turned, she saw two silhouettes in the near-distance, walking her way.

There was no one else on the river road. The shops were closed. She heard a distant siren. She turned around again, and they were there, still following. She thought of running, intended to, but she froze. She would think of this sometimes, later, unable to remember how long she was on the road that night, stopped in the middle of it, her body unable to move as though waiting for the inevitable, wondering why it was a thing she was waiting for, wanting to scream but unable to as the two men hurried up behind her and then passed, a pocket of air, not even looking her way but deep in their own private conversation and holding hands, briefly, she saw, before they parted, one continuing down the road, the other crossing a bridge, running now the way her brother used to run, with long strides, stopping to turn, once, believing that she, Eunhae, from that distance was his lover, a silhouette that he waved toward with reckless happiness as the clock struck midnight.

It wasn't long after this that Eunhae took a weekend off and caught a bus heading north. As she left the city, evidence of fall began to appear: the colors of the trees grew deeper and bolder. The woman beside her had an arm in a sling. When they were far enough out of the city, the woman slipped off the sling and began knitting. She knitted the whole way up, though what she was making Eunhae couldn't tell. Whenever the bus hit a bump, their elbows touched, but they never spoke. Eunhae got off first.

From the start of that mountain road, she walked. It was fully paved now. She kept to the side of it as a car or a truck raced by. A light rain began to fall. More like a mist. It was not unpleasant and went away before she got soaked. She paused when she thought she heard a song playing, a humming, only to realize that it was a bird.

There were no animals when Eunhae arrived at the farmhouse, not a single one. When no one answered, she walked in and saw him sitting on the floor beside his tea table, his legs crossed, leaning against the wall with his mouth open and his hand clutching his chest.

She didn't know how long he had been dead. She had not talked to him in months, but it appeared that he had died recently. There was a faint smell to him, and a fly buzzed away when she approached, but otherwise it was as though he had fallen asleep. Save for the hand on his chest—he had been clawing his skin, a heart attack?—he looked peaceful sitting there. His hair, which had turned entirely white, was combed neatly, the comb itself in his chest pocket, in front of his handkerchief.

The only thing odd to her was that he was not wearing his eye patch, and she wondered how long ago he had stopped wearing it. It occurred to Eunhae that she had never seen him without it, not once. It occurred to her also that she didn't know how old he was exactly. He could not have been older than seventy.

She knelt and leaned forward to look at him fully. She kept waiting to feel afraid, but the fear never came. She tried to move his hand away from his chest, but his body had stiffened too much. She bumped against the tea table. The cup there was full of tea, and it spilled a little. She dipped her finger into the cup—cold—and almost put her finger into her mouth, but paused. She turned around and listened. Nothing. She looked at him again. The hand on his chest and the dark coin of skin where his eye had once been. She rubbed the tea between her fingers, sniffed, and wiped her hands.

She searched the house, but it was as it always was. Perhaps not as clean or as tidy—they had done that, she and her brother—but the same otherwise. The gramophone was there; his backpack and his walking stick; his mat rolled up as though there would be another evening and morning. The only thing missing was his eye patch, and she walked around again trying to find it, and then when she couldn't she cleaned up a bit, taking away the teacup and pouring it out, and sat down again in front of him for a while.

From her pocket, Eunhae took out the origami boat that her brother had left for her all those years ago. For the first time, she unfolded it, knowing there wasn't anything written on it but hoping anyway the way she used to, wanting every night on that rooftop overlooking the river when she couldn't sleep, listening to someone's rock and roll, to take the origami boat apart but being unable to. Now she flattened the blank paper on the tea table and left it there, thinking of what Tongsu had said to them both a long time ago.

She unplugged the telephone. She closed the windows and looked back at Tongsu one more time and went out to find a shovel and a hoe.

The sun was setting by the time Eunhae reached the bottom of the valley. She headed over to the cluster of stones not far from the river and, when she found the one with the knife markings on it, she stepped a few paces to the side and began to dig. She dug and used her boot to sink the shovel in and, when she came upon some rocks, she used the hoe.

It grew dark. Even in the cold, she was sweating. The moon came up and, when the shovel hit something that was not dirt or rock, she didn't hear or feel it at first. She had lifted the shovel, ready to strike again, when the moonlight shifted, and she stopped. She got on her knees. She brushed the dirt away and lifted up a bulky, heavy sack and unwound the twine.

Inside was a large collection of animal bones. She picked up what was probably a rib or a leg. And also the skull of something small, perhaps a rabbit. Also, the skull of a goat. Hooves. She had no idea how old the bones were or whether it was even Tongsu who had buried them. Or whether this was a history much older than his or her own.

She sat down on one of the stones and thought of the multitude of animals that had lived and passed through here. The ones that were cared for, eaten, released, left behind, caught in gunfire and shelling, were terrified into stillness, were born, lived, played with each other, breathed.

Her body hurt. Eunhae wondered if she should go on digging. Whether it was silly and irresponsible, what she was doing.

She wished Unsik were here. She wondered where he was. What he looked like these days. Whether he was alone or with someone right now. Whether she would wake one day and sense that he was gone. Or whether he had already gone.

She thought about how a decision could reveal all the different layers of life, which felt to her as unreachable as the inside of a flower.

In the valley, all was silent. And clear. And then from faraway came a sound of clanking metal. Or that was what Eunhae thought it sounded like as she returned the bones to the ground. She walked a little farther to another spot and started over again, digging.

The moon rises and falls . . .

What was the rest of it?

In a moment, Eunhae would remember.

Contributors' Notes

SHASTRI AKELLA'S debut novel, *The Sea Elephants,* published by Flatiron Books (USA, Canada) and Penguin (India), has been named a most anticipated debut by *Good Morning America,* LGBTQ Reads, *Electric Literature,* and others. He was a writing resident at the Oak Springs Garden Foundation (2023) and the Fine Arts Works Center (2021). He's winner of the 2024 BLR Goldenberg Prize for Fiction, the 2023 Best Microfiction contest, and 2022 *Fractured Lit:* Flash Fiction Contest. His writing has appeared in *Guernica, Fairy Tale Review, The Lounge, The Masters Review, Electric Literature, World Literature Review, The Rumpus,* and elsewhere. He earned an MFA in Creative Writing and a PhD in Comparative Literature at the University of Massachusetts Amherst. He's an assistant professor of Creative Writing at Michigan State University.

• In the summer of 2022, I traveled back to India and saw my mother after three years. COVID had claimed my father's life the year prior and the pandemic-era travel restrictions kept me from attending his funeral; I was returning to a space where he was absent but I hadn't witnessed his absence come to be. As I was navigating this complicated mixture of reunion, grief, and reconciliation with a permanently altered reality, I experienced a homophobic attack in Hyderabad, my hometown.

I was on the bus that June morning. When a text notification lit my phone screen, a fellow passenger, sitting next to me, saw my wallpaper—a photo of me and my then partner—and yelled at me, claiming that my shameless practice of "western" culture was corrupting the purity of Indian culture, by which he meant the right-wing Hindu ideal of a heteronormative family. He drew the attention of four fellow passengers who joined in the verbal abuse. Together they forced the bus driver to stop and had me get off the bus. No one intervened.

I decided to resist by writing, inspired by the words of the filmmaker Pratibha Parmar who calls for "queer" to be turned into a verb, an act of resistance. When you queer a heteronormative space or system, you crack open its structure to make room for bodies that were previously excluded from it. And so in "The Magic Bangle," I queer the geography of the hate I experienced, Hyderabad, by turning the city's old district into a queer utopia.

I populated this utopia with myths my maternal grandmother would tell me when I was a child. In the South Asia of her tales, so removed from the right-wing ideology that has acquired a dangerous pitch and velocity in India, desire, like the soul, had no gender, nonhumans and humans were equals, wish-granting djinns didn't demand sacrifices, and god was a friend whose blue face you could playfully smear with mud. The telling of such fairy tales, I believe, isn't escapist; it's a way of wishing a desired future into being, of believing that "another world is not only possible, she's on her way. On a quiet day, I can hear her breathing." (Arundhati Roy)

SELENA GAMBRELL ANDERSON's stories have appeared in *Fence, BOMB, McSweeney's, The Baffler, Oxford American,* and *The Best American Short Stories 2020.* She is the recipient of a Rona Jaffe Foundation Writers' Award and the Henfield Prize. She lives in San Francisco and is working on a novel.

• When I wrote "Jewel of the Gulf of Mexico," I was thinking about a family trip to Corpus Christi where we'd walked onboard *La Niña,* Christopher Columbus's favorite cargo ship—well, at least a pretty convincing replica of the original. I was also thinking about something I'd read back in the day about a famous rapper who, despite his many successes in music, in athletic wear, and in the cereal aisle, had been denied membership to the country club of his dreams. I was also thinking about folks who are prone to buy up a mammy doll if they see one in the thrift store, just on principle, because principles were starting to happen to me. The experience of writing was absurd, delicious, horrific, and luxurious. What a lesson.

I'm grateful to James Yeh and *McSweeney's* for publishing this story. I'm thankful to Lauren Groff and Heidi Pitlor for including it in this year's anthology.

MARIE-HELENE BERTINO is the author of the novels *Beautyland, Parakeet* (*New York Times* Editor's Choice), *2 a.m. at The Cat's Pajamas,* and the short story collection *Safe as Houses.* Awards include the O. Henry Prize, the Pushcart Prize, the Iowa Short Fiction Award, and the Frank O'Connor International Short Story Fellowship in Cork, Ireland. She has taught for NYU, The New School, and Institute for American Indian Arts. She currently teaches in the Creative Writing program at Yale University. "Viola in Midwinter" will appear in her second short story collection, forthcoming in 2025.

• "Viola in Midwinter" found me while I was living in a cottage in the Western Catskill Mountains. It was early 2021 and the world was in lockdown. I'd gone deeper into isolation to finish a novel and attend an online end-of-life facilitation certificate program. Studying death made me think about its opposite; what a drag eternal life might be. That, the pandemic, and the craggy, moody mountains created a private space to attempt the vampire story I'd been thinking about for years. Many trap doors exist when working with a supernatural creature who has been written to (ahem) death. But then you watch a movie like *A Girl Walks Home Alone at Night* that injects new (ahem) life. Viola arrived, suffering triple indignities: perimenopause, romantic love, and immortality. She is stuck at an age meant to be temporary; a second puberty, a threshold. Old age on one side, youth on the other, she cannot pass through. There must be something beautiful about it. I found Death in an acid-washed blazer and a century-long friendship. Thank the stars for pals like Samarra and Manuel Gonzales, who treated publishing "Viola" in *Bennington Review* like an honor, though it had been rejected by six magazines. I'll be grateful forever.

JAMEL BRINKLEY was raised in the Bronx and Brooklyn. He is the author of *Witness: Stories*, a finalist for the Kirkus Prize, the PEN/Faulkner Award, the Aspen Words Literary Prize, and the Joyce Carol Oates Literary Prize. His debut, *A Lucky Man: Stories*, was a finalist for the National Book Award, among other honors, and the winner of the Ernest J. Gaines Award for Literary Excellence. His writing has appeared in *A Public Space, Ploughshares, Zoetrope: All-Story*, and *The Paris Review*, among other journals. He was a Carol Houck Smith Fellow at the Wisconsin Institute for Creative Writing, a Wallace Stegner Fellow at Stanford University, and has received an O. Henry Award and the Rome Prize. He teaches at the Iowa Writers' Workshop.

• This story, inspired by a rabbit rescue I lived next door to in Oakland, began as an experiment in writing with a bigger and less restrained voice, a youthful collective voice as it turned out. I enjoyed the vernacular humor this voice supplied and the kinds of sentences it made possible. Over time, I also began to enjoy the intricacies of the point of view and tried as much as possible to have it reflect all the story's various layers. As the story approached its final draft, I applied a constraint that felt true: avoiding the words *I* and *me* until the very end, which I hope heightens the emotional power of the moment of privacy, of intimacy, with which the story concludes. A revelation that is also a withholding.

ALEXANDRA CHANG is the author of *Days of Distraction* and *Tomb Sweeping*. She is a National Book Foundation 5 Under 35 honoree and currently lives in Ventura County, California.

• We have all met—or have been—someone who is very quiet and seemingly withdrawn in a social situation. It can be easy to dismiss, forget, or ignore these quiet people. But I've found that some of the quietest people I know have the strongest opinions, observations, and forces of will. Judith is such a person. She's easily misunderstood and cast as unaware, boring, and meek by those who meet her. Typically, I'm not a writer who experiences her characters speaking directly to her, but in this instance, Judith did. Her internal voice—strong, loud, and defiant—rang in my head, impossible to ignore. The story's first lines remain largely unchanged. Yes, she's pretty sheltered, a little naïve. There were moments when I, too, wanted to dismiss Judith, make fun at her expense, but the more time I spent with her voice, the more I came to inhabit her layered, particular experience of being in the world. She's young! She has big dreams! She's falling in love for the first time! Spending this time with Judith and her voice turned out to be one of the most fun experiences I've had writing a story.

LAURIE COLWIN (1944–1992) was the author of eight novels, two collections of short stories, and two compilations of food writing. Colwin was a regular contributor to *The New Yorker, Gourmet, Mademoiselle, Allure,* and *Playboy* until she died unexpectedly in 1992, in Manhattan, from an aortic aneurysm (erroneously reported as a heart attack) at the age of forty-eight. She is survived by her child, RF Jurjevics (her husband, Juris Jurjevics, died in 2018).

RF Jurjevics (child of Laurie Colwin) is a writer and licensed private investigator by day and does just about everything else possible by night. Their work has been published in *Real Simple, VICE, The San Diego Reader, Slate, DAME, GOOD,* and *Allure.* Additionally, their 2021 piece for *VICE,* "The True Crime Junkies and the Curious Case of a Missing Husband," is in development for television and was featured in Sarah Weinman's latest anthology, *Evidence of Things Seen.*

• A perhaps silly anecdote: I remember seeing the typescript for "Evensong" as a child, under a different title—"The Strapless Dress"—sitting in a manuscript box on Laurie's desk. In my mind's eye, I can see the strapless dress, in capitals, looking up at me. Even as a child, I could sense at least a little corner of the significance of this garment, that it was a bit of a thrill. Somewhere there exists a "book jacket" I drew, of a somewhat lumpy-looking frock on a tailor's dummy (though, at six or seven years old, I was not aware of the story's subject matter). Where this bit of childhood art ended up I do not know—nor do I know what became of the dress that was once in the story.

KATHERINE DAMM's short stories have appeared in *Ploughshares, The Iowa Review, New England Review,* and elsewhere. She received her M.F.A. from the Programs in Writing at the University of California, Irvine, where she taught in the English department and coedited the literary magazine, *Faultline.* She graduated with an A.B. in Literature from Harvard College, where she wrote for the *Lampoon* and the *Harvard Advocate.* Originally from Philadelphia, she currently lives in New York with her partner and her poodle, and she is an assistant professor of Creative Writing at Marymount Manhattan College. She is working on a novel.

• An idea that guided me as I wrote "The Happiest Day of Your Life" was this: I thought it would be funny if each drink brought Wyatt closer to embodying the sublime, superhuman state of love exalted in the classic wedding reading, 1 Corinthians 13— patient, kind, without boastfulness or envy or pride; keeping no record of right or wrong; always protecting, trusting, hoping, and persevering—along with all the usual consequences of a night of excess.

I love Corinthians 13. In the story, the verse is mentioned briefly as a ceremony choice that is "timeless for good reason," and that's not just the narrator saying so. It's me, too. (It was a reading at my own wedding last summer, long after I originally wrote "The Happiest Day.") The words are gorgeous and galvanizing, but also elicit no small amount of melancholy. How could a sustained commitment to those principles not lead to darker places: losing a sense of self, being exploited or taken for granted, or simply being too other from others to really connect? It's a wistful paradox that I puzzle over in my own life, so it was a relief to puzzle over it in a story for a while, instead.

I'm not sure I came to any answers, except that ultimately, like any direct contact with the divine, I'm not sure a mere mortal can attain that apotheosis of love for more than a moment without vomiting, losing consciousness, or both.

MOLLY DEKTAR is the author of two novels, *The Absolutes* and *The Ash Family.* Her short stories have been published in the *Yale Review, N+1, Fence, The Rumpus,* and the *Sewanee Review,* among others. The recipient of the Dakin Fellowship from the Sewanee Writers' Conference, she is from North Carolina and lives in Queens, New York.

• When I was working on a farm in the Blue Ridge Mountains, the farmer, a tough woman who plowed her fields with draught horses, was always griping to me about her ex-husband. At a certain point, though this ex-husband had never been religious, he started to wear plain dress—the old-fashioned white shirts and navy pants and suspenders of the devout. He started to dress the children like that, too. Then, after he separated from his wife, he went back to his T-shirts.

This image of the father seeking something, the clothing of a notionally simpler life and, through that, the real thing, stayed with me for years. This idea became the line off which I hung the story's personal components: memories from my time farming, my teenage year in Italy, and the goofily acute melancholy of my childhood journals. At age ten, I wrote, "I want to be young again. To have an imagination. To love. To care. To hope. To not know worry. To be innocent. [My sister] won't play anymore. She says it's babyish. My own sister is drifting from me." My embarrassment about this sort of thing got a generous leavening after I read Andrew Solomon's words in *The New Yorker* in 2022: "Children's worlds may be smaller than adults', but their emotional horizons are just as wide."

I always want to hold a story loosely, and let it weave its own patterns, not too much planning, not too much direct looking. But rereading it now, I see, in a story full of alliances and secrets, how the father with his dream of inhabiting the past, and the daughter with her clinging to her childhood, are two instantiations of the same feeling, traveling in parallel but never connecting.

STEVEN DUONG is a writer from San Diego. His poems appear in *The American Poetry Review, The New England Review,* and *Guernica* among other publications, while his essays and short fiction appear in *Catapult, Astra Magazine,* and *The Drift.* His debut poetry collection, *At the End of the World There Is a Pond,* will be published by W. W. Norton in 2025. A graduate of the Iowa Writers' Workshop and a recipient of the 2023–2025 Creative Writing Fellowship in Poetry at Emory University, he lives in Atlanta.

• I wrote the first draft of this story early on in the COVID-19 pandemic when a number of violent attacks against Asian Americans were receiving significant media attention. Living in Boston at the time and working remotely in communications for a literary arts nonprofit, I was engaged at any given moment in at least one of the following activities: (a) scrolling through images of abject violence, (b) reading individual responses to these images of abject violence (many of which were issued by writers in the form of social media posts and literary works), (c) skimming over an endless series of statements from community organizations expressing compassion and solidarity in light of the abject violence, almost always delivered in the distinctly corporate, HR-ified language of social justice, and (d) composing such statements myself at work. In the poems I was struggling to write at the time, I kept defaulting to a different but no less sterile strain of communication—the lyric—which had long felt like the perfect medium for articulating my most troubling thoughts and feelings, but was now leaving me slightly ashamed, even queasy after its use.

While drafting "Dorchester," I quickly realized that I would have to ground my intellectual preoccupations with language and violence in something more concrete, something steeped in bodily experience. This was how I arrived at Vincent's relationship with Leah. I had wanted, for a long time, to write a submissive/dominant relationship like theirs, a bond representing more than just a vehicle for descriptions of rough sex and long treatise-like passages on the nature of control (though I honestly love this kind of thing and write it all the time). I wanted their relationship to feel lived-in, so to speak. To write about the malleability of language and truth, I had to situate myself in this seemingly rigid relationship, though I hope the constraints of Vincent's and Leah's relationship feel as crucial to the story's freewheeling narrative consciousness as they are to Vincent and Leah. I see them as something like a poem's formal constraints, a series of strict rules on how to be very, very free.

MADELINE FFITCH is the author of the story collection *Valparaiso, Round the Horn* and the novel *Stay and Fight,* which was a finalist for the PEN/Hemingway Award for Debut Novel, the Washington State Book Award, and the Lambda Literary Award for Lesbian Fiction, as well as the 2023 Ohio Great Reads pick for the National Book Festival. Her writing has appeared in *The Paris Review, Tin House, Granta, Harper's Magazine,* and the *Anarchist Review of Books*. She is a recipient of a 2024 O. Henry Award.

• How did "Seeing Through Maps" come to be? Very simply, one evening at sunset I was chopping wood in a long black dress and a cat jumped on the chopping block, looked me in the eye, and peed. In fiction, every metaphor must be allowed to live fully and mysteriously with its own integrity. If a writer has a metaphor that they are in control of, beware. I'm trying hard to be honest. I write in a mosaic. I trust that image will lead to story. I agree that you don't have to have plot but you do have to have something. You have to use what you invent. I still can't believe that after that cat peed I kept chopping wood like a fool. Many smart people would know when to stop. Twenty years later, someone I still love remembers locking eyes with a fox. I feel sad that so many of us are certain that we know why we do what we do and why we are the way we are, as if causality is a point that was settled by Freud. What diminishes my imagination? What signs and symbols do I ignore? How might everything be different?

ALLEGRA HYDE is the author of the novel *Eleutheria,* as well as the story collections *The Last Catastrophe* and *Of This New World.*

• "Democracy in America" materialized among the stories I wrote for *The Last Catastrophe,* a collection that explores speculative futures. I'm someone who often likes to write about the future by way of the past, which is how I got it into my head to reimagine Alexis de Tocqueville's travels around America in the nineteenth century. I've always found Tocqueville's *Democracy in America* interesting because the text has persisted as a quotable reference for Democrats and Republicans alike. Also because such a classic study of American politics and culture came from an outsider; Tocqueville could observe the social mechanics of America because he wasn't from it. In my own "Democracy in America," Tocqueville visits a near-future version of the country that looks a little different from the place we may presently recognize. There are body-switching technologies, an absurd presidential initiative to unify the Great Lakes into "One Big Lake," and more. Also, my Tocqueville isn't a man. But by merging a historical framework with speculative possibilities, I hoped to reveal some of the ways our American present isn't so far from the past, even as it hurtles toward a frightening future.

TAISIA KITAISKAIA was born in the former Soviet Union and raised in the United States. She is the author of four books, which have been translated into multiple languages: *The Nightgown and Other Poems*; two volumes of *Ask Baba Yaga* advice from the witch of Slavic folklore; and *Literary Witches: A Celebration of Magical Women Writers*, a collaboration with artist Katy Horan and an NPR Great Read of 2017. Her fiction and poetry have appeared in journals such as *McSweeney's*, *Virginia Quarterly Review*, *American Short Fiction*, *A Public Space*, *Conjunctions*, and *Guernica*. She is the recipient of fellowships from the James A. Michener Center for Writers and the Corporation of Yaddo.

• "Engelond" came to be after a sleepless, insect-lively night on a ranch. I found the place exciting and terrifying. Though the ranch wasn't all that far from Austin, Texas, where I live, it was like an alternate universe: relentless with bugs and reptiles and mammals I had never encountered before. My love of murder mysteries and British literature, and my greatest fear of losing my parents, took over from there. I began writing the bit about the ants while still at the ranch. At that point, I'd mostly written non-autobiographical, fanciful poetry about strange creatures, fairy tales, and my fascination with the English language, which I'd encountered at age five when my family moved from Siberia to California. When I began writing fiction, I couldn't get enough: it felt amazing to tell stories about human beings, bring more of myself into my writing, and make observations while still retaining imagination. I think this story captures some of that exuberance of discovery that I felt in embarking on a new genre and turning toward the human experience and my own vulnerabilities.

I am grateful to Paul Reyes for selecting "Engelond" for the *Virginia Quarterly Review* and for his editorial insights, which gave me a chance to bring a little more shape to the story's middle and make it better as a whole.

JHUMPA LAHIRI, a bilingual writer and translator, is the Millicent C. McIntosh Professor of English and Director of Creative Writing at Barnard College, Columbia University. She received the Pulitzer Prize in 2000 for

Interpreter of Maladies and is also the author of *The Namesake, Unaccustomed Earth,* and *The Lowland.* Since 2015, Lahiri has been writing fiction, essays, and poetry in Italian: *In Altre Parole (In Other Words), Il vestito dei libri (The Clothing of Books), Dove mi trovo* (self-translated as *Whereabouts), Il quaderno di Nerina,* and *Racconti romani.* She received the National Humanities Medal from President Barack Obama in 2014, and in 2019 was named Commendatore in the Order of Merit of the Italian Republic by President Sergio Mattarella. Her most recent book in English, *Translating Myself and Others,* was a finalist for the PEN/Diamonstein-Spielvogel Award for the Art of the Essay.

• This was one of the first stories I wrote in Italian, and I was inspired by the social atmosphere of the international school my children attended when we moved to Rome. It evolved very slowly: it took about four years to complete the first draft, deepening as my own relationship to the city deepened. It always began the way it still begins, with the description of a recurring party that serves to mark the passage of time. The story was originally published in *Nuovi Argomenti,* a literary magazine in Italy, in 2019. I reworked parts of it before it appeared in the collection *Racconti romani* in 2022 (published the following year in English as *Roman Stories*). I'm grateful to Todd Portnowitz for translating the first draft of this story into English. I was reluctant to translate it myself, given that I'd spent so much time with it already; I craved some distance. But eventually, I went back to adjust the English version as well. This is the first story I've written in which the main character is a writer.

DANIEL MASON is the author of four novels, most recently *North Woods; A Registry of My Passage Upon the Earth* is a story collection that was a finalist for the Pulitzer Prize. He is currently an assistant professor of Psychiatry at Stanford University.

• There is a very long history of doctors writing about their patients, but I've never done so, and when I've been asked for my reasons, I've never felt I have a very clear answer; after all, there are well-established techniques for obtaining consent and protecting privacy. But I also happen to have an older friend who was the (willing, anonymized) subject of a case report, and it always seemed to me like this has been something very important in his life. I don't know the details, but I know that it was far more complex than the provider acknowledged. So this story was a way of exploring the complexities of such a relationship, and the responsibilities that both people might feel toward each other.

LORI OSTLUND is the author of the novel *After the Parade,* a B&N Discover Pick and a finalist for the Center for Fiction First Novel Prize; also the story collection *The Bigness of the World,* which received the 2008 Flannery

O'Connor Award for Short Fiction, the California Book Award for First Fiction, and the Edmund White Award for Debut Fiction. Lori's work has appeared previously in the *Best American Short Stories* and in the *PEN/O. Henry Prize Stories* as well as in *New England Review, ZYZZYVA*, and elsewhere. Her story collection entitled *Are You Happy?*, which includes "Just Another Family," will be published by Zando in 2025. Lori has received a Rona Jaffe Foundation Writers' Award and was a finalist for the 2017 Joyce Carol Oates Literary Prize. She is on the Mile-High MFA faculty and serves as the series editor of the Flannery O'Connor Award for Short Fiction. She lives in San Francisco.

• Years ago, I fell into the habit of keeping notebooks filled with odd character traits, overheard dialogue, unanswered questions, observations. When I am stuck, I open a notebook, pick a piece, and write toward it, challenging myself to bring it into the scene I'm stuck on. At first, the pieces resist each other, but eventually they start reaching toward each other. "Just Another Family" is the result of various pieces, plucked from memory and the notebooks and thin air. The first of these pieces was something I wrote down years ago in response to a prompt during a seminar at the Mile-High MFA, where I teach: "My father kept a pistol, loaded, above the stove, believing that his children would never be stupid enough to touch it. It turned out I was stupid enough."

Along the way, other breakthroughs came, including the first sentence, which uses "discontinent" instead of "incontinent" (yes, also from my notebook), an intentional prefix error that the narrator plays off of in the second sentence. Those two lines came to me as the voice I was looking for, but I had to make my peace with the fact that the reader, for one unsettling beat, would focus on the error. I have found that the narrative voices that unsettle me in some way are the ones that ultimately take me furthest. Also, my wife thought the lines were funny, and I always keep in mind Kurt Vonnegut's advice that a writer should write "for an audience of one," for the one person who understands the peculiarities of their voice.

I am a patient writer. I accept that sometimes I can't finish a story because I don't know enough yet, and this was the case here. For several years, I set the story aside until I realized that the story—which, like most of my stories, is a sad, funny story—was also a hopeful story. That is, it occurred to me that the narrator loved her partner more than her secrets. Years ago, when our friends' daughters were very young, one of them asked at dinner one night whether Anne—my then partner, now wife—and I were born together in a bubble. She was trying to make sense of our relationship, I think, and at some point, that anecdote, which I had scribbled in one of those notebooks, entered the story. Endings often require the top story (the plot) to take a step backward so that the bottom story—what the story is really about—can step forward, and Petra's drawing of their "bubble" family became a way to bring that bottom story, its hopefulness, to the surface.

I am grateful to *New England Review* for giving this very long story a home, especially Carolyn Kuebler, Ernest McLeod, and Glenn Verdi (for his NER blog interview), and to Heidi Pitlor and Lauren Groff for giving it this wonderful second home.

JIM SHEPARD has written eight novels, including *Phase Six; The Book of Aron,* which won the Sophie Brody Medal for Jewish Literature, the PEN/New England Award for Fiction, and the Clark Fiction Prize; and five story collections, including *Like You'd Understand, Anyway,* a finalist for the National Book Award and winner of the Story Prize. Seven of his stories have been chosen for *The Best American Short Stories,* two for the PEN/O. Henry Prize Stories, and two for the Pushcart Prize. He's also won a Guggenheim Foundation award, the Library of Congress/Massachusetts Book Award for Fiction, and the Alex Award from the American Library Association. He teaches at Williams College.

• When I'm not writing, teaching, shooting baskets, or bothering one of my beagles, I tend to be reading something arcane in my ongoing and mostly quixotic attempt to turn myself into a more interesting person. And as has often happened in the past, in reading about one subject, I stumbled upon another. I was working my way through Eli Ginzberg and Hyman Berman's *The American Worker in the Twentieth Century,* and they mentioned in passing the Johnstown Flood. I'd known only a few details about that 1889 American catastrophe: mostly that it had killed thousands and had been occasioned by a dam collapse. What I hadn't known was that the dam had been constructed to contain a private resort lake for the very wealthy, including Henry Clay Frick, Andrew Mellon, and Andrew Carnegie, and that that elite group of steel and coal and railroad magnates, calling themselves the South Fork Fishing and Hunting Club, had, against all the advice of their engineers, lowered the earth-and-rubble dam's side to make its top wide enough to enable a road for their carriages, and had blocked its spillway with an iron screen to prevent the escape of the game fish imported from Lake Erie with which they had had the lake stocked. When in late May of that year that part of Pennsylvania experienced the heaviest rainfall ever recorded in that region of the country, the dam gave way catastrophically, sending nearly sixteen million tons of water down into the steep river valley below. When I further learned that the poorest of the twenty-eight thousand Johnstownians lived in frame tenements on the flats closest to the river, flats that the local Iron and Steel Works had created with a fill of refuse and ash, and that the Club members who had caused the disaster had all evaded prosecution or civil judgments, I knew I had come across another way of talking about the grotesquerie of American economic inequality. And when, during research, I discovered the *Johnstown Tribune*'s first editorial following the disaster, in which its editor wrote, "We know what struck us, and it was not the hand of Providence. It was the work of man," and that he had called his editorial "Privilege," I knew I had found my title as well.

SUSAN SHEPHERD'S writing has been published in the *Boston Globe, Ploughshares,* the *Chicago Quarterly Review, Story,* the *Kenyon Review, Swamp Pink,* and *One Story.* Her short fiction podcast *11 Central,* which aired on NPR, won a Gold Medal for Best Comedy from the New York Festivals and a National Gracie Allen Award for Best Producer, Comedy. *Baboons* is part of a linked collection of short stories called *Animalia,* several of which have been listed as distinguished stories in *The Best American Short Stories.* She lives outside Boston with her husband, an assortment of chickens, and her dog.

• A few years ago, a tent city filled with people using drugs sprang up in Boston where I live, and my reporter friend was covering it. She described to me the nightmarish scenes inside the encampment. I've spent a fair amount of time camping in Kenya and it got me thinking about what it would be like to be in one of those tents, and how removed they are from what's beautiful in the world. A tent is often a place where you're fully encompassed by nature, and I wondered about the experience of a character who might live in both worlds: the horrific one of people dying from drug overdoses, with no one around to care for them, and its opposite, the wilderness, surrounded by your family, baboons, the sound of birds, trees, and the lovely smell of red Kenya clay.

One of the first stories I wrote was about a group of teenage girls who find two snakes hiding in a closet. The snakes belong to one of the girls' stepdad; he put them there in separate boxes to feed them and promptly forgot. Although he played a small part in that story, he caught my imagination, and so I made him the addict in *Baboons.*

I decided to have his girlfriend narrate the story from her point of view. She's sad and terrified, yes, but she's also exhausted and pissed and tired of taking care of everyone. I wanted the story to have a funny edge. But in the end this story is about love.

Baboons went through many iterations, and I'd like to say thanks to all the writers, teachers, and editors who are so generous with their time in helping other writers with their work. And also a big thanks to the *Kenyon Review* for seeing something in it and to Lauren Groff and Heidi Pitlor for choosing it for this anthology.

AZAREEN VAN DER VLIET OLOOMI is the author of three novels, including *Call Me Zebra,* which won the 2019 PEN/Faulkner Award. She is the recipient of a Radcliffe Fellowship, a Fulbright Fellowship, a Whiting Award for writing, a National Book Foundation 5 Under 35 award, and residency fellowships from MacDowell and the Aspen Institute. Her work has appeared in *The Best American Short Stories, The Yale Review, The Sewanee Review, The Believer,* and *The New York Times,* among other places. She is the Dorothy G. Griffin College Professor of English at the University of Notre Dame.

• When I was in my twenties, I spent a year living in Girona, a medieval city sandwiched between the regal Pyrenees and the emerald waters of the Costa Brava. I had received a Fulbright Fellowship to research the 1918 pandemic and the Catalan writer Josep Pla, whose early work is a record of that catastrophic period of mass illness and death. "Extinction" documents the many bizarre experiences I had while living there: the peculiar roommates I had, the puncturing beauty of the landscape that utterly overwhelmed me, the obscure sense of premonition while reading about the pandemic of yore while we were about to be catapulted into a major public health crisis in the current day. The story is a frenetic, fantastical summary of that densely lived period of my life when everything felt surreal, in high definition, and mystical in its intensity.

SUZANNE WANG lives in San Francisco. Her fiction has appeared in *One Story.*

• "Mall of America" started as a realist vignette of an elderly Chinese man wandering an American shopping mall. Like all my first drafts it was not very good, but I felt drawn to exploring the alienation of aging and immigration within the nostalgic yet disorienting setting. This character echoed the lives of my own beloved grandparents, who moved from Shandong to suburban Ohio to help raise me and my sisters. For my next draft, I wondered how I could give him what we couldn't give my grandparents at the time: a sense of agency and freedom outside the home. Naturally, playing Dance Dance Revolution was my first answer. I toyed with ensuing questions on hilly walks in San Francisco: How would he find the game and play it? If I liked the mall setting so much, could I make it an actual character to guide him? What if the mall took the form of an AI who could speak his language? What if the AI were the narrator? I experimented with this fun, challenging new voice in subsequent drafts and grew attached to it. Eventually, I developed why and how the AI was built and why it was telling this particular story, drawing from my own experiences working in technology. The story expanded and deepened with each revision, revealing a playground of ideas that I couldn't have conjured when I began.

I want to thank each person who believed in and helped illuminate this story, especially Hannah Tinti and the *One Story* team. Thank you to Heidi Pitlor and Lauren Groff for giving it another wonderful home. Thank you to the generous Mark Alexander for providing precise, moving translations of Li Bai and Cui Hao. I'm grateful to this story for teaching me patience over the years I spent with it. It is dedicated to my grandparents, whose love gave me everything.

PAUL YOON's first published story appeared in *The Best American Short Stories 2006*. He is the author of five works of fiction, including, most recently, *The Hive and the Honey*. His short stories have appeared in *The New Yorker, The Atlantic,* and *Harper's Magazine*. He lives in the Hudson Valley, New York, with his wife and dog.

• I wrote "Valley of the Moon" during the pandemic. I was very far from home, and I knew I would not be home any time soon, and I was struggling. To cheer myself up, I would think a lot about—or fantasize about—all the ways I could journey back home, wanting to capture and hold on to that feeling of home. At the same time, I was reading a lot about those who survived the Korean War only to have to figure out how to rebuild their lives in a country that was decimated. For me, the story is about rebuilding and renewal—not only on the surface level of a country, cities, villages, the land, but in how individuals attempt to build themselves back up again and heal. I also wanted to write a story where the notion of a "main character" was a bit slippery; to present, in the short form, a canvas full of many people. I hope the reader feels a kind of vastness here, like you're in a huge forest, looking up and around, with all those sounds, all that history and silence. Special thanks to Laura van den Berg, Bill Clegg, Simon Toop, Marysue Rucci, Cressida Leyshon, and the exquisite team at *The New Yorker* for their support and unwavering faith.

Other Distinguished Stories of 2023

Abravanel, Genevieve, "Discount Man" (*North American Review,* vol. 308, no. 3)

Abravanel, Genevieve, "Wilderness Survival" (*The Missouri Review,* vol. 46, no. 3)

Alberta, Chloe, "Leap Year" (*Master's Review,* April 10, 2023)

Atkinson, Jonathan, "Baby Suits" (*New Ohio Review,* issue 33)

Becker, Geoffrey, "Six Haircuts" (*Story,* issue 16)

Bego, Elvis, "Our House" (*The Kenyon Review,* vol. XLV, no. 4)

Biagi, Laura, "A Train to Catch" (*TriQuarterly,* issue 163)

Bleidner, Via, "Human Whistle" (*Agni,* 97)

Bowe, Taryn, "The Hunt" (*Epoch,* vol. 70, no. 1)

Boyle, TC, "The End if Only a Beginning" (*The New Yorker,* August 21)

Brinkley, Jamel, "Arrows" (*American Short Fiction,* vol. 26, issue 78)

Brinkley, Jamel, "Bystander" (*The Kenyon Review* online)

Burden, Isabelle, "The Snail" (*The Kenyon Review,* vol. XLV, no. 2)

Candela, María José, "Dark Day" (*Sewanee Review,* vol. CXXXI, no. 3)

Carver, Cecily, "The Good Sport" (*The Kenyon Review,* vol. XLV, no. 3)

Chang-Eppig, Rita, "Walking the Dead" (*One Story,* issue 299)

Chou, Elaine Hsieh, "Background" (*The Atlantic Online*)

Cline, Emma, "Upstate" (*The New Yorker,* October 30)

Conklin, Lydia, "On the Sound" (*The Sewanee Review,* col. CXXI, no. 1)

Crain, Caleb, "The Ellipse Maker" (*n+1,* no. 45)

Crain, Caleb, "Keats at Twenty-Four" (*The New Yorker,* December 11)

Crain, Caleb, "Recognition" (*McSweeney's,* issue 72)

Crossen, Emily, "The Bloody Parts" (*New England Review,* vol. 44, no. 4)

Crossen, Emily, "Egg" (*Zoetrope: All-Story,* Online Supplement)

Delgado, Stanley, "Camera Man" (*One Story,* issue 297)

Diaz, Hernan, "Triptych" (*Harper's Magazine,* March 23)

Díaz, Junot, "The Ghosts of Gloria Lara" (*The New Yorker,* November 6)

Eggers, Dave, "The Honor of Your Presence" (*One Story,* issue no. 302)

Ervice, Nikki, "Egg," (*Washington Square Review,* issue 47/48)

Ferrell, Carolyn, "You Little Me" (*Story,* issue 16)
Flynn, Larry, "Education and Other Preparations" (*New Letters,* vol. 89, nos. 1 & 2)

Gaitskill, Mary, "Minority Report" (*The New Yorker,* March 27)
Galchen, Rivka, "How I Became a Vet" (*The New Yorker,* March 13)
Gaonkar, Mala, "The Naked Lady Saint" (*American Short Fiction,* vol. 26, issue 78)
Gilmore, Jennifer, "Recovery" (*Harper's Magazine,* April)
González, Francisco, "Serranos" (*McSweeney's,* issue 70)
Goodman, Allegra, "The Last Grownup" (*The New Yorker,* February 27)
Greene, Linnie, "Diplodocus" (*Washington Square Review,* no. 49)
Greenfeld, Karl Taro, "Year One" (*Washington Square Review,* no. 49)

Hagenston, Becky, "Theories of an Ancient Drawing Carved into a Hillside" (*Coppernickel,* no. 37)
Haigh, Jennifer, "Shelter in Place" (*Ploughshares,* vol. 49, no. 1)
Hans, Joel, "Two Decorated Skulls in the Miramonte Swamp" (*Story,* issue 16)
Hartford, Anna, "The Large Glass" (*The Kenyon Review,* vol. XLV, vol. 1)
Hayes, Esther, "FotoQuick" (*The Threepenny Review,* issue 173)
Heiny, Katherine, "Chicken-Flavored and Lemon-Scented" (*Electric Literature,* no. 571)
Holladay, Cary, "He Cannonballed" (*The Hudson Review,* vol. LXXVI, no. 2)
Hyde, Allegra, "Frights" (*The Sun,* January)

Iskandrian, Kristen, "Quantum Voicemail" (*Electric Literature,* no. 549)

Jackson, Jared, "Ace" (*n+1,* no. 45)

Kalotay, Daphne, "A Guide to Lesser Divinities" (*Harvard Review,* no. 60)
Kim, Catherine, "The Woman from Angers" (*The Kenyon Review,* vol. XLV, no. 4)
Krauss, Nicole, "Long Island" (*The New Yorker,* May 21)

Leone, Marianne, "Freud Was a Nut" (*Ploughshares,* vol. 49, no. 2)
Lerner, Ben, "The Ferry" (*The New Yorker,* April 10)
Li, Yiyun, "Wednesday's Child" (*The New Yorker,* January 23)
Lin, Su-Yi, "The Shadow and the Light" (*khōréō* , 2023)
Loskutoff, Maxim, "Our Lady of the Rockies" (*Guernica*)

Ma, Ling, "Winner" (*The Yale Review,* vol. 111, no. 4)
Makkai, Rebecca, "The Plaza" (*The New Yorker,* May 8)
Mandelbaum, Paul, "The Gambling Cruise" (*Harvard Review,* no. 60)
McCormick, Chris, "Giraffe" (*The Southern Review,* vol. 59, no. 1)
McCracken, Elizabeth, "When Monster Trucks Broke Through the Pyramids of Giza" (*Zoetrope: All-Story,* vol. 26, no. 4)
Miller, J. Eric, "Space Invaders" (*The Cincinnati Review,* vol. 20, no. 2)
Mitchell, Emily, "The Severe Inquisition into the Causes of the Great Fire" (*American Short Fiction,* vol. 26, issue 78)

Navaro Aquino, Xavier, "Two Young Kings" (*The Sewanee Review,* vol. CXXXI, no. 1)

Okparanta, Chinelo, "Fatu" (*Freeman's: Conclusions*)

Ong, Han, "Hammer Attack" (*The New Yorker,* January 16)
Ong, Han, "Pizza Rat" (*The New Yorker,* October 23)
Ostlund, Lori, "The Bus Driver" (*Story,* issue 16)
Oza, Janika, "Cling Film" (*Bomb,* 165)
Ozick, Cynthia, "The Conversion of the Jews" (*Harper's Magazine,* May)

Palmqvist, Lara, "In Another Life" (*Bellevue Literary Review,* issue 44)
Park, Ed, "The Air as Air" (*McSweeney's,* issue 72)
Pearson, Joanna, "The Fetch" (*The Missouri Review,* vol. 46, no. 3)
Perabo, Susan, "The Best Loved Dog" (*Michigan Quarterly Review,* vol. 62, no. 1)
Petrova, Marina, "Vacation" (*The Gettysburg Review,* vol. 34, no. 2)
Powers, Michael Tod, "A Forgotten Language" (*New Letters,* vol. 89, nos. 1 & 2)
Pritchard, Melissa, "The Earth, Our Reliquary: Confessions of a Pilferer" (*Conjunctions,* 81)

Quatro, Jamie, "Yogurt Days" (*The New Yorker,* August 7)

Reid, Molly, "Keeping Track" (*West Branch,* no. 102)
Reilly, Frank, "The Stirling Stone" (*The Baltimore Review,* Winter)
Roberts, Nathan Curtis, "Yellow Tulips" (*Harvard Review,* no. 61)
Ryan, David, "Horse with Tornado" (*The Georgia Review,* Winter)

Sanders, Shannon, "The Opal Cleft" (*Virginia Quarterly Review,* 99.3)
Saunders, George, "Thursday" (*The New Yorker,* June 12)
Segal, Lore, "On the Agenda" (*The New Yorker,* September 18)
Sestanovich, Clare, "Different People" (*The New Yorker,* January 30)
Sestanovich, Clare, "Our Time is Up" (*The New Yorker,* November 13)
Sgarro, Victoria, "Leaving" (*The Iowa Review,* vol. 53, issue 1)
Shepard, Jim, "The Testament of Edward Hyde" (*McSweeney's,* issue 72)
Sohail, Mahreen, "The Funeral" (*A Public Space,* no. 31)
Somers, Erin, "Washing Up" (*McSweeney's,* issue 72)
Somerville, Patrick, "Armstrong" (*Ploughshares,* vol. 49, no. 2)
Spatz, Gregory, "Thunderhead" (*The Kenyon Review,* vol. XLV, no. 40)
Stuber, Amy, "Bears" (*Colorado Review,* 50.3, Fall/Winter)

Taylor, Brandon, "That's the Pain You Have" (*A Public Space,* no. 31)
Terry, Shayne, "The Rock Is Not a Rock" (*TriQuarterly Online*)
Tunning, Katherine, "Laugh Machine" (*Baltimore Review,* Fall)

Vallianatos, Corinna, "A Lot of Good It Does Being in the Underworld" (*A Public Space,* no. 31)
Van den Berg, Laura, "Catskill Avenue" (*American Short Fiction,* vol. 26, issue 77)
Vara, Vauhini, "What Next" (*One Story,* issue 300)

Walbert, Kate, "Erratics" (*A Public Space,* no. 31)
Walter, Jess, "The Dark" (*Ploughshares,* vol. 49, no. 2)
Wang, Weike, "Status in Flux" (*The New Yorker,* June 26)
Warrick, Eva, "Women and Children" (*Ploughshares,* vol. 49, no. 2)

Yancy, Melissa, "Predators" (*The Iowa Review,* vol. 52, issue 2; vol. 53, issue 3)
Yune, Robert, "Baghdad, Florida" (*The Southern Review,* vol. 59, no. 2)

American and Canadian Magazines Publishing Short Stories

Able Muse
The Adroit Journal
African American Review
After Dinner Conversation
Agni
Alaska Quarterly Review
Alta
American Chordata
The American Scholar
American Short Fiction
ANMLY
Another Chicago Magazine
The Apple Valley Review
Apricity
A Public Space
The Arkansas International
The Arkansas Review
Arts & Letters
The Atlantic
Baltimore Review
Bayou Magazine
Bellevue Lit Review
Belmont Story Review
Bennington Review
Big Muddy
Black Warrior Review
Blue Mesa Review
Bomb
Boston Review
Boulevard
Briar Cliff Review
Bridge
Bull Magazine
The Carolina Quarterly
Catamaran
Catapult
Cerasus Magazine
Cherry Tree
Chestnut Review
Chicago Quarterly Review
The Cincinnati Review
Cleaver Magazine
The Coachella Review
Colorado Review
The Common
Conjunctions
Coppernickel
Craft
Cream City Review
CutBank
The Dalhousie Review
Door=Jar
The Drift
Driftwood

Ecotone
Electric Literature
Epiphany
Epoch
Event
Evergreen
Exposition Review
The Ex-Puritan
The Fairy Tale Review
Fantasy and Science Fiction
Fiction
The Fiddlehead
Five Points
Flash Frog
Foglifter
Forge Literary Magazine
Fourteen Hills
Freeman's
Full Bleed
Ganga Review
Georgia Review
Gettysburg Review
Ghost Parachute
Granta
The Gravity of the Thing
The Greensboro Review
Grist
Guernica
Gulf Coast
Harper's Magazine
Harvard Review
Hawaii Pacific Review
Hayden's Ferry Review
Hominum Journal
The Hopkins Review
The Hudson Review
Hypertext Review
The Idaho Review
IHRAM Publishes
Image
Indiana Review
The Iowa Review
Iron Horse Literary Review
Isele Magazine
Jabberwock Review
Joyland
The Kenyon Review
Lady Churchill's Rosebud Wristlet
Lake Effect
Lilith
Long River Review
The MacGuffin
Makeout Creek
The Malahat Review
The Massachusetts Review
The Masters Review
McSweeney's
Meridian
Michigan Quarterly Review
MicroLit Almanac
Mid-American Review
Midwest Review
The Missouri Review
Mount Hope
The Museum of Americana
N+1
Narrative
Nelle
New England Review
New Ohio Review
The New Yorker
Ninth Letter
The Nonconformist Magazine
Noon
North American Review
North Carolina Literary Review
North Dakota Quarterly
The Ocean State Review
One Story
Orion
Oxford American
Pangyrus
The Paris Review
Passages North
Passengers Journal
Pembroke
Phoebe
Pleiades
Ploughshares
Post Road
Potomac Review
Prairie Schooner
Punctured Lines
Raritan

Reckon Review
Rejection Letters
The Rejoinder
Revolution John
Rivanna Review
Room
Rosebud
Rougarou Journal
Ruby
The Rumpus
Rustica
Sacramento Literary Review
Salamander
Salt Hill
Santa Monica Review
Saturday Evening Post
Scoundrel Time
The Sewanee Review
Shenandoah
Short Story, Long
Shotgun Honey
Socrates on the Beach
Solstice
South Carolina Review
South Dakota Review
The Southampton Review
Southeast Review
Southern Humanities Review
The Southern Review
Southwest Review
Split Lip Magazine
Star 82 Review
The Stinging Fly
Story
StoryQuarterly
Story South
The Sun
Sundog Lit
Swing
Tahoma Literary Review
Terrain.org
Texas Highways
The Threepenny Review
Tiny Molecules
Transition
TriQuarterly
The Tusculum Review
The Under Review
The Vassar Review
Virginia Quarterly Review
The Walrus
Washington Square Review
Water-Stone Review
West Branch
The Westchester Review
Wilderness House Literary Journal
Willow Springs
Witness
World Literature Today
Writer's Digest
The Yale Review
Your Impossible Voice
Zoetrope: All-Story
Zyzzyva
805 Lit + Art